FOREVER

FOREVER

The Porn Star Brothers Series

L.J. DIVA

★ ROYAL STAR PUBLISHING ★

Chances is an imprint of Royal Star Publishing
www.royalstarpublishing.com.au

First edition paperback published in 2018
All Rights Reserved, Copyright ©L.J. Diva 2018

Trade Paperback ISBN: 978-1-925683-52-3
Dust Jacket Hardcover ISBN: 978-1-922307-32-3
E-book ISBN: 978-1-925683-51-6
A catalogue record for this book is available from the National Library of Australia.

Cover design: Royal Star Publishing and Odyssey Books
Cover photos: stockcreations/Shutterstock.com
Typesetting in Minion Pro by Royal Star Publishing

Dedications

In 2014 a vague idea to write a book about a porn star came to me. In 2015 the idea brewed and grew and when my idol, Jackie Collins, passed away, the idea flourished with a vengeance.

Jackie Collins is the only inspiration in my life when it comes to writing. She had the passion, the brains, the ballsy rollicking attitude, and the kind of life that made me want to *be* her.

Without her, these books would not exist, for I would not have had the inspiration to follow in the same 'write whatever you want' league. Without her, I will continue trying to write the kind of books she wrote. Real, ballsy, and bonkbustingly good.

Jackie,

the Porn Star Brothers book series is dedicated to you as so many of my other books are. I thank you for the inspiration you have given me and hope you continue giving me, to go on and write more. I hope that you are well and having a good laugh wherever you are. I miss you and will continue doing so. Sometimes I think I feel you egging me on with my writing. Maybe that's true, and maybe it's just my rampant imagination; the same imagination that has given me the books I have written so far in my life. And sometimes, I really wished I could be you. You will forever be my idol and inspiration and I thank you.

RIP, Miss Jackie C.

And to the three Stefanovic brothers, Carlos, Pedro, and Tomas, without whom I would not have had names for my porn stars.

October 1977

Jenny Stephanopoulos fluttered around her beautiful suite in the *Elegance Hotel* in Athens, Greece. She had so much to do before heading home to Mykonos for the weddings of her children. Helping her future daughters-in-law find dresses, and helping her sons find rings. There were arrangements to get to, and she had started with a phone call to Father Bowen of the Greek Orthodox Church to see if they could have the ceremonies the following weekend. They could, and so dates were set.

She looked up as Spiros, her husband, opened the door and let in Carlos, their eldest, and his future wife, Vivian, the gorgeous woman her son had chosen for his bride. Vivian Villiers was forty, a world-famous model with rolling brown curls down to her pert backside. She had a body men could only dream about holding, and women could only dream about having.

Jenny glanced from Vivian's gorgeous peach-coloured dress, the latest style no less, to her own demure blue woollen frock and cardigan. It was almost November, the chill was in the air, and the dress was all Jenny had that was on the fancier side. Not that she *didn't* have nice clothes, she had what she needed for their lifestyle, and Spiros had provided her with a nice life. But now that things had changed, maybe she could update her style and bring it into 1977, for a fresh start to 1978.

It had only been a week since Spiros's grandfather, Giorgio

Stephanopoulos, had finally dealt with the man behind her sons' troubles. Stefano Papadopoulos, at one time Spiros's uncle, had kidnapped her boys in the vain hope of killing them himself so he would inherit Giorgio's estate. His plans had been thwarted, and now he was dead. And, as his only relatives, the Stephanopouloses had inherited his estate. Within weeks they would have money to burn, and Jenny planned on burning it to her heart's content.

She sat at the table by the large floor-to-ceiling window to go over her notes. They had decided to stay in Athens for another week after dealing with Stefano and wrapping things up with the FBI who had become involved, using the time to acquaint themselves with the future in-laws, and letting Angie and Tomas recover from their health issues. She and Spiros had their suite, while the boys and their partners had suites of their own. She glanced from her list to the view to her son. Carlos Spiros Stephanopoulos, twenty-four, and a world-famous porn star. *Oh, how I hate that the boys have fallen into that,* she thought, watching Carlos with his father.

Vivian glanced up from Carlos's side and moved over to join Jenny at the table. "So, we're still on for shopping?" She still wasn't used to the idea of having in-laws as Carlos had only proposed a week earlier, plus she was suffering the effects of morning sickness. As much as she loved shopping, she wasn't sure she could tolerate being out all day.

Jenny eyed her up and down. "We are unless you and Angelina aren't well enough. How are you dealing with the morning sickness?"

Viv smiled softly. "It's not too bad. The ginger tablets help, so it doesn't last long." She shifted in her chair. "Um, are you okay with this?" she asked quietly, her emerald cat-shaped eyes glancing at Carlos talking to his father. "None of us have done things in a traditional way." Delicately licking her lips, she looked Jenny boldly in the eyes. "Having your eldest and youngest getting their partners pregnant and *then* marrying them isn't exactly the right way in the eyes of God."

Jenny thought about it before speaking. "True. But while we go to church once a week it doesn't mean we don't understand things don't always go to plan. God knows you love each other and that's all that matters. Well…" a pause, "that and abiding by your vows. I hope you plan on taking them seriously." She studied Viv closely for a moment before continuing. "I'd hate for my sons to get divorced in a few years. I want this to be forever for them." While she waited for Viv's reply, she watched Spiros answer the door again.

"I don't plan on divorcing him, Mrs Stephanopoulos." With another glance at Carlos, who was slapping Tomas on the back in a hug before he and Roger sat beside him on the couch, she continued with a smile. "This is it, for both of us." She turned back to Jenny. "Forever."

Jenny smiled. As much as she felt slightly uncomfortable with Vivian's age, only nine years younger than herself, she saw the love that Carlos had for her, and that was all that mattered. She hoped.

Tomas popped up from the couch and walked over to his mother to kiss her cheek. "Hey, Mama. Having fun making plans?" He glanced at his future sister-in-law. "Viv."

"Tomas," Viv greeted warmly with a smile.

Tomas stood behind Jenny with his hands on her shoulders. She had been his biggest supporter in coming out to the family, and he would forever be grateful. He was also grateful that she had persuaded Spiros to be okay with it too. He looked back at his father and watched him closely as he conversed with Roger. Roger Dencott, the Australian working in Miami porn, was the love of his life. They had met the day he arrived in Miami and had quickly gotten to know each other before falling into bed. While Spiros seemed to accept Roger, and had been warm and cordial this last week, Tomas still had reservations. Carlos had definitely taken to Roger, and they sat chatting like lifelong friends. Pedro had no problem with him either.

Spiros noticed Tomas watching and gave his son a soft smile. It had been hard for him to see his middle child go through the fear of abandonment by his father, and Spiros knew that feeling well. He vowed to never do that to his own children and accepted that Tomas was different from his brothers. While they loved women, Tomas loved men; one man in particular who was sitting on the couch beside Carlos.

His eyes went back to Roger, and he saw how comfortable he was with his eldest. Roger had been accepted smoothly, and while it was not the way he, Spiros Giorgio Stephanopoulos, had been raised, or the way he had raised his sons, he knew it was important to Jenny, the love of his life, and Tomas, the spitting identical twin to himself. So he had let all past issues go and accepted Tomas for the man he was, *and* accepted the man he loved. Spiros glanced warmly from Roger to Tomas and smiled his approval.

Jenny squeezed Tomas's hand. She felt the tenseness as he gripped her shoulders and watched him watch his father and brother with his lover. It had been a week since the introductions, and things had gone well. Spiros had some grumbles the first few days, but after spending time with Roger and Tomas, seeing how in love they were, he had softened and now seemed to accept Roger as another son.

Tomas finally looked into his mother's blue eyes.

"Nervous?" she asked. "Or still getting over your illness?" She had been absolutely mortified to find out that Tomas's first sexual encounter could result in a stalker who could poison her son and frame his lover. Luiz Manning had been Andros Poulos's illegitimate child, making him Angelina's half-brother, and he'd become obsessed with Tomas after being dumped in Mykonos, not only by his new male lover, but his fiancée Bertha St John. More so after he killed four men and framed Roger for it just to get Roger out of Tomas's life. When Tomas was hospitalised after falling ill, Luiz kidnapped and absconded with him only to be shot dead by one of Stefano Papadopoulos's henchmen. She had taken Tomas to a top doctor in poisons for a full blood work and made sure he ate three healthy meals a day to get his strength back. And he seemed to be doing well, except when he became nervous about Roger being around his father.

Tomas smiled down at the warm face of his loving mother. "Why would I be nervous?"

"Because you're digging your fingers into my shoulders, and you always go a little green around the gills when you watch your father with Roger." She watched his expression soften. "There's no need to be, you know."

His smile broadened. "Not with you here." Leaning down, he

wrapped his arms around her, his face beside hers. "I love you, Mama. And I'm fine. The doctors you took me to saw to that."

Gently rubbing her face against his, she thought back over the five traumatic months they had just come through. "Good. I wasn't about to let my baby be any sicker than what that bastard made you. I'm just glad he's dead. That they're all dead. All of the bastards that made my babies' lives a misery are dead. But it's over now, and you're okay and safe and healthy. *All* of my babies are safe and healthy." She kissed his cheek as the door was banged upon.

"I'll get it," he called out and all but skipped across the room to reveal Pedro and Angelina, who was fresh out of her sling, standing there.

"Hey, bro," Pedro said as they walked in and hugged each other. He loped over to his father and planted a kiss on both cheeks before heading for his mother to do the same.

"My baby," she said as he bent down to hug her. "Do you have everything you need? We're heading home the day after tomorrow."

"Yes, Mama. I'm ready to go." He helped Angie into a seat at the table, kissed her head, and bounded over to the menfolk where he jumped onto the other single chair. "Hey, all. What are we doing today?"

"How are you today, dear?" Jenny asked Angie, watching as she rubbed her shoulder. "How's the arm and the morning sickness?"

"The arm's still a little achy, but good," Angelina replied. "But the morning sickness is a bitch. That's why we're late."

"We're on no timetable, so the both of you take all the time you need in the mornings," Jenny told her. "I certainly had to, especially with Carlos. I was so sick with him, being my first, and, of course, having never been pregnant before my body was out of control. I couldn't stop it, and it had me out of commission for three months."

"Ugh," Angelina groaned while Viv pulled a face. "I don't want it to last for three months."

"Well, you may not suffer the way I did." Jenny patted her hand. "It wasn't as bad with Tomas, and with Pedro, I barely had any."

"I'm not sure if I can get through *three* children just to not have morning sickness," Viv told her. "I'm not even sure if I'll be having any more after this one."

Jenny looked at her sharply. "Why wouldn't you be having more?"

Viv blushed. "Well…my age for a start…I'm surprised I became pregnant now."

"Yes…" Jenny softened. "I suppose that is a factor." Turning back to Angelina she said, "Are the ginger pills not working?"

"They help," Angelina replied. "But they don't stop it completely, and I don't want to vomit on my father's lawyer when I see him tomorrow."

Jenny laughed softly. "I'm sure you won't. Have you decided what you're going to do about his estate?"

Angie shrugged. "I know what he did and that part I'm not interested in. I don't want our home, so I'll have to clear that out, and as for the club, Pedro suggested keeping it as an investment."

"Do you really want to deal with running a club while you're finishing Juilliard?" Jenny asked, shuffling through some papers. Because Angelina was closer to her son's age at eighteen, she felt more like a daughter than Viv. Not that Viv wasn't nice, she was just too old. And besides, Angelina was of Greek heritage.

"Yeah," Angie muttered. "I don't really want to deal with it, but I'm not that fussed either way. Not even sure if I want to go back to Santorini."

"Then don't. Tell your father's lawyer to deal with it all," Viv told her. "Who said you had to go back there?" She quite liked Angelina, the wee slip of a girl who was going to be her sister-in-law. Since Viv was an only child like Angie, she was looking forward to having a sister and brothers.

"Exactly," Jenny agreed. "If you don't want to go back, don't. Get the lawyer to sell everything off and then set the money up for your futures *and* your children's futures. Surely you won't be having one child as well?" While she had hoped to contain her excitement over the upcoming grandchildren, she also hoped that there would be more down the road, but didn't want to push either of the girls. With Angie still so young, more children would more than likely be a definite. But with Viv, not so much.

Angie smiled. She hadn't felt the love and support of a mother in a long time. And Jenny Stephanopoulos was offering it in spades. *I'm lucky to be marrying into such an awesome family,* she thought, *because the one I come from sure as hell wasn't.* "I think the reason Pedro suggested keeping it was because we met there."

"It's also where Andros drugged him, assaulted him, and you hit him over the head," Jenny reminded her. "Is it *really* a place you want those memories of?" Her child's welfare was all that mattered, not some stupid nightclub.

"That's why I also suggested we move from our apartment in New York," Angie replied. "Too many bad memories. Pedro's looking into apartments in the same neighbourhood, so it's still close to school and 69."

"Will you still go back, with the baby due in June?" Viv jumped in. "I know modelling's not a nine to five job, but I can take time off. Can you?"

Angie shrugged. "School won't start until September, so we'll have some time to settle in with a new baby by then."

"It will still be a big workload, a baby *and* school. Will you be able to do it part-time, or will you get a nanny?" Secretly, Jenny hoped to be asked to help and hell, even if she wasn't, she'd still be there for her son and grandchild.

"I hope so," Angie told her. "If not, we'll have to figure it out when the time comes."

"So, what are you boys planning for today while the girls are off shopping?" Spiros asked his three strapping sons and Roger. While he still wasn't sure of the whole homosexual thing, he vowed to love Tomas no matter what. And if that happened to be his son falling in love with a man, then so be it.

"Going and getting Viv's ring." Carlos kept his voice low. "She said to surprise her, so I plan on it. And since Mama insisted on us getting married in Mykonos as soon as possible, I gotta get a suit as well."

"Same here." Pedro put his feet up on the coffee table and his hands behind his head. "We may as well get that done today since none of us brought suits with us."

"Looks like we'd better hit the jewellery store and the tux shop then," Tomas said from his spot between Carlos and Roger on the couch. "We go home the day after tomorrow, and we've gotten nothing done all week."

"That's 'cause we had so much to catch up on," Carlos said. "And we gave you and Angie time to get better. Speaking of," he glanced at Pedro, "Has she sorted out her father's affairs yet?"

"Sees the lawyer tomorrow," Pedro replied. "We've been talking about it, and she's still unsure of what to do. Get rid of everything most likely."

Angie turned around in her seat. "We were just talking about that."

Pedro turned his head.

She continued, "As much as you said to keep the nightclub because it's where we met, I'm not sure I want the responsibility."

Pedro kneeled on the chair to lean on the back and face her. "Even though I'd like you to keep it, I'm not fussed either way. If it would be too much for you to take on then sell it." He flashed his goofy Stephanopoulos grin. "Whatever you want I'll support."

She smiled back. "With everything else we'll be doing I don't want to have to worry about a nightclub on the other side of the world. So...I think we'll sell it."

"Speaking of everything else we have to worry about," Jenny added to the conversation. "Have you invited all your friends to the weddings?"

"There are only a few school friends from Santorini and Maggie from New York," Angie said.

"Will she be coming with Mike?" Pedro asked her.

"She told me she was when I rang to invite them," Angie said. "She'll only be allowed to take a few days off, so won't stay for the whole weekend."

"When will they be coming in?" Jenny checked the guest lists. "We leave for Mykonos the day after tomorrow which is Wednesday, and then the first wedding is on Friday."

"She said she'd fly in Friday night or Saturday morning, and then fly back out Sunday," Angie told her.

"Right, so she'll be staying one night then. We'd better make sure there are enough rooms so she and what's his name…?" she glanced at Angie, "Mike, can have a room each."

"There should be enough room since Giorgio rented the entire hotel for a week," Spiros said, comfortable in his lounge chair.

"Yes," Jenny replied. "That was very kind of him to do so."

"He wanted to contribute to the weddings without interfering," Spiros said. "But even that was too much."

"Nonsense." Jenny waved a hand. "It's only the Windmill Hotel. It has lovely rooms and a nice view. Plus, it's close to the church and reception venue, since the reception venue is on the hotel grounds. I thought it was most appropriate for the guests and very kind of him. Do you know if he's coming to the weddings?"

Spiros sighed. He hadn't been on good terms with his grandfather for nearly three decades, but after involving him in their troubles with Stefano, Giorgio made it clear he didn't want to be where he wasn't welcome. If the family wanted him, he would be there, but he would not force himself on his grandson and great-grandsons and their future. "You know I called him and invited him after that conversation we all had the other day. It was up to the boys whether they wanted him in their lives or not, and it was decided to invite him to the weddings, so he at least had something. That's how come he booked out the hotel for a week, so we had a reception venue as well, and we didn't have to go to the trouble of finding it all ourselves. That's his gift to the boys."

"Yes, but is he *coming*?" Jenny asked impatiently. "We've nearly filled up the hotel with guests, most of which are family."

"Well, they're certainly not *my* family," Spiros said. "My brothers refused to come, and my sisters didn't even get to talk to me. Their husbands answered for them."

"Angry about Giorgio giving his belongings away, or that you chose to leave Greece nearly thirty years ago?" Jenny asked, scanning the guest list for her in-laws.

"The latter," Spiros replied. "You know none of us have talked since we came back. They were angry at me inheriting the meat shop, so why would they talk to me?"

"What about our cousins?" Carlos's interest was piqued. They had never met any of their cousins personally, but had been in the same space at the funeral for their grandfather. He remembered his cousins being ushered away from them by frowning adults he was told were his uncles.

"They're not interested," Spiros said. "I was shunned, so you were shunned. It's not an ideal situation, but it was what it was. They were invited; they told me where to go. It's unfortunate, but the way it is."

"So, what about Stefano's fortune? Are they annoyed about that?" Jenny crossed her in-laws' names from the maybe list.

"I don't think they've been told." Spiros chuckled. "I also don't think Giorgio's told them what he's done with his own estate."

"That's not going to end well." Jenny moved on to the list of bridal shops in the city. "But will Giorgio turn up?"

A sigh left Spiros once more. "I *don't know.* It will be up to him."

"He doesn't have much time left. And he more than likely won't see his great-great-grandchildren be born," Jenny added.

"I know, but as I said, it's up to him," Spiros repeated.

Jenny picked up a list that was very special indeed. Everyone had a job on that list, and she was hoping to pull it off without a hitch. "Well, it looks like we'd better get some more things crossed off. Boys, you have your tuxes to get today. Don't forget to buy them and not rent them. And we girls have gown shopping to do. Plus, getting shoes and bags and all the other things you'll need. And then my family are flying in tomorrow or the day after, and they'll be helping."

"Are *all* our cousins coming?" Pedro piped up excitedly. "We haven't seen them since we left Australia."

"Yes. Your grandparents, aunts and uncles, cousins, all of them are coming because it's probably going to be the only time we're all in the same room again." Jenny Stephanopoulos, née Marsh, came from a huge Australian family. With six brothers and five sisters, they had over fifty children between them. And some of *them* were also getting married or having children of their own. The hundred room hotel was going to be packed to the rafters. "It's going to be very rowdy and full. Prepare yourselves for nearly a hundred people."

"Jesus, Mama." Carlos leant forward so he could look past Tomas and Roger. "They're *all* coming? Was there anyone you *didn't* invite?"

Jenny smiled. "Of course not. *Everyone* was invited. It was up to them if they refused or not." She glanced back at the list and saw Roger's family crossed off. They had disowned their son after finding out he was gay, and even though she had called and invited them, they had refused to have anything to do with their son. *Which is a pity,* she thought. *That people can't be more open-minded. It is the '70s after all. Free love, good times, and all that.*

"So, Grandma and Grandpa, six uncles and aunts, five aunts and uncles, and all of the kids are coming?" Pedro was still kneeling in his seat. *"Everyone?"* He remembered the huge family barbeques back in Australia and running around their backyard with his cousins. *"Every* one of them?"

"*Every* one of them is coming." Jenny gathered the papers into their folder and walked over to her son. Laughing at his excited puppy dog expression, she laid her hand on his cheek. "You'll get to see your grandparents, your aunts and uncles and all the cousins again. Just like when you were kids."

"Do they know about Tomas…?" Roger asked. "And me?" He slid his fingers through Tomas's, wondering what the answer would be.

Jenny sat on the arm of Pedro's chair and saw Viv join Carlos, and Angie sit next to Pedro on the other side of the chair. "I did tell them. I also told them that if they had a problem with it to not bother coming. I wasn't going to put up with their vitriol if they didn't agree with the way we do things. But, considering there were a few gay uncles in the family, I don't think anyone minded."

"There were what!" Carlos exclaimed. "I never knew that."

Jenny laughed lightly. "Neither did most of us. But we guessed they were queer as we called it then, and it didn't worry us all that much. Mum didn't worry about it either. She liked her brothers and that was all that mattered."

"Whoa!" Pedro breathed and glanced at his brothers in amazement. "The things you learn from being in *this* family."

November 1977

Tomas put the finishing touches to his brother's tux; a pocket kerchief, and a set of gold initialled cufflinks that were his and Pedro's present to Carlos on his wedding day. The big day had finally come, and for Carlos and Vivian, it was about to get bigger.

"I can't believe you guys bought me a pair of cufflinks for a wedding present," Carlos said as Tomas spun him around. They were facing the full-length mirror in Carlos's bedroom in the family home. He glanced down at the left one as Pedro walked in, resplendent in his tux.

"Why shouldn't we give our big bro a present on his wedding day?" Pedro grinned and shoved his hands into his pockets before standing beside Tomas, so all three Stephanopoulos brothers were in the frame. "It's a hell of a weekend and besides," Pedro's grin grew larger, "let's hope it's the only time you get married."

Tomas smiled in agreement as he brushed down Carlos's tux then put his arms around his brothers. "It's a big weekend for all of us. Do you have the rings?"

Carlos stepped over to the bedside cupboard and withdrew a small velvet box. Opening it, he showed off the two gold wedding bands with inset diamonds for his and hers.

"Matches the engagement ring you bought her." Pedro eyed the rings nestled in the small cushion.

"Didn't you see them the other day?" Carlos asked.

"No, I was busy buying my own," he replied, staring at the box.

Carlos handed the box to Tomas. "Now, don't lose them, little brother, it's your job to hang onto them until the ceremony."

Tomas gazed at them for a moment, feeling a twinge in his heart before gently closing the box and placing it in his jacket pocket. "I won't." Glancing up he saw Roger standing next to his father in the doorway and caught the look in his lover's eyes; the same look he knew he had in his own. A need and want and desire to get married like everyone else. Yet that was not an option if you were gay.

Spiros enjoyed the moment of his three sons standing in their tuxedos preparing for the big day. Although this was Carlos's day, Tomas and Pedro were dressed to the nines as well, and he knew it was time to be their father. Stepping over to Carlos he took him by the arms and kissed both cheeks. "I know that because your mother is Australian, the weddings this weekend will be slightly tamer than most Greek weddings, but we still need to uphold *some* traditions. So, while all of the guests will be Australian or American, you boys are still Greek and are expected to maintain that heritage since there will be no one else there to do so."

He gazed into his son's eyes. So much like his beautiful Jenny's. "You are my eldest, Carlos, I expect you to be a man now you are getting married and have a child on the way. The time for messing around with women is over. The time for whoring yourself out on the big screen is over." A frown came to his face at the thought of what his sons had done. "The time for you to man up is upon you because from tonight, you will be a married man."

Carlos blinked slowly. Even though he loved Viv and wanted to spend the rest of his life with her, the realisation of the situation was just now sinking in. Sinking in now he had his tux on, sinking in now he had his father giving him a pre-wedding lecture, and his brothers were beside him in tuxes to match his own. "Papa," he started then stopped.

"No, Carlos," Spiros went on. "You need to be a man and provide for your wife and child now. You need a job that will provide what your family *needs,* and not what your own desires want. Stability and not pornography."

"Papa." Carlos licked his lips. "It's not something I'm going to be in forever. As Viv said, I may choose to be a stay-at-home dad. I don't know yet. We have the next few months to think about things and put a plan into action, so there's no rush. Okay?" He took his father's hands and kissed each one before kissing both of his cheeks. "I love you, Papa, but leave it. This weekend is all about celebrating. Your sons are getting married. Then we have Christmas and New Year's, and then Viv and I will start making plans. But until then, can you just leave talk of jobs and work and plans until the new year? Please, Papa?"

Spiros relented. "Okay. But you know I had to give you that speech for your mother's sake. Otherwise, she would have hounded me about why I didn't."

The boys grinned. "Yes, Papa," Carlos said with a knowing wink at his brothers. "It was all for Mama's sake."

*****

Jenny walked around Vivian's room at the Windmill Hotel. It was a gorgeous suite overlooking the back terrace, reception hall on the right, cascading gardens down to the seaside, and dotted windmills on the left. She took a moment to smell the aromas wafting through the French doors before shutting them. Deep ocean, succulent flowers, and all kinds of food floated along and made her mouth water. Turning from the closed doors, she saw Vivian emerge from the bathroom in a light pearl grey silk pantsuit with matching heels, and a white lace ruffled blouse. When they'd gone shopping, Vivian had thought it more appropriate, not only for her age, but since she was far from virginal.

Compared with her future daughter-in-law, Jenny was feeling a little matronly in her own silk calf-length blue dress with its long sleeves and pearl buttons. Skin-coloured stockings and blue silk pumps finished off the outfit. She smoothed it down and watched Viv place a delicate antique watch on her left wrist. "All done?"

Viv looked up. The baby's breath and miniature roses wound through her stylishly rolled, but loose up-do had a halo effect, making her look even more breathtakingly gorgeous than she already was. "All done," she breathed and gave herself the once over in the mirror. "How do I look? It's appropriate for a wedding, right? Even a Greek one?" She spun around, distress on her face. "What if I'm not Greek enough?"

Jenny went from a frown to a laugh. "Well, I'm not either. The wedding takes into account some Greek traditions, but not all of them." She moved to Viv's side. "Don't worry. I've planned it perfectly. Hell, I've had twenty-five years to do it."

With a knock at the door, Angelina walked in.

Viv sighed and glanced her way then back at Jenny. "I just hope there won't be any problems with the priest about me not being Greek and all."

Jenny shrugged. "Neither am I, but they eventually accepted me. Although in part, I think it was because of who I was related to. But I also think I've proven myself in the community. Besides," she grasped Viv's hands, "there will be more Australians than Greeks, so don't worry." Turning to Angelina, she added, "Feeling better?"

Angelina smiled wanly. "A little." She was looking a little washed-out in the off-white dress she'd chosen. "Don't worry Viv, how do you think I feel? I *am* Greek, but my father tried to kill my husband-to-be and ended up dead. And my ex-step-grandfather killed my illegitimate half-brother, so I have no family coming either."

Jenny held out her arms for Angelina to come into the circle. "We're your family now, believe that." Looking from Angie to Viv to include her she continued, "Whenever you need anything, whenever you want anything, we're your family, we're here. We pull together in times of need, and after everything we've all been through, we need to pull together now more than ever. If you need help with the babies, just ask, and I'll be there." She hugged Angelina close. "Especially with you still being so young and wanting to continue studying. It's going to be hard, and you'll need lots of help, so don't hesitate to ask." She turned her attention to Viv and held out her hand again, waiting while Viv took hers. "That goes for you too. Babies can be a lot to deal with at any age."

Viv smiled, feeling warmth flow through her at Jenny's love and support. She couldn't remember the last time she felt that from a parent and hadn't been sure if she'd get it from Jenny. She was feeling the ice melt. Even though she hadn't detected hatred or resentment, she hadn't detected an overdose of love either. *Probably my age*, she thought. *After all, who doesn't love me?*

There was another knock on the door and Sarah Marsh, Jenny's mother, walked in. "It's nearly five. Are you ready yet? Don't we have to be at the church for a five-thirty start?" She gave Viv the once over. "My, what a lovely pantsuit, Vivian. It's very becoming."

"Thank you, Mrs Marsh," Viv murmured. "I thought it was appropriate." Not only did Viv have Jenny to contend with, but at least seventy other family members. *Oh, good grief,* she thought, *how am I going to deal with all of them?*

"I'll call Spiros and let him know we're leaving." Jenny went over to the phone and dialled home, waiting for the connection.

"Hello."

"Spiros, we're ready and will be leaving for the church shortly. How are the boys?"

Spiros glanced behind him and saw all three still regaling themselves in Carlos's mirror. He couldn't stop a smile from forming on his lips. "They're our boys," he said. "Exactly how they always are. Fighting over a mirror to see which one looks best."

Jenny laughed lightly. "Oh, they're definitely our boys. I'll see you soon." Replacing the phone in its cradle, she turned to the others. "Grab your coats, it's time to go." After gathering their things they left and entered the melee that was the Marsh family in the hotel lobby. "Okay everyone, time to leave. It's about a ten-minute walk, so it will warm you up. Let's go." Sliding on her coat, she took Viv by the arm and led the way down the cobblestone street to the island's Greek Orthodox Church where she, Viv and Angelina entered by the back door, and Sarah led the rest of the family around to the front.

While Viv gave herself the once over in the mirror, Jenny went in search of Spiros and the boys, finding them in the nave near the door, greeting everyone as they came in and seated themselves. "Oh, look at you boys!" Jenny exclaimed, feeling her heart explode with pride at how devastatingly handsome and tall they looked in their tuxedos.

"Mama," all three answered, but grinned at their mother's affection.

Jenny took Carlos into her arms. "Oh, my baby's getting married," she murmured. Leaning back, she ran a hand through his hair. "My firstborn is getting married, my baby's getting married."

"Mama," Carlos admonished, his grin growing bigger. "Pedro's the baby of the family. I'm the man."

"Better not let Papa hear you say that," Tomas quietly told him. "You'd never hear the end of it."

"And *I'm not a baby,*" Pedro admonished right back.

"But you're not yet an adult. Not until February," Jenny reminded him. "Until then, you are *all* my babies." She kissed Carlos on each cheek, then Tomas and Pedro, and waved at Roger as she walked up to Spiros. "We're ready on this end."

Spiros slid an arm around her waist. "Just a few more minutes and we'll be ready to go." They saw the altar boys close the doors.

Father Bowen stepped forward. "Are we both ready?"

"Once everyone is seated we'll start," Jenny told him and watched as he nodded and wandered down the aisle to the altar.

"Does he know about Tomas?" Spiros asked as they faced the front.

"Probably, but not from me," Jenny replied.

"Will he have a problem with it?" Spiros went on as they walked past everyone, making sure they all had their places.

"Who knows," Jenny muttered, waving at family members. "But if he does he'll have me to answer to."

"And what about Sunday?"

"As far as I'm concerned that's all set." She smiled brightly at the boys. "Take your places; we're almost ready." With one last look at the whole Marsh family that had filled both sides of the church, Jenny dashed back to the waiting room to Angelina and Viv. "Ready to go?"

Viv froze. *Oh, my God, oh, my God, oh, my God,* sped through her mind. *I'm about to get married. Oh, my God, I'm about to get married. Oh, my God, can I say oh, my God in a church, wait, I'm not saying oh, my God, I'm thinking oh, my God. Oh, my God, can I think oh, my God in a church?*

"Viv?"

She turned to see Jenny and Angelina waiting for her.

"Viv?" Jenny stepped over to her. "Are you all right?" Taking her by the arms, she peered closely. "You're not going to be sick, are you?"

"No," Viv said slowly. "I'm just…" a breath, "I'm just…" another breath, "oh, my God I've never been married before, and it's really hitting me now."

Jenny smiled. "It is a big step. But you love Carlos, don't you?"

Viv stared into her future mother-in-law's eyes. "Yes. God yes, I love him. I love him so much."

"And this is the next step in that love," Jenny said, giving her arm a quick squeeze. "Don't worry, don't fear, just love."

Viv nodded slowly and regained her composure.

"Now," Jenny told her, "let's go." She led Viv and Angelina down the hallway at the side of the church that led around to the front doors. The priest, Carlos, Spiros, Tomas and Pedro were there waiting.

Carlos's eyes grew wide at the sight of his betrothed as she walked forward. "Oh, Viv." His eyes roamed up and down, his heart beat in double, no, triple time, and he took a deep breath.

A shy smile spread across Viv's face as she stood before him clutching her small bouquet of white roses. "Look at you. Incredibly gorgeous as always," she said lightly.

Tomas took his position by Carlos's side, and Pedro stood by his.

Spiros stepped around to Jenny's side with Angelina on her left. The betrothal service was about to start.

"Do you, Carlos Spiros Stephanopoulos come of your own free will?" Father Bowen asked.

Carlos licked his lips nervously, tore his gaze from Viv to look at the Father. "I do."

Father Bowen gazed upon Vivian's beauty. "And do you, Vivian Marcella Villiers come of your own free will?"

She smiled brightly as she gazed upon Carlos's freshly shaven face. "I do."

"Then we shall continue." Father Bowen turned and walked slowly down the aisle with Vivian and Carlos behind him. Tomas followed Carlos with Pedro following him as best men. Jenny and Angelina followed Vivian. Spiros trailed behind, closed the doors, and took his seat as they stopped at the altar.

"Do you, koumbaro, have the rings?" the priest asked Tomas.

"I do." Tomas removed the box from his pocket, opened it, and handed the rings to the priest.

Father Bowen picked up each one, blessed them, and placed them upon the right ring finger of Carlos and Vivian before exchanging them three times. This symbolised that their lives would be entwined forever. He started chanting a prayer and placed his vestment over Viv and Carlos's crossed hands. Once he was finished, he lit two candles and handed one each to the bride and groom to hold throughout the rest of the ceremony. Then he gathered two crowns, known as stefanas, held them up in front of the couple, and made three cross signs above them before holding them in front so they could kiss the crowns before he placed them on their heads. The stefanas were made of evergreen leaves to symbolise fertility, with orange blossoms to signify purity. There were small olive branches and herbs, all tied together with a white ribbon.

Tomas was beckoned forward to perform his duty, switching the stefanas back and forth three times before stepping back to Carlos's side.

Father Bowen continued with Bible readings before presenting a cup of red wine for the bride and groom to drink from, then a spoon of honey nuts from which they ate.

Jenny glanced at her son and future daughter-in-law, tears welling in her eyes as she saw the joy and love in their eyes as the priest led them around the altar table three times in the dance of Isaiah. It symbolised that the couple would follow the word of God as they started their new life together. Once they circled, they stood before the altar, and the priest lifted the crowns and used the Bible to uncouple the joining of hands, representing that only God was able to divide them.

Jenny's eyes wandered over to Spiros and saw him look her way. He smiled, and she remembered that day twenty-five years earlier in the little Greek Orthodox Church in Armidale, New South Wales. They had married in May, and she'd had Carlos nine months later. She wiped her tears away and remembered the overwhelming love that had taken hold of her that day; threatened to overload and overtake her, threatening to send her into a flood of tears as she gave herself to the man she loved. Glancing back at the happy couple, she saw the priest finish up and move on to the westernised Bible passages before Viv and Carlos said their vows. Jenny had made sure that not all of the ceremony was traditional Greek.

"Do you, Carlos Spiros Stephanopoulos, take Vivian Marcella Villiers, to be your lawful wedded wife? To have and to hold, for richer or poorer, in sickness and in health, till death do you part?"

Carlos gazed lovingly at Viv. "I do."

"And do you, Vivian Marcella Villiers, take Carlos Spiros Stephanopoulos, to be your lawful wedded husband? To have and to hold, for richer or poorer, in sickness and in health, till death do you part?"

Viv gazed back at her betrothed. "I do."

"Then by the power vested in me, I now pronounce you, husband and wife. You may kiss the bride."

Carlos turned to his new wife and stared into her eyes. "Hello, wife."

Sliding her arms around his neck, Viv replied, "Hello, husband."

Their lips met as arms entwined and the church broke into applause. Viv's mouth broke loose, and her head flew back in laughter as Carlos spun her around.

Jenny jumped forward to embrace Carlos. "Oh, my baby." She hugged him fiercely. "I can't believe you're married." She held an arm out for Viv and pulled her into the hug. "Welcome to the family."

"Thank you," Viv murmured as Tomas, Pedro and Spiros joined the hug.

Amongst hugs and kisses, the bride and groom made their way down the aisle, through the family, and into the night as husband and wife.

*****

"Here's to Carlos and Vivian, long may they live," Spiros declared, his drink held high.

"To Carlos and Vivian," everyone murmured and threw back their shot glasses of ouzo.

"Let the festivities begin," Spiros told the group and a traditional Greek band burst into life.

"Oh, my God, that was horrible." Roger shook his head as he swallowed the ouzo.

Tomas agreed, putting his glass down and refusing a refill. "That's why we don't drink it." He watched his father lead his in-laws in a circle dance, and as they passed their table waved for Carlos and Viv to join in.

Viv laughingly allowed Carlos to pull her into the circle, and she held hands with Spiros on her right.

Tomas watched the celebration from his seat at the head table for a few moments more before turning back to Roger on his right. "I wish we could do this." His fingers wound through Roger's, and he leant in closer to talk.

"Have a wedding reception?" Roger asked, wrapping an arm around his lover and gazing into his deep brown eyes.

Tomas smiled shyly. "Not just a reception, but a wedding."

"A wedding, huh?" Roger mused. "Are you proposing, Mr Stephanopoulos?"

Tomas blushed and gazed down at his hand entwined with Roger's. "I was kind of hoping you would."

"Oh, really," Roger teased. "Not up to doing what your brothers did and whipping out an engagement ring?"

The blush deepened. "Well," Tomas said, "I was hoping since you were older and wiser…"

"And sexier," Roger cut in.

That made Tomas laugh. "Oh, definitely sexier than my brothers."

"Ew, not what I was talking about," Roger told him, glancing over at Carlos and Pedro in the middle of the circle dance. "But now that you mention it…"

"Ew, Roger, stop kidding." Tomas punched him lightly on the arm. "I'm being serious."

"Well, in all seriousness, you know we can't get married," Roger said, taking a swig of the champagne the waiter had dropped off. It annihilated the taste of the ouzo.

A deep sigh left Tomas, and his eyes found his brother and Viv dancing with each other in the circle. Pedro and Angelina, his mother and father were around them, and the Marsh family around them. "I know." His eyes welled, his lips quivered, and he quickly walked out of the reception room and stood on the terrace overlooking the ocean.

Roger followed and put his arms around Tomas. "Would it mean that much to you if we could get married, or *be* married?"

Tomas choked on a sob. "Yes. After everything I went through with Luiz, and being poisoned and kidnapped, all I thought of was you and getting back to you and being with you. I love you, Roger. I want to be with you for the rest of my life, but I can't be…legally." He sobbed. "And Pedro proposed to Angie, and Carlos to Viv, and the girls are pregnant, and now they're getting married and what about us? What about me?" He looked over his left shoulder and into Roger's eyes. "What about *me*? Doesn't this Stephanopoulos brother get to be happy and married? Don't *I* matter? Don't *I* count?" Tears flowed down his face; hot rolling tears of pain and loneliness.

"Oh, my love," Roger crooned, nuzzling Tomas with his cheek as he leant over his shoulder. Gazing across the ocean, he tried to soothe Tomas's tears. "I love you, too, and I wish to God we could be married, but it doesn't work that way. Gays aren't allowed to be unless it's to a member of the opposite sex. We can't, no matter how much we want it."

Tomas's sobs deepened. "It's not fair. It's not fair."

"I know, my love, I know."

Jenny stood watching her son sob his heart out in his lover's arms and felt her heart shatter into a million itty bitty pieces. Oh, how she ached for him. Just when he had found the love of his life and settled into who he was meant to be as a man, and an adult, his emotions threaten to overload and leave him behind. *Society* was threatening to leave him behind. But if it was the last thing she did, and she knew it wouldn't be, Jenny Stephanopoulos was going to do something about it. *She* was not going to leave her son behind! With a swipe at her tears, she re-entered the reception hall and left them to their moment.

"Mama," Pedro called, running over to her as she reached the table. "Come join."

With a teary laugh, she let him sweep her back into the circle dance that was still going, and joined with Spiros and her mother until the music stopped a few minutes later for dinner.

After everyone was seated, and with Tomas and Roger back from their alone time, Spiros led the celebratory meal with a mention of himself. "We have lamb of all kinds for these celebrations. Lambs from my butcher shop, *Stephanopoulos Meats* no less, so you know that it will be the best in Greece. There is pig and fresh fish, alcohol for everyone's tastes, and desserts to make your mouth water. So, dig in, and then tell me what you think of the lamb."

"Spiros," Jenny chastised. "This isn't about you." She pulled him down into his seat, and everyone dug in to the succulent Lamb Yuovetsi. A savoury meal of lamb, braised and marinated with ouzo and tomato, topped with Kefalotyri cheese, and side dishes of vegetables and spiced beans. Everyone talked among themselves while they ate.

"So...what do you think of Roger?" Matthew Marsh, Jenny's father, asked his wife as he sliced into the lamb on his plate. "Did we even guess Tomas was that way?"

"Hush," Sarah whispered, looking from Tomas to her husband. "I always wondered why he didn't have a girlfriend, but he just didn't seem interested either way. I should have realised considering my brothers were that way, even though no one told us they were gay, of course." She took a sip of champagne. "But we all knew they were strange. The clothes they wore for a start. Tight pants and shirts, or shorts and t-shirts. Plus, they walked weirdly, and you never saw them with women."

She watched those at the head table. Spiros and Jenny at the end, followed by Pedro and Angelina, Vivian and Carlos, then Tomas and

Roger. Her gaze lingered on Tomas and Roger. *They look like normal young men growing up in the '70s, and Roger is Australian,* she thought. *They don't look queer at all.*

When Jenny had rung to invite them to the weddings, she had told her all about the future in-laws, and that one of them was a man. Jenny had warned her and the rest of the family that if they weren't happy with them being gay, then not to come. She didn't have an issue with it personally, having gay brothers and all, but had found out on the flight over what the rest of the family had thought. She turned back to Matthew. "Do *you* have a problem with him being gay?" She saw two of her daughters look her way. They were sitting opposite them at table two. There were twelve in all, with table one belonging to the bride and groom.

"Well, I guess it is the '70s," Matthew replied, watching Jenny continually glance down the table at Tomas and Roger with a secret smile on her face. "She's up to something. Do you know what it is?"

Sarah glanced over at Jenny. "No, but then it might be a surprise."

"Oh, I really don't think I could eat this." Angelina moaned softly and pushed her lamb aside. "The smell is turning me off."

"Same here," Viv told her quietly, finishing off the vegetables and spiced beans. "The vegetables I can handle, the lamb I cannot."

"Is morning sickness all day sickness now?" Carlos asked them, finishing his meal off with favourite beer, as Jenny had seen to it that their favourite food and beverages were served.

Viv groaned delicately and dabbed her mouth before putting her napkin on her plate. "It must be. The smell of the lamb is just…ugh."

"Or is it the smell of meat in general?" Angie asked, pushing her plate away. "I smelt the pork and fish before, it was the same. It made me sick."

"Then just have vegetables tomorrow night." Pedro leant toward her. "Coz we get to do this all again tomorrow."

Viv and Angelina both looked at him. "Ugh," they groaned in unison.

"Who'd have thunk it," Antonio DeLuca, Carlos's old bartending mate told a couple called Beth and David, who were relatives of

Carlos. "That Carlos could pull a chick like Vivian Villiers." He took a swig of beer. "She's sixteen years older than him, you know."

David laughed. He was the boys' cousin and knew even when they were younger, running around the streets of Armidale, that Carlos was a stud with girls. "Oh, man, where have you been? He's been like that all his life. He could pull any chick he wanted and had them waiting in a line around the block when he did a kissing booth for the school fate one year. He was fourteen, and it wasn't long before they left to come here. Pedro was a bit too young for it, as were the girls in his class, but while they all had a crush on Pedro coz he's so adorable, they had a bigger crush on Carlos. And of course, Tomas was never interested in girls, or boys for that matter. But look how he's turned out." He shrugged. "Aunt Jenny doesn't have a problem with how her sons have turned out, or who they're with, so why should we?" He picked up his own beer and took a long swallow.

"Yeah, but dude," Antonio went on, watching the delicious Viv get nuzzled by Carlos. "She's hot *and* older. What I wouldn't give to get a real woman like her. An *older* woman. I wonder if she has sisters."

David laughed again and shook his head. "From the way Carlos went on about her when he was fourteen, I don't think so."

"That's a pity, but Jesus, Vivian Villiers." Antonio's jealousy burned through his body and out of his eyes. "Bloody lucky bastard."

"Cheers to that." David held up his beer bottle and clinked it with Antonio's.

After a delicious dessert of baklava and strong Greek coffee, Carlos stood and dinged his champagne glass with his knife. "Everyone, can I have your attention." He waited while the noise died down. "I want to thank you all for coming tonight. I know it was a last-minute thing and Mama made all the calls and probably threatened you all with bodily harm if you didn't come." The crowd tittered as Jenny blushed a deep red. "But it's been a long time since we saw you all and believe me, memories have come flooding back for all of us." He moved to wave at his brothers to include them. "Now, a lot of you know what we do, and a lot of you know Viv is a supermodel." She blushed. "But tonight is all about our love and us coming together in this union called marriage. Because for me, there will never be anyone else I will ever want more, or love more, or need more, than this amazingly beautiful woman beside me tonight."

He gazed down at her smiling face as the family clapped. "Viv, you are my everything." He took her face in his left hand, and she nuzzled it. "You are my life, my wife, the mother of my future children, and I love you. I would risk my life for you. I will *and* would do anything and everything to protect you." She kissed his hand. "And I am so glad that you accepted my proposal. I am so glad that you are my wife." He picked up his champagne glass and faced the crowd. "And I am so glad that all of my family is here to enjoy it." He spied his great-grandfather in the back of the reception room. "Especially my father's grandfather, Giorgio Stephanopoulos, who is not long for this world." He raised his glass to Giorgio who nodded his gratitude in return as everyone glanced to the back of the room. "Thank you, everyone, for coming and sharing our special day." The room cheered.

"Okay." Carlos put down his glass. "Now it's time for the best man's speech." He looked at Tomas and slapped him on the shoulder. "Take it away, little brother."

"What!" Tomas looked up in shock. "I haven't…I didn't…I can't…"

"Who cares if you don't have anything prepared, just say what you think," Carlos told him as he sat down.

Tomas glanced wildly at Roger who encouraged him to stand up. "Ah." Tomas looked down the table to see encouraging nods. "Ah…I…" He stood. "Didn't know I'd need to do a speech, so haven't prepared anything," he told the crowd.

"Tell us about Carlos's porn star career," someone yelled out from the back of the room. Quiet laughter filled the space.

"Ah," Tomas said and then had an idea. "I can't tell you about that because if you've already seen it, you'd know all about it." More laughter. "But I can tell you all about how he had a poster of the gorgeous Vivian Villiers on his wall when he was fourteen and what he did with it when he was alone."

"Don't you dare," Carlos threatened darkly.

"We already know," a man yelled out. He was Chris Marsh and

had gone to school with his cousins as he was the same age as Carlos.

Carlos flew into a standing position. "Don't you dare," he told Chris, "or I will kill you both!" The other cousins laughed, for they all knew how Carlos had masturbated over that poster night after night because he'd been walked in on by Chris, Tomas, Pedro, and other cousins.

"That's what you get for not locking the door when you're doing it," Cousin Dean called out. He was Tomas's age and had also gone to the same school and had been one of the group to walk in on Carlos. "Next time you do it, lock your damn door."

Raucous laughter followed, and Carlos went a deep red. Even Viv was blushing as she knew all about it. They looked at each other in embarrassment.

"Okay, okay." Tomas put his hands up to calm the room. "Who knew, that when the great sex machine, Carlos Stephanopoulos, was fourteen, with a poster of the amazingly gorgeous supermodel Vivian Villiers on his wall," Carlos threw him another threatening look, "that ten years later, after moving to Mykonos, that he would meet that gorgeous woman herself, the great Vivian Villiers, and capture her heart."

"Aw," went through the room as Viv and Carlos gazed into each other's eyes.

Tomas went on. "That the gorgeous Vivian Villiers would be taken with the half Greek island stud of Carlos Stephanopoulos."

"Must have been his ten-inch cock," Chris called out. "It was used to seeing her after all." Wild applause went around the room, and Tomas tried to contain his laughter and remain serious, but one look at a laughing Pedro and he joined in.

Carlos stood. "*Not funny people!*" he admonished and pointed to Chris. "I'm gonna get you for this."

"Yeah! What with? Your ten-inch cock," Chris replied and all the male cousins joined in with jibes and jeers.

"Well, that cock got Vivian Villiers, and it also got Berry Wilder, the first girl *you* liked and wanted to date," Carlos told him.

The laughter died down to oohs and aahs.

"What!" Redness swept over Chris's face as his cousin's words sank in. "You what?"

Berry Wilder, named Berry for the colour of her hair but whose real name was Bethany, was a girl in their grade at school. She'd always had a massive crush on Carlos, but Chris had a massive crush on her.

"*What?*" Carlos repeated. "You don't remember Berry?" Teasing his cousin, he went in for the kill. "Did *you* ever get Berry after I left?" Seeing Chris's blank face, he went on. "What's that? No? No, that's because she had a taste of the great Carlos before I left."

Chris's expression darkened. "Oh, you dirty bastard," he said. "I'm gonna get you for that." Cousins oohed and aahed for many knew of the triangle that was Berry, Chris and Carlos.

"Let me get back on track," Tomas called out to calm the situation, and putting a hand on Carlos's shoulder, pushed him down into his chair. He knew Carlos and Chris had a feud back in school, but had figured it was long over. "I want to propose a toast to Viv and Carlos. A match made in heaven." He raised his glass and waited while the others followed suit. "To Viv and Carlos."

"Viv and Carlos."

He led a round of applause and sat down. "I had no idea that was about to happen," he told Carlos. "You should *not* have made me give a speech."

Carlos laughed. "Don't worry about it. I was just shit stirring, but if Chris has a problem, we'll sort it out later." A glass dinged to their left, and they turned to see Pedro standing.

"Everyone, I want to make a toast now." Pedro looked around the room. "Since I was too young to know about the Berry Wilder incident," guffaws all around, "I won't go into it." He grinned and faced Carlos. "What I'd like to say is that Carlos has been the best big brother anyone could hope for. He has taught me things—"

"Like how to be a manwhore," Chris yelled out.

Pedro tried not to laugh and kept going. "Like how to be a manwhore," the laughter leaked out, "how to be strong, and independent, and go after what I wanted. Which I did." He encompassed Viv into his gaze. "To

Carlos and Viv. May your life be better, brighter, happier, and may your children never follow in their daddy's footsteps." More blushing and guffaws. "To Carlos and Viv."

"Carlos and Viv!"

"I love you, man." Pedro walked around Angelina and Viv to embrace Carlos.

"I love you, too." Carlos hugged him back as Pedro pulled Tomas into the hug. "I love both of you." He held them, and after a few moments, he let go and turned to Viv. "Welcome to the family, Viv." Leaning down he kissed her cheek before going back to his chair.

Jenny squeezed his shoulder as she and Spiros stood. "Our turn. Listen up, everyone. We're going to make the last toast, and then we'll party all night." She lifted her glass with Spiros right beside her.

"Carlos," he said, looking down at his eldest. "You carry my name, you carry my family jewels—"

"Oh, my God, Spiros," Jenny interrupted, blushing a deep red to the oohs and aahs of her family.

Spiros winked at her. "Well, it's true." He looked once more at his laughing son. "*And* you carry the bloodline. The blood of all the Stephanopouloses is in your veins, and now you are passing them down to your child. May the child be strong, may your love be deep, and may your marriage be for eternity."

"Aw, Papa," Carlos muttered, embarrassed, but flattered by his father's speech.

"My turn," Jenny called. "My baby. My firstborn." Tears sprang to her eyes. "My baby boy born nearly twenty-five years ago. You have shown strength, maturity, and boundless love. Not just for your family, but in your love for Viv." She glanced from one to the other as she wiped her tears away. "A love that I pray will last for your lifetime and be a testament to how well I..." She blushed and threw a quick glance at Spiros. "*We* raised you. To be a man, an adult, and a provider. May your love last forever. To Carlos and Viv."

"Carlos and Viv!"

After a sip of champagne, Jenny moved to her son and stood crying tears of joy in his arms. Spiros was right behind her.

"Oh, Mama." Carlos fiercely hugged his mother, feeling every ounce of motherly love emoting from her pores. "I love you so much."

"I love you, too. Oh, my baby." She kissed his face all over. "I love you so much. I still remember pushing your big head out of my loins."

"Mama!" Carlos exclaimed with wide eyes. "Don't say that. I don't want to hear stuff like that."

"Why not?" Jenny pulled back to look him in the eye. "It's true. Your head was big, and it hurt like hell." She pinched both his cheeks. "But look at you. I'd do it all over again in a second."

"Mama." He reddened. "Thank you, for all of this. For the way you raised us to love each other and protect and defend. You and Papa made me the man that I am." He kissed both of her cheeks. "I love you."

"I love you, too." Jenny turned to Viv. "I know I've said it before, but welcome to the family." She reached out to squeeze her hand. "I know you make my son happy and that makes me happy."

Viv touched her other hand to her chest at the sentiment and stood to hug her. "Thank you, so much."

Spiros spied his grandfather at the back of the room. "I think there's someone you should go and talk to." He saw Carlos's perplexed expression and nodded toward the back of the room.

Carlos turned to see his great-grandfather. "Yes." He turned back to his father. "We will. Come on, Viv." He took her hand from his mother's. "Let's go say hello." They made their way to the back of the reception hall to stand by the side of his great-grandfather.

"Ah, Carlos, Vivian," the old man rasped, holding out a hand for Carlos to take. "Congratulations."

"Thank you." Carlos sat in the empty seat beside him and pulled Viv onto his lap. "I know you paid for the hotel for the week. Thank you for that too."

"It was nothing. Just a small contribution to the family. After all these years of missing out, it was the least I could do," Giorgio told him.

Carlos studied the man before him. Old, bald, near his end. He couldn't see any resemblance to himself or his brothers or father, except in the twinkle of the eye and the goofy Stephanopoulos grin.

Giorgio waved a withered hand across in front of him. "Your mother outdid herself with the reception. And you do it all again tomorrow." He gazed upon his great-grandson with newfound affection.

Carlos glanced around and agreed. "Leave it to Mama to organise something like this in a week, and get all of the family here."

"Not all." Giorgio's sadness was evident. "Your Greek side isn't here."

Carlos smiled and gently squeezed his hand. "But that's where you're wrong, Great-grandfather." The old man looked up. "I have my great-grandfather, my father, my two brothers, the people that matter, and that's more than enough."

Giorgio's heart swelled with pride, and he clasped Carlos's hand between both of his. "Yes, yes, my boy, you do. You have those who matter." He took Viv's hand and placed it on Carlos's and then enclosed them both within his. "You have all that matters."

*****

In Los Angeles, Harry and Harriet DeVille, Carlos's porn star bosses, were celebrating *and* commiserating the marriage of Carlos and Vivian. They had invited the entire cast and crew to join them, since none were invited to the ceremony itself, and popped bottle after bottle of champagne to drink to the newly married couple.

"I am so glad Carlos found someone," Aneeka Ne Masta, famed African American photographer friend of Harry, held her glass aloft. "They were so happy in Athens."

"Mmm," Tony Vega, a *DeVille* bodyguard mumbled. "She deserves more than that pretty boy idiot. Look at all the trouble he caused." Sitting on the couch in Harry's lounge room overlooking the penis-shaped pool in the back yard and Los Angeles beyond that, he crossed his arms and grumbled.

Aneeka smiled down at him. "Yes, he caused trouble, but it was not his fault. You were there, you know that."

Harry cracked another bottle and took a plate of hors d'oeuvre from Suzy, his maid. "Well, I don't care if he didn't cause it or start it, the boy is still a *DeVille* member, and we will celebrate."

Harriet played with the pearls around her throat. "How I wish I were there, but his mother banned us from attending."

"She did no such thing, Harriet," Harry scolded. "We just weren't invited."

"She did too. But I'm his mother here in L.A.," Harriet whined, delicately sipping her champagne.

"Oh, for *heaven's sake,* Harriet," Harry complained. "*You're not his mother*, Jenny Stephanopoulos is, and there is no way we were going to be invited." He made sure everyone had a full glass. "Drink up everyone, and celebrate the wedding of our dear friend, Vivian Villiers, to our biggest porn star ever, Carlos Stephanopoulos."

*****

At two o'clock Saturday morning, the reception was still blasting away, but Carlos had had enough and wanted to be with his wife.

"Mama, Papa, we're going now. Thank you for everything, we loved it." Kissing both parents on the cheek, he stepped back for Viv to give her thanks.

"Yes, thank you, both so much." She hugged and kissed them both. "But I've had enough, and I really need to rest." She slipped her arm through Carlos's and stared up into his big blue eyes. "Plus, I want to go and be with my new husband."

Jenny touched her hand to her chest. "Of course you both do. Go, go, go be a married couple and we'll see you tomorrow afternoon for Pedro's wedding. Go, go." She ushered them along. "Just go and don't stop for anyone."

Arm in arm, Carlos and Viv stopped at his grandparent's table to kiss them goodnight, before sidestepping the rest of the family and the handfuls of rice and rose petals they threw at them. Laughing, they made a quick stop at Giorgio's table before making a break for it and running for the hotel, up the stairs, and to Viv's suite before stopping to take a breath.

"Ah, come here my gorgeous, amazing, incredible wife." Carlos spun her into his arms and captured her.

She laughed and wound her arms around his neck. "Only gorgeous, amazing and incredible?" she asked. "Is that all?"

"No." Carlos shook his head. "No, that is not all my sexy, vivacious, saucy wife."

Her laughter grew louder. "And I love you my gorgeous," she kissed him, "amazing," another kiss, "incredible," another kiss, "sexy," a longer kiss, "vivacious," and even longer kiss, "saucy husband." The kiss deepened, and they held on tight for endless moments until they parted.

Carlos slid his hands through her brunette locks, pulling the pins with him, allowing the curls to fall freely down her back.

Her fingers slid his bow tie off and followed it up with his tux jacket.

His hands slid to her blazer buttons and deftly removed the coat from her body.

Her hands slid through his shirt buttons, opening them and removing the shirt from his manly five-ten frame.

Carlos sighed as she slid her hands over him, feeling their softness, their womanly touch, and felt himself harden. He unbuttoned her lacy blouse and slid it off her shoulders, and his hands and lips left a blazing trail of kisses along her collarbone and onto her shoulders. He received a small sigh in return and let the blouse fall before moving to her pants. They joined her blouse and jacket on the floor, and she stood before him in her lacy teddy.

His penis strained for release, and so did he. "Jesus, Viv," he breathed as her hands unzipped his pants and pushed both them and his underwear down to the ground.

Viv saw the ten inches of goodness and stroked it, tearing a groan from his throat. They had abstained for the week; a decision they'd both made as much as that screwed up their reunion. She had been too sick, but had also wanted to wait. And now, here they were together…finally. "I love you," she whispered, stroking him into release.

"Jesus Viv, we could have…"

"Shhh." Her lips went to his mouth. "It's not time yet." Sliding her teddy straps over her shoulders, she wiggled it to the floor, revealing pert breasts and pearl-grey panties. "Your turn."

He groaned and licked his lips. "Oh, God, Viv." His lips found hers and launched themselves to her neck. They slid over her collarbone and shoulder, finding their way to her breasts.

"Oh, God," they groaned together.

Her hands slid over his well-muscled back and into his golden-brown hair, hanging on as he sucked her nipple into a hard bud. She grew wetter than she already was and longed for his ten inches to do their magic.

His lips slid down her body to her navel, and as his tongue poked and prodded, his fingers slipped into the lacy concoction covering her womanhood and ripped them down her legs.

"Oh, God, Carlos, take me," she cried as his tongue did the deed. "Oh, God." She flung her head back making her golden-brown hair cascade down over her pert ass.

His lips and tongue moved upwards. His hands took hold of her ass and lifted. Lifted her upwards, upwards and onto him as he stood proudly. All ten glorious inches of him.

She cried out at the sensations. The sensation of ten inches sliding inside of her as she wrapped her legs around his waist and her arms around his neck. It had been weeks since they'd made love and waiting for this night was torture. But to make love for the first time as husband and wife had been worth it. Worth the trauma and drama. Worth waiting until she was forty to find the man of her dreams.

His hands slid along her legs, across her ass, and up her lithe back into her hair. "Oh, God, Viv. I love you so much," he said against her lips.

"Take me," she gasped. "I'm yours."

He stepped out of his pants, over to the bed, and lowered them gently onto the rose-covered sheets.

*****

"Okay, everyone," Jenny told her family. "It's five o'clock, time for bed. Morning's nearly here, and we need to get some sleep so we can do this all again tonight." She glanced around the room. Pedro and

Angelina had left not long after Carlos and Viv, and so had Tomas and Roger. Spiros was still going strong, teaching her family Greek dances, but she was flagging and needed sleep. *Thank God I'm staying here at the hotel through most of this,* she thought. The boys had stayed with Spiros in their home, and she had stayed with the girls and her family at the hotel.

"What do you *mean*, time for bed, we're still celebrating," Spiros called from the circle dance that was going on. "I could do this all night."

"You have," Jenny called back. "It's five o'clock in the morning, time to stop." She waved at the band to stop, and they wound down the music. They were glad to be going home as well.

Grumbles went around the room, but it was evident they were flagging. Several brothers and sisters had gone, as had cousins and Jenny's parents not long after the boys. Only the young ones kept going. They applauded for the band before gathering their things.

Spiros came over to Jenny. "My love. Have you had enough?" He kissed both cheeks and wrapped his arms around her.

She breathed him in. "Yes. My feet are killing me, my back is killing me, and you've had way too much to drink." Jenny glanced over his shoulder. "Don't forget to be up by four this afternoon," she called to her family as they departed. They waved in return, and she picked up her purse from the table and Spiros's jacket from his chair. "Time for you to get home and check that Pedro and Tomas are there. Let's hope Pedro's been a good boy and waited." She wrapped her arm around him and led him from the room.

"Ha!" he huffed. "Like he waited." Sliding his arms into his jacket as his wife dutifully put it on him, he kissed her goodnight.

"Don't forget to call me when you get home to let me know if the boys are there." She saw his uneasy gait. "Can you make it home?"

He gave a drunken salute. "I will make it home. I can get home blind, so I can get home drunk." He weaved his way down the driveway and headed for town.

Shaking her head, an amused smile on her lips, she headed inside and up to her suite, watching out for wayward relatives along the way.

Unlocking the door to her room, she stepped inside and sighed. *One down, one to go,* she thought, sliding off her dress and leaving her shoes by the foot of the bed. Sliding into her night dress, she waited for Spiros's call, and after getting it twenty minutes later, pulled the comforter over her and fell asleep.

*****

Saturday morning dawned bright and cool, but the Stephanopoulos clan did not rise and shine. They slept until three when Pedro woke. He was used to sleeping during the day, and this was the hour when Angie woke him, after coming home from school, and pounded away on his disco stick.

The Stephanopoulos grin spread across his face, and his eyes opened to her, but she wasn't there. Disorientated, he breathed and realised that she *wasn't* there. For she was at the hotel waiting for him. Waiting for him to meet her at the church for their traditional Greek service. Basically, a replica of Carlos's wedding. Rolling onto his back, he stretched his arms above his head and worked the muscles in his back, then stretched out one leg at a time. He saw his hard-on standing to attention under the sheet and wondered if he should do something about it. The boys had their own wing of the house, and he didn't hear Tomas or Roger up yet. But then they had each other to take their morning wood out on.

The grin came back as he thought about Angie and making love to her again. They had abstained like Carlos and Viv. Angie's arm was still healing and the morning sickness had packed a punch. But tonight, they would be husband and wife and things would be different. Needing release, his hand snaked under the sheet to do the deed.

*****

Tomas trailed soft light kisses along Roger's arm to his shoulder, to his neck, and across his cheek. His tongue played with nipples and chest hair for a few minutes, eliciting a groan from the man he was playing with before making his way down his body to go under the sheet to take Roger into his mouth. He sucked and teased and played until he had what he wanted.

And Roger wanted more of what *he* was getting. "Oh, God, Tomas."

"Shh," Tomas told his lover. "Shhh." Rolling Roger over, he entered from behind. Normally Roger was in charge of this, being the one to penetrate, but it was time for Tomas to take the reins and get used to being the giver and not just the taker. His leg slid between Roger's, and his hand found what his mouth had been around just moments before, getting another groan from the man beside him.

Keeping his thrusts even and strong, they came together, and after withdrawing, Tomas collapsed onto Roger as he turned.

Taking Tomas into his arms and kissing him savagely on the mouth, Roger stopped for breath. "God, I love you."

Tomas lay panting. "I love you, too." Snuggling into Roger's chest, he felt his own heave. "If we could do that as a married couple it would be even better."

Roger paused, thinking about the words. "Is it not good enough now?"

Tomas's head flew up. "Of course it is. I didn't mean it like that." Returning Roger's kiss, he sighed. "I just wish…" Snuggling into Roger's neck he melted. "I wish we could get married…that's all."

Roger held him tight. "I know. But since this is what we have, let's make it the best there is."

*****

At the hotel, Jenny woke to another day and another wedding. Her baby was getting married. To a baby younger than him. *God,* she thought, *how are they going to cope? They're both so young.* Flinging back the covers, she showered and dressed in a rose-pink dress, similar in style to the blue one from yesterday, and made her way to Angelina's room.

*****

An alarm buzzed incessantly, and an arm reached out to stop it. When it did, the arm slid back under the sheets and across the stomach of Vivian Villiers.

"Mmm." She moved. "We need to get up."

"I am up," Carlos told her and proceeded to thoroughly wake her up.

"Carlos." She sighed afterwards. "Your brother's getting married, we need to get up and get ready. And you need to get to the house."

"Mmm," he moaned. "We need to get up."

"I am up," Viv told him and proceeded to thoroughly wake him up.

"Viv," he sighed afterwards. "My brother's getting married. We need to get up and get ready. And I need to get to the house."

"Oooh, you little." She bashed him over the head with her pillow.

*****

Angelina woke to the sound of her alarm. Turning it off, she rolled over and groaned. "Ah…what's today? Why do I have to get up?"

Because it's your wedding day, her brain told her.

Her eyes flew open. *Oh, my God, it's my wedding day. What the… but…I…what the hell. Oh, my God.* The millions of thoughts flying through her head slowed down, and she grasped onto the one thought that mattered.

Pedro.

Today she was marrying Pedro. The amazing, gorgeous, incredible man that she loved. Her lips curled into a smile, and her hand slid under the covers to her stomach. She was also pregnant with his child. A baby Poulos Stephanopoulos.

Poulos?

Did she even want that name anymore?

Probably not, but since Greece was considering reforms and laws against women taking their husband's surname it was a chance to change it. *But Pedro is only half Greek, and Mrs Stephanopoulos took her husband's name, although they got married in Australia and*

Pedro and I live in America. I could still take it and legally change it there. And if not, she thought stubbornly, *I'll do it anyway and still call myself Mrs Pedro Stephanopoulos.*

There was a knock at the door, and she reluctantly slid out of bed, wrapped her dressing gown around herself, and opened the door to her future mother- and grandparents-in-law as well as Viv.

"Ready to get married?" Jenny asked.

*****

Carlos found his way down familiar cobblestone streets to the house he'd called home for ten years. And after Roger let him in, he made his way into Pedro's room. "Hey, little bro, ready to get married?"

Pedro turned his head dazedly from the mirror to his brother. He was standing in the middle of his room without a shirt, socks or shoes, and his pants hanging open.

"Geez, Pedro, why aren't you ready yet?" Carlos shoved him aside to check himself in the mirror.

"Because he's freaking out about getting married." Tomas walked into the room. "Papa's not up yet. Pedro's freaking out, and we have," he glanced at his watch, "an hour to go." He picked up Pedro's shirt and helped him into it.

"Papa's not up?" Carlos asked. "What time did he get to bed?"

"About five-thirty this morning," Roger said from his spot in the doorway. "Woke up the house."

"That's 'cause he was still singing." Tomas laughed. "And then he very loudly told Mama that her babies were tucked into bed and then nothing. He must have fallen asleep." He held out Pedro's tux jacket, and his brother slid his arms in.

"I'd better wake him up then." Carlos grinned and made his way to his parents' room to find his fully clothed father face down and snoring. Carlos laughed, picked up the phone from the bed where it had been left, and replaced it in its cradle. "Aw, Papa." He jumped on him like he did as a kid and Spiros stirred.

"Who's that, go 'way."

Pedro and Tomas came into the room and saw Carlos jumping on their father, and with wicked grins at each other, dived for the bed. "Bombs away," they yelled, landing on top of Carlos and their father.

"What, what," Spiros sputtered, finally waking. "What is this? What are my grown adult children doing jumping on me?"

"To wake you up!" they exclaimed in unison, bouncing up and down.

"All right, all right. I'm up. Let me up." He waved them away and sat up. "Ah…what time is it?"

"Ten past four," Tomas told him and slid off the bed. "You need to have a shower and get dressed. We have another wedding to go to."

With a groan, Spiros flopped backwards on the bed. "Wedding. I'm too old for another wedding."

"No, you're not," Carlos said, and he and Tomas grabbed his arms and hauled him up to his feet. They marched him into the bathroom and shut the door.

"God, we haven't done that since we were kids," Carlos said as they walked back into Pedro's room. "Brings back memories."

"Yeah," Pedro agreed, sliding his bowtie around his neck. "Good memories."

Tomas smiled softly. "*Really* good memories." All three brothers looked at each other.

"Yeah," Carlos added and pulled Tomas into his arms. "Really good. Now, Pedro, our little bro." They turned to their brother. "We have something for you." He pulled a small velvet box from his jacket. "As your best men, and as your brothers, we bought you these." Handing over the box, he waited for Pedro to open it.

Pedro lit up when he saw what was in it. "Hey, you got me initialled cufflinks too. Aw, guys!"

Carlos and Tomas took one each and clicked them into place. "Why not?" Carlos asked, slapping him on the back. "Think of it as a new Stephanopoulos tradition."

"Cufflinks?" Pedro raised a questioning brow. "A tradition?"

Tomas felt a twinge at the turn of phrase. If they were a tradition for getting married, then he would never get a pair, essentially being left out. He breathed slowly.

"You seriously think cufflinks could be a new family tradition?" Pedro asked.

Carlos shrugged. "Why not? We can do it with our sons and grandsons and pass it on down. Besides, when else have we given each other stuff?"

"Chicken pox," Tomas said.

"Measles," Pedro added.

"Nits," Tomas replied.

"School sores," Pedro pointed out, glancing at Tomas who nodded in agreement.

"All right, all right." Carlos put his hands up in protest. "Something that's non-medical." He waited for their replies.

"Besides normal birthday and Christmas presents?" Tomas asked dubiously.

Carlos sighed in defeat. "All right. Why can't we give cufflinks as a tradition?"

Pedro glanced at Tomas and shrugged. "Guess there's no reason why we can't," he told his eldest brother and tried to ignore the sad expression on Tomas's face. He saw Roger's in the background and could tell he was on the same wavelength as Tomas.

"Good, it's set then. This is a new Stephanopoulos tradition," Carlos said. "Now, let's get Papa dressed." He wandered off with Pedro on his heels, leaving Tomas and Roger behind.

"It hurt, didn't it?" Roger came up behind his lover. "Because you can't get married you'll never be a part of that tradition." Gently laying his hands on Tomas's shoulders, he added, "I'm sorry."

Tomas choked back a sob and wiped his face. "I don't want to talk about it right now or I will..." He breathed. "Burst into tears and not stop."

Carlos and Pedro came to collect them ten minutes later. "Ready to go?"

With a nod, Tomas and Roger followed Carlos and Pedro, and a freshly showered and clean shaven Spiros, out the door and down to the church.

*****

With a finishing touch of baby's breath, Jenny stepped back and gazed at Angelina. "Oh, my," she breathed. "You look beautiful."

A shy smile slid over Angie's face. "Will Pedro think that?"

"Oh, sweetie." Jenny grasped her hand. "Of course he will. Are you ready?"

With a nod from Angelina, they set off for the church. The family had gone ahead minutes earlier, and they were running a little late due to nerves and morning sickness. Jenny led them down the streets and into the back door to the bride's room where Viv had stood the day before. "I'll go and check that everyone's ready." Hurrying into the church, she saw her family finding their places, and Spiros and the boys coming through the doors. She made her way to their sides. "Are you ready?" she asked all of them and then her face crumpled upon seeing Pedro in his tux. "My baby's getting married."

"Mama," all three boys groaned as she took her baby into her arms.

"Stop it," she chastised. "I'm entitled to be emotional, my baby boy's getting married." She looked at him closely. "Now, did you have something to eat?"

"Yes, Mama."

"And did you get a good sleep?" She dusted off his jacket.

"Mama!" He rolled his eyes and looked at his brothers for support.

"Did your father have a talk with you?" She smoothed his shirt and straightened his tie.

He froze and glanced at his father. "You mean the same talk he gave to Carlos yesterday?" he asked slowly.

Jenny turned her head to stare at her husband. "Spiros!"

"I did, I did," he lied, quickly straightening his cuffs and tie and brushing imaginary lint off his jacket.

"Oh, for God's sake," Jenny said, not caring about using the "g" word in church, and turned back to Pedro. "Did you hear your father's talk to Carlos yesterday?"

"Yes, Mama." Pedro nodded. "We all did."

"Right, well, I guess we'll just have to leave it at that. Are you ready to get married?"

The Stephanopoulos grin grew ear to ear. "Absolutely."

"Right." She kissed both cheeks. "I'll go and get Angelina." Jenny hurried back to the bride's room. "The boys are ready, are you?" She saw Viv straightening the train on Angelina's simple white gown. The silk clung to her tiny body and flared out in a scallop shape behind her. It had a white fur bolero jacket over it. Her long dark hair was braided around her head with the baby's breath in it. A small bouquet of white roses was clasped tightly in her hands.

"Yes," she breathed after a moment. "I think so."

Jenny took her in her arms. "I know marriage is a big deal, and so is having a baby. And you're just a baby that's doing both of those things. But it *will* be okay." She pulled back and stared Angelina in the eye. "It *will* be all okay."

Angelina saw the strength in Jenny's face and felt it flow through into her. She breathed deeply and nodded. "Okay, I'm ready."

Jenny smiled and led Angelina from the room, down the hall, and around to the door where the boys, Spiros, and the priest were waiting.

Pedro's mouth dropped as Angie came into view. The delicate little girl he'd fallen so in love with was now a beautiful young woman. And she was going to be his. His heart swelled with pride, love, and happiness. "Oh, Angie," he breathed, his face crumpling. "You're so beautiful."

She came to a stop in front of him and smiled shyly. "And you look so handsome." Hanging on to her bouquet for dear life, she gazed up at her six-foot tall husband-to-be who towered over her tiny five-five frame.

"Then shall we start," the priest said. "Do you, Pedro Matthew Stephanopoulos come here of your own free will?"

Pedro gazed down at Angelina, a huge smile on his twenty-year-old face. "I do."

"And do you, Angelina Maria Poulos," she winced at that name, "come here of your own free will?"

Her smile crept across her face. "I do."

"Then we shall proceed." Father Bowen led them down the aisle with Carlos and Viv, and Jenny and Tomas, following. Spiros brought up the rear.

The same ceremony as the day before followed, starting with Carlos as the koumbaro, handing over the rings to the priest to be blessed before placing them on the right ring fingers of the bride and groom and exchanging them three times. When he was done, he slapped Pedro on the arm and stood back beside his brother, getting a huge grin in return.

Father Bowen sealed the rings and moved onto lighting the candles and crowning the couple with the stefanas.

Jenny had told Bowen that the same ones would be used, so not to throw them out. She stared at her baby boy through the crowning, watching him and Angelina bow their heads as the priest made the cross symbol. Watched as Carlos switched it three times, and watched the pain in Tomas's eyes as he stood by Carlos. *Oh, my poor baby, Tomas,* she thought. *If only you could do this.* A quick glance at Roger, who was sitting beside her husband, told her he felt the same way.

Roger was staring forlornly at Tomas, feeling every bit of pain that his lover was feeling. *If only I could make your dreams come true, my love,* he thought and noticed Jenny watching him. Her painful expressions reflected his own.

Jenny moved her gaze back to her children as Father Bowen led them around the altar. She flashed back to the day nearly twenty-one years earlier when she had given birth to her baby boy. Fortunately, the birth has gone smoothly, and after four hours he'd just slipped out like an eel. Her hand flew to her mouth to stifle the giggle, and she coughed softly to cover it.

The boys glanced her way, and she smiled as Bowen lifted the crowns and laid them on the altar table.

Picking up his Bible, he read a passage and led into the vows. "Do you, Pedro Matthew Stephanopoulos, take Angelina Maria Poulos, to be your lawful wedded wife? To have and to hold, for richer or poorer, in sickness and in health, till death do you part?"

Pedro lovingly looked down at the radiating beauty of Angelina who gazed up at him with the same love he had for her. "I do."

Her smile brightened.

"And do you, Angelina Maria Poulos, take Pedro Matthew Stephanopoulos, to be your lawful wedded husband? To have and to hold, for richer or poorer, in sickness and in health, till death do you part?"

Her heart pounded in her chest as she stared up at the man beside her. The love of her life, the man who made her fall so completely and totally in love with him that no other man had mattered, nor ever would. "I do."

Jenny's heart broke a little. Her baby was now a married man. With a baby of his own on the way, and a wife who was barely old enough to look after herself let alone a husband and baby. She took in Angelina's slim appearance and dark hair. Just how she imagined a daughter would look…if she'd had one. Her heart twinged with the pain and sadness of not having a daughter. Even though she had three fine sons, she had longed for a girl. And now here, in front of her, was the picture-perfect daughter she had always wanted. She gasped in as Angie and Pedro kissed and couldn't stop herself from crying. Her chin quivered, and her hand flew to her mouth to cover her sadness. Tears rolled like hot daggers down her cheeks.

Her son and new daughter-in-law turned to the crowd, and Pedro spied the distress on his mother's face. "Mama." He stepped over to her and pulled her into his arms. "Don't cry. I'm still your baby boy."

"I know," she wailed. "My baby's gotten married."

"Jenny." Spiros enveloped both of them. "Let them walk down the aisle. Hush now, dry your tears and let him go." He extracted Pedro from her arms and encouraged his son to lead them down the aisle.

Through her tears, Jenny watched her son take his new bride and walk past their family and friends with Carlos and Viv following. Tomas held out his arm to her, tears in his own eyes.

Her heart went out to him as she took his arm and they walked down the aisle with Spiros and Roger behind them. She patted his hand. "I know this is hard for you." She kept her voice low. "I know this is so hard." They stepped out of the church, and Pedro and Angie led the way back to the hotel's reception room.

"I'll deal with it," Tomas murmured, sucking in air and wiping his tears.

"Yes." She patted his hand once more. "So will I."

*****

In New York, Greta Von Burro was reminiscing about the night she met Pedro.

Stephanie Martison, her director-producer, Thomas Derbon from publicity and management, and Carson Trumack, the company's star-maker all sat around her office.

Greta was *the* porn queen of New York, and she had successfully scored Pedro Stefan as her star. Of course, it helped that he was Carlo Stefan's little brother and gorgeous to the extreme.

"He's getting married," Stephanie wailed around her fifteenth champagne. They had been going hard at it for an hour, bemoaning the fact their biggest star was walking down the aisle.

Thomas sighed as he sipped his tenth alcoholic beverage. "I can't believe I didn't get to tap that." He'd been out of the closet for years and had made no secret of the fact he fancied Pedro. Of course, Angelina had set him straight, but that hadn't stopped him hoping.

"Well, good for them." Carson held his glass aloft. "Cheers to them. And for God's sake Stephanie, get a grip. You and Thomas are pathetic." He glanced from the forty-something brunette Stephanie, drunkenly sprawled across her seat, to late-thirties Thomas wiping away tears. The ones that didn't fall into his drink that is. He shook his head in a mix of amusement and disgust. "You're grown ass adult women, get a grip and grow a pair." Stephanie's sad, lonely expression, and Thomas's drunken scowl simply made him laugh. "Pathetic."

"Oh, shut up, Carson," Greta snapped. "You may not have been interested in Pedro, but the rest of us were, *are.*" She polished off a bottle of champagne and immediately opened another. Not bothering to pour it into a glass, she drank from the bottle. This was unusual for the American-born, Swedish-descended blonde, but she hadn't reached her fifties without a lot of hard work. And if she managed to fuck a few of her acquisitions along the way, all the better for her. But not in the last decade or so. She'd become too old for them, and they'd refused when she tried forcing them. Some had reluctantly agreed, others had played ball and played hard, threatening to go to her rivals if sex was a part of the job requirement.

She sighed, planted her feet on the coffee table, and waved the bottle around. "He was the one I wanted so desperately," she moaned. "All I wanted was him."

"And you didn't get him coz you can't have him," Carson told her. "At least you can watch and dream and wish you could. But for the love of God, can we just cheer to them instead of commiserating. He's not dead. He *will* be back in the new year."

"But for how long?" Stephanie wailed. "He's married now with a baby. What's gonna happen then? Oh, God." She stared wild-eyed as the thought came to her. "What if he leaves and doesn't do any more movies?"

"We have him for eight more," Thomas interjected.

"But after that?" Stephanie went on. "Once he's a father will he want to fuck on screen? Will we get to see him naked…and long and strong and bulging?" Sobbing into her sixteenth drink, she collapsed on the arm of her chair. "What if he doesn't want us anymore?" she wailed. "I can't lose him."

"You!" Greta slurred. "*I* can't lose him. He's making me filthy rich."

"You already were," Carson mumbled behind his drink.

"Yes, but he's making me what I took years to earn. And he's only done two movies."

*****

Back at the reception hall, the family finally settled down to raise their glasses to Pedro and Angelina before digging into another meal of lamb, pork, fish and vegetables.

Once again, they sat at the head table, but the seating had been rearranged, with Pedro and Angie in the middle, Carlos and Viv to his right, and Tomas and Roger to his left. Jenny and Spiros sat beside them down on the left side, keeping an eye on their children.

"I can't believe we're doing this again," Carlos told Pedro. "Like last night wasn't enough, now we're here again, this time with my baby brother sitting in the prime position."

Pedro nodded in agreement. "Absolutely. It's weird. It's like the last five months haven't happened. I mean, *what* the hell happened? *You* leave under criminal charges. I leave under assault charges, Tomas leaves of his own free will. We all end up in porn, and all end up in relationships, and now," he picked up his bottle of beer, "here's to us as married couples." He clinked his bottle against Carlos's.

"Here's to us," Carlos repeated and took a swig of beer as he glanced around the room of all his Australian relatives. His gaze ended up on Viv as she ploughed through her vegetables. "Feeling better? You've piled up on the veggies."

She nodded due to her mouth being full and kept shovelling food in. "Starving," she managed around a concoction of beans and spinach.

Carlos watched with a smile on his face. "So, no morning sickness then?"

She shook her head. "Not so far." Another spoonful went in.

Angelina delicately picked at her own plate of food, a vast difference to Viv.

"Not hungry again?" Pedro asked, sliding an arm around his brand-new wife's waist, watching her put some more potato in her mouth. He worried for her and the baby's health.

"I am, and I'm not," she said after swallowing. "I'm starving, but want to keep it down, so I'm taking it slow." She gazed up into his electric blue eyes. "I'm okay. I just don't want to be sick at our reception. I'll finish it off." Digging her fork into another piece, she placed it in her mouth and looked over the crowd. She spied Maggie and Mike at one of the back tables and waved her fingers at them. They were sitting with Giorgio and a few other friends of hers. She wasn't sure why Pedro's great-grandfather was so far away from the only family there. Something about not wanting to interfere, Pedro had told her. She sipped her water and glanced at Tomas on her left with Roger, Jenny and Spiros beside him.

The Stephanopoulos clan, along with the Marshes, was a family she could definitely get used to being in. Loving, caring, supportive, huge, unlike her own. At eighteen, she was an orphan, no siblings that she knew of, except, apparently, Luiz who was older than her. *But after what he'd done to poor Tomas I'm glad he's dead. Just like our father. A tyrant who wanted everything his way and to hell with what anyone else wanted. Who the hell else did he impregnate?* she wondered and quickly went through what her father's lawyer had said. That she inherited everything and no one else could claim it. *Well, if he's so certain about that, then I have nothing to worry about. Right?*

Jenny finished her meal and spied the thoughtful look on Angie's face. *The poor girl, all alone in the world. No father, no mother, and, apparently, related to the vile, horrible Luiz.* She glanced at Tomas as she sipped her champagne and wondered what was going through his mind. Whether he thought of Luiz or whether he had been abolished as a bad dream. She hoped the latter, and hoped Tomas didn't hold it against his new sister-in-law for any reason. She didn't want a feud in her family and was not going to allow it. Watching Angelina push her plate away and dab her napkin to her lips, she took note of how perfect she was for her son. Both had the same dark hair and white skin and looked right together. She heard Spiros push back his chair.

"Everyone, can I have your attention." Spiros dinged his glass. "Time for toasts." He turned his attention to Pedro and Angelina. "To my son and his new bride. As your mother and I have mentioned, we both think you are way too young for such an adult responsibility. But we have seen from your determination that you are prepared to make it work. You are a man now, Pedro, and that means you are not only responsible for yourself, but your wife and child."

Pedro and Angie glanced at each other as he continued.

"But just as you are responsible for your family, remember that we will always be here to help you. Whatever you need, whenever you need us, we will be there to help you both. We are Greek, we are family, it's what we do." His hand slid to his wife's shoulder, and she laid her hand on it. "To Pedro and Angelina."

"Pedro and Angelina."

Jenny rose and cleared her throat. "As everyone knows, when Pedro was born, it was only after a four-hour labour, and he slipped out like an eel."

"Ew, Mama," Pedro complained as the family snickered.

"And he's been slippery ever since," Jenny continued, laughing at her son's discomfort. "Always batting those big blue eyes at me to get out of trouble. Always wriggling his way out of situations with that big goofy Stephanopoulos grin of his. He's grown into such an incredible young man even though he will *always* be my baby boy. And now, he's a husband and father-to-be, and he's chosen Angelina as his life partner." She gazed at both of them. "To my baby boy and his new wife. To Pedro and Angelina."

Cheers went around the reception, and Carlos stood.

"When I was four years old," he told everyone, "Mama went to the hospital and came home four days later with another baby. She'd only just come home with Tomas two years earlier, but now she'd brought home another one. And do you think I liked it?" he joked. "Of course not. For that meant even *more* competition when trying to get a girl." Laughter littered the room. "And as we grew older, he would follow me around and pester me with lots of questions about what everything was and what it did. And believe me, it got *incredibly* annoying, *especially* when I was trying to score with a girl. He'd pop up right behind or in front of us and start asking questions. He nearly put me off my game."

"Clearly didn't work," Pedro retorted, knocking back his beer.

"No." Carlos laughed. "It didn't. But lo and behold my little brother ended up following me into the industry I'm currently in. And who the hell thought we'd end up in the industry we're in?"

"We all did," Chris yelled out.

"All right, enough out of you," Carlos called back before continuing. "But that annoying little kid turned into quite an incredibly gifted young man."

"Yeah, an inch bigger than you," David added to the toast.

"Oh, for God's sake." Carlos was exasperated. "I meant with his music." Turning back to a laughing Pedro and Angelina he continued. "That annoying little kid turned into one hell of a brother. And now he's found the woman that he wants to spend the rest of his life with. To my baby brother and Angelina."

"Baby brother and Angelina." The crowd burst out laughing.

Dessert followed, and so did raucous celebrations during which Pedro and Angie wound their way through the crowd to Giorgio.

"Great-grandfather." Pedro kissed both cheeks and sat beside him, wrapping an arm around Angie as she stood by his side. "I know we haven't had long to get to know each other, but thank you for coming. And for paying for all of this."

Giorgio smiled and awkwardly waved his hand. "I've missed out on a lot. But being invited to your and your brother's weddings more than makes up for it." He looked at Angie. "And you, young lady, need family now more than ever. You have made my great-grandson very happy."

She smiled down at Pedro and lovingly slid her hand over his shoulder. "I hope so. Because he's made *me* very happy indeed." Leaning down she kissed his upturned smiling face.

"Yes, yes," the old man rasped. "I see that he has. Now go, go have fun."

"Actually, we're not going far." Pedro laughed and walked around two seats to Mike Gatos, his bartending co-worker from *Studio 69*. "Mike, glad you could make it." They hugged and slapped each other on the back as Angie hugged Maggie Boltworth, her friend from Juilliard.

"Oh, my God, you look so beautiful," Maggie cried. "Look at you. I'm so jealous." Her eyes turned to Pedro. "And look at you," she purred, as he kissed her cheek. "Still as gorgeous as ever."

Pedro laughed, and Mike pretended to be hurt. "Still a flirt I see, Maggie," Pedro said. "What about this guy here?" He gave Mike a punch on the arm. "You've still got him, haven't you?"

Maggie beamed and slid her arm through Mike's. "Yeah. So, how's everything been?"

"Good," Angie told her. "We dealt with my father's estate. We're selling the club."

"But are you coming back to Juilliard?" Maggie asked.

"And are you coming back to 69?" Mike asked Pedro. "The club's boring without you and everyone misses you."

Pedro grinned. "I miss everyone too. We'll be back in a week or two, and we'll sort everything out." His arm slid around Angie's tiny waist. "We have our baby on the way, so we'll need to make plans."

"And I'll definitely be coming back to school if they'll have me," Angie added.

"Of course they'll have you," Maggie said. "They'd be stupid not to."

After a few more moments of chatting with them, Angie introduced Pedro to her old high school friends also sitting at the table. They all oohed and aahed over him as they had been the night of her going away party when he'd DJd, and they'd had the run-in with her father and made their getaway.

With a glance at his watch, he went back to his great-grandfather and thanked him once more before bidding him goodnight. He led Angie over to his parents, thanked them and said goodnight. It was one in the morning and time to retire.

"You two go and enjoy yourselves, and don't forget the family service at the church at three tomorrow afternoon." Jenny brushed down his coat.

"No, Mama, we won't." He kissed both cheeks and led Angie over to his grandparents to say goodnight before they left. Making their way up to the suite Pedro opened the door and swung Angie into his arms.

She giggled. "Oh, my God, Pedro."

"What? You are my new bride, and I'm carrying you over the threshold."

"But it's just our suite, not our home." She shut the door behind them.

He walked over to the rose-petal-covered bed with its covers pulled back and gently placed her on her feet.

"Oh, wow, look at the bed." She picked up a petal and held it under her nose, soaking in the aroma. "And look, little chocolates and chocolate-covered strawberries." Reaching into the bowl of brown-covered berries on the bedside table, she moved one to her lips and bit into it. Her eyes closed. "Oh, my God, chocolate."

Pedro gently pulled at her braids, removing the pins and undoing them to let her hair fall in wavy cascades down her back as she ate the whole bowl of strawberries. His fingers slid through from top to bottom.

"Oh, my God, did you want one?" She held up the last one.

He laughed lightly. "No, you eat it. You obviously need it." He turned her and untied the white fur bolero and slid it from her shoulders. "God, you're beautiful, Angie."

She blushed as red as the strawberries and helped him out of his jacket and shirt. "So are you," she whispered, running her fingers over his smooth skin.

His hands slid up her arms, and his head bowed, resting his forehead on hers. "I love you," came from between his lips as they landed on their mate. Slow, sensual, light. He kissed her gently as he unbuttoned her dress and slid it down over her tiny frame. It fell into a puddle of white silk to reveal a sleek, long, white lace slip. He breathed in her essence and kneeled before her, his lips and hands moving to her stomach where their baby grew. "Oh, Angie," he murmured against her. "I love you so much."

Her fingers grabbed hold of his hair, and she moaned softly. "Oh, Pedro. I love you, too. So much." Through hooded eyes, she saw the sparkle of her engagement and wedding rings. "I can't believe we're married."

Standing, he held her like the delicate flower she was, watching while she gazed at her right hand. "Neither can I. I love you, Angie." His lips found hers and gently moved in time with her wants and needs as her hands slid over his arms and around his neck. He bent over and wound his arms around her as his tongue invaded her mouth. Hers returned the favour as he picked her up into his arms and carefully kneeled on the bed. He laid her down against the rose petals. Sliding down beside her, they didn't break their embrace.

*****

The party continued, but Carlos and Viv took their leave an hour later.

"Don't forget the family service at the church at three," Jenny reminded them as she kissed them goodnight.

"Yes, Mama," Carlos said. Holding Viv's hand, he moved off through the crowd saying goodbye as he went.

Jenny checked her watch. Two o'clock. She had to end the party soon, so they all had time for a decent sleep before the service. It was more than likely the last time the whole family would be together. Spying Tomas and Roger walk out onto the terrace, she thought about the next day and smiled. It was going to be one hell of a service. She stepped over to the door and moved into the shadows.

"What is it, my love?" Roger asked, standing behind Tomas at the balcony. It was the same scene playing out from the night before.

Hot, painful tears overflowed and rolled down Tomas's cheeks. "I don't know if I can keep doing this."

"Doing what?" Roger rested his hands lightly on Tomas's shoulders. "Being happy for your brothers?"

Tomas shook his head. "Being happy around weddings and married people in general. I just don't know how much I can take," he sobbed. "I want to be married so desperately, I want to be able to walk down the aisle, and say vows to my husband, and exchange rings, and be married to the man that I love for the rest of my life. I want that with you," he told Roger, and moved into his arms to sob on his shoulder.

"There, there." Roger patted him on the back softly. "I know. I want that too. I want to be married to you and call myself your husband. But we can't."

"It's not fair," Tomas wailed. "It's not fair, Roger."

"I know." Roger slid his hand over Tomas's back, soothing him. "I know."

Jenny wiped away her tears and turned, then pretended to be coming out the door. "Ah, there you two are. With your brothers having gone, why don't you go home as well?" She stood behind them to give them a moment.

Tomas wiped his face and turned to his mother. "You sure, Mama?"

"Go." She pulled him into her arms. "Oh, my baby. Go home and don't forget about the family service later today. You'll see me in the morning because I'll be home, and we'll go together." She pulled back and placed her hands on his cheeks. "It will all be better tomorrow, Tomas. I promise." Replacing her hands with kisses, she stepped back. "You two go. I'll see you later."

"Okay, Mama." Tomas was a little perturbed by his mother's words, but allowed Roger to lead him away.

"Night, Mrs Stephanopoulos," Roger called, and they headed off for the road to take them home. He noticed Tomas was silent on the way. "You okay? Still thinking about before?"

"Huh?" Tomas came out of his thoughts. "Just thinking about what Mama said."

"Which was?"

"It will all be better tomorrow," Tomas repeated.

"Well, maybe she meant being a new day and all."

"Mmm? No. She meant something by it." They arrived home, and Tomas opened the door and let them in. "I think she's up to something."

Roger slid his jacket off as they made their way into Tomas's room, and quickly stripped off the rest of his clothes as Tomas laid his watch on the bedside cupboard, lost once again in thought.

"Let it go," Roger said, sliding Tomas's jacket off and turning him around to unbutton his shirt. "Your parents aren't here yet. Let's use this time wisely."

Tomas came out of his head to see Roger naked and hard and tugging his pants down. "But don't you…" He broke off as Roger kneeled before him and took him into his mouth. "Oh, God."

*****

After watching her son and Roger walk away, Jenny had waited a few minutes more before stopping the celebration. "Okay, everyone, we're ending this early so you can all have a good sleep. Set your alarms for *two o'clock* this afternoon because the service is at three. And wear your party clothes." She took the next half hour to usher everyone upstairs before finally turning to her husband. "I'll go and grab my things and then we can go home."

He grabbed another drink from the tray of the passing waiter. "I'll just wait down here."

With an exasperated shake of her head, she went quickly up to her room, packed her bag with everything she'd brought with her two days earlier, and went back downstairs to have a quick chat with the evening manager about what she wanted for the next night. He promised to have it done, and after thanking him, she gathered Spiros from his seat, and they set off home. "You have enjoyed yourself way too much," she told him, putting her arm through his. "You need to save yourself for this afternoon."

"I have more than enough energy to party for the rest of my life." Spiros kissed her hand. "I am Greek, that's what we do."

Laughing, she patted his hand. "Why don't you try and keep that energy for later."

"Do you mean later this afternoon, or later when we get home?" His hand moved and gave her a quick pat on the behind.

"Spiros!" Her eyes went wide. "You wouldn't!"

His eyes glittered. "And why wouldn't I? You are my wife, you are beautiful, and I am a man who wants you."

They arrived home.

"But Tomas and Roger are home. And we have to get some sleep for later." Fumbling for her key, she quickly opened the door.

He pushed her against the doorjamb. "That never stopped us when they were little." He breathed into his wife's neck. "I have missed you, Jenny Stephanopoulos." His mouth invaded her neck, and she felt herself throb.

"Oh, Spiros, we can't." His hand slid up her dress, but she pushed it away. "Not here," she whispered, and quickly led him inside, closed the door, and took him to their wing of the house.

Spiros couldn't contain himself any longer. He had to have his wife now. Sliding her dress up and over her head, he fumbled with her undergarments as she yanked open his shirt. He was still in fine form physically, well-toned from carting sides of animal around in the butcher shop, and he had no problem getting it up.

Jenny groaned as his lips took hold of her, moving roughly from her mouth to her neck to her still pert breasts. Oh, how she loved the feel of her man and being in his hands. They were experts in her body and knew exactly how to please her. Her own hands slid over his shoulders, through his thick hair, and down his back until he straightened, pushed off his pants and underwear, picked up his wife and slid her onto his hard shaft.

She gasped, she groaned, she flung her head back and revelled in the twelve inches of Spiros Giorgio Stephanopoulos. "Oh, God Spiros."

He knelt on the bed and laid her down, sliding deeper as he went.

"Oh, God," she cried, delighting in the length and strength of her husband. It had been months since they'd been together. Since before Carlos had left, and with all of the stress and strain of Pedro and Tomas leaving, they had not been intimate. But now, he was proving just how good he was at being her husband. "Oh, God, oh, God." She felt him inside, a Greek powerhouse of muscle and fire. Burning her, searing her, branding her.

"Oh, Jenny," he groaned. "Oh, Jenny." Using his knees to power, he thrust hard, gaining momentum with every move. "Oh, God." He felt himself coming. "Oh, God." He pushed himself up on his hands and brought his right knee up, lifting his wife's left leg for better access. "Oh, God, Jenny."

Jenny clung on. She knew the best and only way was to let Spiros do his thing. For his thing was always right and delivered her the most exquisite orgasms every time. And she hadn't had one in months. Hooking her legs up, she spread them, and he moved higher between them. Her hands went to his ass and dug in.

His hand went to her breast and fondled the large nipple his mouth loved to delight in. His mouth found her nipple and his twelve-inch cock found her G-spot, bringing her to a screaming orgasm.

Tomas awoke. His head lifted from Roger's chest, and he heard his mother and father screaming. "Oh, my God," he whispered. "Roger, wake up. Mama and Papa. Something's wrong."

Roger sleepily awoke. "What's going on? What's wrong?"

"Shh, something's happening to Mama and Papa."

Roger listened to the screams and raised his brows in amusement. "Have you *never* heard your parents having sex before?"

Tomas cocked his head to listen as the *oh, my Gods* slowed down and disappeared. "Oh, my God, they didn't?"

Roger chuckled. "Oh, *they did.* And why shouldn't they? They're adults."

"They're *not* adults," Tomas disagreed. "They're my parents. They shouldn't be having sex. How embarrassing."

"How do you think they made you and your brothers?" Roger asked him. "By magic?"

Tomas felt the blood rush across his face. "No...but...they're *old.* They *shouldn't* be having sex, least of all like that."

"Like what?" Roger asked. "Like their three sons! I'd say after raising you three they're quite entitled to hot fast sex. Now hush and go back to sleep."

Tomas was embarrassed. It was one thing for him and Roger to have sex, but his *parents. Oh, God, how embarrassing.* "But," he started.

"Hush," Roger demanded. "Sleep, this is your parents' house, and they're entitled."

Tomas snuggled back into Roger's chest. "It's still embarrassing."

Spiros came to a slow stop with both of them panting. He stretched out on his wife and lay fully on her. Her arms slid over him as his mouth met hers and their tongues did the dance of love. The same dance their privates had just finished.

Jenny's legs entwined with his and her fingers dug into his back. "Mmm," she mumbled under his mouth. "Mmm."

They stayed that way for several minutes, relishing in each other as they hadn't done in months.

Finally, Spiros pulled out and rolled on to his back, panting lightly. "Oh, God, that was good."

Jenny breathed in. The fire was still raging inside of her and she wanted more. Remembering to set her alarm clock first, she rolled on top of her husband and kissed him.

"Mmm, what are you doing?" He broke away from her mouth.

"Have you not had enough of the famous Stephanopoulos jewels?"

"Not tonight," she told him, kissing his mouth and trailing down to his chest, lightly spattered with thick, coarse hair. She rubbed her breasts in it, feeling the roughness set her nipples alight. "Oh, God," she groaned, feeling him rise between her legs. Pushing herself up and down his body, she sent both into a raging inferno that threatened to send them both out of control. "Oh, God." She pushed up from his chest, and he lifted her hips and guided her onto him. Sliding down twelve inches she felt every sensation it caused and then some. "Oh, God."

He bucked, sending her skyward, and waited while she came down. And bucked and bucked until she met his thrusts with bucks of her own.

It was always a little uncomfortable, sitting like this on her husband. His size and length penetrated her deeply, and she wondered if he would do damage to her innermost lady parts. But the feeling of him inside her always outweighed any worries she had because the orgasm was worth it. "Oh, my God," she cried.

Tomas's eyes flew open. "Oh, my God," he mumbled. "Not again." He buried his head in Roger's neck and flung the covers over their heads to block out the noise while Roger chuckled.

"Oh, my God." Gasping, she sucked in air as he stopped and sat.

His mouth devoured her breasts, chest and neck before settling on her mouth. "I love you, Jenny Stephanopoulos," he murmured against her. "I love you so much."

"Oh, Spiros," she breathed. "I love you, too." They fell into a tumbled mess.

But it wasn't long before Jenny's alarm went off at one o'clock, and rolling reluctantly from her husband's arms, she slipped out of bed and into the shower. While getting dressed, she tried cajoling Spiros out of bed. Her hand slid across his chest and twisted a nipple. "Come now, we have work to do."

Swatting his wife's hand away, he reluctantly rose and found his way into the shower while she went into the kitchen to make a light lunch.

Dressed in an apron, she cracked and beat eggs, cut up bacon and tomatoes, and popped bread into the toaster before going to Tomas's door and knocking. "Boys?"

"Yes," mumbled through the door.

She opened the door and stuck her head through. "I'm making a light lunch of scrambled eggs and toast. Come and eat before we go."

"Okay," her weary-eyed son said.

Back in the kitchen, she started serving up four meals as Spiros walked in wearing his pants and shirt. The boys followed in velvet robes. She glanced up and set Spiros's and her plates on the table. "Take a seat, boys." Getting theirs from the kitchen, she poured juice and coffee for all.

"Geez, Mama," Tomas groaned. "This is more than a light lunch."

"Don't be silly." She sat down. "It's only scrambled eggs, bacon and fried tomatoes on toast. "That *is* light."

Roger and Spiros were already digging in, but Tomas eyed them balefully. "Ugh, *how could you* with everything else we've eaten in the last two days?"

Roger swallowed his mouthful and followed it with juice. "I'm hungry."

"Well, I'm not." Tomas pushed his plate away. "Sorry, Mama."

"Don't apologise," Spiros waved his fork, "eat it. You eat what your mother makes, and it does not go to waste. Eat," he commanded his son.

Tomas eyed him dolefully before glancing at his mother and Roger. Sliding the plate back in front of him he began to pick at it. But five minutes later he handed most of it to Roger to finish off.

Jenny watched him, noticing the dull expression while she drank her coffee. Her eyes moved to the large windmill clock. "It's just after two. We need to leave at quarter to three. You boys go and have showers and get into your tuxes and I'll clean up."

Tomas sighed from the pit of his stomach, his coffee cup in hand. "Why do we need to wear tuxes to a family service? We can just wear suits."

"Because it's a special family service," Jenny told him.

"But it's only church," he went on. "Nothing else. No party, no wedding, no nothing."

Jenny felt the panic start to rise at the word wedding. "Because it's special," she repeated sharply, getting a look of concern from all three of them. "It's a family service, and we'll be having a party afterwards. And since it will probably be the *only* time we get to all be in the same room as the same time, we're going to dress up and make it special. *God knows* if we'll ever see them again. So, you'll get into your tuxes and stop complaining." She looked at his shocked face, trying to maintain some composure. "Don't you feel well? Is that why you're reluctant?"

He blinked. "Um, no. I just…" He gazed back at his mother, unsure there was even a need to say anything. "I just wasn't hungry, that's all," he ended up saying.

She softened. "Go and have a shower; you'll feel better after you've freshened up and shaved. Put some nice aftershave on and do your hair." She stood and ran a hand through Tomas's hair, looking down into his sad face as he looked up. "You'll feel better later. I promise you." Kissing him on the forehead, she ushered him away. "Go on, freshen up. You'll feel better." She watched them go as she gathered the dishes then turned to Spiros. "Throw these in the dishwasher. I'm going to call the hotel." In quick, hushed tones, she spoke to her mother to make sure arrangements were completed on that end before finishing her hair and make-up, and donning the matching coat to her dress. Glancing at the clock, she saw it was twenty minutes to the hour. "Boys, you have five minutes before we leave."

Tomas groaned. They were tucking in shirts and tying ties in his bedroom, having showered, shaved and coifed their hair in thirty minutes. Sharing a bathroom had helped with the timing, even though there had been some hijinks. They finished up.

"I still don't know why we need to wear tuxes." Tomas sighed. "It's just a church service." He pulled on his jacket and straightened his cuffs.

Roger did the same. "Because it's your family and you all haven't seen each other in over a decade. Your mother brought everyone here for her boys' weddings."

"*Two* of her boys' weddings," Tomas corrected, fixing Roger's tie. "Today's not a wedding, it's just a service."

"Doesn't matter." Roger laid his hands on his lover's hips. "Your mother's obviously gone to a lot of bother getting all of this set up for her boys, and bringing the family over at the last minute couldn't have been easy. Besides, it's probably going to be a good service if it's just for family."

"Mmm," Tomas mumbled and laid his hands on Roger's chest. "I don't feel good about it."

Jenny knocked on the door and poked her head through. "Ready? Your father's just left to make sure the boys made it in case they'd forgotten about it in the throes of passion. Come along." She saw the boys blush, and guided them out of their room and out the front door where she linked arms with them before they set off, excited for what was about to happen, and hoped the boys would be too. "You're awfully quiet," she said to Tomas who was on her left. "Still not feeling well?" They strode along the cobblestones towards the church.

He sighed, having no idea what *was* wrong. "I'm all right. I just…"

"Yes."

He moved his head from side to side. "I can't put my finger on it."

"Maybe he's still embarrassed at having heard his parents in the wee hours of the morning." Roger grinned.

"Roger!" Tomas's head flew in his direction. *"Don't tell her that."*

"And what's wrong with your father and me still having sex?" she asked him. "We're only in our late forties and early fifties, we're not ancient. Besides," she tugged Tomas's arm, "*you two* have certainly done your fair share of conjoining in the last few days. Don't think I don't know about that." They saw the church at the end of the road.

"Mama, oh, my God." Tomas blushed. "*How could you!* Oh, my God, *we're* supposed to have sex, not hear *my parents* having sex." He bowed his head in embarrassment and the afternoon sun made his black hair shine.

"Oh, for God's sake, Tomas." Jenny laughed. "We're not dead. And besides, how do you think we made you and your brothers?"

"That's what I told him last night," Roger mentioned as they approached the church and saw Spiros standing in front of the closed doors.

"Is everything ready?" Jenny called as the three of them ascended the steps.

"Everything's ready and in place," Spiros said. "Are *you* ready?" He kept his eyes on his son.

Tomas frowned. He knew something was going on and wanted to know what his parents were up to. "Why do *we* need to be ready for a family service?" He looked from Spiros to Jenny. "What are you two up to?"

Jenny's bright smile slid across her face. "Something very, very special," was all she said as Spiros turned and opened the doors.

Stepping into the foyer of the church they were confronted by Pedro and Angelina on their left, and Carlos and Viv on their right. The boys wore their tuxes, the girls, beautiful silk pantsuits.

Spiros closed the doors and Jenny slid out of the boys' arms and joined them together before standing with Spiros in front of them.

"What's going on?" Tomas asked, and clung to Roger's hand for support as he looked from Pedro to Carlos to his parents.

"Tomas." Jenny's smile continued as she gazed at her son. Clasping her hands in front of her, she continued. "I have seen your pain and heard your words the last few days, and it has *killed* me inside that you cannot have what your brothers have." She watched his expression fall as he glanced at Carlos and Pedro with glossy eyes. Roger put a protective arm around him, and she went on. "So…in the preparations for *their* weddings…I also made preparations for yours."

Tomas frowned and licked his lips. "Mama," he said quietly. "You know we can't."

"Poppycock!" she exclaimed, making everyone look at her. "I know that the marriage itself will not be legal in the eyes of the law, but that *does not* stop my son from having a wedding to the man he loves. Which is why I arranged it all while we were in Athens."

Tears rolled down Tomas's cheeks as Pedro and Carlos stepped forward.

"I saw the look on your face when Carlos gave me my cufflinks and said it would be a new Stephanopoulos tradition." Pedro pulled a velvet box from his pants pocket and opened it to reveal initialled gold cufflinks just like theirs. "But I knew that today," he clipped the left one on, "that you would be getting yours." He clipped the right one on. "So now, you are part of the Stephanopoulos cufflink tradition." He wiped away the tears pouring down his brother's face. "You can stop crying now because you're about to make me cry." He kissed both of Tomas's wet cheeks and hugged him tightly.

Tomas sobbed. His brain did not fully comprehend what was happening, so he was struggling to keep up. He gasped for breath as Pedro pulled away.

"And." Carlos stepped forward, and everyone turned to look at him. "Since you're a guy and coming into the family," he told Roger, "we bought you your own pair of cufflinks." Carlos whipped open the box for Roger to gaze down upon his own pair of initialled cufflinks. "We put RD on them since we weren't sure if you'd take the Stephanopoulos name or not," Carlos joked as he clipped on the first one. "Or whether Tomas would become a Dencott." He finished the other and pocketed the box. "But you deserved your own pair."

Roger stared from the cufflinks to Carlos, to his cuffs to Tomas, who was still in shock about it all. "Thank you," he told Carlos. "I know…" He tried to get his brain to function through his shock. "Thank you. We only just met this week, and you've been a family for so long…" He turned to the others. "Thank you all."

Tomas clasped Roger's hands and held his cuff links next to his lover's. Gold with black onyx and diamond initials. TS. RD. They radiated happiness at each other, almost forgetting they were surrounded by family.

"We know it's only been a week since we met," Jenny interrupted the moment between her son and his partner. "But after our chat last week, and hearing how much Tomas loves you," she put a hand on her son's arm, "I knew I wanted to give you something that would bring you together as a couple. Even if it's not legal. So," her excitement started building, "you will get to walk down the aisle, you will get to exchange vows and rings, and you will get to sign a marriage certificate."

"But how?" Tomas butted in through his tears. "It won't be legal."

"Well," she said, blushing at her secret. "You'll get to sign it. Mainly because I managed to score a spare one from the registry office when no one was looking. So at least you'll have something to hang on the wall."

"Jennifer Melissa Marsh Stephanopoulos, do you mean to say you stole it?" Spiros was shocked by his wife's behaviour, but still had a twinkle in his eye.

And Jenny was shocked from being called by her full name. "Well, I haven't heard that since we were married," she said, looking from her husband to her crying son. "Tomas." She took him into her arms. "I would *and will* do anything for you. For *all* of my babies." Stepping back, she wiped her tears. "And today is *your* wedding day. You *are not* going to miss out on something so special."

Tomas burst into tears. He couldn't help it. Sobbing in his mother's arms, he let all of his pain wash away. Pedro, Carlos and Spiros gathered around him, soothing him with their words and hand movements. His family were what he needed, and he'd needed them a lot in the last few weeks. Being apart for months, and then going through hell, made him realise how much he'd missed home and family.

"Oh, my baby," Jenny murmured. "My baby."

"I thought that was me," Pedro joked as he stood in the huddle.

That made everyone laugh, and Tomas pulled back. "It *is* you." He wiped his face. "You *are* the baby, look at you." His eyes roamed up and down. "You're my little brother, and I love you. C'mere." He pulled Pedro into a hug. "And you, too," he told Carlos, and the three brothers stood hugging each other.

Jenny dried her tears of happiness. "Oh, you're all my babies," she cried, so ecstatic that her sons were all together and as close as ever. "Let's get this wedding happening, shall we?" She watched her sons dry their faces and step back beside their partners who were also teary-eyed. "Now, let's proceed." She waited for Spiros.

"Do you," Spiros started, "Tomas Giorgio Stephanopoulos, come here of your own free will?" His heart surged for his son, his spitting image in every way.

"Well…Mama dragged us," Tomas joked, but then he looked at Roger. "But I do."

"And Roger…oh…what's your middle name?" Spiros asked his future son-in-law.

"Wallace," Roger told him reluctantly.

"Wallace?" Jenny's interest was piqued.

"After my father and grandfather," he said, red creeping over his face.

"Yes." Jenny softened. "I did call and ask if they'd like to come. They said no. I'm sorry." Her heart broke for her son-in-law to be.

Roger blanched. "So am I."

Tomas slid his hand through the crook of his arm. He knew that Roger's parents had disowned him for being gay, and no one else had accepted him. Until now.

"Okay," Spiros breathed and continued. "Do you, Roger Wallace Dencott, come here of your own free will?"

With teary eyes, Roger looked into his lover's and said, "I do."

"Oh, my baby," Jenny cried softly, feeling her heart explode for her son.

"Then let the wedding progress," Spiros said, and he and Jenny turned to the closed doors that led to the altar. They opened them and moved down the aisle past their family and friends.

"Oh, my God," Tomas gasped as they moved forward. "Everyone's here." He clung to Roger's arm as he looked at all of his Australian family.

Pedro and Carlos followed them, with Angie and Viv closing the doors and following their husbands.

Jenny and Spiros stood in front of the altar table, and everyone took their places. Tomas and Roger smiled brightly at each other. Pedro stood beside Tomas as best man, Angelina beside him. Carlos stood to Roger's right as best man, with Viv beside him. Sarah and Matthew beamed from their places as did everyone else in the family.

"While this is not technically a traditional wedding," Jenny began, "we will use the same traditions as with the previous weddings. Koumbaros, the rings."

Pedro and Carlos stepped forward and provided gold wedding

bands which they laid upon the open Bible in their father's hands.

"Oh," Tomas cried, so overwhelmed by it all. "You got us rings as well."

"Of course," Carlos told him. "We got everything."

Spiros made a cross symbol over the rings and murmured a blessing, then Pedro and Carlos placed the rings on the right fingers of the grooms, exchanging them three times. Spiros sealed the rings by chanting a prayer and making another cross symbol.

Jenny lit two candles and handed one each to Tomas and Roger who held hands the whole time. Next, she picked up the stefanas and made the cross symbol over the boys' heads before they kissed them and Jenny placed them on their heads.

Tomas gazed at his mother and the love radiating from her. *I can't believe she's done this,* he thought as Pedro and Carlos moved forward to exchange the stefanas. *I can't believe she went to all of this trouble for me. Her gay son.* He glanced at Roger, happiness beaming out of him. *I can't believe I get to marry the man I love, in front of all my family, with my brothers being best men, and Mama and Papa presenting the ceremony.* He looked up at the statue of Jesus Christ on the church wall in front of him. *And what would* you *think of all this?*

Spiros was chanting something about responsibilities of marriage, and Jenny was filling the cup with red wine, which she presented to the boys to drink from. This was followed by the spoonful of nuts and honey, and then they circled the altar three times.

Each time they circled, Tomas would glance across the church to his family, seeing the mixture of happiness and surprise. Every one of them was there, even Giorgio was up the back with a small smile on his face. But no one from Roger's family. He glanced at Roger, hoping he wasn't too disappointed at having no relatives at his wedding. But then from what he'd been told, even his younger siblings wanted nothing to do with, in their words, 'the filthy poof of a brother'.

Jenny lifted the crowns from the boys' heads and laid them on the altar table then Spiros handed her the Bible. "Before the usual vows, I'm going to read from Corinthians because I believe it's very appropriate today."

She took a breath before starting. "Love is patient, love is kind. It does not envy, it does not boast, it is not proud. It is not rude, it is not self-seeking, it is not easily angered, it keeps no record of wrongs. Love does not delight in evil but rejoices with the truth. It always protects, always trusts, always hopes, always perseveres. Love never fails. But where there are prophecies, they will cease; where there are tongues, they will be stilled; where there is knowledge, it will pass away...And now these three remain: Faith, Hope, and Love. But the greatest of these is Love."

Once she finished the passage, she moved on, watching tears flow down her son's face. "Do you, Tomas Giorgio Stephanopoulos, take Roger Wallace Dencott, to be your wedded husband? To have and to hold, for richer or poorer, in sickness and in health, till death do you part?" The joy and happiness that washed over his face blinded her as he gazed ever so lovingly at Roger.

"I do."

"Oh," she cried softly, a hand going to her chest. "My baby." That elicited a giggle from her boys. "And do you, Roger Wallace Dencott, take Tomas Giorgio Stephanopoulos, to be your wedded husband? To have and to hold, for richer or poorer, in sickness and in health, till death do you part."

Roger looked from Spiros and Jenny, his in-laws, to the man standing beside him. The man whose hand he had in his. The man whose brown eyes he drowned in and wanted to keep drowning in for the rest of his life. "I do."

"Oh," Jenny cried once more, wiping away her tears she went on as they smiled at her. "Now, I'm going to ask Tomas and Roger if they have anything they want to say to each other."

"What?" Tomas's eye grew wide. "We don't..." He looked at Roger in a panic.

"Relax," Roger said and faced his lover who did just that. Drowning in Tomas's eyes, he continued, "I knew when I saw you that night in the club that you were very special indeed, and when you turned up at the studio, and we chatted, I knew you were someone *extraordinary* indeed. And after our first date I knew," he kissed

Tomas's hand, "that I had already fallen in love with you." He watched everyone's face crumple with joyful tears and laughed a little. "I knew that you were the only man for me, Tomas Stephanopoulos. And I am *so* glad that you feel the same about me." Staring longingly into his lover's teary eyes, he finished off with, "I promise to love you, protect you, and respect you, for as long as I shall live."

"Oh, Roger," Tomas sobbed, a hand flying to his mouth. "I love you so much," more sobs, "so much. I can't imagine living my life with anyone else. You have shown me what unconditional love really is and you expect nothing more. You helped me through a time I didn't know what to do with, and have made me so incredibly happy." Sniffing, he wiped his eyes so he could see Roger. "I love you so much, and am so grateful that you're in my life. And I promise to love you and honour you for the *rest* of my life." He touched his fingers to Roger's face and mouthed the words *I love you.*

Roger kissed his fingers and mouthed them right back.

Spiros cleared his throat, and everyone dabbed their eyes. "And so, by the power vested in me as a Greek, and as your father," he told Tomas. "I now pronounce you husband and…ah…" Everyone looked at him. "Husband?" he questioned with a slight shrug. "You may now kiss the…"

"Groom," the boys finished off for him before Tomas and Roger enveloped each other in a kiss.

Everyone cheered and stood up, applauding as Tomas and Roger broke free from each other and made their way down the aisle, clinging to each other, stopping to hug and kiss grandparents, aunts, uncles and cousins.

Spiros and Jenny followed with Carlos and Viv behind them, and Pedro and Angelina behind them. The rest of the family followed as the grooms stopped at the back of the church for Tomas to kiss his great-grandfather's cheeks.

Giorgio took both boys' hands and placed them together between his, said a silent blessing, crossed his fingers over theirs, and let them go.

Spiros and Jenny were right behind them and saw the motion.

"That is the Stephanopoulos blessing," Spiros told the boys. "*Very* rare indeed. You *are* blessed."

The boys looked over their shoulders at him before glancing back at Giorgio who smiled his approval, then moving on out the door.

"Giorgio," Spiros said, "see you at the reception." He received a nod in return and kept walking. They made their way back to the reception room and took their places.

Pedro and Carlos held out Tomas and Roger's seats with flair and waited for their newly married brother and brother-in-law to sit. They drew out the chairs for their wives and then sat, waiting while their parents took their places.

Once everyone was seated, Spiros called for attention. "All right everyone. And now let *day three* of the festivities begin." A cheer went through the crowd, and the Greek band started playing. The food was the same as the last two days, and dessert and hot coffee followed.

Tomas was blown away by the whole thing, having, for the last two days, been miserable about his brothers getting married and him not being able to. He saw the love from his grandparents as they raised their glasses to him, and a couple of male cousins pretended to suck cock by giving their beer bottles a blow job. "Oh, my God." He choked on his own beer.

"What?" Roger looked up and saw the direction Tomas was looking in. He spied his new cousins-in-law sucking pretend cock and blew them a kiss before giving his new husband one.

"Roger." Tomas laughed and clasped Roger's right hand in his.

"What?" Roger gazed adoringly into his husband's eyes. His left arm around him, his right hand clutched in his. "What, my love? My husband."

The grin spread across Tomas's face as he sat staring back at his husband. "My husband," he repeated, unbelieving. "*My* husband."

"Yes," Roger replied. "*My* husband." Of all things in his life he'd never believed that this would be one of them. Marrying the man he loved. The man he desired. The man he wanted more than anything in the world. And that man was now his husband. While not legally, they had rings and a marriage certificate to show it, as well as their love for each other. His right hand broke free so his fingers could trace Tomas's cheek bone down to his lips. The lips that loved him, the lips that kissed him. "I love you, *so* much, Tomas Stephanopoulos Dencott," he whispered.

"Ah," Tomas said softly, "I love it." His hands clenched Roger's leg as Roger's mouth found his.

"Whoo," went around the room and they broke apart, blushing at the cheering crowd.

"Time for the best man's speech, I think." Pedro stood up and calmed the crowd.

Tomas turned around to watch his brother, leaning back against Roger who had his arms around him.

Pedro held his champagne glass up. "As you all know, to Carlos I was the annoying kid brother," laughter went around the room, "but to Tomas, I was the best friend. He taught me the alphabet and how to count. He played ball with me, and held my hand when we crossed streets while Carlos raced ahead." He got a chuckle out of Carlos and a loving smile from Tomas and went on. "For many a year, especially through our young school years, Tomas was *my* best friend. Always there when I needed help, always there to help with school projects, always there when I needed *him*. Especially," he threw a glance at his parents, "when we moved here to Mykonos. When we started school, he was there by my side to hold my hand, to help me with my Greek, to help me understand the culture that for some reason he knew better than we did. He was there for me because Carlos wasn't. He was too busy hitting on all the girls who thought he was some god from the heavens with his blue eyes and golden-brown hair."

"He still is," a female voice called from the crowd, and everyone laughed.

"Well, *he* thinks he is," Pedro retorted to the audience before looking down once more at his brother. "But the real God was Tomas. The brother who was there for me when I needed him. Through the times I needed him for. And while we may not have been so close these last few years since we've grown up, and I may have emulated Carlos more, I will always forever be grateful to my big brother Tomas. And I am *so* glad that just like us, you have found someone to love and share your life with. And Roger, welcome to the family. To Tomas and Roger." Lifting his glass, he cheered his brother and brother-in-law.

"Oh, Pedro." Tomas leapt to his feet and hugged his brother. "I love you."

"Love you, too," Pedro told him before letting go.

"Okay, sit down, my turn." Carlos stood and waited for them to sit. Tomas and Roger turned his way. "When I was two, Mama came home with a little baby boy that looked nothing like me. He had Papa's black hair and brown eyes and a naturally tanned complexion."

"Oh," Jenny guffawed. "Feeling un-Greek again, Carlos?"

"Yes, Mama," Carlos replied indignantly. "He looked *nothing* like me, and that's why I asked you where you'd gotten him from." The whole room laughed.

"The butcher shop. He was on sale at a bargain price," Spiros said, poker-faced, to more laughter.

"Spiros," Jenny chastised before laughing.

The boys rolled their eyes and Carlos continued. "As Tomas grew older, I realised that I *was* the golden boy." Pedro and Tomas groaned. "All right, all right," Carlos went on. "Even after blue-eyed Pedro came along, I realised I was special." More groans. He waved a dismissive hand. "But what I realised as I got older, was how special my younger brother was in his own right. Besides being a spitting image of Papa, he was quiet, thoughtful, careful and caring, and was always there for little brother Pedro when I wasn't. And as always, there for me when *I* needed him, even if it was a rare occasion. Now, after much debate and waiting, we see that he has chosen his own path in life. To be the man he was meant to be, and to be *with* the man he was meant to be with." He raised his glass. "To Tomas and Roger. May you live long, love longer, and always be in our hearts."

"Tomas and Roger!"

A few 'oh, my Gods' went around the table, including from Tomas who covered his mouth as hot tears fell. He jumped up and hugged Carlos, with Pedro joining in behind him. "Oh, God, I don't believe you two," he cried through his tears. "Both of you, really." The brothers held on, crying together, laughing together.

Jenny looked on in tears, dabbing her face with her fiftieth tissue. She watched her boys bring Roger into the hug, all crying, all laughing, and watched Angelina, who was seated beside her, sob as well. Reaching out, she took Angie's hand and squeezed.

Angie turned to Jenny in tears. "That's was beautiful."

"I know," Jenny sobbed back.

The boys finally pulled apart and sat down as Spiros stood, wiping his own tears. "Dating for Tomas was never a problem. He just wasn't interested. But we knew that when he found the right person, he would find himself in a relationship. So, when that ended up being with a man, no one was more surprised than me." He watched his son intently. "But after everything that my three sons had been through, and who had put them through it, family proved to be more important than ever. And if it meant my son was happier with a man than a woman, then so be it. I will not disown or disinherit my sons for their choices as my father did. I will support and love and be there when they need me. Tomas, I am your father," he saw his son's tears, "I love you, and I will support you, and all the choices you make. To Tomas and Roger." After cheers and champagne, Spiros called out, "Now we celebrate, let's dance." The band started up, and he walked around to a crying Tomas, hugging his son tight. "I love you, don't ever doubt that."

"Oh, Papa," Tomas said, crying into his shoulder. "I love you, too."

"And Roger." Spiros pulled back. "Welcome to the family." He pulled him into the embrace. "You are a son now."

"Thank you," Roger managed through his tears.

"Both of you, stop crying and come dance." He led them to the dance floor and started a circle dance which the whole family joined in. Hours flew past until Jenny finally looked at her watch. It was two o'clock, and time to send her sons off. Retrieving her room key from her purse, she approached Tomas and Roger who were having a quiet moment at the terrace doors. She smiled at Tomas's happiness and ran her hand through his hair. "I love you so much," she told him.

He took her hand and kissed it. "I love you, too, Mama, and I can't believe you've done this."

"I'll always do best by my babies, and you know you're such a good boy." She took his hand in hers and handed the key to him. "And that's why I've organised something special for you both. Take this key. It's to the suite I had, but it's yours now. Go and spend your wedding night together."

"What?" Tomas stared from her to the key before taking it. "Mama, no."

"Why not?" she asked him. "You deserve a night or two together as a married couple, so go. Go and share your first night together."

He cried more tears of happiness. "I love you so much. You've done so much for us. Always supported me with my choices." He glanced at Roger. "Even this one. And now you've thrown us a wedding reception." He waved a hand at everything around them. "I can't believe you did this."

"Why wouldn't I? You're my son, I love you, now don't worry about anything. Just go and have your night together."

His face crumpled, and he hugged her again. "Thank you. Thank you so much."

"You're very welcome, my baby boy." She rubbed his back. "Now, go."

He took Roger's hand, and they left for their suite, avoiding everyone by leaving through the terrace door and skirting the building. Smiling and holding hands, they made their way into the hotel and up to Jenny's old suite. Tomas opened the door, and they entered to see candlelight, bottles of champagne, bowls of chocolate-covered strawberries, and a rose-petal-covered bed. "Oh, my God," Tomas breathed, moving over to the bed. "Look at this, oh, it's so beautiful." He touched the petals, the fresh white linen, the candles, the chocolates and strawberries. "Oh." His face crumpled for the hundredth time. "Mama did this for us. Oh." He turned to Roger. "Mama did all of this."

Roger took his crying husband into his arms. "Yes, she did because she's an amazing woman." Patting his back, he held him for a few moments more. "But let's stop talking about your mother and worry about us and our wedding night." He wiped Tomas's face and then helped him out of his jacket before removing his own. "It's time for us to get down to business," he told his smiling husband. His fingers moved to the buttons on the shirt around the body he wanted desperately, and swiftly undid each one to reveal the body he sought. "Oh, God," he groaned his acceptance, and his hands took on a mind of their own, moving over the light pattering of dark hair across his lover's chest. "Oh, God." He breathed and reached toward his husband, laying his forehead against his. "I love you so much, Tomas." Gazing into his eyes, so deep, so dark, so full of love. "My husband." His fingers lingered.

"My husband," Tomas repeated, undoing Roger's shirt and sliding it over his shoulders to fall to the floor. His hands planted themselves on the muscular chest underneath them. His right hand over Roger's pulsating heart, he breathed in deeply. Breathed in the scent of his man. The scent of love. The scent of eternity. His eyes had closed for the moment, but opened to see Roger gazing deeply into his. "I love you," came out as barely a whisper.

Roger's fingers made their way up Tomas's side, over his shoulder, and to his face. He looked at the man he loved. The man so taken with him, the man so in love with him. *How in the hell did I get so lucky to have found a man like Tomas Stephanopoulos? The Greek god that has so captured my heart.* His fingers traced across Tomas's lips before his own settled in their place. He was slow and sure, and his tongue found its way home. They joined, and their hands slid to pants and unzipped zips, unsnapped buttons, and freed the men within to stroke their way into throbbing vessels of man love.

Roger barely broke from Tomas as he directed him onto the bed, his lips never leaving his as he lay beside his lover; his husband, and took him into his arms. Long, lithe, and joined in every way, they became husband and husband in every way.

*****

Jenny looked around her extended dining table to see her family all back together. It had been a week since the weddings, and the boys had all stayed at the hotel as a honeymoon. All of her family, bar her parents, had flown back to Australia, and they were celebrating Sunday lunch in the Stephanopoulos household once more.

Carlos was to her right with Vivian beside him. Angelina was between Viv and Pedro who was next to his father. Sarah and Matthew were to her left, with Roger and Tomas, then Giorgio who had been invited.

Thank God for an extendable table. This is more people than we've had in years. She thought back to that day in June, the last day Carlos was there, and all three boys were on her right, her parents to her left. Their last dinner together before the shit hit the fan, he'd run, then there was two. And just when things couldn't get more depressing, Pedro disappeared in the middle of the night just like his brother. And not long after Tomas had left of his own free will.

She glanced at each one as she thought about them. Carlos, her eldest, the golden god with his short hairdo. How he'd fought for so many years against haircuts and would scream if anyone came near his golden mane. He was laughing at something Viv said, throwing his head back, blue eyes twinkling, his face alight with happiness. No wonder, with Vivian Villiers, supermodel, as his new wife.

Jenny's gaze went to her elder daughter-in-law. Her hair was in a loose updo, and she was wearing a powder blue pantsuit and matching blouse. She was as much in love with Carlos as Carlos was with himself. *Perfect pair,* she thought, and moved on to Angelina, the frail little girl that was her younger daughter-in-law. Eighteen, married and pregnant. And wife to her baby Pedro who was only twenty.

Dear God, where have the years gone? She rested her elbows on the table and laced her fingers in front of her chin in thought. *My baby hasn't even reached legal adulthood yet and he's married with a child on the way.* She took in the difference between her eldest and youngest. *They may both have my blue eyes, but Carlos is golden-brown like me, making him an attractive match to Vivian's luscious brown locks, while Pedro's black like his father, making him so physically compatible with Angelina's dark hair and pale complexion. It's just like his.*

A soft smile slid over her lips. *My babies. My eldest, my youngest. Both about to become fathers.* With a silent sigh, her gaze moved to her husband. A strong, virile man in his early fifties who had worked hard to support his family for the last twenty-five years. Dark brown eyes stared back, and the Stephanopoulos grin greeted her. She saw the love he had for her in the depths of those eyes.

Beside him was his grandfather, barely holding on, but not for much longer. Giorgio knew his end was coming and had held on to see his great-grandsons get married. *I'm glad he at least has that,* wandered through her mind. *His other grandchildren don't care about him and Stefano sure as hell didn't. Why didn't he come near us, why wait until Stefano does such horrendous things to my children, his great-grandchildren, nearly killing them, before seeing us, having anything to do with us?* She took in his hunched form, crippled hands, and sallow skin. An oxygen tank was attached to his wheelchair, and narrow tubes were down his nose. No, not long for this world.

She watched him take hold of Spiros's right hand and Tomas's left. "You are so much like my Giorgio," he told Tomas. "In every way." The words rasped painfully from his throat as he had declined quickly in the week since the weddings. "It is so good to see you." He squeezed Tomas's hand. "You bring back good memories of my Giorgio when he was young. When he was a good boy. Always be a good boy, Tomas. Always be like my Giorgio."

"I will, Grandfather," Tomas told him, being the man Jenny had raised him to be.

She gazed proudly at her middle son. The man he had grown into, the man he had always been destined to become, and her heart was bursting with pride. All of the things Pedro and Carlos had said at the reception were true. He had been the best big brother to Pedro, and the weird kid that looked nothing like him to Carlos. But for all of their personality differences, as they had grown older, they took into account what their mother and father had taught them. To be men, to respect women, including their mama, and to be the best person they could be. And Tomas was being that now.

Tomas glanced at Roger and beamed as Roger beamed back.

They're so perfect for each other, she thought, taking in Roger's dark-brown hair and eyes. *God, Tomas is so happy.* She watched Roger put his arm around Tomas's shoulders and lace his fingers with his husband's. His husband. Recalling the ceremony, her eyes welled with tears. There was no way in hell she was going to let her son miss out on a wedding because he had chosen to be with a man. Not that organising an extra wedding had been hard. All she'd had to do was let the priest know they needed the church on Sunday for a family service and was allowed to slot it in at three. Naturally, a healthy donation didn't hurt. A sly smile turned up her lips. There was no way in hell she was going to let some priest say no to her son getting married. Besides, what he didn't know wouldn't hurt him. And since the doors were all locked, no one would have been any wiser if they'd seen Tomas and Roger escort her into the church. Her eyes travelled to Roger's fingers as they played with Tomas's. *His body language says it all; he's in love with my son.*

Tomas's fingers played back, and he flashed Roger a smile.

Oh, God, he's so happy after being miserable for so long, she thought. Her father engaged Roger in a conversation that Tomas joined in on. Her father had always been there for her when she needed him, and she'd looked for that quality in a husband. But Spiros didn't have a father. He'd been disowned and made the vow to not do the same. He had told her he would be there for her and their children when they needed him, and he had come through. Glancing to Spiros talking to Giorgio and Pedro, she went back to her father and couldn't believe how easy it had been for him to accept Roger. In fact, they both had so easily.

Her eyes moved to her mother and saw her blue eyes looking back. She had always been on the same wavelength as her mother, and each one knew what the other was thinking or doing at the same time.

Sarah smiled and took her daughter's hands. "You are so blessed, my baby. So, so blessed."

Jenny squeezed back, fully aware of just how blessed she was. Glancing around the table, she saw empty plates and glasses. "Who's ready for dessert?" Standing, she gathered Carlos's and her mother's plate.

"I'll help." Viv sprang up and collected cutlery.

Angelina grabbed her own plate and set it on Pedro's.

"You'll make a good little housewife." Pedro gazed adoringly at her and patted her on the ass.

She snorted. "Is that what you think I'll be?" She leaned across the table for Spiros's plate. "In your dreams, little boy."

Sarah gathered her husband's plate, and Roger grabbed Tomas's.

"What are you doing?" Tomas asked as Roger stood. "You don't have to help."

"Yeah," Carlos added. "You're a man, let the little women clean up."

"Say what!" Jenny exclaimed. "No, no, no." She came back from the kitchen and stood with her hand on her hip next to Carlos. "Little women?" She tipped his chin with her finger. "Where'd you get this *little women* business? We didn't raise you that way, Carlos Spiros Stephanopoulos. We raised you to clean up after yourself. Not to have a sexist attitude."

He blushed a deep red. "Sorry, Mama, just joking."

"Besides," Jenny added, watching Viv come back to her seat. "I seriously doubt Vivian's going to let you get away with an attitude like that."

Carlos glanced from his mother to his wife, pleading with his big blue eyes.

Viv scoffed. "Don't look at me like that, your mother's right. Don't think you're gonna get away with that garbage."

He sighed in defeat, and his shoulders sagged. "Sorry, Mama, sorry, Viv."

Roger tried to defuse the situation. "I want to help. I'm an in-law now, and it's not fair for me to sit on my backside like my lazy brothers-in-law while your mother's doing all the work."

"Oi," Pedro and Carlos objected. "Who you calling lazy?"

"You two," Roger told them and carried a pile of crockery into the kitchen.

Jenny followed him and returned with a huge dish of baklava while Roger carried a stack of bowls. "He's right," she said to her sons. "You're all just being lazy because we have guests and there are more women here. We are *not* doing your chores, Carlos. *You* are on dishwashing duty."

"Mama!" Shock flew over his face. "I *don't think so.*"

Pedro burst out laughing. "Ha! Suck that Carlos."

"And *you* are on dish *drying* duty," Spiros told Pedro.

"What!?" Pedro's eyes grew wide. "But I—"

"And Tomas can put them away," Jenny added, dealing out the ten-layer baklava and sending bowls around the table.

"Ah, geez!" Tomas balled up his and Roger's napkins and threw one each at Pedro and Carlos. "Thanks a lot for dragging *me* into this."

"Enough!" Spiros called out. "While you are in this house you will do as your mother tells you. Now—"

"You don't," Pedro interrupted, and the boys agreed.

"Yeah, since when have you ever listened to Mama?" Carlos asked.

"I listen to your mother all the time," Spiros cut in. "And if she says you boys do the dishes, then I will agree and tell you to do the dishes. Now, let's have this delicious baklava and no more whining." He dug into his dessert to Giorgio's chuckle. "What are you laughing at?" he asked his grandfather.

Giorgio came to a hacking stop. "Just like your father."

"Us or Papa?" Tomas asked.

"All of you," Giorgio told him. "The three of you are just like your father, and he's just like his. Whining about everything. Doing chores, working in the meat shop." He managed to spoon up some dessert. "Brings back memories."

"Good ones, I hope," Jenny said from her end of the table.

Giorgio thoughtfully chewed his food, gazing upon his granddaughter-in-law. When he swallowed, he replied, "Very good memories."

Jenny smiled and took a breath. "Speaking of memories, I'm hoping we can make some new ones in the lead-up to the new year and then your birthdays," she told the boys. "Your father and I have discussed it—"

"More like you told Papa what you wanted to do and made him go along with it," Carlos muttered.

"Oi!" She swatted his arm. "But for the record—" The boys jeered. "I told him what I wanted to do and he agreed that it would be a good thing all round."

"All round what, Mama?" Tomas asked, enjoying the amazing home-cooked dessert his mother had made. Regardless of how many places he'd had it, his mother's was always the best.

"Best all round for everyone," Jenny went on. "And," pause, "I hope that all of you will entertain me and my plans, at least until your birthdays."

Everyone was watching her, waiting for her to continue.

"I know that with Angelina going back to school, and Pedro working at night, that the two of you are going to need help and lots of it." She watched them as she talked. "And I," she glanced at Spiros, "we," she looked back at her babies, "have decided to go to New York with the two of you to help out until the new year." There were open mouths all round. "You are both still so young, and will need help setting up a nursery and learning how to do things, so I want to come, no." She shook her head. "I *will* come to New York with the two of you to help you settle down up until the new year. And I'm hoping," she glanced at all of her sons, "that *all of you* will take the rest of the year off to stay in New York as well, so we can celebrate an American Thanksgiving instead of a Greek one, and *then* Christmas together as always, and then New Year's." Studying their shocked faces, she added. "I think spending New Year's in New York will be fun. I've never been to New York." Folding her hands in front of her face she waited for their replies.

Jaws moved up and down in shock as eyes stayed saucer wide.

"But I…oh," Carlos started then stopped.

"And we're ah…in…Miami," Tomas added.

"Would you do that for us?" Angelina managed. The thought of having a mother-in-law interfering in her pregnancy was not a good one. But since it was Jenny Stephanopoulos, and she was more than a mother-in-law, more of a mother that she had so desperately waited for, for so long, she desperately wanted it to happen. To have a mother by her side, teaching and showing her how to get through a pregnancy and helping to pick out the right equipment and clothes and toys that she had no idea about would be a truly wonderful present.

Jenny tilted her head. "Oh, sweetie, of course, I would. The two of you are babies *having* a baby, and with you not having your own mother around to help, you only have my mother and me to help." She turned and patted her mother's hand. "How about a holiday in New York, Mum?"

"Sounds wonderful." Sarah grabbed her daughter's hand.

"The *two* of you…" Angelina couldn't believe her luck. Not one but *two* mothers to help her settle into being a mother.

"Of course," Jenny continued. "You two are going to need more help than Viv and Carlos. Viv's established and older, and you're barely starting out. Besides," now she aimed her blue eyes at her Carlos's matching ones. "I also expect the two of you to spend the next two months in New York with us, because after everything that's happened with Stefano, there's no way I'm going to be away from my sons this Christmas-New Year period. Especially now I have two daughters-in-law *and* a son-in-law and speaking of," she now aimed at Tomas and Roger, "I also expect the two of you to come and stay with us. I don't care what your bosses want you to do, you can leave that rubbish until next year, but until the new year, I want you all to be in New York with your brother and me plus your grandparents. So, no arguments, because it's happening," she told her astounded children.

Angelina excitedly turned to Pedro. "Oh, we have to, we have to. I have no idea about looking after babies, and your mother can teach me so much. After all, she popped your big head out after four hours."

"Like an eel," Jenny added.

"Ew," chorused through the room.

Pedro stared into his bride's brown eyes and saw all the fear of being a teenage mother to the delight of having a mother figure around to help. "Ah, Mama," he glanced at her, "We only have one bedroom, and were planning on finding a new place when we get back."

"Don't worry about that," Jenny told him. "I've already booked us all into a huge apartment block nearby, and I'll help you look for an appropriate apartment."

"But Harry and—" wandered out of Carlos's mouth.

"Bugger Harry bloody DeVille," Jenny spat. "You're taking the rest of the year off, and *that's* final. So are you two." She pointed to Tomas and Roger. "I don't care what the Seralifts want, they can bloody well wait. So can Von Burro. My children have been through hell this year, and we are all spending Christmas and New Year's together, and *that's* final. Now, about your birthdays. Any idea what you all want to do?"

"Oooh, I know," Angie piped up excitedly. "69 will probably have a big party anyway, so why not have them all there? The latest music, food, drink, it would be great. You should see Pedro on his decks, Mrs Stephanopoulos, he's so good." Her hand slid over his, and she received a grin in return. "Everybody loves him, but he only plays for me."

"Oh, God, how corny." Carlos rolled his eyes. "We've seen him play, Angie, and believe me, he plays for himself to boost his ego and make himself feel better. It's all for attention."

"At least I can do something other than swing my cock around," Pedro retorted.

"All right, enough of that." Jenny stopped it before it escalated. "This is my plan, and that's the way it's happening. We have spent twenty-four Christmases as a family, and we will spend another twenty-four more as a family, and that's all there is to it. We are *not* going to let some thug like Stefano Papadopoulos keep our family apart. Nor will Von Burro, Seralift or DeVille. You got that!" she told her sons. "We will all fly to New York in a couple of days and stay in a lovely apartment building that I've chosen. We have an apartment each, and we'll spend time together doing family things like we used to. Because," she zoned in on the girls, "we now have a son-in-law, and two lovely daughters-in-law who are pregnant and in need of help. We have welcomed them into the family, so we will spend our first Christmas together...*as a family*," she emphasised. "Do I make myself clear?"

Silence...

"Yes, Mama," finally came three replies, out of three mouths, belonging to three heads that now turned to their father. "And what do you say, Papa?"

Spiros looked from one son to another until his gaze landed on his wife. "This means everything to your mother, and so you will respect her wishes and do as she says."

The boys looked from their father to their mother and back again, seeing the look that was transferring back and forth between their parents. They knew from experience that look meant business, that they were on the same wavelength, and nothing and no one would break the bond that formed in that look.

"So…you're coming to New York too, Papa?" Tomas asked.

Spiros broke his connection with Jenny to look at his son. "Not yet. I need to set up the shop to run while I'm not here. I'll come a week or two before Christmas, so that will give your mother time to spoil all of you and set the girls up with baby products that I know she will lavish on them."

"Absolutely," Jenny agreed. "Lots of spoiling. It is Christmas after all. Lots of shopping, lots of baby stuff. And maybe a makeover for the holiday season." She fluffed her hair a little and saw Viv's eyes light up. "It is Christmas, so we need to look our best."

"You already do." Spiros gazed upon his beautiful wife.

She smiled. He always knew when to say the right things. "So," she continued. "No excuses for not coming to New York. You are *all* coming, and we leave in a few days."

"And Mr and Mrs Marsh too?" Angelina asked, going by the comment made earlier.

"None of this Mr and Mrs nonsense. You can call us Sarah and Matthew, or Grandma and Grandpa. All of you," Sarah told the brand-new in-laws.

"Oh." Angelina saddened. "I don't have grandparents."

"You do now," Sarah said. "So call us Grandma and Grandpa."

Angie's face brightened like the sun after the clouds had parted. "Thank you…Grandma," she said tentatively. "Are you coming for the whole time, too?"

"Of course," Sarah replied. "We're retired and have no plans back home."

"Weren't having Christmas or New Year's with the others?" Jenny asked.

"Not this year," Sarah told her. "After everything that's happened, and the weddings, when you suggested all going to New York, we decided it would make a great trip. The more, the merrier."

"So it's settled." Jenny addressed the table. "We're all flying to New York in three days' time, and you can tell your bosses where to shove it if they complain."

The boys all shrugged. "All right," they agreed.

"Good. Then there's one last thing we need to address right now. Vivian, Angelina, Roger." She looked at each surprised face. "You have all come into the family as partners, then in-laws, now you *are* family. So no more of this Mr and Mrs Stephanopoulos. We are Jenny and Spiros. But if you don't feel comfortable calling us that, maybe Mr and Mrs S will be better for you. Or even," she looked at Angelina, "Mama and Papa. If that's not too much for you," she told a teary Angelina. "The choice is up to you three. Whatever feels comfortable, but no more Mr and Mrs Stephanopoulos. You are family now." Taking in Angelina and Vivian, she contained. "You are our daughters and you," she looked at Roger, "are our son."

Tomas beamed brightly at his husband as Roger looked from Jenny to him and their hands entwined.

Carlos slid an arm around Viv, and Pedro gazed at an excited Angie.

"I raised my boys to be loving and respectful men and husbands. They have chosen the three of you as their life partners, wives, and husband, and have brought you into the family. You are now *a part* of this family. And that's the way it always will be. Welcome."

Spiros and Giorgio held their glasses aloft. "Kalos irthate."

*****

"Oh, my God," Jenny breathed, her eyes taking in everything they could. "It's all so beautiful." Her head spun to Pedro and Angelina seated beside her in the back of the stretch limo on their way from JFK Airport in New York. "I can see why you love it so much." Staring out the window, she looked up and down the streets and buildings at the place she would call home for the next two months.

"You should see it in summer Mrs Steph…oh…Mama…it's all so beautiful," Angelina stumbled, still getting used to calling her mother-in-law, Mama. "The sun shines, the park is green, and everything comes alive."

Pedro smiled at Angelina and saw his brothers smile as well. Angie was more and more family every day.

Jenny squeezed her hand. "I guess this will be your first winter here too. We must go shopping for winter coats. Do you boys have enough to get through winter? You all left in summer so you wouldn't have worried about winter clothes." She gazed at her sons and their partners all seated in the black limo she had hired at the airport. They were taking New York, and they were taking it in style.

Roger and Tomas shook their heads. "Don't really need one in Miami," Roger said.

"I can do with a new wardrobe," Carlos told her. "You paying?"

A sly smile crossed Jenny's lips. "More like Stefano Papadopoulos is paying. I plan on blowing his money big time. So, whatever my boys want, they can have, all courtesy of your ex-great-uncle." She looked at her parents. "Same goes for you two. Let's blow this cash and buy whatever we want. Including accommodation."

They pulled up to a seven-level apartment building, and the driver came around to open the door.

"Thank you." Jenny smiled brightly. "Boys, help him with your luggage."

"Not that there's much." Pedro stumbled out of the car behind Angelina and his grandparents. "We have one case each."

"Doesn't matter, help anyway." Gazing up at the old-style Victorian block with turrets and angles, Jenny knew it was perfect. Situated on 5th Avenue, apparently, known as millionaire's row, it was across the park from Pedro and Angie's current apartment.

The doorman stepped forward as they all stood staring up at the impressive building.

"Apparently, it was renovated last year, so now there are apartments on each floor," Jenny dazedly said as she eyed the brickwork. "Nothing like Mykonos."

"Or Australia," Sarah added from beside her.

"You must be Mrs Stephanopoulos," the doorman said, doffing his hat. "I'm Brewster. Martin Brewster, your doorman."

Jenny finally stopped staring at the building. "Oh, yes, hello. Yes, I'm Jenny Stephanopoulos. These are my parents Sarah and Matthew Marsh. They'll be in Apartment 1."

"How do?" Brewster asked.

"Fine, thank you," Sarah replied.

"My sons Tomas and Roger will have Apartment 2." She pointed them out. "My son and daughter-in-law Carlos and Vivian will have Apartment 3."

"Ms Villiers, pleasure." Brewster doffed his hat again. "Big fan."

"Why, thank you." She beamed from her fur coat. "Always nice to meet fans."

"And my son and daughter-in-law Pedro and Angelina, they will have Apartment 4. I'll be in the penthouse."

"Of course, ma'am. Please, let's get out of this chilly air and inside." Holding the door open he ushered them into the warm lobby.

"My, this is nice," Sarah murmured at the monogrammed floor design and patterned wallpaper.

"Ooh, a chandelier," Angelina cooed. "*So* nice."

"Now, this is your main entrance." Brewster led them to the elevator. "There is a back entrance on this level as it leads to the garage for your cars. But you will need to go in the alley behind us to get in." He waited while everyone gathered themselves in the elevator. "The garage holds ten cars and has spots for five visitors." A second later the door opened. "Apartment 1, Mr and Mrs Marsh."

"Already?" Sarah said. "That was quick."

"The elevator was updated when the building was renovated last year," Brewster said. "Everything was. Piping, water, heat, electricity. You won't be hot or cold. You have everything."

The boys moved out of the way for their grandparents to step out.

"We'll be up in a few minutes," Sarah told them as the doors shut.

"Second floor apartment." Brewster opened the door.

"See you in a few minutes, Mama," Tomas said as he and Roger moved into the small foyer that held their door.

"I'll leave the door unlocked," Jenny called before the doors shut.

"Is that safe?" Angelina asked. "With what we went through with that nutjob getting into our building, she still managed to get in despite security."

"The building is safe," Brewster informed her. His portly belly all but shoved Carlos out the door on the third floor. "I have unlocked your doors for your arrival, and your keys are on the kitchen counter with a basket of fruit." He gave Viv the once over. "Ms Villiers." Tilting his hat, he shut the gate, and they were on the fourth-floor, depositing Pedro and Angie.

"Come up when you're ready," Jenny told them before the door closed once more. "I can't wait to see the penthouse. Is it as nice as the others?"

"See for yourself, ma'am." He opened the door, deposited her bags in the foyer, and waited for her to open the door.

Stepping inside she gasped at the view. "Oh, my, it is."

"I'll just leave your bags here, ma'am." He left Jenny's two suitcases inside the door and closed it behind him.

*****

Tomas was staring at the view while Roger was putting their cases in the main bedroom. "I can't believe how nice this is. Look at the view."

Roger came out. "You should see the bedroom. King-size bed, Egyptian silk sheets, down comforter, plus a black marble ensuite." He gazed at the living-dining-kitchen combo with its luxurious finishes of marble and what looked like velvet. "This is like some posh hotel you can never afford to live in." He stood beside his husband, casting a quick eye over Central Park. "Nice."

Tomas stared glassy-eyed. "What do you mean, *nice*? *Look* at this. I've never been to New York before, and I'm with Mama, everything's new and awesome, and I can't wait to go places. We can jog around the park for exercise, and I wonder if there's a gym nearby."

"I think it's the Y," Roger replied, feeling a chill from staring out the window. The late afternoon sun glinted off the tops of the trees and left shadows dancing down the street. Cold shadows, full of foreboding. He sat on one of the couches and placed his feet on the coffee table. "Couch is comfy. I wonder if there's food."

"How can you be thinking about food when we have *this*?" Tomas finally turned from the window to take in the rest of the apartment.

"I meant in the fridge," Roger said. "So we can make breakfast or dinner."

Tomas fell into his husband's lap and snuggled up. "Let's have breakfast and lunch and dinner every day at somewhere new. I don't want to cook or clean. Let's go and explore the city. I'm sure Pedro and Angie know a few places."

"Like 69," Roger added. "I can't wait to go there."

"Mmm." Tomas lifted his head. "I suppose we should go and see what Pedro does. One night. But not yet. I want to get settled in to the city first. See if there's anywhere else we can go. I want to take it all in. I'm a sponge. I want to soak it in."

"Mmm." Roger nuzzled his neck and received a giggle in return. "I know what I want to soak in."

"Roger." Tomas planted a kiss on his lips. "We need to get upstairs."

"I'm sure your mother won't mind if we turn up late." Roger kissed back. "Besides, you should see the bathtub. I'd love to soak *you* in while we soak in that baby."

*****

"Oh, my God, Viv, check this out." Carlos was running room to room. "This must be costing Mama a fortune." He stopped in the doorway to the master bedroom and watched Viv unpack her two cases. "You wanna unpack mine while you're there?" He leaned on the doorjamb, arms crossed, left leg bent over right, biting his lip.

She threw him a dirty look. "I already packed it in L.A. when I flew out, you can do the rest." Hanging her ankle length grey fur coat in the closet, she closed the door.

"Leave any space for me?" Carlos wandered over and grabbed her by the waist.

She laughed and slid her arms around his neck. "That closet is big enough for *all* of my clothes, but since I only have two cases full, there's plenty of room." Her fingers made their way through his golden locks before sliding over his unshaven face to land on his lips, and she noticed the glint from her rings, which she had switched to her left hand ring finger, as had Carlos. A relieving sigh escaped her. "I can't believe we're married."

"I can't believe I have Vivian Villiers as my wife," he replied. Fingers deftly slid to pants buttons and zip and found their way in.

"Down boy." Slapping his hands away she adjusted her clothes. "We have to meet your mother in the penthouse, and I can't wait to see how glamorous that is. It's two-stories you know. Now, I'm going to freshen up, and you can put away your clothes."

*****

"Oh, Pedro." Angie glanced around the lushly decorated apartment. "This is beautiful."

He took in the thick comfortable couches, elegant wood dining table and kitchen, the chandeliers, the marble-patterned floor, wallpapered walls, and one spectacular view. "At least we're close to Juilliard and 69. Right across from our old place, so it should be fairly easy to get our stuff."

"Ugh," she groaned as she gazed across the park toward their old building. "I don't want to go there. I never want to go back again." Shivering delicately, she pulled her cardigan tighter around her.

Pedro came up behind her and wrapped his arms around her tiny frame. "You don't have to. We'll go and do it. Besides, it's not much. Should all fit in a taxi, so I can take Carlos or Tomas and be back in half an hour or so."

Angelina relished in the warmth of her husband's embrace and felt him kissing the top of her head. Smiling, she turned her face up for a kiss on the lips and received what she was hoping for.

"We'd better empty our cases so I can take them and fill them up with what's left." He rubbed his cheek across her head, feeling the electricity from her hair.

"It's not much," she said. "Just my violin, maybe another case of clothes, and the rest of your stuff."

"Mmm." He kissed her head again. "Let's get up to Mama and let her know what we're doing." They made their way to the elevator, and it opened to reveal everyone else.

"Going up?" Roger asked with a grin as he opened the gate.

"Let's go see the penthouse," Viv said as they boarded. "I wonder if it's fancier than the apartment. What's yours like?"

It turned out they were all furnished the same, so nobody was missing out on anything over the others. They walked through the penthouse door to find their mother on the phone.

"Yes, right." She glanced at them with tears in her eyes. "I'll tell them."

"Tell them he loved them and was glad he at least had that time with them." Spiros came down the line. "And not to be upset or feel guilty. He was old…we all knew it was coming."

Jenny saw the concern on their faces as each stood in the sitting area watching her. "They just walked in. I'll tell them. What are you going to do with the body?"

There were gasps and a few flinches at the word *body,* and several hands flew to mouths.

"Cremation," Spiros said simply. "He didn't want anyone knowing, and he was sure my siblings wouldn't care enough to do something. He asked me to scatter his ashes across the water."

Jenny nodded briefly. "That sounds nice. You do what you need to do and then come when you can. It's lovely here. We're opposite Central Park, and it's so green. And the city is so busy. Definitely different to Mykonos."

"I'll be there when I can, my love. You look after yourself and our children, and I'll see you soon."

"Okay."

"I love you."

"I love you, too…" Jenny slowly replaced the phone in its cradle, and a half sob left her.

"Mama." Carlos stepped forward as the head of the family until their father arrived.

Dazedly, she looked up into the distraught faces of her children and parents. "Your great-grandfather…died…" Shocked murmurs spread through them. "While we were…en route here."

"Oh, my darling." Sarah went to her daughter's side. "Come, sit." She led her around the sofa and sat them both down.

"Oh, Mama." Carlos sat opposite his mother and grandmother.

"What now?" Viv sat beside him, and he took her hand.

Matthew moved to stand behind his daughter and wife, and Angelina and Pedro squeezed in beside Jenny on the couch. Tomas and Roger sat next to Viv.

"Ah…" Jenny breathed in, trying to compose her thoughts. "He asked your father, and his carer to…ah…cremate him and sprinkle his ashes across the sea." She remembered Spiros's words. "He told your father to pass on that he loved you all very much and was glad he at least saw you marry, and that he's glad he also had Sunday to say his goodbyes."

"He was old," Tomas murmured. "In more ways than one."

"Yeah," Pedro breathed. "He looked like he didn't have long."

"Pedro," Carlos chastised with a sharp turn of his head. "Don't say—"

"No," Jenny stopped him, and he stared at her with a stunned expression. "Pedro is right. Your great-grandfather had a very long and very complicated life. It aged him; dramatically after his son died." She shook her head. "I first saw him at the funeral for your grandfather, he still had a head of hair and could walk fine. That was only ten years ago, and you boys saw him these last weeks. So old, so worn out, so ready to go." She frowned. "His life aged him. His wife and daughter's deaths aged him, his son's death aged him even more."

"So, what now?" Matthew asked his daughter.

She came out of her mind. "We ah…" Wiping away her tears, she continued. "We get on with what we were doing. We are here to set up Angie and Pedro and to celebrate Christmas and New Year's, and to have fun and blow lots of money." She laughed lightly, but the laughter never reached her eyes. "Carlos, I want you, Tomas, and

Roger to take Pedro over to his apartment and pack his and Angie's things and bring them back." She turned to her youngest. "I want you here tonight. I want you and Angie in your apartment and safe."

Glancing at her watch, which she had changed to New York time, she added, "You should be back within the hour if you go now." Picking up her purse from the coffee table she pulled out a handful of notes. "Take a cab across the park. I don't want you walking. And take one back," she told Carlos. "We'll stay here and keep warm." She saw the boys look at each other. "What?"

"*We* don't need to go do we?" Carlos asked slowly through pouting lips.

"Oh, for God's sake, Carlos, help your brother. That's what I raised you to do." She frowned, but a small laugh escaped her, and she watched him reluctantly get to his feet. "Stop being a child and go."

Pedro gazed down at Angie. "Will you okay here, babe?"

She giggled. "Of course, silly. It's not like I'll be on my own."

"Okay." He kissed her. "Back soon."

They watched the door close behind the boys and Jenny heaved a sigh of relief. "I don't know about all of you." She closed her eyes briefly. "But I would prefer to stay in tonight."

"Absolutely," Sarah agreed.

Matthew finally sat in an easy chair. "We'll stay until you kick us out," he said.

Jenny spied Angelina wringing her hands. "What's wrong?" She laid a hand on her daughter's.

"Nothing...it's just..." Angie faltered and grasped Jenny's hand with a death grip.

"Go on."

"Everyone's...leaving...my mother, my father, a brother I never knew I had, now Pedro's great-grandfather..." Angie frowned. "And I don't know...how to..."

"Deal with it?" Jenny filled in the blanks.

"Comfort you..." Angelina blinked slowly, waiting for her mother-in-law's reaction.

"Oh." Jenny's face crumpled. "Sweetie, come here." Taking Angelina into her arms, she hugged her tight. "You don't need to comfort me. Giorgio was Giorgio. In the grand scheme of things, he didn't matter, the people who *do* matter are still here with us, and *that's* what's important." She stroked Angie's hair. "You don't need to comfort me. I'm okay. And so are you." Glancing down she added, "Okay?"

Angie smiled and snuggled into her mother-in-law's shoulder for a few moments more. "Okay."

"Okay. Then we'd better get some food going because I know my boys and they will be hungry. Come, let's look in the fridge and see what we have." She stood and collected Viv on their way to the kitchen. "Okay, let's see." Opening the fridge door, she spied fresh beef, lots of vegetables, fruit, milk, juice and a variety of condiments. "Viv, can you see what's in the cupboards?"

"Sure." Viv opened the top cabinets to reveal cereals, pasta, tinned fruit and vegetables, plus an assortment of herbs and spices.

"Well, I spy pasta, pasta sauce, and beef, so, let's make pasta." While she gathered the beef and fresh tomatoes, Viv pulled out packets of pasta and jars of pasta sauce from the cupboard.

Sarah searched for pots and found a large pasta pot and a saucepan for the sauce. Within ten minutes the water was boiling, and the pasta went in. Jenny finished frying off the beef and poured two jars of sauce on top before slicing and dicing the fresh tomatoes to be added near the end. "Another ten to fifteen minutes I think."

"The boys have been gone for thirty, so they'll definitely be hungry when they get back." Viv glanced out the floor-to-ceiling windows that stretched across the whole floor. "It's almost dark outside."

"And probably quite cold," Sarah put in. "I hope they grabbed their coats on the way out."

*****

They had, but had slipped them off upon entering Pedro's pad.

"Nice place, bro," Carlos said, looking around. "Seventh floor, nice view."

"Yeah, but it's time to move on." Pedro moved into the bedroom and grabbed Angie's second suitcase, throwing it on the bed, he started grabbing clothes from the closet and shoving them in the case.

"Hey, take it easy, let me do that," Roger told him as he walked into the room. "You grab your stuff from the bathroom." As Pedro disappeared, Roger went to work, expertly folding Angie's clothes into her case.

"Where'd you learn to pack like that?" Tomas marvelled at the speed of Roger's expertise as he stood at the end of the bed.

"Years of practice," Roger replied, quickly folding the last pieces in and shutting the lid. "Anything else?" he asked Pedro as he came out of the bathroom.

"Yeah," he said, grabbing Angie's bag from the closet. "Her toiletries, and she has her shoes and personal stuff." He grabbed his own bag and jammed his clothes in before digging for personal papers. "She also has a violin."

"Found it." Tomas laid it on the bed.

"Got all your mail and whatever else was in the living room." Carlos came in.

Pedro pulled paperwork from the drawer, jammed them into his bag, and zipped it up. "I think that's it."

"Take one last look around and make sure," Tomas said, his hands still on the violin case. "You don't want to get home and then have to come back because you've forgotten something."

"Yeah," Pedro mumbled and quickly went from room to room, through every drawer and cupboard. "Nope, let's go." They gathered the things and went downstairs to the waiting cab, where they piled everything into the trunk.

"Thanks for waiting." Carlos climbed into the front.

"No problem," the cabbie replied. "Especially since you said you'd double the fare if I waited."

"Absolutely," Carlos said. "Back to 5th Avenue."

The driver took them down Central Park West to the 79th St transverse and up 5th Avenue back to their building. "That's $28.50 and doubled."

Carlos dug the notes Jenny had given him from his pocket. "Here, sixty bucks, keep the change. And thanks." He climbed out and helped the others lug bags and cases up to Pedro's apartment before heading upstairs.

"Finally," Matthew called. "Come and eat."

Jenny pulled garlic bread from the oven. "Food's ready, take a seat."

Everyone gathered around the table as the girls set out plates of pasta and Jenny put two plates of garlic bread on the table.

"Yum." Pedro scooped up two slices. "You always outdo yourself, Mama."

"Wasn't just me," she told him, sitting down. "We all made this."

Carlos swallowed his third spoonful. "Delicious as always, Mama. Viv, I didn't know you could cook?"

She laughed at the napkin tucked in his shirt. "There are a lot of things you're yet to learn about your new wife, Carlos Stephanopoulos."

"Mmm," he mumbled around another mouthful. "Well, I certainly didn't know cooking was one of your magic tricks."

"Oh, I have many tricks, Carlos," she purred in a sultry voice.

"Enough with the magic and more with the eating," Jenny said, dishing out more pasta to her son.

*****

Three days later, they celebrated Thanksgiving on a cold November day. Snow lightly fluttered on the breeze, blanketing the park in a thin layer of white, and everyone was ensconced in the penthouse with a roaring fire and delicious aromas wafting in from the kitchen.

They'd spent the last few days hanging out, walking around the local neighbourhoods, and had fun buying Pedro a brand-new car, all courtesy of Stefano Papadopoulos. This time he had chosen a black and gold Pontiac Firebird Trans Am special edition that featured in the *Smokey and the Bandit* movie. And his brothers had helped him choose. It took pride of place down in the garage as it was the only car there. For now, that was, as Jenny reminded him he could hardly put a baby seat in the back of it.

Jenny checked on the turkeys. Instead of one big one that would take all day to cook, she'd bought several smaller ones and cut them up to save on cooking time. Pans of veggies sat roasting alongside them in the oven, merrily sizzling away as they tanned themselves in the glow of the gas fire. "Another half hour or so," she called across the expansive suite.

The penthouse was incredibly furnished. The dining, sitting and living areas all faced the park. The kitchen was at the back with a laundry and small bathroom, plus an office behind the living room. A lushly decorated master suite plus two bedrooms and a bathroom were upstairs. The living room boasted the roaring fireplace with multiple couches and easy chairs, while the sitting area had two couches and two easy chairs. It was fit for royalty, and Jenny liked it very much.

Definitely somewhere I could call home, she thought, gazing across the room at her sons and in-laws seated around the fire. Her parents had the couch in the sitting room where Sarah was knitting, and Matthew was reading a book. Putting the kitchen towel on the bench, she smiled. *My boys are so happy, so happy being married, so happy in love, so happy with their lives, except for the porn. I'm not happy with that, and I wish they'd stop. Hopefully, I can get them to.* She walked over to her parents and was about to sit down when the phone rang. "Ah, I'll get it." She grabbed the phone and saw her children perk up. "Hello."

"Hello, my love, happy Thanksgiving. I'm sorry I can't be there yet."

Her lips curled into a smile. "Hello, I'm sorry you can't be here too. When will you get here?" She missed her husband terribly. The days may have been full, but the nights were cold and lonely.

"In a week or two, and then we'll all be together once more."

"I can't wait." They spoke for a few minutes more before she replaced the phone and gazed over her children. All six of them made her burst with pride. "That was your father. He'll be here in a week or so." She wandered over to the fireplace and stood staring into the crackling flames. "I hope he enjoys New York as much as I do."

"We've only been here three days and haven't seen much." Carlos snuggled deeper into the couch he was sitting on with Viv, and pulled the light crocheted blanket over them and tucked it in.

"Yes, but you've enjoyed snuggling in front of the fire every day," Viv replied, playing footsies under the blanket.

"That's because *we* don't have a fire," he told her. "How come the penthouse has a fire, and we all don't?"

Jenny laughed lightly. "Because it's the penthouse and you all have heating."

"Mmm," Carlos mumbled. "And that's why we're here every day, in the penthouse, snuggling in front of the fire." He slid his arm around his wife and pulled her closer.

"And I don't mind one bit," Jenny said to them. "I love having my babies back around me." Turning to Pedro and Angelina, snuggled under their own blanket on their own couch, she asked, "And when do you two go back to work and school?"

"Next week," Pedro said. "I called Eddie yesterday, told him we were back. He threatened to fire me for being gone so long, but when I told him the whole story, he said to come back next week. Apparently, attendance has been down since I've been gone and he can't wait to get me back behind the decks. He's putting out fliers letting everyone know I'm back in town."

"Will you be working Christmas and New Year's?" Jenny sat on the ottoman that matched the couches.

"I bargained with him." Pedro's eyes twinkled. "And bargained hard. Because I've had over a month off, he's letting me off Christmas Eve and Christmas Day, but I have to work a double shift at New Years. They're planning on doing a twenty-four-hour party from midday New Year's Eve to midday New Year's Day, so I'll be working."

"Well!" Jenny huffed. "At least we get you for Christmas. What about your *other* boss?" An eyebrow arched.

Angie giggled as Pedro um-ed and ah-ed.

"Well…" Pedro's voice rose slightly. "She didn't like me having the extra time off, but I told her to make sure the movies would be ready to go in January, and I'd make them back to back to get them out of the way before the baby comes, because after that, I wouldn't be interested."

"Good!" Jenny exclaimed. "Take it well, did she?" There was a touch of snarkiness to her tone.

"Not particularly." Pedro grinned and hugged Angie tighter. "But after I reminded her of my ordeal at the hands of Andros Poulos and Nedro Scarvo, for who she was partially responsible since she hadn't bothered checking into him before wanting his house, she relented and told me she'd have the movies ready to go. If I do one a week, I can get them out of the way before the baby comes."

"One a week?" Tomas piped up from his spot beside Roger on the third couch. "We did one a night, five nights a week, nearly."

"Well, it's not like it's work," Roger teased, his arm around Tomas's shoulders. His fingers laced with his husband's as they sat under a blanket.

Tomas blushed and looked up into his man's eyes. "Mmm, that's true."

"Okay, don't need to know," Jenny quipped with a wave of her hand.

"Ew, gross bro," Carlos added. "We don't need to know about your sex life."

"At least *I* have sex with my real-life partner in the movies *I* make and *not* some stranger," Tomas retorted. "How many women have you screwed?"

Carlos blushed. "Not the point. Even if I film one a week, I also write them."

Viv had raised a brow at Tomas's question and was now left wondering. "What *is* going to happen?" she asked Carlos. "Tomas has a valid point. You've been busy having sex with different women in the movies, but now what? We're married with a baby on the way. What will you do when you go back to work?" The queasy feeling in the pit of her stomach was more than morning sickness. She knew that this was going to be discussed, but a part of her had expected him to stop fucking altogether.

"Ugh." He stared into her inquisitive face. "I…have a contract," he said slowly.

"For how many?" she asked.

Carlos blinked, thinking. "I don't actually know. I know Harry wanted the Golden Gods series written and filmed. And I've finished the scripts for them."

"Good," Viv told him. "So, once you finish the films you're contracted to do, you can quit porn?"

"Ah, what?" Carlos was surprised. She had mentioned him being a stay-at-home dad, but not actually quitting porn. Especially since she and Connie had got him into it. "But I like writing movies and helping to set up the stages and then seeing the finished product. And it makes good money."

"I have no problem with you writing the movies, or being a set designer, or even producing or directing them," Viv said. "What I have a problem with is you being *in them*."

He blinked, digesting what she'd just said. "And what about modelling? Will you give that up?"

"Not forever," she said. "I plan on taking a year or so off once I grow too big and I'll be with the baby while it's little. And when I feel that I'm ready, I'll get back into it."

"What about the travelling?" he asked, completely unaware of everyone's eyes on them. "Will you travel for work?"

She humoured him with a smile. "Not if I can help it, and even if I have to, I'll keep it to short trips. I've already thought about it. Looks like it's time to think about your porn career now there's a baby on the way." She turned to Pedro. "That goes for you too, but at least you've *started* thinking about it. Whereas you," she told her husband, "need to make a decision."

Carlos sat in thought. He knew they would have to change with the baby coming, but hadn't even realised that meant giving up being an actor in the movies even though his father had mentioned it in his pre-wedding speech. Sure, he could write, he'd rewritten *Cabana*, and had come up with the *Meat Shop* ideas. Plus, *The Golden Gods* scripts were done. So, what now…?

"And you two?" Jenny asked Tomas and Roger. "Will you two continue?"

Roger glanced at Tomas snuggled in his arms. "We don't have a baby on the way, and I do studio work as well as star on screen. If we chose to stop, we could still work behind the cameras, or Tomas could keep on training."

"Personally, I'd like to see you give it up," Jenny said. "I find it disgusting and don't like it. Why do you even need to do it now?"

The boys looked from her to their partners as they thought about it.

"Well," Pedro started. "I was kinda talked into it because Carlos was doing it. So," he shrugged, "I don't *need* to do it."

"Then for heaven's sake, don't," Jenny pleaded.

"Mama, I have a contract and eight more movies. I have to finish them. You and Papa are the ones who taught us to finish what we start. But," he looked at Angie snuggled under his arm, "once they're done that will be it. No more porn."

Angie glanced up, all toasty warm. "Really?"

"Really," he repeated, staring lovingly back at his bride. "I get paid well to DJ at 69, and that's what I love most. So, I'll finish my contract and be done with it."

"Yes," she hissed, fist pumping herself. "As much as I love seeing you on the screen..."

"It's time for him to be a husband and father," Jenny finished. "Now that wasn't so hard. Was it Carlos? Your turn, if your brother can make the decision, so can you."

Carlos sighed. While he enjoyed sex immensely, he knew that Viv was the one he wanted to be with. And what would be the point in fucking strangers now that he had the stunningly gorgeous Vivian Villiers as his wife? Finally, he spoke. "I have a contract too, as I said, but..." He glanced at Viv. "I do like writing and stage setting as well. I'll have a chat with Harry about finishing off my contract and then moving into behind-the-scenes work."

Vivian's smile brightened the room. "Thank you. Now, that wasn't so hard, was it?"

He chuckled. "No, I guess not. Not when I have you to fuck every day, so a stranger is just not going to cut it."

"Language," Jenny reminded him then stopped. "Jesus, I sound like my mother."

"I heard that," Sarah called and the boys laughed.

"And to get out of that," Jenny said, "it's time for lunch."

*****

Two days later, Jenny treated her family to a shopping spree at *Barney's*. After speaking to the manager and being given several personal shoppers, the boys headed for the menswear floor while the girls headed for fashion and shoes. Jenny was determined to have the best money could buy, and she was going to buy as much as possible. She spied Viv homing in on the fur coats. "Oh, they are beautiful," she said, eyeing a gorgeous black ankle-length coat.

"They are," Viv replied, sliding a white rabbit fur over her shoulders. "And so warm."

After everyone had tried them on, they decided upon an ankle-length each, plus a hip-length blazer style each, and Angelina chose a bolero as well.

Moving on to the rest of the floor, Viv sent Jenny into the change room with multiple dresses. "They're the latest style, and the length will keep you warm."

Jenny felt a chill about her ankles. "I do prefer pants in winter. Are there any out there?" She eyed the teal dress she had on. "Pick colours that will go with all the tops." Sliding out of her dress she tried on a deep blue button up with cap shoulders and slightly ballooned sleeve with cuffs. Pearl buttons went all the way down the front. The skirt silently whooshed around her ankles, but while she loved the colour, she wasn't sure about the style.

Viv and the personal shopper returned with a rack full of pantsuits and matching blouses in a dozen colours.

"Oh, goodness," Jenny cried when she saw the clothes. "So many. Where do I even begin?"

Viv picked up a deep rose-pink pantsuit and matching silk blouse. "With this." Handing it to Jenny, she watched her disappear behind the curtain. "Apparently, they have matching shoes and bags too."

"Oooh, we'll have to look at those." Angelina stepped out of a changeroom in a geometric pattern blouse, and a pair of pants in a deep shade of green that picked up on one of the colours on the blouse.

"Oh, that's fantastic, Angie," Viv said. "That blouse is made for you."

Angie swept her long hair back and eyed herself critically in the mirror. "You think?"

"Absolutely," Viv enthused.

Angie heard the curtain swish back. "What do you think, Mama?" Even after the last few weeks, she was still unsure about calling her mother-in-law that. She glanced at Jenny, and her eyes went wide. "You look beautiful."

Jenny smoothed the rose pants and tailored blazer. "Oh, thank you, sweetie." Taking a look at Angie, she added, "That blouse looks fabulous on you." She stood by her side, grasping her arms as they stared into the mirror. "We *both* look fabulous."

"You certainly do," Viv said. "That suit's a keeper. Next!"

*****

Meanwhile, the boys were having a ball being sized for pants and shirts. Three-piece suits were suddenly all the rage thanks to *Saturday Night Fever*, and since Roger already had a white one, he had Tomas fitted out for one. They chose different collars and cuffs, and helped their grandfather pick out some things as well.

"I don't need all of this," Matthew protested. "We don't wear these things in Australia. I'll be the laughing stock of Armidale."

"No, you won't," Pedro told him. "You'll be the big fashion star instead. Wearing the latest trend before it even hits Aussie shores." Straightening the jacket, he looked over his grandfather's shoulder in the mirror. "See, you'll be a hit." He turned him around.

Turning, Matthew looked at his reflection and shook his head at the slate blue three-piece suit and pale blue shirt. He couldn't really come up with anything bad to say.

"I am *loving* these suits." Carlos walked out of the changeroom and did a spin. "How *hot* do I look?" He flicked the cuffs of his shirt up.

"Not as hot as *you* think you look," Tomas said and looked at himself in the mirror. He wasn't sure if the three-piece style was for him.

"And I think I'm hot because I *am*." Carlos did a few more spins and pretended to walk down a catwalk.

Pedro rolled his eyes. "Only in your own head," he muttered and went to try on a suit. After finishing with the suits and shirts, the boys moved on to the coat section.

"They have fur coats?" Matthew asked, watching Carlos slide a coat over his shoulder.

The personal shopper helped him adjust it. "Yes, we do. They're huge in New York this year."

"Yeah," Pedro agreed. "Leon, one of the guys I work with, wears a lot of faux fur. I don't know whether he's got the real thing, though."

"He works at 69 with you?" Roger asked and watched Tomas turn his nose up at the fur and pick up a sturdy black overcoat from a rack.

"Yeah," Pedro replied. "He's one of the waiters, as gay as a hatter, so you guys would love him."

The personal shopper's eyes widened, and he breathed, "I thought you looked familiar." Eyeing Pedro up and down he added, "I didn't recognise you with your clothes on." Everyone turned to him, and he blushed. "I go to 69, you're the DJ."

"Yeah," Pedro said for the third time. "I am. I've been on my honeymoon, but I'll be back next week."

The personal shopper was crestfallen, for he had always fancied Pedro. After all, it wasn't often that you had an extremely tall, lithe, well-built man like Pedro strut around in tiny gold shorts and boots. "Oh, you're married..." Disappointment rained down over him.

"Yes, to my girlfriend. But we're now back and ready to work." He picked up a leather jacket. "This is cool."

"It is." Carlos spun around. He was wearing one and walking up and down his imaginary catwalk. "Have we ever had clothes as fancy as this?"

"Nope," Tomas said from a few racks away, all wrapped up in a trench coat with tartan lining. "But that jacket does look good."

"Well, you know your mother wants you to have whatever you want, so you may as well get everything now." Matthew glanced at his watch. "We have a few hours before meeting up for lunch. "Will you boys want shoes next?"

*****

The girls moved on to the shoe and bag department, and with help from the assistants, as well as the personal shopper, were able to find the matching bags, hats and shoes to go with the clothes they'd bought. Then it was on to the jewellery department where Jenny spied watches she could buy for everyone for Christmas, and some dazzling diamond studs she might like for herself. "I need to purchase a present for Spiros, maybe a watch, would that be appropriate?"

"Of course." Sarah tried on a bracelet. "He's not really a jewellery kind of man anyway, so a watch *would be* appropriate."

"Mmm," Jenny eyed a few more pieces and added them to the list. "Are we finished here?"

"I just have to decide between the pink and the blue bead necklace set," Angelina said, staring at the two as they lay side by side on the counter.

"Why choose? We'll take them both," Jenny told the assistant and surprised a wide-eyed Angie. "Do we need make-up?"

"Why not?" Viv said. "The beauty counter is downstairs, and the latest fragrance is *to die* for, apparently."

"Okay, let's wrap this up. I'll go and grab a watch and pay for the boys' things. You girls head down to the beauty counter. Then we'll have lunch and hit the salon. See you in a few minutes," she said to the girls as they said goodbye and walked away. Jenny paid for the jewellery they'd chosen, plus bought the watches and diamond studs she'd had her eye on, and had it all added to the shopping to be delivered to the penthouse later that afternoon. She then hurried up to the men's floor where she found her sons modelling the latest watches. "Do you think your father would like one of them? I need to get him something for Christmas." She stopped behind them at the counter. "Let me see."

They turned to show her the latest designs, but she didn't think they were right for Spiros. After looking for a few minutes, she chose a simple watch for him to wear to work. "And I'm done. What about you boys?"

"What do we get you two for Christmas?" Pedro asked, slinging an arm around Carlos's shoulders.

"We already bought them, remember," Carlos reminded him. "In Athens, when we went shopping."

Pedro thought for a moment. "Oh, yeah, forgot about those."

Jenny laughed. "Well, whatever you *did* get, keep it a secret. Now, the girls are downstairs at the beauty counter, so if you want the latest man scent, you'd better get down there and grab it."

"I got all the scent I need." Carlos flexed his pecs. "It's au naturel."

"It's *oh* disgusting," Pedro told him. "Time to get a new one." He shoved his brother ahead. "We'll meet you downstairs, Mama."

Once they disappeared, she checked the things they'd chosen and made a few more purchases. While she was buying them everything they wanted, she was also getting them some special Christmas gifts.

Meeting them at the beauty counter, she let Viv try the latest make-up on her and smelt a dozen new perfumes. The boys tried the latest aftershaves and cologne for men, and Angelina found exquisite body lotions and washes. After adding several dozen items to the list, they headed up to the top floor for lunch.

The whole floor was a restaurant overlooking the city and parts of Central Park. They lunched on salmon and chicken, a change from all the lamb they'd had in Greece, and drank fine wine and champagne.

Angelina squirmed in her seat as she gazed out the window.

"Have you got worms?" Pedro joked, watching her from across the table.

She giggled. "No, silly, look at the view. I've never eaten here before let alone shopped here."

"We *have* only been here a few months," Pedro reminded her.

"I know. But we've never had the opportunity to shop like this before," she said.

"Neither have I," Jenny told her with a warm smile and got one in return. "But there's a first time for everything." She glanced at her watch. "Time for the salon. Apparently, there's a man's barber here so you boys can have a cut and shave."

"Mmm," Viv murmured. "Carlos needs it. As much as he looks hot with stubble, it's not so hot against my skin. I think I've gotten a burn from you." She nudged him under the table as he sat across from her.

His lips pouted. "I thought you liked my stubble. Or did you lie?" he demanded with narrowed eyes.

Viv laughed and accidentally snorted champagne out her nose. She kept on laughing as she hid behind her napkin and dabbed at her face.

"I, for one, don't want to know about it." Jenny stood and gathered her things. "I'll pay the bill, and we'll go to the salon."

Ten minutes later they parted ways on the fifth floor. The girls luxuriated in facials before getting their hair cut and coloured. The boys had the hot towel treatment after expert shaves and needed only a trim each as they'd had haircuts for their weddings.

Jenny watched the last curler come out of her hair and marvelled how a different style could change the way you looked. A half hour later she was admiring her new look in the mirror. She'd had inches cut off her shoulder-blade length hair, and it was layered and lightly curled to frame her face perfectly.

"Gorgeous," Angie breathed as she stood behind her. "You look so different."

Jenny smiled brightly. "So do you. When was the last time you had a fringe?"

Angelina fluffed her dead straight bangs. Inches had been cut off her hair, and it was layered around her face, while still long in the back. "Not since I was a little girl."

"I think you both look fabulous," Viv said, admiring her own trim and highlights.

The hairdresser finished with Sarah who stood up. "What about me?"

The three of them turned around. "Awesome," Jenny told her, seeing the shorter cut her mother had chosen. "If we're all finished, let's go meet the boys." She paid the bill and then walked out to find the boys waiting. "Oh, look at all of you. Clean shaven and clean cut. My babies look so handsome."

"Mama," came three groans and Roger laughed softly at the carry on.

"What?" she cried. "I'm not allowed to admire my gorgeous babies anymore?"

Carlos spied his mother's new do and nodded at it. "And you look pretty spiffy yourself." The compliment made her smile.

Pedro's eyes were on Angie as she turned around. "I like it, you look so different." He slid his fingers through it. "I didn't think you'd cut so much off, though."

"It was only five inches," she replied, hugging him. "My hair was too long and needed a cut and deep condition."

"And now it's nice and shiny." Pedro let it slide over his hands. "I love it." He kissed her. "And I love you."

"If we're ready to go I think we've been here all day." Jenny put her coat on. "And all our things will be delivered in," she checked her watch, "Oh, God, half an hour, we'd better get home." She ushered them into the elevator and downstairs, managing to hail the driver she'd hired. "Home, please," she told him as they piled in.

An hour later everyone's apartments were piled high with clothes and accessories, and Jenny sat on the bed in the penthouse looking at the special present she'd bought Spiros. She couldn't wait to see his face when he saw it and hoped he loved it as much as she did. Smiling to herself, she hid all the presents away in a box in the huge walk-in closet and went downstairs to prepare dinner.

*****

On Monday night, Pedro was back at work. As much as he loved what he did, a part of him still wanted to be home with Angie and his family. He'd enjoyed the last few weeks of life. Getting married, spending time in Athens and back on Mykonos, even a week hanging out with his brothers. But he needed to get back to work, to start earning a living again.

He saw the regulars, Bev Marie, Sara Holdare, Martine Krevnokov, and Stan Kosnov. It was almost as if he'd never been gone. All the regulars and the staff had welcomed him back as if he had been resurrected from the dead. And, of course, Mike had told everyone about the wedding, so everyone knew he was off the market. Except for Bev.

"I've mished yoo sho mush." Ten champagnes down and Bev was hot to trot, slobbering over him as she flung her arms around his neck. "I luv yoo."

Pedro laughed. "Same old Bev. But I'm off the market now." He flashed his hand. "I'm a married man, so as much as I'm flattered…" He shook his head. "Nothing's gonna happen."

Bev stared at the ring, and her arms slid down to her side. "You…got…married!" Her words were lost in the music.

"Oh, congratulations," Sara yelled out over the music. "When did it happen?" She was next to Bev and saw the green come over her face.

"A few weeks ago," he replied, flashing his pearly whites at her before glancing at Bev as she lurched and vomited all over him.

"Oh, Jesus, Bev!" Sara's hands flew to her mouth.

Pedro didn't move; he couldn't when he had vomit all down his legs.

Luckily, Leon had seen what happened and quickly grabbed the cleaning crew that set up a perimeter around Pedro and gave him wet towels to wipe himself off.

"I'm shorry," an apologetic Bev called, as Sara and a guard moved her on. "I'm sho shorry."

Pedro clenched his jaw, trying to keep a smile on his lips, but it was damn hard.

"Pedro." Eddie came over. "Go take a shower. I got Master Z to take over while you take a break." He watched Pedro take one last wipe at his leg and dump the towels in a heap for the cleaning crew to gather up. "Welcome back," he told him with a chuckle and followed him to the staff room. "Clearly, you were missed."

Pedro threw him a dirty look. "Not funny, Eddie. All the months I was here she never did that. Now I'm back from a month off, and she chucks all over me." He grabbed a towel and hit the shower, being in and out in two minutes and back in fresh gold shorts and boots. Thank God he had a spare set in his locker.

"Well, *she* missed you." Eddie leant against the lockers. "So did my bank balance, kid, so I'm glad you're back. Takings were down and I didn't like it. Which is why I'm already advertising that you'll be doing the New Year's party. You'd better come through. We already have ticket sales and enquiries for that, and I have a feeling we'll sell out in no time." He watched Pedro slick back his hair and spray cologne. "No wonder everyone loves you, looking like that." He eyed the sexy half Greek up and down. "And damn, what *is* that smell?" A delicious aroma wafted into Eddie's nostrils.

"*Fior* for men," Pedro told him. "Mama took us on a shopping spree."

"That's a hundred bucks a bottle." Eddie was astounded. "Not that *you* can't afford it on what I pay you. Five grand a week."

Pedro flashed a grin. "Yeah, it's a hundred bucks a bottle, but Mama can afford it too. She's rich now."

"And when will I meet your mama?" Eddie licked his lips in anticipation of meeting the makers of the stud before him. The Greek *money-making* stud.

"Don't know." Pedro slammed his locker shut. "This isn't Mama's thing, so I don't know if she'll want to come, but Carlos and Tomas are coming at the end of the week, probably Friday."

"Yeah, I heard. Saw he married Vivian Villiers." Eddie followed him out of the staff room, and they watched the crowd while the song finished up. "She's a piece of ass."

Pedro agreed. "She is, but Carlos will flatten you if you try anything."

"On her or him?" Eddie joked. "I've seen his movies. He's a hot piece of ass himself."

"Ew, Eddie!" Pedro frowned. "Don't need to know."

*****

Angelina sat on the couch in the penthouse finishing her reading and watching a late-night show with Jenny. Everyone else was tucked up in their own apartment as it was fast approaching midnight, but she didn't want to be on her own. She *hated* being on her own after what her father had done. But she also knew it was something she was going to have to deal with, with a baby on the way. Closing her book, she laid it on the table and finished off her tea before settling back into the couch.

"Time for bed yet?" Jenny saw her eyelids slide down to halfway.

"Mmm," Angie murmured looking over at Jenny. "Sorry."

"Don't be." Jenny smiled. "It's late, and you should be in bed already. Why don't I walk you downstairs and tuck you in? You have school now."

"No," Angie cried. "I don't want to go yet." A creeping red blush crawled across her face.

"Why not?"

The blush deepened. "Sorry I...don't want to be alone."

Jenny slid her arm around her and kissed her temple. "You're not alone. You have us. But this is something you'll have to get used to doing now Pedro's back at work."

Angie sighed. "I know. I just want to..."

"Ease into it?"

"Yes."

Jenny rubbed her arm. "Fair enough. But what's he going to think when he comes home and you're not there in the morning?"

She shrugged. "That I'm here."

Jenny laughed. "Probably. But what happens when Spiros comes and we want some alone time?"

Angie's eyes widened, and the blush came back. "Oh..."

"Yes...oh... I don't mind you staying here for the rest of the week, but we need to get you back into your own bed by the weekend. Okay?"

Angie nodded. "Okay."

"Right. I'll go make us another tea. You snuggle up on the couch." Taking the cups, she walked into the kitchen and refilled the kettle. While waiting for the water to boil she saw Angie curl up on the couch under a blanket and fall asleep. After pouring another tea for herself, she went over and heard Angie snoring softly. She tucked the blanket around her, turned off the TV and lights, and took her tea upstairs.

*****

Pedro left 69 at 6:30 in the morning, and after a quick breakfast made it back to the apartment to find it empty. "Angie?" He checked both bedrooms, but the place was dead silent. "Must have slept upstairs. Ugh." He collapsed on the bed and yawned. "I should go up." Lying back, he pulled the comforter over him and fell asleep.

*****

Jenny was awake at six, the same time she'd woken every morning to feed Spiros before he went to work. Then she would get the boys up at seven, and get them to school at eight. But now she had no one to get up for, except for Angie down on the couch. Lying back beneath the warm down spreads, she watched the last embers in the fireplace burn out. It was warm and toasty in that bed, and she couldn't wait for Spiros to join her. *He'll be here on the weekend,* she thought, *and we can spend the entire two days in bed.* Snuggling down further, she closed her eyes to dream of her husband but was awoken by her alarm at seven-thirty. With a sigh, she slid out of bed, turned the heating up high to get it going, and stepped into the bathroom for a quick shower. When she came out, the bedroom was as hot as a steam room. "Whew! That definitely works." After dressing, she went down to wake Angie and start making breakfast.

"Angie." She gently shook her shoulders. "Wake up. It's time for school."

Angie mumbled and snuggled deeper under the blanket.

That brought back fond memories for Jenny, and smiling at those memories, she shook her daughter again. "Angie. Time to get up. You have school."

"Mmm, don't wanna," Angie protested, wiping her hand over her face.

"Well, you can always quit," Jenny told her.

That woke her up. "What?" Angie's eyes opened to see Jenny standing over her. "I don't want to quit. I at least want to do one year."

"Then you'll need to get up," Jenny said. "I'll make breakfast. Pedro's probably fast asleep so no waking him. Come, freshen up and we'll get something to eat." Sending Angie to the bathroom at the back of the stairs, she opened the curtains to reveal a wintry

November day, so she turned on the heating system before getting everything out for breakfast.

Half an hour later, her sons rolled in one by one, except for Pedro, after her parents. By now Angie had to go and shower for school.

"Don't forget your books," Jenny called, waving a hand at the coffee table.

"Oh, forgot." Angie rushed over and grabbed them. "See you later." She flew out the door, down one floor, and into her apartment to find Pedro snoring his head off. She quietly showered and dressed, packed her bag, and went down to find Maggie pulling up at the curb.

"Mmm, great breakfast, Mrs S," Roger said, finishing off his French toast. "I definitely need to get back to exercising with all the food I've eaten this last month. What about you, T?" He used his affectionate nickname for his husband and looked at him. "T?"

Tomas stared glumly at his half-eaten breakfast.

Jenny noticed and knew something was wrong. "Tomas? What's wrong?"

He finally looked up through blurry eyes. "I don't feel well."

She rushed to feel his forehead and poke at his glands. "Pain?"

"Sore throat."

"Since when?"

"Overnight."

"Well, you had glandular fever as kids, as well as measles, mumps and chicken pox." Jenny stared into his face. "I'll get you some Panadol, take it and eat your toast. It will help your throat." She bustled around getting the pills and pouring more juice. Not wanting her son to be sick again, she had despaired at not being able to help him the last time he was sick. But she was here now and going to take care of him. "Get these down you and eat your toast." Sitting in her seat, she watched him swallow the pills and feebly eat.

"Oh, does that mean I'll catch it?" Roger asked, watching his husband's face. "We live and breathe the same air. If you've got a bug, then I'll get a bug."

Tomas glassily looked at him. "Sorry."

Roger laughed. "Not your fault. With everything you went through your immune system is down. I'm surprised you didn't pick something up sooner. Maybe we should get back to exercising. Build up your strength again."

Tomas let a weary sigh escape between his lips. "Yeah…maybe…I just don't…"

"You were never sick while you trained," Jenny reminded him. "Maybe ease into it by walking the park. Get your muscles working again after such a long break."

Tomas swallowed, feeling the pain subside. "Maybe. But right now, I just want to lie down and let the pills work. My head is…" He shook it slowly. "Full of cotton wool." Rubbing his jaw, he heaved another sigh and stood. "I'm gonna go back to bed."

"No, you're not." Jenny stood and took him by the arm. "You'll stay here on the couch where I can keep an eye on you, and feed you pills and chicken soup." Leading him to one of the couches, she settled him down, laid a blanket over him, and tucked it under his chin. "You rest, and I'll make a huge pot of homemade soup." With a kiss on the forehead, she went back to the kitchen and quietly took Roger aside while the others watched on. "How long has he not been feeling well?"

"He said last night, and he was fine before that," Roger whispered as he leant against a cupboard. "After you took him to that doctor in Athens he was better."

"Mmm…" Jenny frowned thoughtfully. "It could just be a winter bug. And what you said before about his immune system being down would be right. He would be highly susceptible to germs right now. But I thought with all the good food I've been feeding him it would have boosted him back up."

Roger pondered for a moment. "Normally I'd agree, but he was poisoned over a period of a couple of weeks, so it was slow-acting. It made him so ill, Mrs S. It was horrible not being able to do anything, or even be by his side. And then that damn Luiz had to kidnap him. God knows what germs he could have passed on, or put him in danger of." His brows moved down. "I could kill him."

"So could I," Jenny replied. "One good thing that Stefano did was have his man kill Luiz before he could do any more damage.

Obviously, he's not up to scratch yet, so it looks like I'll just have to feed him and keep giving him pills, and if he's still bad in a couple of days, we'll take him to another doctor." She peered into Roger's face. "How do *you* feel?"

He smiled. "I'm fine, Mrs S, at least for now. We'll take it day by day in case I get whatever it is he's got."

"Let's hope you stay that way." Digging around in the cupboard, she pulled out the soup pot. "I'm going to need chicken and noodles. Who wants to go and get me some?"

Her mother stood and collected the breakfast plates. "We will," she said. "We'll use the walk for our daily constitutional."

"Good. I'll need five chickens and five big packs of noodles." Jenny filled the pot with water and pulled out vegetables from the fridge.

Sarah placed the dishes on the sink. "We'll be back in half an hour." Beckoning to her husband, she left.

"We need to go too, Mama," Carlos said, getting to his feet. "Don't want to hang around germ-ridden people any longer than we have to."

"Will you be back for dinner, or are you eating out again?" Jenny asked as she peeled a potato.

"We'll pop in, but we have plans for *El Viro*, that hot new Italian restaurant," Viv told her before smoothing her blouse and pants.

"Right, I remember you mentioning that. Tell me what it's like in case I want to take Spiros there." Jenny set out the carrots and celery.

"Papa eats Italian?" Carlos joked. "I thought he only ever ate Greek."

Jenny's laugh flooded the room. "It's food, he eats it. But being in Mykonos for so long, it was always Greek food. What else were we going to eat? Although I did try to mix it up every now and then with something else, like pasta, meat pies, and my roast chicken and beef dishes. So, what are your plans for today?"

"I have some meetings for photo shoots and commercials," Viv said. "I'm going to try and do as much as possible before I start growing." She patted her stomach.

Carlos's hand slid over his wife's. "I can't wait for you to show. See your stomach grow with our baby inside it." Happiness flooded his face and lit up the tiny sparks in his eyes. "To know that my baby is growing inside of you just…fills me with…" His heart swelled with an overwhelming warmth that threatened to overflow into tears. "Oh, Viv," he managed.

"Oh, Carlos." Viv melted into his arms and kissed him passionately.

Jenny hid her face and kept on with the vegetables then noticed Roger was starting the dishes. "Roger, you don't have to," Jenny told him.

"No, it's okay. I want to help out. Besides, who do you think does all the cooking and cleaning at home?" He grinned and squirted dish cleaner into the sink.

Jenny sighed. "I did raise the boys to clean up after themselves, but unfortunately I think they take after Spiros too much. Brings home the bacon, but the wife cooks it and cleans up after it as well as the rest of the house."

"I don't mind, really," Roger said, scrubbing a plate and putting it on the rack. "I was used to it living on my own. But who knows, maybe I'll train Tomas one day."

"Get a room, you two," Tomas rasped at his brother and sister-in-law from the couch.

Carlos and Viv finally pulled apart, blushing.

"You shut your mouth," Carlos told him. "We have to put up with *you* two. Besides which, shutting your mouth will stop the germs flying around."

"Enough out of you," Jenny directed at him. "You two go, I'll take care of the patient."

They left as Sarah and Matthew returned, and Jenny set about roasting the chickens before shredding them and putting them in the pot of boiling noodle and vegetable soup.

"How do you feel?" She sat beside Tomas on the couch and felt his forehead.

"A lot better," he said. "My throat's a bit weird." He gazed up at his mother, feeling the love radiate from her.

She stroked his face and her lips curled into a soft smile. "My baby. Soup's ready, so I'll feed you and get some more pills into you to make you better."

"Mama, I don't need you to feed me, I can feed myself." He relished in the touch of her. It had always been light and loving and motherly, and she always knew what to say and do. He held her hand to his face and kissed it.

"When you're sick, I do." She squeezed his hand and went to serve lunch.

*****

Carlos and Viv met with Cabot Conroy, New York's hottest photographer, in his sprawling Greenwich Village studio. It encompassed the entire top floor of the building and overlooked the skyline of Jersey and the Hudson River on one side, and the rest of New York City on the other.

"Cabot." Viv air-kissed him.

"Vivian, *dahling.*" Cabot took in her sable coat and ten inch heels. "You look *fabu*lous." His attention turned to Carlos. "And *who is this* delectable dish?" Cabot dressed the way he was educated. Schoolboy prep with his knit vest, stiffly ironed shirt, khaki pants, a bowtie, tortoiseshell-rimmed glasses, and slicked back blond hair.

Vivian laughed. "This *delectable dish* is my husband, Carlos Stephanopoulos. You might know him as *Carlo Stefan…porn star.*"

Cabot's eyes widened as he admired the man before him. "Carlo Stefan! I've seen your movies. Any chance of ever seeing *you* with a man?"

Carlos had never gotten used to being eyed like a piece of meat, but knew it was a part of the territory. "Not me. Maybe you're thinking of my brother, Tomas. He does his movies with his new husband, Roger Dencott."

"Husband!" Cabot's eyes were now saucer wide. "Since when can fags get married?"

Viv winced at the comment. She'd never heard Cabot speak like that, even though she knew he was of *that* inclination himself and didn't think he'd put his own kind down. Besides, Tomas was her brother-in-law, it wasn't polite, and she was insulted. As she knew Carlos would be. She cast a sideways glance at her husband's face and saw the controlled level of anger.

Carlos narrowed his eyes. Wasn't the man before him a fag? "Since my mother organised for them to have a marriage ceremony and they declared *themselves* husband and husband." He observed Cabot carefully before arching a brow. "Do *you* have a problem with that?"

Cabot pulled back, knowing he'd overstepped the mark with this one. "No. I just haven't heard of two men getting married. It's only the '70s after all. Fags can't get married."

"No," Carlos murmured, eyeing him warily. "*You* can't, legally."

Cabot shifted uncomfortably. "Yes…well."

Vivian diffused the situation. "Cabot, let's get down to business. You're doing the next *Roses Fraîches* ad shoot aren't you?" Sliding off her coat she revealed a tight catsuit in black, a brilliant green blazer, and a multicoloured scarf that finished the ensemble. She laid the coat across the back of a chair in Cabot's plush expansive office.

"Viv, you sexy beast." Cabot looked at her before taking his seat behind the desk. "Yes, I am." He watched as they seated themselves.

"Well, I wanted to stop by to confirm the details and see what ideas you have for it." She flung tendrils of hair over her shoulder. "Something good, I hope."

"Absolutely," he replied, jumping up to grab the storyboard from a shelf. "It's a set of three ads, and we have them planned for morning, noon, and night." He showed them the plan. "The first ad will be for the fresh scent of morning, dewdrops on rose petals, the start of a brand-new day. Then you'll be meeting girlfriends for a lunch date, and then getting all hot and sexy for a night out."

Viv studied each scene. "They look great. Will we get it done in one day?"

"I don't see why not," Cabot said. "But be prepared in case it takes two. And we'll need different sets and outdoor scenes. And then, of course, there's the weather."

"Yes, it has become quite cold, and this ad is for the summer campaign," Viv said. "Hope you have somewhere warm in mind to film."

"Well…" Cabot continued to eye the two of them. "I was thinking of a little tropical island called…Hawaii.”

Viv's eyes grew large. “Oh, I do love Hawaii,” she squealed at Carlos who couldn't help but grin in return.

“Yes,” Cabot went on. “A few days in Hawaii would be perfect to wipe away the winter blues. Are you up for it?”

“Absolutely,” Viv told him. “When?”

“Two weeks' time.” Cabot sat back behind his desk. “Will you be coming, *Mr Porn Star*?” His eyes greedily drank in Carlos's muscular body in.

“I got no plans.” Carlos shrugged. “As long as we're back by Christmas, I don't think anyone would mind.”

“Mind? Why would anyone mind?” Cabot asked, getting a thought in his head.

Carlos breathed in. “My family are in town, and we're all here until New Year's, so we plan on spending the holidays together.”

“Your family?” Cabot repeated. “You mean Pedro and Tomas are in New York as well?” The thought in his head expanded.

“Yes, Pedro's in town with his new wife, Tomas is here as I mentioned, our grandparents and mother are here as well. Our father is coming this weekend.”

“And is this your first time in New York?” Cabot asked.

“Yes, it is.”

“And you scored the *insanely* glamorous Vivian Villiers as your wife. I didn't think you'd ever find a man, dahling,” he said to Viv.

“Oh, I've found plenty of men, *dahling*,” Viv replied. “But none of them were worth it until this one.” She gazed fondly at Carlos and squeezed his hand affectionately.

He flashed a smile and squeezed back.

“Mmm,” Cabot murmured, watching the sparks between them. “Have you two ever done a photo shoot together? Because you *are* gorgeous,” he told Carlos.

“So I've been told,” Carlos quipped.

*****

Carmichael Burns slumped in his seat, put his feet up on his desk, and leant back. A thirty-year vet of the force, he was getting old and tired. Tired of dealing with scum, tired of not always winning. He rubbed his eyes and yawned. Tired from late nights and early starts. Tired of not having a wife to go home to, bills to pay, and a job that seemed to be going nowhere. Tired all the time. Just dead tired. He wearily watched his partner stride toward him, an excited puppy dog expression on his face.

Jamal Devron was a thirty-six-year-old black man not ready to come out of the closet. He thought no one knew, and most people didn't, except Burns had figured it out and told him as long as he didn't rub it in his face, he didn't care.

"Guess what I found out?" he said, coming to a stop at Burns' feet. "Pedro Stephanopoulos is finally back in town and back at work."

Burns wondered why he was so excited. "Gotta crush, have we?"

Devron blanched. "No. I just thought, since the case wasn't wrapped up, and Gardo wanted to know if we'd heard anything, that we should tell him."

"Mmm, hmm." Burns raised a brow. "Doesn't have anything to do with him being young, hot, and a porn star, does it? Or those short gold shorts and gold boots that got you so hot last time?"

Devron sat uncomfortably in his seat. "Knock it off. You told me to never say anything around you, and now you're digging it in. Quit it!"

Burns slowly stood, his bones moaning and groaning. "All right. Let's go get Gardo." They made their way up the three floors to Giancarlo Gardo's office in the precinct.

"Don't tell me you can't do it," Gardo yelled into his phone. "I want it done *now*. I want that scum off the street by tonight. Do you understand me?" The six-foot Mack Truck of a man slammed the phone down and swore under his breath. "What do you two want?"

"Pedro Stephanopoulos is back in town, sir. Started back at 69 last night," Devron excitedly explained. "You wanted to know if we'd heard anything."

Gardo sighed and put his hands on his hips. "Back in town, huh? Any word on the Poulos girl?"

"They were married on Mykonos a few weeks back," Devron told him.

"Well, well, well," Gardo muttered. "Guess with her inheriting her daddy's money he thought he was on to a good thing." He grabbed his coat from the hook on the wall. "Guess we'd better go see him then." Glancing at his watch, he noted the time. "He should be at home sleeping like Sleeping Beauty."

They drove to Pedro's apartment on Central Park West and strode into the foyer. "We're here to see Stephanopoulos on seven," he told the guard as he flashed his badge.

"Stephanopoulos moved last week," the guard said with a shake of his head. "Came in here with three other guys, packed up, and took off in a cab they kept waiting."

"Any idea where he was going?" Gardo looked around the lobby with his hands on his hips.

The guard gave another shake of his head. "Didn't say."

"All right, thanks." Gardo led the way outside. "Get around to 69 and find out where he is. I'm heading off for a bite to eat."

With a nod, Burns and Devron took off for 69 and Gardo made his way to a small delicatessen owned by an Italian family he knew. While munching on salami on rye, he waited for their call on the two-way.

"Gardo, Devron. Turns out he's now on 5th Avenue in an apartment building."

"Where?" Gardo asked around a mouthful of food.

"Opposite the zoo."

"Get going. I'll meet you there."

*****

Angelina sighed her satisfaction. Sliding her hands over her lover's body, she kissed his chest before burying her head in it. "God, I love you."

Pedro laughed before grabbing her hand and kissing it. "I love you, too."

"Mmm…" Another sigh. "I'm so happy."

Wrapping his arms around her, he held her tight. "So am I. God I love you so much, Angie. So much." She'd woken him upon arriving home an hour late after completing extra work, and now they lay in each other's arms as they always did. When he worked and she had school, he'd come home and sleep all day, then she'd come home and wake him up for sex, then he'd work all night and she'd sleep.

Now that they were married it would be no different. As long as he was working and she was going to school, this was their schedule. The only times they had together were an hour in the morning, three hours in the afternoon and then all weekend.

"We should go up to Mama's soon. I want food before I go."

"Mmm." She snuggled in the crook of his arm. "Too warm."

He kissed her hand and checked his watch. "Nearly five. We have some time."

*****

The officers parked outside of the apartment building and entered the lobby to find Martin Brewster standing sentry.

"Can I help you fine officers this cold wintry day?" Brewster eyed the badge Gardo offered and wondered what they were doing there.

"Pedro Stephanopoulos," Gardo said, eyeing the expensive fittings. "Apparently, he lives here now."

"He does." Brewster's curiosity was aroused.

"We need to see him," Gardo added.

"Well, I'm sure you want to, but whether or not you'll get to is a different matter," Brewster informed him.

"And what does that mean?" Gardo asked.

Brewster smirked at the three of them. *They have no idea who's here,* he thought. "I'll just make a call." He dialled the penthouse, and after five rings, Jenny answered.

"Yes, Mr Brewster?"

"There is a detective…" He looked at Gardo.

"Giancarlo Gardo, he knows me."

"Giancarlo Gardo here with two officers," Brewster said.

"And what do they want?" Jenny asked, fretting that her boys were in trouble again.

"To see Mr Pedro Stephanopoulos."

"Right, well." Jenny frowned. "Send them up to the penthouse."

"Of course." Brewster hung up. "Take the elevator to the penthouse."

Gardo frowned. *How the hell could a twenty-year-old kid afford to live in a penthouse?* "Thanks," he grumbled, and they took the elevator up to the top floor.

Jenny scurried around tidying up. Her parents were out, and Roger and Tomas were lying on the couch in front of the fireplace. She filled the kettle with water to boil and placed cups with coffee and tea on a tray. Hearing the doorbell, she removed her apron and smoothed her soft pink dress, checking herself in the mirror before answering the door. "Hello." She stared at the three men who stared back in surprise. "I'm Jenny Stephanopoulos, Pedro's mother. Apparently, you want to see him."

Gardo stared back at the fine-looking woman before him. The pink of the dress brought a becoming glow to her cheeks that were framed by the latest hairstyle. Her slim figure radiated health, and her face radiated happiness. He found himself lost for words. He, Giancarlo Gardo, lost for words, at fifty-three years of age.

Burns had quickly removed his cap at the sight of the woman in the doorway. He hadn't been expecting a woman to answer, let alone a fine example like this one. His eyes took in her curves and the way she held herself. Proud, determined, unafraid of man or cop. And he liked what he saw. He elbowed Devron who quickly removed his cap.

"Ah…yes…ah…" Gardo stumbled and blushed. "I…ah…"

"Wasn't expecting his mother?" Jenny asked lightly. "What can I do for you?"

"We…ah…need to see your son." Gardo finally got his voice back. He cleared his throat. "To finish up something from the ah…"

"Kidnapping? Stalker? Andros Poulos?" Jenny inquired. "Oh, where are my manners. Would you gentlemen like to come in? Pedro's downstairs asleep, but he should be here for dinner. I can offer you coffee or tea. Please, come in." She held the door open.

"Ah…" Gardo hesitated before entering with Burns and Devron

behind him. Gardo took in his surroundings. Expensive, lavish, far more than he could ever afford, or Pedro for that matter.

"And you are?" Jenny inquired.

"Officer Burns, ma'am," Carmichael introduced himself. "My partner, Devron." He nudged him once more. "And Detective Gardo, NYPD."

"Ah, yes. The officers who arrested Andros Poulos for assaulting my daughter-in-law, and the detective who chased after Pedro when he was kidnapped." Her smile lit up the room. "I've heard all about it. Please, come, would you like coffee or tea?" She led them to the kitchen bench and found the kettle had boiled.

"Ah...we..." Gardo couldn't seem to find himself or his words. This was the mother of the porn stars? The three Greek gods were her children?

"Detective?" She poured three cups of water and heaped coffee into two.

"Ah...yes..." He reddened; embarrassed that he couldn't speak in front of her.

"Coffee or tea?"

"Ah...coffee."

She mixed a third cup and handed all three over. "I've heard the boys' stories, I've heard Agent Payday's story, now tell me yours." She waved a hand at the dining table. "Please, take a seat." Taking a plate of cookies with her, she led two of them to the table.

Devron stayed behind. He had been eyeing off the two men he'd seen when he walked in, and recognised them instantly, having seen Tomas Stefan in the flesh in Chicago. With him was his partner, Roger Dencott. After seeing all three Stephanopoulos brothers for himself, he'd gone out and seen every movie, bought them on tape, and proceeded to masturbate to Tomas and Roger's movies. Sitting naked on his couch in front of the TV, he'd willingly stroked himself into a frenzy over the two men. All three brothers were hot, but to add Dencott into it made it better, and now here they were in the flesh, together. The two men he'd fucked his new toy boy to as they re-enacted the movies in front of the TV. Naked, groping each other's balls, and sucking and fucking their way to heaven. Not that his twenty-two-year-old Latino lover wasn't hot enough, but he was just the bit on the side that no one knew about. They'd met at 69 when he'd gone there, and they'd hit it off. He'd been taken by the sultry looks, and his lover had been taken by him being a six-foot cop with handcuffs, which they'd used many times, cuffing his lover to the sofa while he came in behind and his hand worked the front. And they did it all in front of the TV while playing Tomas and Roger's movies. He'd imagined his lover beneath him was Tomas, wanting to pound that flesh with his eight-inch cock and wanting to suck Tomas's twelve inches. Of course, Roger wasn't bad either, but he was into exotic, and he wanted Tomas.

Burns cleared his throat, and Devron came out of his dream world to quickly sit at the table, hoping no one saw his hard-on.

Gardo was recounting the story while Jenny listened intently. He had her full attention, but the blue of her eyes was distracting him, and he grew annoyed when Burns took over during the story, for that's when Jenny moved her eyes away from him and onto Burns.

"Ah, yes, we just need to talk to your son and new daughter-in-law so we can finish up with the paperwork on the stalker, and the death of Miss Poulos's, ah, *Mrs* Stephanopoulos's, father." The correction received a smile from Jenny. "And then we will be done," Gardo managed.

"Excellent," Jenny said, sitting at the head of the table with Gardo to her right and Burns and Devron to her left. "I thought it was all over with Payday as he said he'd sort it all out. I didn't imagine there would be more paperwork to do." She fluttered her lashes. "We've had to deal with so much in the last few months. To find out my husband's ex-uncle was behind all of this, and then we had to deal with him, and then all three of my boys were married, and then my husband's grandfather passed away while we were flying over to New York."

Gardo flinched at every mention of the word husband. Here he was getting all tongue-tied over a married woman. A woman he couldn't have. "I'm sorry about your boys' grandfather." He glanced around the room. "Now you're here. Is *Mr*...Stephanopoulos here as well?" He saw Burns give him the evil eye.

"Oh, no, he had to deal with the funeral and get the meat shop ready before he could leave. But he's coming here this weekend, so we'll spend Christmas and New Year's together as a family," Jenny told him.

"And you'll be staying here the whole time?" Burns jumped in before Gardo could open his mouth again. "It's very luxurious."

"Yes, it is. But after what Stefano Papadopoulos did to my boys, and it seems we were his only living relatives, when we were asked if we wanted his estate I said absolutely. There was *no way* I was going to pass up spending his money on my boys after everything he'd done. I hope he's turning in his grave."

The twinkle in her eye made Burns smile. Jenny Stephanopoulos was proving to be one hell of a woman. Strong, fierce, and protective of her boys.

Sarah and Matthew entered the suite. "Oh, I didn't know you had company."

"These are my parents, Sarah and Matthew Marsh," Jenny introduced them. "This is Detective Gardo and Officers Burns and Devron. They were involved with Andros, and Detective Gardo chased after Pedro and saved him."

"Hello, how do you do? We're so grateful our boys are alive, and since you had a hand in helping with that rescue, thank you," Sarah said.

"Ma'am." Gardo nodded slightly. "Just doing our duty." He and the others had stood when the Marshes had entered.

The door opened. "I can't believe she did that," Pedro said as he and Angelina came through and stopped at the sight of the police, recognising them instantly. "Oh, God, not you lot. What now? Someone else made a complaint against me?" Pedro's face fell, and Angie's went into a momentary panic.

"Pedro, manners," Jenny reminded him. "These officers are here to finish up their paperwork on your case, so you may as well get it done now."

Pedro sighed, hating being chastised in front of others. "Okay. What do you want?" He had one arm around Angie who was hanging on for dear life.

Gardo pulled papers out of his coat pocket while Sarah and Matthew excused themselves to go and sit with Tomas and Roger who were now sitting on the couch watching curiously.

"We need you to sign these, stating that Andros Poulos is dead, the restraining order is over, and that you're happy that everything has been cleared up."

Pedro arched a brow. "What happened to Barbara Weston?"

Gardo thought back. "Once the morgue cleared her for transport her body was shipped back to her parents in Australia. Since you hadn't filed any report, there wasn't much else to do."

"She killed my father," Angelina said. "She crashed Pedro's car into him."

"Ah." Gardo frowned. "Yes, we, ah, confiscated the car for forensic testing. Your brakes had been cut again, and we assume it might have been by Papadopoulos's man who kidnapped you and also did work for Poulos." He studied Angelina. "I'm sorry for your loss, Miss, ah, *Mrs* Stephanopoulos. But from all account of things, you didn't much care for your father after what he did to you. And you're married now, so there's not a whole lot left to do except inform you of this information and sign off on all the paperwork." Throwing a glance over his shoulder at Devron he added, "We heard you were back at work and figured this was the best time to get it out of the way." He held the papers out. "If you could just sign these, we'll be on our way." As much as he *didn't* want to be on his way for he would have loved to have spent more time with the delightful Jenny Stephanopoulos, married or not.

"I'll grab a pen." Jenny hurried over to the phone table and grabbed one so Pedro could sign.

The door opened again. "I can't believe he propositioned me," Carlos said as he and Viv came through the doorway. They stopped when they saw the police. "Hey, I remember you."

"Mr Stephanopoulos number one." Gardo grinned. "Detective Giancarlo Gardo, wrapping up some paperwork with your brother."

"Yeah." Carlos nodded. "He's always been a wanted man, my little brother. Never could stay out of trouble."

"Carlos," Jenny scolded while hiding a smile.

Pedro snorted and finished signing the papers. "Just like my big brother. I *so* take after you, Carlos." The grin was ear to ear as he turned around.

By now, Tomas and Roger had wandered over, curious as to what was happening. "Signing your prison release?" Tomas joked through a swollen throat.

"Fun-nee." Pedro rolled his eyes. "At least I can still talk," he mocked.

"At least I can still blow," Tomas replied and received a wild-eyed look in return from his little brother.

Carlos snorted beside Tomas. "Oh, my God. Like the cops want to know about *your* sex life."

"Yet they've *seen* yours," Tomas rasped at his brother.

"Oh!" Carlos exclaimed, looking back and forth between his brothers. "Well...yeah...I..."

"Have nothing?" Tomas asked and crossed his arms.

Roger stood beside him with a smirk on his face trying not to laugh.

"Boys," Jenny chastised, unable to stop herself from smiling. She loved it when her boys were playful with each other.

Gardo watched the banter between the brothers. Seeing Pedro and Carlos again he now knew exactly where they had gotten their blue eyes from. Their delightful mother. *The other one must take after the father*, he thought.

"All done." Angie flashed her signature across the paper. "It's all over?"

Gardo folded the papers, putting them in his pocket. "All done. Well, that's it. Thank you, Mrs Stephanopoulos, for your warm and welcoming hospitality." He gave a bow of his head. "We will see ourselves out."

"Let me get the door." Jenny rushed to open it for them. "Thank you so much for dropping by to finish this once and for all. I'm glad it's over."

Gardo and Burns stopped in the doorway so they had more time with Jenny. Pedro and Angie wandered into the kitchen, and Carlos and Viv went to say hello to his grandparents, while Devron stopped Roger and Tomas to ask a question.

"Ah, how did you two…" Devron licked his lips and cast a quick glance at his partner who was busy chatting up Jenny. "How did you two get married?"

Roger raised a brow and exchanged a glance with Tomas. "Well, for a start, it's technically not legal, but that didn't stop Mrs S from organising a ceremony on Mykonos, or us having a reception. We exchanged vows and rings and take it seriously. We *are* married, whether the law says so or not."

Devron nodded. "What about now you're back in the states? There are a lot of fag haters out there."

Tomas blanched, but Roger remained determined. "Yes, Officer Devron. And I'm sure *you've* come across them yourself…*haven't you*?" Roger let the words sink in. He had a suspicion that Devron might be gay because he could swear he'd seen him in a friend's photo. A friend who'd regaled them about his trip to New York and the hot black cop he'd fucked for four days straight and what they had done with those cuffs…

Devron blinked, and his left eye twitched. He'd always played it as straight as he could, and while he *was* a fag, he always pretended to be on the side of fag haters so people wouldn't suspect. But did Dencott suspect now? He stared into Roger's eyes and took a step closer. "What are you implying?"

Roger had a couple of inches on him, so he stood toe to toe. "I know David Marks," was all he said.

Devron registered the name and stepped back, now fully aware of how his misadventures could be a dangerous thing.

"Devron," Burns called. "Time to go." He watched his partner standoff from Dencott with a snort and walk toward him, with Dencott watching after him. Devron brushed past them into the foyer, leaving Burns to apologise to Jenny for his partner's rude behaviour. "I'm sorry for Devron's rudeness, Mrs Stephanopoulos. I have no idea what's gotten into him."

"I'm sure you'll straighten him out, Officer Burns," she warmly replied. "Thank you all for stopping by. Goodbye and goodnight." She closed the door and faced Tomas and Roger. "*What* was that about?"

"He asked how we'd gotten married and then brought up fag haters. I realised I recognised him from a friend's photo and that he was gay. So I reminded him of our mutual friend's name." Roger smiled. "It hit a nerve right in the eye."

"Well," Jenny said, cleaning up the table. "I hope we don't have any trouble with him in future then."

*****

"What the fuck was that?" Burns asked Devron once they climbed into their car. He wasn't much of a swearer, preferring to use it only at the appropriate times, but with Devron's bad manners, this was an appropriate time.

"Nothing." Devron sulked, slumping in his seat.

"Gay boys hit on you, did they?" Burns pulled into the traffic.

"No." Devron snorted. "Fuckin' fags!"

"Of which you are one. So why the hostility?" Besides wondering what was up his partner's ass, he was wondering about Gardo's intentions with the delightful, yet married, Jenny Stephanopoulos.

"I told you not to bring that up," Devron shouted angrily, thumping the dashboard in return.

Burns pulled over. "Listen to me very carefully, little man." His tone was low and threatening. "I have told you that I don't give a fuck if you're a fag. You have asked me to not say anything, and I try and abide by that. But today you are out of line. So, whatever the fuck happened back there, pull your damn head out of your ass and grow up. You're a cop, you also happen to be in the closet, but that is *your* choice, so fucking deal with it and stop taking it out on others. Got it?"

Devron gave him the side-eye. "Yeah," he finally mumbled.

*****

Gardo hung his coat up and pulled out the papers from the inside pocket. A gold pen fell from them. He picked it up and rolled it back and forth between his fingers, knowing it belonged to the delightful

Jenny with the blue eyes Stephanopoulos. Oh, yes, he'd taken it on purpose. Taken it with the purpose of seeing her again to return it. He knew it was a flimsy excuse, but he had to do something to see that woman again, for she was warm and homely and vivacious and beautiful. Golden-brown hair in the latest style framed her face perfectly. And then there were those big blue eyes he just wanted to drown in.

He felt himself harden, his cock straining at the memory of Jenny Stephanopoulos and what he'd like to do to her. How could he? She was married with three grown children, and her husband was on his way. He slumped in his seat and continued rolling the pen between his fingers. He would return it before the weekend.

*****

"Are you boys hungry? I made chicken noodle soup today," Jenny said as she went into the kitchen to serve dinner.

"Starving." Pedro grabbed a chair and held it out for Angie before sitting down. "Big bowl for me, Mama."

"Nothing for us, Mama," Carlos said. "We're not staying."

"Let me help, Mrs S." Roger grabbed the bowls and prepared the bread rolls while Tomas took his seat and hung his head in his hands.

"Still sick?" Pedro asked and wrapped his napkin around his head to cover his mouth. "I don't want your germs. Quick, Angie, cover up. You don't want the baby getting sick."

"Silly." She laughed. "I'm not about to get sick because he's got a sore throat."

Sarah carried bowls to the table and sat next to her husband. "But you never know what that sore throat is a precursor to, or whether it's just an allergy."

"Well…considering what he does with Roger, it's no wonder his throat's sore. It was bound to happen, hey, little bro." Carlos slapped him on the arm as he stood behind his chair.

"Carlos! That's disgusting." Jenny frowned. "There'll be no talk like that while I'm around."

"But it's true," Carlos implored. "There's bound to be a sore throat sometime."

Jenny carried her soup to the table. "Enough," she told him. "Aren't you two going out?" She waited while the rest were seated before seating herself.

"Yes, Mama. Just wanted to check in." Carlos kissed her on the cheek. "See you all tomorrow."

Viv waved goodbye as they left.

"Make sure you take your pills," Jenny reminded Tomas. "If you're not better in a few days I'll get the doctor in."

Tomas sighed softly. "I don't need a doctor." He moved his spoon back and forth in the bowl.

"Considering how drab you look, I'd say you do." Jenny worried for her son.

"I'm just not hungry because you've been feeding me all day."

"I only gave you a cup every few hours so you could take a pill. You need to keep your strength up. I want you to get an early night. You can either stay up here where I can keep an eye on you, or I'll tuck you into bed downstairs."

"Mama," Tomas protested.

"No arguments," Jenny told him. "Now finish your soup and go and rest in front of the fire."

They finished their food, and she gathered the bowls and tidied up.

Pedro kissed his mother. "Thanks for the food, I gotta get to work."

"Have a good night. Are you staying, Angie?" Jenny asked.

"Yes, Mama. I'll just get my books and be back." She went with Pedro to collect her things, and they parted ways at the elevator. Jenny was tucking Tomas up on one of the couches when she walked back in and made herself comfortable on the couch facing the TV in the corner.

"Is everyone warm enough? Looks like it's going to be a cold night." Jenny laid a blanket over Angie's lap before sitting beside her with a magazine.

Across the street, Gardo sat in his car and looked up at the penthouse. The lights were on. He flicked the overhead light on to check his watch.

Seven. Pedro would have left by now which would mean the Poulos girl was still home. And then there were the parents and the other son and his partner. Flicking off the light he sighed. *What the hell am I doing sitting across the street from a married woman's place? A woman that I can't have.* He shifted uncomfortably, giving the bulge in his pants more space. *I can't be doing this. What the hell is wrong with me?*

Oh, but how Jenny Stephanopoulos warmed his heart *and* his groin. The amazing Australian woman had captured his attention. Not that it mattered. She was taken, and he had a very strong feeling she was one to take her vows seriously. *So why the hell am I sitting here watching, thinking about her?* Because her blue eyes had captured him so. The exact same shade as two of her sons. Sons that had disappointed her, yet she forgave them and loved them so. *Whereas I would have put them over my knee.* His left brow arched up slowly, and he sniggered.

His right hand absentmindedly rubbed his right thigh as he thought about rubbing the lovely Jenny Stephanopoulos's. The scent of her, the feel of her flesh under his, the way she'd feel in his arms.

"Stop it!" He banged the steering wheel. "You can't think this way. She's a married woman. She is not available for you. She is not yours. Jesus. Fucking, Jesus." Starting the car, he cast one last glance at the penthouse and pulled into the street.

*****

Sheila Manning trundled home from a long day at work, collected her mail, and walked five flights up the stairs to her tiny apartment in an area of Harlem, New York. She'd been there for twenty-six years as she could never afford to move out. Her job at the local supermarket had lasted her most of that time, and the men in her life came and went, including her son Luiz, whom she'd kicked out eight years ago for fucking the underage neighbourhood boys. Luckily, the neighbourhood parents had either never found out, or didn't give a fuck about their own children. Otherwise, she was sure she would have been hunted out and put on the street years ago. That's why she had sent Luiz packing. Kicked him out and told him to get out of New York. His scumbag father didn't want him, and neither did she.

When she was fresh out of college she and her friends had holidayed in Santorini, and she had taken a fancy to a wealthy young man who was going places, and she let him go all he liked until it was time for her to go home. Three months later she found out she was pregnant at twenty-two. Her parents kicked her out, and she'd had to find a job and an apartment all on her own, and that's where she'd been all these years.

Letting herself in, she dumped everything on the table beside her chair, grabbed a drink from the fridge, and sat down to watch TV. It was the only thing that gave her pleasure anymore, besides the alcohol. Nothing else did. Swigging back her rum and coke, she ploughed through the mail. "Junk, junk, bill, junk, flier, bill…wait…" She grabbed the flier from the floor where she'd chucked it and studied it carefully. *Studio 69* was advertising the comeback of Pedro Stefan as their DJ. "Well, well, well," she murmured. "I wonder if little Miss is with him?"

She'd read the papers habitually for the last month, collecting every cutting on Andros Poulos and how he'd died trying to set up his daughter's boyfriend, Pedro Stephanopoulos. She hadn't seen Andros since that holiday in Santorini when she'd become pregnant. And all communications with him about being pregnant with his baby had fallen on deaf ears, except when the lawyer's letter had arrived, informing her that it was not his baby and she was not entitled to anything. That had burned her. He had seemed like such a kind and caring guy when they'd been together. But now…he was dead, and she had read every word in every paper that she could get her hands on, and had made a detailed list of his wealth and properties. After all, he did owe her child support, and he knew all about the baby because she'd sent him a photo after he was born. But now Luiz was dead, along with his father.

Those papers had come in the mail too. The letter saying Luiz had been murdered and did she want to claim the body. She had not, and sent a letter back to that effect. She had disowned him, and besides, she didn't have the money to bury him, so his body was going into a pauper's grave.

They were both dead. Andros Poulos and his son, Luiz Manning. Yet his little Miss and her boyfriend were still alive. And in a massive twist that no one could have seen coming, there was even a story about Luiz being involved in the kidnapping of Pedro's brother Tomas. She chuckled. *Well, what do you know, like father like son. Assholes to the end.*

A thought floated through her mind. *Yes, oh, yes, now that's right.* She thoughtfully tapped her chin. *Little Miss would have inherited daddy's estate. After all these years of missing out on child support, little Miss collects all the earnings. Well, well, well, we can't have that now, can we? Even more so with the fact Luiz was killed while he was with the brother. I wonder how much money that could bring.* The idea floating through her head excited her, and she knew she was on to a winning ticket. She grabbed the phone book and started looking for lawyers.

*****

On Wednesday morning, Tomas awoke feeling better. He'd fallen asleep on the couch in the penthouse, with Roger sleeping on the floor in front of him, and Angie on the couch opposite him. The fire was dying, and there were noises coming from the kitchen. Staying quiet as to not disturb the others, he padded over to his mother who was getting breakfast ready. "Mama, what time is it?"

"Seven-thirty. Feeling better?" She checked his temperature and felt his glands.

"Sore throat's gone, but I still feel blah," he replied, hearing his stomach rumble.

"Let's hope a sore throat was all it was," she said. "You get the others up, and I'll get breakfast going."

Once breakfast was over, and Angelina had left for school, she asked the boys what their plans were. "I need to go and do some things, so you can stay here if you like."

"Will you be gone all day?" Tomas inquired, having enjoyed being looked after by his mother which hadn't happened since he was a kid.

"I should be home for lunch, but I'm not sure what time. I can call."

"No, no. We'll just hang out here all day," Tomas told her. "You go do your thing."

She smiled and took her baby into her arms. "You go and have a nice hot shower, it will do you good. I'll leave the door unlocked when I leave in case you're not back."

"Okay," he said and kissed her cheek.

She watched them go and headed for her room. Considering what she was about to do, she needed to look the part. Flicking clothes aside on the rack in the closet, she chose an emerald green pantsuit and matching blouse, with matching accessories, and an ankle-length fur coat. She styled her hair, applied a layer of make-up, and thirty minutes later she was ready. Meeting the boys on her way out she kissed them goodbye and reminded Tomas to take his pills.

Fifteen minutes later, she alighted from her car and entered the building of *Pine & Sable, Real Estate Agents*. Having called for an appointment the day before, she didn't have to wait long to see Margot Pine and Rich Sable, the owners of the agency. And why would she? They knew she was rich when she'd come to them to rent the whole building.

"Mrs Stephanopoulos, how are you?" Margot extended her hand and Jenny took it warmly.

"Fine, Ms Pine, thank you."

"Good, please come this way." Margot Pine directed her into Rich's office. At forty-five, Margot was five years younger than Rich. Blonde, thin, and alcoholic, she didn't let that get in the way of a business deal.

"Mrs Stephanopoulos." Rich Sable, fifty, tall, broad, and dirty blond came around his desk to greet Jenny. "Good to see you again. Loving the apartments, I hope."

"Oh, absolutely," Jenny told them and sat in the chair they offered. "That's what I'm here to see you about."

"Oh?" Margot and Rich both leaned on his desk in front of Jenny.

"No problems, I hope?" Rich turned on the charm

"Not at all. In fact, I absolutely love them," Jenny said.

"Great. Then what's the problem?" Margot was straight to the point.

Jenny laughed lightly. "There isn't a problem. I have decided that I want them permanently."

"Oh, great, you want to keep staying there." Rich clapped his hands. "That can be arranged. We just need to set up another lease agreement."

"No, Mr Sable. I don't want to continue *leasing* the building," Jenny said. "I want to *buy* it."

Two sets of eyes went wide, looking from Jenny to each other.

"You what?" Rich asked in amazement.

"I want to buy the whole building for my family," Jenny said, crossing her legs carefully.

There was a long pause before, "Oh…well…that's fantastic!" Margot exclaimed. "Just fantastic. We'll get in touch with the owner and see what he wants for it and let you know."

"Could you do that now?" Jenny asked her.

Margot stopped. "What?"

Jenny took a breath and tried not to laugh. "I want to get it over and done with now. If you ring them now, I will buy it now."

"Ugh…well…why not!" Rich exploded. "Just let me make the call." He sat behind his desk and ploughed through his Rolodex before making the call. "Mr Beckmore, Rich Sable. We have your 5th Avenue apartment building for lease and the lovely lady renting it wants to buy it. What will you sell it for? Ah-ha…right… Oh…okay…I'll ask." He held his hand over the mouthpiece. "Two million five."

"I'll take it," Jenny replied. After all, she had the money.

Rich's eyes expanded once more. "Okay." He spoke into the phone. "She'll take it…right…ah-huh…okay…we'll wait here." He set the phone down. "He's sending his accountant and lawyer down to take the cheque in about half an hour."

"I can wait," Jenny said.

"Fantastic! Let's celebrate." Margot clapped her hands and grabbed crystal glasses from a small rack on a sideboard.

"A bit early for that," Jenny told her, watching Margot get a bottle of champagne from the small bar fridge hidden in the sideboard.

"Never too early for champagne." Margot popped it open.

"I haven't signed or paid for it yet," Jenny added, watching Margot knock back a glass of bubbly.

Twenty minutes later, the lawyer and accountant pocketed her cheque, and she signed the papers.

"Thank you very much, gentlemen, you have made me very happy." Jenny shook hands and left, heading for her next stop. She now owned an apartment building. *Her,* little Jenny Stephanopoulos from Australia and Mykonos, now owned an apartment building for her family.

Her driver stopped outside of *Baby King of New York.* New York's finest baby store had all an expectant mother could need. She had raided the city directory for the best stores in town, and this one boasted that it was the best. And from the look of it, it was. She stood staring at the wide array of cots, prams, toys, and blankets that the store had on display.

An assistant came over. "Hi, do you need some help?"

Jenny turned to the young girl, pregnant herself. "Oh, I certainly do," she said, remembering when her boys were young. "My two daughters-in-law are having babies, and I want to buy everything they need, and I want to get them set up now before the babies arrive."

"Oh, that's wonderful," the girl said, "come this way."

Since Jenny didn't know the sex of the babies, she bought gender neutral tones and accessories in cribs, prams, toys and blankets, plus all the necessary bottles, diapers and bags. After paying for delivery and assembly, Jenny walked out two hours later to head home for lunch. She was greeted by Roger and Tomas who'd just come back from a short walk for fresh air. "How are you feeling?" she asked, seeing a red glow in Tomas's cheeks.

"A little better. The fresh air was good." He kissed her on the cheek and snuggled up for a hug.

"Good." She hugged back. "If you're feeling up to it you can help me set up the nurseries in three and four."

Tomas checked his watch. "Won't Pedro be sleeping?"

"Oh, damn, I forgot!" Jenny gasped. "Oh, it will be okay. We'll just be quiet."

"So, where's the stuff?" Roger asked, looking around.

"Coming in…" Jenny looked at the wall clock. "Half an hour, so I have time for a bite to eat."

A half hour later, they directed the men from the baby store into Carlos and Viv's apartment first where they had everything set up within a half hour. Jenny laid blankets in the closet, and set up teddies on the white rocking chair by the window. The pretty rainbow coloured curtains went up, and decorations were hung over the crib.

"Think they'll love it?" Jenny asked Tomas and Roger.

"Yeah." Tomas nodded. "They'll love it." He still couldn't believe his brothers were having babies when they were still babies themselves.

"Good. Now, you're going to need to stand guard at Pedro's bedroom door and make sure he doesn't wake." Jenny directed the men in to Apartment 4, warning them to be quiet. She quietly closed the master bedroom door and made Tomas stand guard while the men worked quietly to get the nursery done on time.

Jenny glanced at her watch. It was nearly three, and she knew Angie would be home soon, so wanted the room done and the men gone before she arrived.

Roger helped her display the toys and blankets, and hung the curtains.

The men were done at ten past three.

"Thank you very much." Jenny ushered them out the door as Angie exited the elevator.

"Oh, what's going on?" She stared wide-eyed at everyone.

"A surprise," Jenny told her. "But I want Pedro to be awake, so I'm not sure I should show you yet."

"What surprise?" Pedro stood in the doorway, yawning, and wearing dark blue silk pyjama pants and nothing else. "I heard voices. What are you all doing in my foyer?"

Jenny sighed. "I didn't want to wake you…but I have a surprise for you. Come." She grabbed their hands and led them to the second bedroom. "Ta-da!"

"Wow," was all Pedro said with raised brows.

"Oh, my God." Angie's hand flew to her mouth, and her eye's teared up. "Oh, my God."

"Wow," Pedro repeated, gazing dazedly at everything. "You did all of this? Just now?"

"Yes. I went to the baby store today and bought everything you'll need for when the baby comes." Pointing to the crib, she started listing things. "You have a crib that changes with the age of the baby, a pram, blankets, bottles, toys. I even bought you a rocking chair." She walked over to the chair and picked up a large and a small teddy bear in pristine white fur. "I bought this one for the baby." She presented Angelina with the small one. "And this one is for the baby's mother." She handed over the other one.

"What!" Angelina took them. "You..." Her lip quivered. "Bought me a teddy bear?"

Jenny watched the tears fall in hot rivulets down her daughter's cheeks. "Oh, baby, come here." She took Angie into her arms. "There, there. Of course I bought you a teddy bear. You didn't think I was going to let you miss out, did you? Oh, sweetie." Patting her back she let Angie cry.

Roger and Tomas backed away, pointing to the ceiling, and Jenny nodded her understanding.

Pedro rubbed Angie's back. "Babe, don't cry. It's just a bear."

"No." Jenny shook her head. "I don't think it is." She pulled back a little. "When was the last time your parents gave you a teddy?"

Angie gasped and sniffed. "When...when I was...ten..."

"Before your mother died?" Jenny asked, wiping Angie's cheeks.

The tears flowed again. "Yes," she sobbed on Jenny's shoulder.

"Oh, Angie," Jenny soothed. "You're still a little girl, and yet you haven't been in such a long time."

Pedro frowned quizzically, not understanding what his mother meant.

"There, there." Jenny patted Angie's back. "It's been a long time."

Finally, Angie pulled back. "I'm sorry."

"Don't be," Jenny told her.

"It's just that all of a sudden it hit me," Angie panicked. "That I'm having a baby. A real-life baby that's going to be a human being." She gulped in air. "And my mother's not here to see it."

Jenny pulled her back into her arms. "Oh, sweetie. But *we're* here, and I know your mother would be grateful that you at least have us." She stroked her hair for a few moments more. "Why don't the two of you freshen up and then come upstairs. Take your time, okay."

"Okay." Angie sniffled.

"We'll be up soon, Mama," Pedro told his mother.

Jenny made her way to the penthouse to find Carlos and Viv. "I have a surprise for you two," she said and led them down to their apartment. "Ta-da!"

"What!" Carlos exclaimed. "Mama, you shouldn't have."

Viv slowly walked around the room and trailed her fingers along the crib. "Oh, Jenny…you shouldn't…you didn't…"

"Nonsense," Jenny said. "I had to. You and Angie are having my grandchildren, and I'm going to spoil you all rotten courtesy of Stefano Papadopoulos."

"Um…" Viv faltered.

"Go on," Jenny encouraged.

"Uh, well, we…'" Viv looked at Carlos then back to Jenny. "We won't be staying in New York. We'll more than likely go back to L.A. after the new year."

"I know," Jenny said, moving to Viv's side. "But this is your home here in New York, and the nursery will always be set up so you never have to worry about it when you come here."

"Oh." Viv revived. "Oh, well, thank you, thank you very much. It's all so lovely." She hugged Jenny. "Thank you so much."

Jenny squeezed back. "You're welcome. Are you up for dinner?"

"No, we have plans, but we can still come up for a while," Carlos said.

"Okay, when you're ready." Jenny went up to the penthouse.

"Oh, my God, Carlos, I can't believe your mother went to all this trouble." Viv picked up the white mother and baby bears from the rocking chair and sat down.

"Well…" Carlos looked around. "That's my mama. She and Papa gave us everything they could, and what they couldn't, we got handed down from cousins so…I guess now Mama's got money… She did say she was going to blow it all on us and the kids."

"I know, but I wasn't expecting a fully set up nursery." Viv gazed around the room, taking it all in. "Especially since we'll be living in L.A."

"Like Mama said, this is here when we'll be here, so we don't have to worry." Carlos kneeled between her legs. "See. I told you Mama liked you."

*****

Pedro and Angie came through the door at four, lugging Angie's books and the two teddy bears. Pedro set her up on the couch with a kiss on the top of her head.

"You guys got a nursery courtesy of Mama too?" Carlos asked.

"Yes," Angie replied. "And these gorgeous teddy bears." She held them up.

"Oh, I got those," Viv said as she walked over to the living room. "Aren't they adorable?"

"Yes." Angie's childlike nature came to the fore. "And so white and fluffy."

"It's going to be hard keeping them clean once the babies start slobbering over them." Viv laughed. "Better keep them away and just for show." She wandered back to Carlos as he stood talking to Pedro, Tomas and Roger near the kitchen. "She seems to be enjoying those teddies."

They all looked over at Angie to see her talking to the big teddy in her right hand, and patting her stomach with the little bear in her left.

"Mmm," Angie murmured. "This one's for you, little baby." She tapped her stomach with the nose of the small bear. "And this one's for me." She squeezed the big bear and laid her head upon it. "Yes, this one's for me and this one's for you." Her voice grew more childish as she spoke to the baby growing inside of her.

"Okay, weirdo," Carlos muttered as they all turned back. "Cuckoo. Got yourself a whack job there, Pedro," he joked to his scowling brother.

"Don't you dare." Jenny pointed her finger at Carlos, and her scowl pulled him back in line. "Don't you *dare* talk about your sister-in-law that way ever again, joke or not. She is an eighteen-year-old child who has lost both of her parents and is in desperate need of parental love. So don't *you dare* make fun of her playing with teddies. She is a baby having a baby, she's hardly going to be adult-like about it like Viv, so don't you dare make fun of her again, Carlos Spiros Stephanopoulos. Same goes for you two." She directed at Tomas and Roger who put their hands up in surrender.

"Mama I—" Carlos was defeated, but alarmed when his mother grabbed him by the arm.

"She needs our support, emotionally and physically, because this is about to hit her hard and if she regresses to being a child for a moment, then there is *nothing* wrong with that. Do you understand me?"

Carlos hadn't seen his mother so passionate yet angry about something since the death of Stefano, and he knew better than to be on her bad side. He blinked a few times and swallowed hard. "Of course, Mama. It was only a joke."

Jenny cast a glance at Angie who was switching between fiercely hugging her teddy and looking at it. She swallowed the growing lump in her throat. "Jokes like that aren't funny, Carlos. They're mean and cruel and unnecessary."

He saw the seriousness on her face, the fire burning in her eyes, and knew something deep was behind it, other than her motherly instincts kicking in. "Yes, Mama."

She finally let go of his arm. "Besides, you have a child of your own on the way, you need to stop acting like a child yourself and be an adult." The fire in her eyes died, and she felt the anger flow away. "It's time for dinner. Boys, set the table." Rushing over to the kitchen bench, she hid her watering eyes from her sons while they cast incredulous glances at each other before setting the table.

What was that? Carlos mouthed to Tomas and Pedro, receiving shaking heads and shrugs in return.

Jenny gathered herself together. "Roger, are you and Tomas staying?"

"Yes, Mrs S." Roger grabbed the plates from the cupboard and set them on the table.

After dinner, Tomas and Roger went down to their apartment so they had time to themselves, and Jenny sat on the couch next to Angie who had a bear in each crook of her arms while doing school work.

"Been a long time since you received any kind of present from a parent, I guess?" Jenny asked.

Angie's hand stopped writing, and she breathed. "Yes," finally came out.

"You're still a baby yourself. No wonder you were so emotional before." Jenny glanced at her and tried to lighten the mood. "I still have the first teddy bear my parents gave me." A smile came to her lips. "I still have the first teddy Spiros gave me, and I still have the boys' toys at home. Maybe I should pack them up and bring them over."

"Pedro had a teddy?" Angie's eyes grew wide.

Jenny thought back. "A small black bear called Raggles. God knows why he called him that, but he did. Carlos had a brown one called Fred, and Tomas had a patchwork one called Ted. Just Ted. But then Tomas wasn't overly interested in teddy bears." She frowned thoughtfully. "Neither were Carlos and Pedro past four or five years of age. But I still have them."

A sad smile crept over Angie's lips. "I still have my stuff. I packed it up when we emptied out the house, I brought some things with me, but I put the rest in storage because I didn't know where we'd be living."

"Well, you do now. Here. So have the stuff sent over. And when I go home after the new year, I'll bring back Pedro's things in February when I'm back for their birthdays."

"*Will you* be going home after New Year's?" Angie grew alarmed. She didn't want to be left on her own, not while pregnant, and certainly not after the baby came.

"At this stage, that's the plan. But then plans *can* change," Jenny said. "Plans can change *a lot.*"

Angie sighed. "They certainly can."

Jenny studied her face. "Will you stay at Juilliard after the baby?"

Biting her lip, Angie shook her head. "I don't know…I really don't know if I can deal with a baby *and* go to school, even part-time if they allow it."

"Do they?"

"I haven't asked."

"You should. You need to be prepared. Think ahead," Jenny told her. "That's all I've been doing for the last twenty-five years since before Carlos was born. Always thinking and planning ahead."

Angie's head nodded slightly. "I guess I should find out. You never know when things are going to pop up and screw with your life."

*****

Sheila Manning left the lawyer's office and took the bus home. She'd taken time out after work to speak to a lawyer, for free, for an hour. Pouring her heart out about her son and former lover, how he'd shunned her and their baby, denying their existence, so there had been no child support and no inheritance upon Andros's death. And so there was no insurance or payout from Luiz's murder. She had been abandoned by her lover, and was abandoned once more in life by the death of her son. Her only child.

"My baby," she'd sobbed to Maurice Blackborn, the lawyer. "My baby, my only child is dead and what compensation do I get?" She'd chosen Blackborn for the apparent success rate he boasted about, and because he was the only one who'd said yes. But then it hadn't been hard to say yes to the potential payday of the Poulos Papadopoulos fortunes. She had shown him all the clippings she'd collected, and how Poulos had once been Papadopoulos's stepson, which made her Luiz heir to two fortunes. "And now he's no more. Shot dead between the eyes by Papadopoulos's man and denied by his father," she sobbed. "My baby's gone, and I have nothing."

Maurice Blackborn's fast working tongue slid across his fat lips as they slid into a Cheshire cat grin. His short fat fingers laced together in front of him, and he sat back in his seat staring glassily at the plain, overweight, dowdy woman in front of him. The Poulos and Papadopoulos fortunes would be the biggest payday yet. But he'd have to do some research on who had what and come up with a nice round figure for himself, *and* Sheila Manning, of course. He was thinking a nice round number with six zeroes after it. *For himself* that is.

"Will you help me?" Sheila sniffed, and wiped her nose with a crumpled tissue she'd found in the bottom of her bag. She stared imploringly at the slicked back, greasy, sleazy lawyer on the other side of the desk. If anyone had the balls to get her the money, he did. And besides, he was all she could afford.

Maurice licked his lips. "Of course, my darling Sheila. But I will need to do some research. You go home and save your money, and I will get to work. You can pay me when it's all over, and I hand you your multimillion dollar cheque."

Dollar signs lit up her eyes. "Oh…multi…you think?"

"Of course, I can get you that much." Maurice stood and escorted her out of his office. "Give me a couple of weeks to look into the legalities of the estates, and I'll get back to you. Goodbye." Closing the door on her, he set about writing a list. Of course, he'd get back to her, she was his payday, so were those estates, and all he needed to do was find out who had inherited them.

December 1977

Gardo took time out Thursday morning to visit Jenny with the excuse of returning her pen. He parked on the street across from her apartment building and glanced up. He didn't even know if she was in there, but knew he had no time to waste. Spiros would be coming in the next day or two. Stepping out of his car, he smoothed his hair, and walked across the street into the building.

"Detective Gardo, welcome back." Martin Brewster forgot no face and no name. He made it his duty to train his brain daily so he could remember the comings and goings of the tenants and any visitors.

"Hello," Gardo replied. "I'm here to see Mrs Stephanopoulos. Is she in?"

"Just let me check." Brewster called the penthouse. He knew she was in as she'd gotten back half an hour ago, but he wasn't about to tell anyone that walked in off the street. Detective or otherwise. She answered. "Mrs Stephanopoulos, Detective Gardo is here to see you…okay…all right…thank you." Hanging up, he told Gardo, "You may go up."

"Thanks," Gardo muttered and made his way into the elevator and up to the penthouse, his stomach quivering the whole way. He quickly checked his suit to make sure it was presentable. Why wouldn't it be? It was a new suit, bought especially for visiting Jenny Stephanopoulos. Not that he normally shelled out the money on a suit he couldn't afford, and God knows why he'd bought a suit just to see a woman. A woman he would never have. But he'd done it anyway, and it was rash and stupid, and he couldn't afford it. The door opened, and he was staring into the sparkling blue eyes of Jenny Stephanopoulos, his dream girl.

"Ah, Detective Gardo." Jenny stood staring at the man before her. Six feet of rock-hard bulk, dark blond hair neatly parted, a face clean shaven except for the moustache. "Do you need to see Pedro? I thought everything was finished off the other day. Oh, where are my manners, do come in." She held the door open, and he slowly stepped in. Closing the door behind him, she waited.

"Ah, actually...I ah..." He glanced everywhere but at her intriguing blue eyes that were set off perfectly by her royal blue pantsuit and blouse. "I needed to," he dug around in his trench coat pocket, "return this." He held the pen aloft. "It seems I collected it by mistake with the papers the other day," he lied.

Jenny stared at the pen in his meaty hand, and it registered. "Oh, I wondered what had happened to it. I was looking for it yesterday. Thank you so much for returning it, but you could have left it downstairs with Brewster." Removing it from his fingers, she walked over to the phone table and replaced it in the pen holder.

"Well...I...ah..." he muttered, unable to get his words, let alone his thoughts, together. "I didn't want to be rude and just leave it," finally came out of his mouth. He felt himself flame up and knew he was making a fool of himself.

"Would you like coffee or tea, Detective?" Jenny walked toward to the kitchen. "I was about to make myself a cup."

"Ah...thank you...yes." Wandering after her, he watched while she filled the kettle and gathered the cups. His heart pounded in his chest, making him warm, and the warmth radiating from the divine Miss Jenny was making his groin grow.

"Do you think you'll catch Nedro Scarvo soon?"

"Mmm?" He pulled out of his daydream. "Sorry."

Jenny poured water over the leaves in the pot. "Do you think you'll catch Nedro Scarvo soon? I know it was all Andros's fault, but Scarvo was the one who supplied the drugs and cut my son's brakes the first time." She indicated for him to sit at the table and carried the tray over.

He waited as she sat, then sat and waited while she served the tea. "He's been on my list for many years. But unfortunately, we can never tie him to anything. It's all hearsay or invalidated." He accepted a cookie that she offered and stirred his black tea.

"Will he ever be caught?" she asked, concerned for the welfare of her son and daughter-in-law. "I have a grandbaby on the way, and I need to know if they're safe."

"Baby?" Gardo looked up in surprise.

Jenny met his look. "Yes. Didn't you know? Angelina is pregnant. Just *one* of the reasons they married and why I made it happen back home. At least with Andros dead they don't have to worry about him, or that horrid Barbara Weston. But what about Scarvo?"

"They're so young," Gardo muttered. "Married and a baby."

"Yes, well, these things happen sometimes. And my son Carlos and Viv are pregnant as well. I think the girls are due at the same time."

"But," Gardo blinked, "he's not much older than…"

"I know," Jenny said, shaking her head. "But they are adults, and they did adult things, now they need to deal with the consequences like adults. Thank God Viv is older and mature. She'll pull Carlos into line. But Angie is still young, a baby herself, and now she's *having* a baby."

"So, you'll be in New York to help them, then?" Gardo asked. *Please say yes,* he thought. *Please say yes, please say yes.*

"For now," Jenny told him. "The plan is to stay until New Year's then go home, come back for their birthdays in February, then come back just before they're due. I'm hoping the family can converge back here for the births."

"The family won't be here otherwise?" Gardo inquired.

"Viv needs to get back to L.A., and Tomas and Roger will probably be back in Miami, so hopefully we can all come together for the next generation."

"When are the girls due?"

"June, I think," Jenny said. "Or sometime before. Fortunately, Angie will be on holiday."

"Is she going to keep on at Juilliard and Pedro at 69?" Gardo finished off his tea and accepted a refill.

"Pedro loves his music, and I'd rather he DJ than do porn movies. In fact, I'm trying to get all the boys out of it. Pedro said it doesn't really worry him, so I think he'll give it up after his contract. And I think Carlos is slowly coming over from the dark side as well. He likes writing and set management better. As for Tomas and Roger, well Roger works behind the scenes and Tomas is a personal trainer, so I'm hoping this…" She heaved a sigh. "This one thing they've found won't last much longer." Offering another cookie, she took one herself and nibbled thoughtfully. "Angie's considering part-time study, but they'd need a nanny, although at this rate she might also finish out the year and not go back."

Gardo sighed. "Young people these days. They've taken the free love thing too far, and none of them wants to deal with the consequences, especially if that means a baby."

"Yes, for many I suppose that would be true. But I think in this case we've raised the boys to understand that if they have sex to use protection, otherwise they'll be a parent before they know it. Now, we obviously couldn't stop them from having sex, but we have drilled it into their heads enough. They're at least with women they love and are prepared to man up and be fathers, and Viv is settled in her life and career, so that's no big deal for her. But while Angie may have her father's money to fall back on, she's very much still a little girl dealing with the loss of her parents, and now this very adult life choice. They are financially set up, but emotionally, that's another matter. And I've told them over and over that Spiros and I are there for them when they need us. That's why I'm here in New York, to help set them up and be settled before the baby comes. Oh, listen to me talk about myself and my family. What about you, Detective? Children?"

Gardo took a deep breath. "Ah…no…"

"Oh, that's a shame. Never married?"

"Never lucky," he managed. "I was like your boys. Married young, went into the force. After a few years we weren't lucky, and when I was shot the first time, she left. Couldn't deal with my job anymore."

"Oh…I'm so sorry." Jenny's heart went out to the man at her table. She knew the pain of love and heartbreak. Knew the pain of loss and heartache.

"So am I."

"You never remarried?" She saw the pain etched all over, in every line, in every crack. And it was deep.

He shook his head. "No. Stayed married to the job, though." Staring into Jenny's eyes, he went on, "This job takes a lot out of you. It works you hard and takes what little sleep you try and get. It robs you of a wife and children, of love and happiness. And while you try and find it wherever you can, it either doesn't work, or it lasts for a short time before that's over too."

Jenny grasped his hand in sympathy. "I'm so sorry."

The warmth sped through his hand, up his arms, and into his body. He laid his hand over hers and held on. This was Giancarlo, the vulnerable man who, like so many others, just wanted to be loved and happy. This was the man who rarely spoke of his pain, and barely anyone knew of it. But here he'd just spilt his guts to the warmest, most inviting, incredible woman he'd ever met, and he was falling. And she was married.

"Would you like another cup before you go?" She pulled her hand away and picked up the teapot. That had become awkward fast. "It's cold out there today, and you need to stay warm."

"Yes, thank you." He felt the awkwardness. "And then I must go."

"Back to Scarvo." Jenny brought the conversation back to something safe. "Do we have anything to fear from him?"

"I doubt it." Gardo downed his third cup and another biscuit. "His house was rented for a movie. Pedro had nothing to do with him personally, all he did was supply Poulos with a brick of coke and have the brakes cut when asked by Poulos."

"All he did?" Jenny's brows rose. "That's far too much as is."

Gardo nodded and watched her gather the cups and plates, knowing their time was over. "I know it's a big deal, Mrs Stephanopoulos, but I really think Scarvo is not interested in Pedro. Let alone being done for his part in this."

Jenny set the tray on the sink. "I hope you're right, Detective. Because I think after the trouble that Andros put Pedro and Angie through, and then Luiz put Tomas and Roger through, and Stefano put *all three* of them through, that it's time my children get back to being happy and living a normal life. The life they had *before* Stefano and Andros."

Gardo stood and placed his chair under the table. "I perfectly understand. And that is why I'm going to give you my card." He fumbled in his pocket and found one. "If anything *does* happen, Scarvo related or otherwise, you call me, and I'll come running." He handed it over. "Anyone looks the wrong way at you, or you think you're being followed, or get harassing phone calls, call me. Twenty-four hours a day, seven days a week."

Jenny glanced from the plain white business card with his name, precinct and phone number on it, to him. "Thank you, Detective. It helps to know that someone cares. Let me show you out." She led him to the door and opened it. "I'll let Pedro and Angie know to keep an eye out just in case. And if anything weird presents itself, we'll be sure to call you. Thank you so much for stopping by, Detective. And thank you for returning my pen."

"Of course." Gardo cleared his throat. "Thank you for the tea. And if there's anything I can ever do, let me know."

"We shall," Jenny said as he walked into the foyer. "Stay warm, Detective, goodbye." She closed and locked the door, tidied up, wiped down the table, and then stood by the window watching Giancarlo Gardo get into his car and drive away.

Oh, my, God, that was strange, she thought, wondering why he'd stopped by. *He could have just left it with Brewster downstairs, so why did he need to see me? And the hand holding moment was awkward. Trust me to be so friendly, I hope he didn't get the wrong idea.* She pondered a few more moments and decided to leave it. Spiros was coming the next day, and she wanted to track down some of his favourite Greek foods so he wouldn't feel so out of place.

Gardo didn't go back to the precinct. Instead, he went to a little dive bar he knew. He was on the job and shouldn't be drinking, but after the feel of Jenny Stephanopoulos in his hands, he more than needed to knock back a few whiskies. "Another." He tapped the glass on the bar and watched the barman refill it then swigged it back. *What a fool I am, going after a married woman. A married woman for fuck's sake. All the women in New York and I had to fall for the mother of the damn porn star I had to save. The woman with the most incredible blue eyes, warm, inviting smile, and a figure to match. And she is bloody married.*

He shook his head and hung it in shame, running his hands through his hair, messing it up. Not that it mattered anymore, he'd only slicked it down to see her. *Jenny with the blue eyes Stephanopoulos. Jenny with the blue eyes…Jenny…Jenny Gardo…oh, for fuck's sake man get a grip. She's not about to leave her husband for you, you fool, and you are a fool. A big boneheaded fool for thinking you could be with a married woman. That she would leave her husband and sons and grandbabies to be with you, you idiot. Who the hell do you think you are? Have another drink, you drunken fool.*

He tapped the bar. *Oh, you're a drunken fool all right. Drunk on love and lust and the throbbing in your pants.* He blearily looked at his watch. Not even *close* to knock-off time, and the woman he occasionally saw would be at work. Yeah, there was a woman. He didn't see her often, but she accommodated him when he needed accommodating, and after spending time with Jenny, he needed accommodating now. He decided to pay her a visit at work, knowing full well he'd get some alone time with her. After all, he was a cop. All he needed to do was flash his badge, and no one would say a thing.

Gardo strode into the supermarket and looked around for the woman he was after. He spied her in the far lane and proceeded over, but the manager got in the way.

"Can I help you, sir?" the thirty-something asked.

Gardo held up his badge. "I need to speak to Sheila Manning about a crime she reported. Is there somewhere private I can talk to her?"

The manager froze at the badge in his face and gazed up at Gardo. "Um, of course. You can use my office. This way." They walked to the end lane. "Ms Manning, this detective is here to see you. You can take him to my office, and I'll finish up here."

Sheila looked up from serving her customer to see the man she'd be serving next. There was only one reason Gardo was there, and it was for sex. "Sure," she told the manager and changed places. "This way." She led Gardo to the back of the small store and closed the office door after him.

"Get your knickers down and turn around." He was already unbuckling his belt.

"Don't waste time, do you?" She sighed and lifted her uniform.

He grabbed her arm and pushed her against the desk, yanking her underwear down. Pulling himself out of his pants, he planted his cock in the place it needed to be, hammering home his erection. Thirty seconds later he was done and adjusting his clothes.

"That it?" She pulled up her knickers and pushed down her dress.

"I get off at eight. I'll be around then."

"Will you be staying?" While she didn't mind the odd night here and there, she didn't always want *or* need a man. But just as he needed a womanly figure to bury himself in, sometimes she needed a manly figure to be buried by. Sometimes you needed physical affection whether you thought you needed it or not.

Gardo sighed. "I don't know. Depend on what you offer. Time to get back."

Sheila unlocked the door and escorted Gardo back to the front. "I hope you catch him soon. I don't feel safe knowing there's some dirty perve hanging around."

"No, I'm sure you don't." Gardo played along as the manager came up. "You've been very helpful, Ms Manning. Hopefully, your statement will help catch the man."

"I hope so," Sheila murmured and went back to work.

"Everything all right?" the manager asked Gardo, his eyes going back and forth between the detective and his employee.

"Ms Manning has been a big help in trying to catch a dirty perve," Gardo said. "You should be happy that you have such a vigilant worker. Good day." He left the manager staring from him to Sheila with wide, unbelieving eyes.

*****

"Will you boys be here when your father arrives tomorrow?" Jenny asked them all at dinner.

"Do you know what time he gets in?" Carlos asked, popping a piece of juicy, succulent steak into his mouth and briefly closed his eyes in happiness. *God, Mama knows how to cook,* he thought. *I wonder if she'll teach Viv all her tricks.*

"Not yet. He said he'll ring before his plane leaves and from what I remember, it was about a nine-hour flight," Jenny said.

"We're heading to 69 to see Pedro play, but we don't have to go until late," Vivian added. "It doesn't start until, what, eight?"

"Opens seven-thirty, gets going at eight, but the party *really* gets going about midnight," Pedro replied. "Especially on Friday and Saturday nights when everyone doesn't have work, or school the next day." He glanced at Angelina beside him. "You comin', babe?"

She nodded and finished her mouthful of food. "Maggie's coming, we're going together."

"Are all of you going together, or separately?" Jenny cut into her French potatoes.

"Hadn't thought about it." Carlos sipped his beer and shrugged. "If we decide on a time to go and come home we could use the service car."

"I would prefer that you at least go together, so Angie and Maggie aren't on their own, and then if they do come home before everyone else, someone should see them back here before you continue other plans," Jenny said.

"We can probably do that, Mrs S," Roger spoke up. "T and I are going, but I doubt we'll stay all night. We can bring them home." He glanced at his husband for his acknowledgement.

"Are you feeling up to going to a night club, bro?" Pedro asked Tomas. "Got the energy to keep up with your much younger and more energetic brother?"

Tomas rolled his eyes and lay his cutlery on his plate. "You're not as good as you think you are, *baby* bro."

"*Are* you well enough, Tomas?" Jenny repeated the question.

"My sore throat is gone, but I still feel a bit blech," he said. "Like something's still hanging around. But I'm hungry again, and food tastes good. You always know what to do with food to make it amazing, Mama."

"Of course I do," Jenny said modestly. "I learned from *my* mother, and my husband's mother, and a whole bunch of recipe books."

"Will you teach me how to cook, Mama?" Angelina asked, finishing off her food.

"And Viv," Carlos added. "Please, for the love of God, teach Viv how to cook like you."

"Hey." Viv swatted him with her napkin in protest. "I know how to cook."

"Toast is *not* cooking," Carlos said, getting another hit from the napkin.

"I can teach you all how to cook." Jenny laughed. "*Including* my sons."

"Ah, no, not me," Pedro replied.

"Nope. I'll leave it up to Roger," Tomas added.

"I didn't raise my sons to be lazy," Jenny reminded them. "I raised you to clean up after yourselves and help around the house."

"Mama, that's what women are for," Carlos cheekily told her.

"Oi!" Four napkins flew at him.

"Joking!" he cried in protest and ducked to avoid more.

*****

Friday morning the call came through.

"My plane leaves in half an hour," Spiros said down the line. "Not sure how long it will take, but they told me I'd be in around four or five in the afternoon, your time."

"Oh, that's fantastic. You'll see the kids before they all go out, and then we get to spend the night together. God, I've missed you." She ached for him, having spent weeks not by his side.

"I've missed you too, my love…wait…they've just called my flight.

I have to go. I'll see you tonight."

Jenny hung up the phone and glanced around the warm living room. It was cold enough outside that there was frost on the windows.

"Was that Papa?" Tomas asked from his seat on the couch next to Roger and his grandparents opposite him. "What time's he getting in?"

Jenny turned and smiled. "Yes. He's leaving now, so he'll be in this afternoon. I'd better get this place cleaned up. Now, the cleaner comes in an hour, and I need to go shopping for some Greek food. What will all of you be doing today?" She hurried around looking in the fridge and pantry, making lists as she went.

"Nothing," Tomas said. "We're resting before tonight."

"And how do you feel?" Jenny asked.

"Okay," he replied. "Not like I used to feel, but I'll be better in a few days."

"I hope so," Jenny said, still worrying about her son. "Right then, your job is to make sure everyone's here when I go for your father. I'll be picking him up."

"Sure. When will you be going?" Tomas asked.

"Not sure. I'll call the airport after lunch to get the time. I hope the weather won't delay it." She marked off her list. "Once everyone's gone we'll have the night alone."

After doing her shopping and having lunch, Jenny called the airport and was told the plane was due to arrive around four-thirty. Leaving Tomas in charge, she left at four and made her way to the airport and through to the international terminal to wait for her husband. Finally, after a fifteen-minute delay, the plane landed, and the passengers disembarked. Waiting for her husband, she smoothed the forest green pantsuit and turtleneck under her matching overcoat and waited until she saw him. "Spiros," she called, standing on her tiptoes and waving her hand. "Darling, over here."

Having heard his name, he glanced in her direction, but glanced away before looking back with a vague recognition in his eyes. "Jenny?"

She ran for him, excitedly clapping her hands. "Oh, my darling husband, how I've missed you." Flying into his arms, she plastered kisses all over his face.

"Jenny?" He pushed her back and took in the new haircut, make-up and clothing. "Look at you. I almost didn't recognise you."

"Well, I did tell you I was having a makeover when I came. It was high time for a new hairstyle, and now I can afford clothes. Oh, just wait until you see the penthouse. It's fabulous. Now, where's your bag?"

They retrieved his case from the carousel, and she led him out to the limo where the puzzled look on his face deepened. "Jenny, you have gone to way too much trouble. A limousine?" He sat beside her in the back, and the driver shut the door.

"Nonsense," she said, getting comfortable. "I said I was going to blow Stefano's money and that's exactly what I'm doing."

Spiros sighed. Even now he still had a bad feeling about taking the Papadopoulos estate. But Jenny had fought a fair argument. After what Stefano did to their sons, he owed them, and she was taking. The uneasy stirrings in his gut told him that for all the good she wanted to do, something bad was still destined to happen.

"Stop sighing." She patted his hand. "And luxuriate in money we've never had, in a place we've never been in, and new things to experience. We're home."

They pulled up to the apartment, and the driver opened the door and removed Spiros's case from the trunk.

"Isn't it gorgeous?" Jenny linked her arm through his, and they stood staring up at the seven-storey building. "And Central Park is across the road, and they have a zoo." She spun around to look and pointed into the park. "The zoo's just right in there. But let's go upstairs, it's chilly out." After thanking the driver, she escorted Spiros into the lobby. "Darling, this is Mr Brewster, our doorman. Mr Brewster, my husband, Spiros Stephanopoulos."

Brewster bowed his head. "Mr Stephanopoulos. How do."

Spiros took in his portly frame. "Good, thank you."

"I can't wait to show you the penthouse, you'll love it. Come on." She pulled him into the elevator.

Pedro heard it. He had his ear plastered to the elevator doors on the penthouse floor. "They're coming," he called and skidded into the suite, slamming the door behind him. He lined up with Angie, his brothers, Viv, Roger and his grandparents. "Okay, get ready." They heard the elevator doors open, then two voices, and jostled for prime viewing position.

"And here is our penthouse." Jenny opened the door to find family standing there.

"Papa!" The boys ran to a surprised Spiros who hugged his sons fiercely.

He had missed them and his beloved wife. "Oh, it is good to see you, my sons." He let them go to kiss the girls. "Vivian, Angelina."

"Papa." Angie hugged him tightly, and he left a kiss on her head.

"Sarah, Matthew, Roger." He kissed and hugged his way through the family to see the view from the floor-to-ceiling windows. Walking over to them, he stared. "This *is* spectacular."

"Isn't it." Jenny slid her arm through his. "The bedroom's upstairs and has the same view," she said under her breath. He looked at her, and she raised her brows saucily.

"Then we will have to see that view as well," he replied, warming in his pants.

"It's particularly spectacular at night with all the lights on," she added, "and you're all warm and snuggled up in bed."

The stirrings continued. "We'll *definitely* have to do that."

"Can you two think of sex later? I need to eat so I can get to work," Pedro called.

"Ew, Pedro." Carlos punched him on the arm.

"Ew, no, no." Tomas covered his ears. "I've already heard them having sex, no, no, oh, my God."

That stopped both boys.

"When did you hear…?" Pedro asked in surprise.

"Your wedding night," Tomas replied. "No, no, don't wanna know." He hurried into the kitchen away from the talk.

Pedro and Carlos exchanged amused glances.

"Yes," Jenny agreed. "Let's have dinner. You must be starving. Sit down everyone." She hurried into the kitchen after Tomas and started dishing out the lamb and vegetables.

With Spiros at the head of the table once more, everyone dug in, following up dinner with Jenny's baklava.

At six, Pedro rushed off for 69, and at seven-thirty everyone else left. Sarah and Matthew were staying in, but the rest went to get ready to watch Pedro do his thing.

With the dishes dried and put away, Jenny hung up the towel and sighed. "Finally." Going to her husband at the table, she slid into his lap. "I have a very special night planned. So why don't I show you the bedroom and you can shower while I unpack your bag. And then I'll shower and put something…*special* on." Kissing his lips, she ran her tongue over them. He caught it between his teeth before letting go. "How does that sound?"

"Sounds like my wife wants to get me into bed." Spiros slid a hand under her blazer.

"I do," Jenny whispered and took him upstairs, locking the front door and collecting his case on the way. "And this…is the bedroom." She closed the door and watched him take it all in.

"It's bigger than our whole house," he said, looking from the fireplace to the sparkling view that now lit up the windows.

"Hardly." Jenny laughed. "But I do have a surprise for you, so go and have a shower, and I'll unpack." Directing him to the bathroom, she swiftly unpacked his case, laid out the bed, and propped up more pillows. She turned the lights down and lit a fire in the grate. She was just pulling the curtains over when he came back into the bedroom. Jenny couldn't wait. "You get settled on the bed and try not to fall asleep," she told him and quickly undressed and showered. After smothering herself in scented lotion, she grabbed her dark fur coat from the closet and slipped it on before parading back into the room.

Spiros turned from the fire to his wife. His eyes went wide at the shapely legs poking out of the opening as she held the coat closed in front of her.

"You like?" she asked.

"Is that fur?" He felt his own fur-covered monster rise.

"Yes." Jenny danced around the bed, flinging a leg here, flinging a leg there. "Wanna feel?"

"Yes." He sat up a little higher.

She sashayed around to his side and shook her booty at him. "Feel."

His hands slid over the fur, and he felt himself rise higher. "Oh, Jenny," he breathed.

Seeing the passion in his eyes, she kneeled on the bed and flung her leg over, straddling him, and allowing the coat to fall open. She let his hands take her.

Her nakedness aroused him to full attention, and Spiros let his hands do the talking. They caressed, they groped, his thumbs found her nipples and rubbed, they were the apprentices, and his cock was the master. "Oh, Jenny." His mouth found the nape of her neck and attacked.

"Oh, Spiros." The fires burned down below, ready for her husband to take her. But she took him instead. Pushing him back against the pillow, her mouth captured his and ravished him. Her tongue sought solace, but found it was not alone. She made small sounds against him as his hands did damage to her body under the fur.

The fur did damage against his bare flesh, and her intimate womanhood beckoned him in.

"Mmm, mmm, Spiros." The kiss deepened and intensified by the light of the fire. The heat it perpetrated sped around the room and into them. "Mmm, mmm." She moved to his chest, kissing the black-hair-covered body of her husband. Her hands and lips moved lower, and she rubbed herself against him, feeling every hard muscle against her soft flesh.

"Oh, Jenny." He wanted to burst. His wife's mouth, hands, and body on and against his was too much. He surged, wanting her, taking her in his arms, he pulled her back up to his mouth, and his cock found the place it sought.

"Ah," she cried softly, feeling him enter. "Ah, oh, God." Her breasts were mashed against the fur of his chest. Her mouth was taken over by his. Her body was manipulated into moving up and down, feeling every single one of his twelve inches inside of her and the pleasure they were inflicting. The fur slid down her shoulders, and her head flung back in defeat. "Take me," she gasped, her body on full display. The fur erotically electrified her flesh, her nipples, her mind.

His hands moved her, his mouth besieged her, his manhood owned her.

"Ah, oh, God," came over and over in short breaths. "Oh, God."

Just before the peak, he pulled back. Stopped. Waited while she registered that she'd stopped being made love to.

Her head lolled forward. "Don't stop."

In one deft move, he rolled her so he was on top of her, the coat pinning her arms, trapping her so he could take her.

"Oh, God," she cried as the twelve inches of man plundered shamelessly, seeking its home, seeking its release. Her body rocked back and forth as her husband took her again and again and again. "Oh, God, Spiros." She came to the brink knowing she was going to explode. "Oh, God."

"Oh, God, Jenny." Spiros knew he was ready. Knew *she* was ready. "Oh, Jenny. Oh, God, I'm coming, I'm coming, come with me, come with me, Jenny."

They cried out together as the explosion shook them. Spiros thundered home, rocking Jenny with his momentum. "Oh, God," he gasped, slowing. "Oh, God." He stopped and collapsed on top of her. "Oh, God." His tongue plundered, capturing her in a passionate embrace. His arms wrapped around her, keeping her tight against him. "Oh, God, I love you, Jenny."

They kissed for a few minutes more while hearts slowed down, while they caught their breath.

"Mmm," Jenny breathed. "Oh, God, I love you, too." He was still inside of her throbbing. *Unless that's me throbbing,* the thought wandered through her mind. *It could be both of us.*

He pulled his head back to gaze into her eyes. His fingers stroked her hair away from her forehead, and he studied her features as if he hadn't seen them in years. "I love you, Jenny Stephanopoulos."

Her hands slid over his back, down over his ass and back up along his strong muscular arms that were around her. "I love you, Spiros Stephanopoulos."

*****

Carlos and Vivian, Tomas and Roger, stood in the crowd at *Studio 69*, with Angelina and Maggie in front of them.

"What the bloody…" Carlos let the sentence trail off.

Tomas bit both of his lips to stop himself from laughing at the spectacle that was his brother. On stage, in tiny gold shorts that showed his size, and gold lace-up boots, he was pounding out the beats.

The place was packed, but, being the brothers of Pedro, and porn star kings, they were allowed entry without hassle, and now they stood watching Pedro work.

"He knows his stuff." Roger watched closely. "He can definitely handle those decks."

"He can," Tomas assured him. "He knows what he's doing, and he does it extremely well. But, oh, my God, that outfit."

Angelina turned around a huge grin on his face. "He *hates* that outfit."

"But, Jesus, we gotta get a photo of him in it," Carlos said. "Anyone got a camera?"

"Eddie's taken publicity shots. You can probably get some of those," Angelina said loud enough to be heard over the music. "Eddie will probably want you to go on stage and show off. You're all porn stars after all."

"I love the décor." Viv was taking notice of all the celebrities around her. "And did you see who's here? The who's who of New York."

Pedro clapped his hands and spun around, dancing to the song he was currently playing. He'd been back at work for a week and loved it. Loved the way the music made him feel, loved the way it made everything better, and he'd missed it like crazy. He danced into a double spin and waved a hand in the air, egging the crowd on. He saw

Angie with Maggie in the middle of the room under the massive disco ball, and his brothers and their partners behind them. "Ladies and gentlemen," he said into the mic and turned down the music. "I can see my brothers Carlos and Tomas in the crowd. They're also known as Carlo and Tomas Stefan." The crowd went wild around them. "Carlos is with his new wife, Vivian Villiers, the gorgeous supermodel." She waved at the attention. "And my brother Tomas is here with his new husband, Roger Dencott, who is his partner in his movies." The crowd screamed louder, and Roger put a protective arm around Tomas. "And, of course, my beautiful new wife Angelina is here with her best friend Maggie, who's dating Mike, the bartender."

"Whoo." Mike waved his hands in the air from behind the bar.

"So, let's get my family of models and porn stars up on stage to play a few tracks and show you how they can move on a dance floor. Come on up." He waved for them to come up onstage, and amidst the cheering crowd, they moved through and climbed the stairs at the side of the stage.

Pedro was having a ball dancing, and Viv took her moment to take centre stage and thrust her ass off. She flung her hair, waved her arms, and kicked her legs high. Carlos stood back and watched, surprised at this wild woman who had just emerged from his wife. She spied him watching and pulled him to the centre of the stage where she thrust and ground against him. He obliged, and they showed 69 what they had.

"Oh, Jesus, trust Carlos to become the star," Tomas shouted to Pedro and Roger.

"That's Carlos." Pedro grinned, dancing with Angie who was swaying back and forth.

Roger took Tomas's hand. "Come on, T, let's join them."

"No, Roger, I—" Tomas pleaded.

"No, you don't. I know you can dance." Roger pulled him to centre stage and danced. "That's how we first met, remember."

Tomas finally got into the mood, and they moved together as though no one was watching. Their platform shoes stomped the floor while their tight shirts and even tighter pants showed everyone exactly what they had.

*****

Jenny lay in her husband's arms, content, serene, insanely happy. Her fingers slid up and down his fur-covered torso. She smiled and buried her face in that fur.

"I take it you're happy." Spiros kissed the top of her head. The fur coat was across their lower half, covering them.

Jenny's fingers snaked down below that coat. "Very."

Spiros captured her hand and held it on top of his member, capturing her hand around him. They moved, and so did he. "I have missed you so much."

"I've missed you for months." Her fingers moved back and forth.

"Months? We were together after Pedro's wedding and Tomas's. In fact, we were together until the day you left." His hand manipulated hers.

"I know." Jenny stared into the warmth of the fire. "But we hadn't been together since *before* Carlos left. During that time, all those months, I missed you. I missed you terribly because you shut yourself off from the kids, from me. I felt all alone and lonely, and I missed you."

Spiros thought back across all those months. "I'm sorry," he finally said. "I am so sorry I was not the husband I should have been. I am so sorry that I was not more loving, more needy. I'm sorry I shut you off." He kissed her again. "I'm so sorry I was not the husband I had been and should have been."

"I know." Jenny manipulated him down below. "But you can make it up to me now."

He rose to the occasion with a sharp intake of breath. "Oh, my God, Jenny Stephanopoulos. You definitely know how to make me do what you want me to." He rolled her over and entered.

*****

Viv shook her ass while flinging her dress back and forth. Waving her arms, kicking her legs, she danced as if no one was watching and didn't care if anyone was. She kicked her leg up, and Carlos caught it in the crook of his arm, pulling her close so they could thrust their way through the song.

They were still on stage, covered in glitter bombs, and showing the crowd what they had. Tomas and Roger had gone back to the dance floor to catch up with a couple of friends of Roger's who had come up from Miami to see Pedro play.

Angie and Maggie were on the dance floor in front of the stage. Pedro had told her to stay close so he could keep an eye on her, and she planned on it.

Shaking her hair, she felt so free. Free from fears of her father, free from fears of Pedro being done for drugs, free from the restraints of school. As much as she loved music and Juilliard, she just wasn't sure she wanted to be there anymore. Out was the red crocheted dress she'd seduced Pedro in, and in was the latest style in disco dresses for teens and young women. Snug, but not skin-tight, metallic lamé, polyester, and mid-thigh length. The shopping spree Jenny had taken her on provided her with more than enough clothes to fill the huge walk-in closet in the suite. She hadn't even thought of maternity wear, and Jenny had told her she'd take her shopping for those later in the new year. She was barely three months, so she had time before she grew. Grabbing Maggie by the hand, she spun them both around, and they fell into a giggling heap on the floor.

Pedro saw them collapse and waved for Leon to roll over and see what had happened.

Leon saw the wave and roller-skated over to the giggling girls. "And what are you two fine young things doing on the floor? You know what happens on this floor, right?" He helped Angelina up.

"Ew, did you have to tell us that, Leon?" she asked, helping Maggie up. She grabbed both their hands and started skipping around in circles.

"Well, let me tell you," Leon purred. "I wouldn't mind doing the dirty on this floor with that brother-in-law of yours." His head whipped around as they turned, trying to get a longer look at Carlos on stage. "He is F.I.N.E fine!"

"But he's straight," Angie reminded him. "If you want gay, try Tomas and Roger."

Leon's eyes grew wide. "Oh, I wouldn't mind me some of those twelve inches either. Have you *seen* their movies, oh, my, God, hot, hot, hot." He fanned his face.

"And speaking of hot," Maggie said. "Can you get us a couple of juices?"

"Sure thing, Miss M. Say, when are you and Mike going to get hitched?" Leon asked, circling her.

Her eyes widened. So did her mouth. "Married?" she managed. "Who said anything about getting married?"

Leon put his hands up. "Just askin' since these two did it." He nodded at Angie. "I figured you two would be next."

She blushed furiously. "We haven't ever…oh…just go and get our drinks." She pushed Leon away, and he rolled toward the bar.

Angie giggled. "So you two haven't even slept together?"

Maggie blushed harder. "No, we haven't," she snapped. "At least I won't end up like you."

Angie's face fell. "What do you mean…like me?"

"Eighteen and pregnant," Maggie said. "You two had sex, and you got pregnant. You're eighteen, he's twenty. Why would I want to worry about adult stuff like that for? If Mike loves me, he'll wait."

Angie felt her temper rise and her brows drop. "*We* didn't plan on a baby you know. And if you're dumb enough to think Mike will wait until you're thirty you've got another think coming."

Maggie frowned at Angie's words. "Who said anything about waiting until I'm thirty? I just want to concentrate on my studies and finish school. Sex is a big deal. So are the consequences." Leon came back with the drinks, and she took hers and sipped it. "Look, Angie, this may be what you did, but it's not what I'm going to do." She watched Angie's hands go to her stomach. "That's not a decision I want to deal with yet. And if Mike loves me, he'll understand and wait."

Angie looked down at her stomach, her hands slid over it and her fingers spread out. She was flat now, but knew by Pedro's birthday she would be showing.

"Look, I didn't say it to upset you," Maggie said. "I'm just nowhere near being ready for it."

Angelina finally looked up. "What? And you think *I* am?" Feeling the emotions rush over her, she bolted for the door that led to the offices, coming to a stop in Stew's. It was where she'd stayed during the issues with her father, sleeping on the couch through the night to be taken home by Pedro in the morning.

He rushed in now. "Angie," he panted. "What's wrong?" Slick with sweat, he'd seen Angie rush backstage and had quickly brought in DJ Master Z to fill in for a few minutes. "Babe?"

The tears flowed forth. "I'm having a baby. Oh, my, God, I'm having a baby." The sobs racked her body, and he pulled her into his arms.

"Oh, Angie, oh, babe. Mama said there would come a time it would hit you hard. Looks like this could be it." Everyone else piled into the room.

"Angie, are you all right?" Viv rushed to her side.

"It just hit her about being pregnant," Pedro said, relinquishing her to Viv.

"It's all my fault," Maggie wailed. "I was talking about not wanting to get pregnant like her, so Mike and I are waiting to have sex. I think she took it as an insult. I didn't mean it."

"I know," Angie sobbed from Viv's embrace. "It's just that it hit me all of a sudden. That by the time everyone's birthday rolls around I'll be five months pregnant for Valentine's Day, and I won't be able to dance anymore, or come here, or wear nice clothes, or go out with you." She gazed at Maggie.

"There, there." Viv patted her back. "I'll be that far along too, so we'll be beached whales together for their birthdays."

Angie looked into Viv's emerald eyes. "But you're so put together."

Viv laughed. "*Now*. Just because I'm forty doesn't mean I'll deal with this any better than you. I have a modelling career, I'll have to get my body back in shape, and God knows how long that will take." She touched her hand to Angie's tear-stained face. "I know it's going to be tough, but you'll have Jenny with you. I'll be off on my own on the other side of the country. Do you think *I* know what to do?"

Angie finally cracked a smile. "I guess not."

"There, that's better," Viv said. "Tears all gone. Wait until you get stretch marks. *Then* you can cry."

Angie's eyes widened and she gasped. "Oh, my, God. I'll be getting what?"

Viv's laughter continued. "Oh, sweetie, don't worry, there's a cream out that helps women not get them. It's expensive, but we can afford it."

Pedro glanced at the clock. "I gotta get back on stage, babe, it's after midnight. Why don't you and Maggie go home? Do some of that girl talk you like so much."

Angie giggled through her tears. "Silly, we don't "do" girl talk," she made quote marks, "but I am losing my momentum, so we might grab some food before we go."

"We can take you," Tomas told her. "We told Mama we would, and I'm kinda over the whole disco club scene anyway." He glanced at Roger. "Do you mind?"

"No." Roger shook his head. "We've caught up with friends and seen Pedro play. Cool gig you've got here, bro," he told Pedro. "I'm just a *little* bit jealous."

"That's because he looks so hot in those shorts," Angie teased.

"Ugh," Pedro groaned, his head falling back and his eyes closing momentarily. "I *hate* these shorts. They're so tight." He pulled them down to make his package less obvious. "But at least I have the body to wear them." A collective groan went around the group.

"Always comes back to the body." Tomas turned for the door. "Time to go."

"Yep." Carlos grabbed Viv's hand. "You always know it's time to leave when Pedro starts talking about how hot he is and what a great body he has."

"Not my fault if I have a body that's hot," Pedro protested. "Just because you're short like Mama and Tomas looks like Papa." The boys stopped short and turned around, throwing daggers at him that he ignored. "Looks like I got all the good looks in the family."

"But those hot looks didn't get you the *hottest woman* in the family," Carlos said, holding up his hand that held Viv's.

"Hey," Angie protested.

"That would be Mama," Tomas told them. "*No* woman will ever be hotter than Mama, and you know it." Everyone looked at him in surprise.

"Ew, Tomas," Carlos complained. "That's gross. I don't even want to think of Mama that way. Jesus." He led Viv out the door.

"You know it's true, Carlos," Tomas argued as he followed him. "Papa always says Mama's the hottest woman in the family and that's the way it will always be."

"Yeah, well…" Carlos stopped before the door that led to the dance floor. "That's for *Papa* to say, not for *you* to repeat and back up."

"Well…" Viv weighed in on the subject. "Have you actually *looked* at your mother since her makeover? She *is* quite hot and very stylish now. And," she looked around the group, "she's caught the attention of that detective friend of yours." She zeroed in on Pedro. "*He's* taken a fancy to your mother."

Alarm spread over Pedro's face. "Ew! What! *You can't be serious!* Gardo? Interested in Mama? Get out!" He studied Viv's face. "You *can't be serious?*"

Viv nodded. "I am *dead* serious. I saw the way he and that older cop watched her the other day, showering her with attention. He's got it *so* bad."

"But she's married," Tomas said, puzzled as to why a man would be interested in his mother when she was a married woman.

"That doesn't stop men when they want a woman," Viv told him.

"But…she's…Mama!" Carlos was incredulous. "*Mama…*"

"*Why* does that make a difference?" Viv asked her stunned husband. "She's actually quite a looker now after the makeover."

"Mama?" asked all three stunned and perplexed Stephanopoulos boys.

Viv laughed so hard her eyes watered. "*Yes! Your mother* is quite a looker now, and two cops were captivated by her." She shook her head in disbelief. "You boys *really* don't see your mother as a woman, do you?"

"Ew, Viv, she's Mama. Mama is…" Carlos faltered.

"A hot woman," Viv answered.

"Mama!" Carlos finished with a horrified look. "And that's all there is to it." He waved a hand. "She's Mama, and *we're* dancing. Let's go." He dragged a laughing Viv out onto the dance floor.

"I gotta get back on stage. You okay, babe?" Pedro kissed Angie.

"Yeah, I'm okay." She sighed softly. "We'll just get something to eat then go."

"Okay. Tomas, I'm putting her into yours and Roger's care, so make sure you do what you said." He quickly squeezed Tomas's shoulder and went back on stage.

"Better get you girls something to eat and get you home," Roger said, taking charge.

*****

Jenny moved up and down on top of her husband. Her hands gripped his, the fur coat lay around her bottom, all but forgotten. She was relishing in her husband, and this was their third time for the night. Making up for all the months they had gone without. Without love, without sex, without each other. She shuddered and collapsed on top of him, breathing out as he breathed in. "God, that's so good."

"It always is," Spiros gasped, feeling the delightful breasts of his wife pressed against him. God how he loved those breasts. So full, so giving, so pliable under his expert hands. Not that his hands were experts when they had met. Hell, he'd been a virgin just like she was. And he had no idea what to do with a woman, having never had one before leaving Mykonos all those years ago. But he had learned the curves of his wife's body, and relearned when it changed with the swelling of his children. Sons that gave her a very warm and welcoming womanly body indeed. Her breasts had swelled and stayed larger, much to his delight. Her hips were curved and feminine. Her body had trained under his guidance, and that was only after Jenny had trained him. All courtesy of the Kama Sutra and lots of practice after their wedding night. Of course, it helped that he was packing twelve inches of manhood, but he had worried that it would hurt her their first time. And she had been scared, having never been with a man, let alone seen a penis, naked and in person before. But they had fumbled their way through it, and many more times after Jenny Stephanopoulos née Marsh found out what her husband's penis could do. She couldn't get enough of it, and had promptly bought the Kama Sutra book. They hadn't looked back since.

His fingers slid up her spine and moved back down to cup the globes of her bottom. Her beautiful body that bore him three children had grown better with age, and she was the only one for him. The only one that made him feel like a man. The only one to make him *feel* like he was home, regardless of where he may actually have been. Australia, Greece, and now New York. It didn't matter where they physically were, as long as they were with each other, they were home.

A sigh of contentment escaped from between her lips as they smiled in the light of love. "Happy?" Jenny ran her fingers up and down his arm.

"Very."

"Good." She lifted her head to gaze into his deep brown eyes. "Because the night is still young."

*****

Tomas and Roger dropped Angie and Maggie off on the fourth floor and went back down to their own apartment. Showering, they soaped off the stench of cigarettes and alcohol and lathered each other in suds. They made love, kissing, moving, touching until they were done. Stepping out and towelling down, they didn't talk. They didn't need to, for they knew what to do and how to do it.

Roger carefully carried a giggling Tomas into the bedroom and laid him down on their king-size bed, pulling the covers over them before sliding down beside his lover and taking him into his arms. His mouth met Tomas's and gently probed his apart. His tongue wandered inside and masturbated against his husband's. His hands claimed flesh, and they moved over hot Greek skin and slid over

Tomas's ass and between his legs, pushing against his ball sack, making him thrust forward. Roger repeated the motion before moving his hand around to the front, joining them together, claiming Tomas's manhood for his own.

Rolling Tomas over, he traced kisses down his spine to his butt, plying the fleshy taut globes until receiving a groan and a buck upward.

Tomas grasped the sheets and spread his legs, his ass in the air. He couldn't wait for Roger to enter, but Roger was taking his time, and it was driving him nuts.

Roger played until he was ready. Spreading Tomas's legs, he lay between them, using his knees to keep them where he wanted them. Slowly, his hands, then mouth, made their way up Tomas's body. Up the long, strong spine, over the masculine well-muscled shoulders, and along bulging biceps until his hands found their way onto his lover's. Fingers laced through fingers, and he tightened his grip as his mouth did damage at the base of his husband's neck.

"Oh, God," Tomas breathed in and out rapidly. "Roger…"

Slowly sliding one knee up at a time, spreading Tomas's legs apart and up until they were almost like frogs joining, he entered from behind.

Tomas's eyes flew open as Roger moved inside of him. "Oh, God." His muscles tightened around Roger and his fingers spread out in reflex. He flung his head back and gasped for air. "Oh, God."

Roger settled, feeling the tight muscles around him. A home he could count on. A home that welcomed him anytime. His face was beside his lover's, breathing the same air as they gently thrust in slow motion. Fingers gripped fingers, legs spread further, bodies moved back and forth in unison until the final explosion overtook them, making them collapse as one.

*****

Gardo groaned. His body swelled with lust and desire and throbbed its way back and forth on top of the woman beneath him. His cock pulsated in double time as it grew longer in the warmth of the woman he loved. Another groan. A thrust. His hands explored the body, plentiful round breasts, long supple legs, fingers that did damage up and down his spine.

"Giancarlo," she whispered. "I love you…"

"Oh," another groan, "I love you, Jenny." And with pounding thrusts he bolted home to a thunderous win across the finish line, galloping to a stop as his seed finished flowing into her. The woman he loved.

"Who's Jenny?"

He breathed. "Huh? What?" he mumbled into the ear of his lover, his hands moving up and down her side. His bulky masculine six-foot frame was solid, with a layer of fat over it. While he wasn't in the best shape of his life, as he had been decades before, he could still run like a cop. A cop full of muscles.

"Who's Jenny?"

His eyes finally rose to see Sheila lying beneath him. "What! Ah, huh?" He lifted his head and glanced around the small bedroom of her apartment. "Ah…" He grunted and rolled off, pulling the sheet up. "What'd you say?"

Holding the sheet over herself, she repeated once more. "Who's Jenny? You said her name." Not that she really cared. It's not like they were a couple, just an occasional fuck for recreation.

"Ah…no one." His feet slid to the floor, and he pulled on his shorts and pants. "That was good, but I gotta go." Grabbing his shirt, he shoved his feet into his shoes, not worrying about putting his socks on.

"Not a problem." She picked up her dressing gown and wrapped herself in it. "Is she another lover? I don't mind if she is since we're not…you know."

Gardo snatched his jacket and walked through the tiny living room to the door. "Ah, no, she's not." He adjusted his clothes before putting his trench coat on.

Sheila followed him and stopped in the small hallway. "Just don't drag me into the middle of whatever it is you have with her. I don't wanna be having sex with a man in a relationship."

He finally glanced at her. While Sheila Manning wasn't his type, he'd found himself drawn to her after dealing with a crime in her building. Like him, she was alone and in need of some company from the opposite sex. And that's all it was. Sex. That's all it ever had been on the odd occasion when he felt lonely. She wasn't a prize catch or anything, but she was homely and accommodating. *Very* accommodating as it turned out. He had no problem getting inside her with his thick stump. Definitely not a long bow like the Stephanopoulos boys, but he had the width, and, apparently, that was all that counted, bringing Sheila to orgasm every time they fucked. All he had to do was find his way inside, and before he'd slid right in, she was moaning and groaning and writhing under him as if she was having an epileptic fit, moaning his name, or biting her tongue. And he liked a bit of tongue around his stump of a cock. She knew how to get her mouth around it, while her tongue went to work on him, making him rise, tormenting him to come. And come he did, and take it *she* did. No, Sheila Manning may not have been a prize worth fighting for, but she was certainly good for fucking when the need arose, and the need had been rising a lot lately. Since the lovely Jenny with the blue eyes had come to town, he had to plant it somewhere, and since he couldn't plant it in Jenny, he had to find other accommodations. So Sheila was it. And she was always good for it.

"I'm not in a relationship," he finally said. "It's just…I've met someone, but she's taken and I…" His gaze wandered.

"Married?"

"What?" He looked at her.

"Is she married?" She leant against the hallway wall, staring at him curiously.

He blinked. "Yes."

"Have you had sex?" Sheila was intrigued. In the whole time she had known him, and been screwing him, he'd never called her by another name. Or thought of anyone else while they were doing it.

"No," he said gruffly. "She's married. Nothing's happened."

"But you want something to happen?" She inched closer.

"What? No…yes…I don't know." His gruff frown was in place,

matching his tone.

"Oh, yes, you do," Sheila came back. "You called me Jenny while we were having sex. Is that her name? Jenny?"

Gardo frowned harder, his nostrils flared, and he huffed. "Her name is none of your business, and I'll thank you to not repeat it or ask any more questions. I'll see you…whenever." He stepped through the doorway into the hall. "I'll call."

Sheila watched him storm down the hall and into the stairwell. For several floors, she heard the stomp of his gait as he barged down the stairs. She closed and locked the door and took another shower. While she enjoyed sex with him, for what it was, she sometimes felt the need for a shower afterwards.

Soaping herself, she thought about their time. He'd been better, more loving. His hands had done things they'd never done before. He'd *kissed her* as he'd never done before, and if that was from meeting a woman who happened to be married, then she hoped he never actually had sex with this Jenny person otherwise she'd go without. "Mmm," she murmured. "I wonder who this Jenny is."

*****

It was Sunday, the fourth of December, and Jenny was in her element. She'd had a massive Christmas tree delivered the day before along with boxes of decorations she'd picked out during the week. She'd waited until her husband was there to bring the family together to decorate.

"A little to the left," she called out as Spiros and the boys wrangled the ten-foot tree. "Tilt it right…there…nearly…okay…there." She eyed the tree from different sides as her boys huffed and puffed. "Perfect. Now, make sure it's stable so it doesn't fall over." It was going to be set in the corner of the living room once it had been decorated.

While Jenny had always done the tree early in Australia and then Mykonos, she didn't mind being behind schedule this time.

"All set, Mama," Carlos called, backing out from under the tree. He stood and brushed off his hands.

Viv laughed from her seat on the couch near the fireplace.

"What's so funny?" he asked her.

"You have a tree coming out of your hair," she replied, watching while he frowned, then ran a hand through his hair, disentangling small branches and leaves.

"Carlos, don't make a mess," Jenny chastised, opening a box of tinsel. "Who wants to wrap the tinsel?"

"Oooh, me." Angie clapped her hands in excitement. It had been nearly a decade since she'd celebrated any kind of Christmas as her father didn't bother with decorations after her mother died.

"Here's a big one for you." Jenny pulled a red and green twenty-foot piece from the box. "Start at the bottom and work your way up."

Angie took the tinsel and excitedly started around the tree, giggling like a child as she went. She grabbed another piece when Jenny handed it to her, but needed Pedro's help to wrap it around the top.

He lifted her, and carried her around the tree so she could wrap it. When she was done, he lowered her, kissing her on the way down.

She giggled and kissed him back.

"We don't have any mistletoe," Tomas told them, hanging balls on the tree.

"Who needs mistletoe?" Pedro quipped, kissing his wife once more before nipping at her neck.

"Pedro." She giggled harder, wrapping her arms around him. This was not only her first Christmas with her husband, but with a real family as well.

Jenny glanced at her, and her smile grew wider. *Aw, my babies are happy,* she thought, looking to Tomas and Roger hanging decorations, to Viv and Carlos sitting on the couch drinking tea. Yes, her babies were happy and so was she. Spiros came to her side, slid an arm around her waist, and kissed her on the cheek. She relished in her husband's love. It nourished her down to her soul. Turning her face so he could plant one on her mouth, she kissed him back before putting her arm around his strong shoulders. "Love you," she whispered, gazing into his eyes.

Pulling her into his arms, he kissed her again. "I love you, Jenny

Stephanopoulos."

Putting her other arm around his neck they kissed again, growing deeper and more passionate before hearing awkward groans from their sons.

"Ew, Mama, Papa, save it for later," Pedro complained, digging around in the decorations boxes. He found reindeer ornaments and handed two to Angie.

"Why should we?" Spiros asked, not leaving his wife's embrace. "We have to watch the three of you kiss your partners. Why are we not allowed to kiss ours?"

"Because you're Mama and Papa," Carlos said looking up from his seat on the couch. "Parents don't kiss."

"Or have sex," Tomas muttered under his breath.

Roger heard and laughed. "Poor T," he said to his husband. "How do you think you were made?"

"Ew, Roger, stop it. I don't want to think about my parents having sex." Tomas hung a fat Santa on the tree and adjusted it so the branch didn't slant.

Roger slid his arms around his husband and nibbled his ear. "But you obviously got your talents from somewhere, so it had to come from your father, and your mother clearly knows a good thing when *she's on it.*"

Tomas looked at Roger in horror. *"How could you say that?"*

Roger snickered. "Come on, T. You and your brothers all have huge cocks. It had to come from your father, and *he clearly* knows how to please your mother."

"No, no, no, don't wanna hear." Tomas stuck his fingers in his ears and went to get more decorations.

"And why shouldn't we kiss!" Jenny exclaimed at Carlos's remarks. "You and Pedro will be parents. Are you going to stop kissing Viv and Angie?" She watched his puzzled expression. "If you say parents shouldn't kiss then you won't be kissing Viv come this time next year."

"Yeah, but…" Carlos started, unsure of where to go next.

"Ha! Knew it! You never have a valid argument to back up what you say," Jenny said. "Carlos was always like that, Viv. Loves saying people shouldn't do things and yet does them himself. And when told that would mean he'd have to give it up, he'd baulk and have no comeback." She handed over more decorations. "Want to decorate? We have stockings and decorative scenes for the fireplace mantel. I want to do the whole apartment, not just the living room."

Viv relinquished her seat, and took a Santa in his sleigh with nine reindeer and placed it on the mantel. "I don't know the last time I decorated for Christmas."

"Do you not celebrate it?" Jenny asked, pulling a dancing Santa from a box.

"I do. I just think I couldn't be bothered if I was the only one there. And for many years I celebrated in a different country for photo shoots, so I never got around to it."

"It will be different now with a baby." Jenny pulled out embroidered stockings. "Once you have kids, Christmas becomes a whole different entity. You'll be decorating, making biscuits in the shape of trees and Santas. There'll be paper flying everywhere as fat little fingers rip at it to get to what's inside, and then they won't even care what's inside because they'll play with the wrapping instead."

"Did Carlos have fat little fingers?" Viv asked, picking up a box.

"He certainly did." Jenny opened the lid on the box to reveal the balls to Viv. They were labelled like the stockings.

Viv's eyes went wide as she saw one with her name on it.

"Pedro and Tomas didn't; their fingers were small, but Carlos was a fat little porker when he was little." Jenny hid her grin unsuccessfully.

"Mama!" Carlos exclaimed in horror.

"I'll show you later," Jenny went on, ready to tease her sons. "I brought the baby albums with me."

"What!" three manly voices rang out in alarm.

Jenny looked at each of her stunned sons. "Oh, yes. I brought your baby albums to show your wives and husband. I didn't get a chance in Mykonos. I was busy planning your weddings."

"I can't wait to see fat little Carlos then." Viv laughed. "He definitely grew out of it."

Jenny looked at her scowling son affectionately. "He did. Took a few years, but by the time he was ten he was lean and mean." She looked around at the decorations left. The dining, kitchen and sitting area were done. A small tree had gone into the bedroom, and she'd had pre-decorated trees delivered to the other apartments the day before, so no one went without. "We just have the balls, the star, and the stockings to go, so let's start from the top of the family. Spiros, come and get your ball."

Spiros wandered over and picked up his gold glittered ball from the box. Jenny followed suit. Standing on a small ladder, they placed their balls at the top of the tree side by side. With a smile and a kiss, they turned for Carlos and Viv.

"You two are next." Jenny held the box out to them. "Not quite a quarter way down." She watched them take their green glittered balls and place them under hers and Spiros's.

"It was so nice of your mother to add my name to the set," Viv murmured to Carlos.

He kissed her temple in return. "Why wouldn't she? You're family now. You deserve a bauble."

Viv smiled in return and stepped back to look at the tree.

"Tomas and Roger." Jenny carried the box over to them.

Roger teared up. "Thanks for including me, Mrs S. I haven't celebrated Christmas with my family for ten years or so. And the last couple were with the Seralifts." He picked up his ball to see it matched Tomas's; red with glitter and his name emblazoned across it.

Jenny laid a hand on his arm. "No more. No more Christmases with the bloody Seralifts. No more without family. You have a family now. Us. And I expect you to spend every Christmas at home with us. That's the one rule we have for our boys. You spend birthdays, Mothers and Father's Day, and Christmas and New Year's at home, and the rest of the time you can do what you want."

"Unless I'm working." Pedro pulled a face. "I have Christmas home, but not New Year's."

"Then we'll come to you," Jenny told him. "We will *not* spend this year apart, especially after what's happened in the past few months."

They waited for Tomas and Roger to place their balls and kiss, arms around each other. Tomas laid his head on Roger's shoulder, a soft smile on his lips.

"All right, you two love birds, out of the way." Pedro took his blue glitter ball and hung it under his brother's. "Angie."

Angie glanced down at the blue glitter ball in the box, unable to pick it up as tears flowed silently down her cheeks.

Jenny saw them and put an arm around the girl's shoulders. "You're a part of the family now," she said quietly. "You get a Christmas ball as the same applies to you. You're a member of the family. *We* are your family."

Angie heard the words spoken so gently and lovingly that she cried harder and buried her head in Jenny's shoulder.

Jenny handed the box to Pedro and took Angie into her arms to let her sob. "It's been hard for you," Jenny soothed. "So hard. And so much has happened this year. *To* you, *for* you. You left home and moved halfway around the world. Started school, became pregnant, got married, and now you're back in New York celebrating a Christmas you wouldn't normally be celebrating."

Spiros silently went to Jenny's side and put his arms around them both, tears in his own eyes. He kissed his wife and then kissed the top of Angelina's head, making her cry harder.

Pedro teared up. It was hard seeing his wife so emotional. Part of him knew why, but he hadn't lost his parents, so would never fully understand.

Jenny looked up to see Tomas and Roger beside Pedro, and Carlos and Viv beside them. All teary-eyed, wiping their faces and sniffing, arms around each other. Sarah and Matthew were right there with them. "You've had it hardest of all," she continued softly. "You lost your mother when you were young, and have now lost your father at eighteen. You have no siblings, no parents, no family of your own blood. You have it hardest of all of us." She stroked Angie's long shiny hair.

"I'm all alone," Angie sobbed, unable to control her tears, feeling pain and loneliness like never before.

"No, you're not. Not anymore," Jenny soothed. "You now have

parents who will look after you. You have a husband who will love you and support you in everything you do. You have brothers who will protect you." She looked up to see Tomas, Roger and Carlos tearfully nod. "And you have a sister to look up to." She saw Viv put her hand to her chest and try to control her tears. "And you have grandparents that look after all of us."

"Of course we will." Sarah sobbed into her hanky.

"See, you have more than enough family now," Jenny went on, rubbing her cheek against Angie's soft hair. "You have more than enough family to go around. You're not alone, Angie, not anymore." She gently pulled back and looked into Angie's tear stained face. "From this year, from this Christmas, you are not alone anymore. You have us." She wiped her daughter's face. "You have family… Okay?"

Angie rasped in a breath. "Yes." She breathed heavily trying to calm herself down. But it didn't work. As she looked from Jenny and Spiros to Sarah and Matthew, Carlos and Viv, Tomas and Roger, and finally her husband, who was openly crying himself, fresh tears poured forth.

"Now, now, no more of that," Jenny told her, pointing to the box in Pedro's hand. "Hang your ball next to Pedro's."

Angie wiped her face and carefully picked up the blue ball from the box, trying not to drop it, and hung it next to her husband's.

Four rows of balls hung down the tree, and now Jenny took the box and offered it to her parents as Angie sought refuge in her husband's arms.

He held on tight and kissed her head.

Sarah and Matthew took their balls and hung them to the right of Jenny's ball before stepping back for the family to admire the handiwork.

Jenny turned more balls over in the box to reveal Spiros's parents and grandparents.

He glanced down and frowned in disbelief. "But you've…"

"*Now* is different," Jenny said, silently imploring her husband. "Times have changed. We need to move on and complete the family tree, until the next generation comes along that is."

Spiros teared up and kissed his wife for the amazing gesture. He took purple balls with his grandparents' names, Giorgio Snr and Stephania, and hung them next to his ball. Then he placed the orange balls with his parent's names, Giorgio Jnr and Katyana, to the left of Carlos and Viv's balls.

There were six balls left out of the box of twenty. Five of them were blank for future grandchildren, but one of them was not. Jenny picked up the lone silver bauble and placed it under Pedro and Angie's balls. Even at home, she had done this. Hung the silver ball at the bottom of the family tree. That's why she'd had a box of them monogrammed, so she would have the tradition of the family placing the balls on the tree while they lived here in New York. And with Viv, Angelina and Roger in the family, she would need to add more balls back home as well, unless she took them all with her. Her lips quivered at the sight of the ball with the name Alena across it, said a small prayer, crossed herself, and stood back.

"Who's—" Viv whispered in her husband's ear, but Carlos cut her off by grabbing her hand and shaking his head. Her eyes widened, and she nodded.

Angie glanced at Pedro, who turned his head to look at Tomas and Carlos, leaving the three new in-laws bewildered by what was happening.

Not that *they* knew. Whenever the boys had asked at Christmas, their father would tell them she was a member of the family that was no longer with them, and to not ask again because it was painful for their mother. But every year when they were kids, they'd ask again, and get the same message. Don't ever ask again, would be said to them by their father. Eventually, they stopped asking, but never stopped wondering who the bauble was for.

Jenny wiped her face. "Okay, who wants to put the star on the tree?"

After a few moments of silence, Angie piped up. "Can I, Mama?"

That brought a smile to Jenny's face. "Of course you can, sweetie. Pedro, help her up the ladder and hang onto her." She removed the star from the box and handed it up to Angie who was being held tightly by Pedro.

Angie reached and stretched and finally popped it on, jamming it down until it didn't move. "How's that?"

"Perfect," Jenny declared. "All that's left are the stockings. Spiros, would you do the honour of hanging ours?" She picked up the stockings, gold and glittered like their balls. They had sticky hooks attached, so all Spiros had to do was stick them on the edge of the mantel.

"Perfect. Carlos and Viv, here are yours."

They hung their glittery green stockings next in line.

"Tomas and Roger." Jenny handed over sparkling red stockings. "And Pedro and Angie." Handing over the blue stockings to her youngest children she held the last one, a silver glittered stocking, and became overwhelmed. It was never filled on Christmas Day and never would be, but it had to be hung anyway. Holding it to her mouth for a moment to kiss it, she hung it at the end of the mantel in line behind the others and stepped back. Taking a deep breath, and swiping at the tears rolling down her face, she said, "Well, that's it. Everything is done." She quickly packed up the boxes. "Boys, can you pop all of these into the office for now? I'll find a place to store them later." They gathered the boxes, casting curious glances her way, and took them into the office.

"Who's Alena?" Roger asked quietly, placing his boxes on the desk.

"We don't know," Carlos replied. "And we were told for many years to never ask until we stopped asking."

"We think she's a member of the family that's no longer with us, like our grandparents," Tomas added. "But we don't know."

"Well…isn't it a bit weird then?" Roger went on.

Carlos sighed, hands on hips as he thought about it. "There are a lot of dead people in our family. And now Mama's put Papa's parents and grandparents on the tree."

"She's never done that before," Pedro said, crossing his arms.

"But our great-grandfather was in our lives the last few weeks of *his* life, so maybe because there *has* been so much loss she added them…for Papa," Tomas told them.

Carlos muttered, "You may be right. There has been loss, not just for Angie, but for all of us." He looked at Pedro. "I keep forgetting she's eighteen and still a little girl emotionally. Mama seems to know, though."

"Angie's…" Pedro thought for a moment. "Very adult and mature and strong. It's just that with everything happening at the same time it's hitting her in waves and hitting her hard. Being pregnant, eighteen, married *and* losing her father has been tough for her. And it's been rough all around."

Carlos sighed and ran a hand through his hair, finding another piece of tree. "Yeah. It would be. Come on, let's get back before they think we're lost." He led the way back into the warmth of the living room.

"Now that the tree's finished can you boys push it back into the corner?" Jenny asked. The tree would be in the corner of the room, to the right of the fireplace against the wall to the office. The boys groaned. "Don't complain." A frown crossed her forehead. "You're all big, strong, Greek Australian men, you can do it," she encouraged and watched Carlos direct Tomas under the tree to push the base.

With a protest, Tomas crawled under the tree and pushed the tub it was sitting in, while the others gently pushed on the thick branches in the middle.

"Stop there," Jenny called. "That's perfect." Springing around, she checked each table, couch, window, and desk to make sure all were decorated. She marvelled at how much the stores were selling and had brought everything. And with three weeks to go, Christmas would be here before they knew it.

"When are the presents going under?" Pedro jumped onto the couch beside Angie.

"Not until Christmas Eve as usual," Jenny reminded him. "So make sure to get all of your shopping done before then so you can come up and put them under. You have all done your shopping?"

Ums and ahs went around the children.

"Oh, for goodness sake. Haven't you even started your shopping?" Jenny asked them.

"Well…" Carlos started.

"Sort of," Tomas added.

"Nope!" Pedro ended the sentence.

Jenny shook her head. "My boys. Marriage has not changed you one little bit."

After a delicious meal of roast chicken and vegetables with pudding for dessert, they sat around the fireplace talking Christmas, their plans for the next three weeks, and munching on Christmas biscuits.

Jenny and Spiros had the couch facing the window with Angelina and Pedro snuggled up next to them. Roger, Tomas, Viv and Carlos had the couch facing the fire, and Sarah and Matthew had the couch facing Jenny.

"So, what's everyone's plan for the next three weeks? Because you are all going to be here Christmas Eve and Christmas Day," Jenny said.

"I have some photo shoots to get done before the new year and an ad to film…so I'll be busy." Viv was comfortably squashed between Carlos and Tomas.

"And Christmas shopping?" Jenny asked.

"I've done most of it. Just have to get a few extra things," Viv replied.

"Boys." Jenny turned to Roger and Tomas. "What are your plans?"

"We're meeting up with some friends who are in town," Roger said. "We ran into them the other night at 69. They'll be in town another week, so we'll go to a party or two with them. Other than that, just getting out and seeing the city as we have been."

"Got your shopping done?" Jenny asked.

"Well…" Roger looked at Tomas. "Except for you guys I have no one to buy for, so we're trying to come up with original ideas for presents."

"Will you be calling your family?" Jenny asked, nibbling on a green tree biscuit.

Roger looked from her to Tomas and back and shrugged. "*You* are my family."

Tomas took his hand and smiled, snuggling into his chest. He was so beyond happy that he had found Roger, and now with them being married and all together as a family, it made his heart sing at how well his lover had been accepted into the family as another son.

Jenny smiled at the happiness radiating from her son as he sat in his husband's arms, curled up under a blanket. She shifted her attention to Angelina, who was snuggled under her arm, and her baby boy. "I know you two are busy with school and work, but how are you managing?"

Spiros had his left arm around his wife's shoulders and knew Angelina meant more to Jenny than just as a daughter-in-law. He had watched her face during the hanging of the balls and stockings and knew she was hurting as she did every year. And God how he wished he could change things, but he couldn't. He hurt too, and being the stoic head of the family, had buried his feelings deep inside to keep the rest of the family together while his wife fell apart. But this year she was holding up well, or as well as could be expected, and he knew it was all because Angelina was now in the family.

"I have no idea what to get anyone and Pedro's no help." Angie playfully swatted his hand. "You're useless at coming up with presents."

"He always was." Carlos smirked. "For my birthday one year, he gave me a ticket to some girly movie because he'd been told the girls got naked in it."

Pedro laughed and remembered back. "That's what I was told. How was *I* to know that wasn't the case."

"The fact that it was rated c for children's," Tomas told him. "It was a kids' movie with kid actors, and the girls stripped down to their bathers." He looked at Roger and shook his head in amusement. "Pedro has no idea."

"Well, look, you come up with a list of stuff to buy, and I'll take you shopping either after school or next weekend," Jenny said to Angie. "Since Pedro has no idea about presents, looks like it's up to us girls to get the shopping done. What do you say?" She glanced from Angie to Viv to her mother. "Viv? Mum? Up for Christmas shopping in the next few weeks?"

"Sure," Viv enthused. "Us girls will get the shopping done in no time. As long as it's not when I fly to Hawaii for the ad campaign. But that will only be two days or so." She was happy to be included.

"I've already sent home a whole bunch of presents last month to all the kids and grandkids," Sarah said.

"I hope they arrived safe and unbroken." Jenny remembered back two weeks previously, standing in the post office checking in twenty big boxes of presents.

"So do I," Sarah murmured. "Now I just have to buy for all of you."

"We can get that done next weekend if everyone's free. Roger, want to come along?" She included him in the trip.

"Ah…" He was surprised. "Well, I'm not a girl…"

Jenny laughed. "No, but you're welcome to come as an in-law."

"Oh." He glanced from her to Tomas, thinking about what sort of present he wanted to buy for his lover. "Sure, why not."

"Great, it's settled then. Next weekend is shopping time," Jenny stated.

*****

The following Saturday, the girls and Roger hit up *Macy's* department store.

"Okay, let's get something for the boys." Jenny led them to each floor where they bought books, records, and personal items for their husbands. Since Jenny had already bought Spiros and the boys' presents weeks before, it was more for Roger and the girls, since it was their first Christmas buying for their husbands.

"I want something special," Angie said, looking at the latest jewellery for men. Thick chains, pendants and rings were all the rage, but none of the boys wore jewellery. "Would he wear jewellery?" she asked the group.

"If you bought it for him he would," Jenny said. "What about buying them the same thing? Since they gave each other initialled cufflinks for the weddings, what about initialled tie clips, rings, pendants, or even money clips, wallets, bags. What do the boys use most of all?"

"A bag," Angie thought out loud. "To carry his stuff to work."

"I'm sure we could find a nice leather one for him." Jenny led the way to the men's bag and luggage department where they found beautiful leather totes, briefcases, satchels and carryalls. She eyed the luggage sets proudly displayed against the wall in different leathers and colours. "Just beautiful," she murmured, thinking about the ratty suitcase Spiros had used to come over. "That reminds me, I'd better take Spiros clothes shopping for new suits and casual wear."

"Found one," Angie called out, holding up a beautiful black leather satchel bag with a strap so he could sling it over his shoulder.

"Oh, that's lovely," Jenny breathed, fingering the soft buttery material.

"It has a couple of pockets on the outside for his keys and stuff, and," Angie opened it wide, "two segments and a small pocket on the inside. I think it will even fit some records. It's big enough, isn't it?"

"Should be," Viv said, wondering if she should get Carlos a bag as well.

"I think I'll get it." Angie went off to pay for the bag.

Roger was looking at overnight bags before moving on to luggage. "I wonder if I should get him one of these," he murmured, touching a black leather doctor's style bag. But Jenny had his arm and directed him over to the satchels.

"I think this would be perfect." She pointed to a deep brown carryall satchel style bag with gold buckles and two outside pockets. "It's different to the one Angie's getting, so you won't be copying, and he can use it for training."

Roger picked up the bag and studied it. "It is beautiful. The stitching and workmanship are divine."

"Yes, it is," Jenny agreed. "Get it."

Roger nodded, thinking some more. "Okay, I will." He joined Angie at the counter while Jenny helped Viv.

"Found anything?" she asked.

"I'm not sure if he even needs a bag." Viv sighed. "But I'm looking at the two of these, and I can't decide which one." She pointed to dark blue and dark green bags. "They're both leather, both Italian made, and are all the latest rage in Paris and London, and now they're here in New York."

Jenny touched them both, checked inside, and stood back. "The blue. Come on." She grabbed Viv's hand while Viv grabbed the blue bag and they went up to the counter. "Hello again," she said to the assistant. "We would like to get all three of these bags monogrammed. Can you do that by next weekend?" Pointing to all three bags on the counter, she waited.

"Of course," the assistant said, and pulled out an order form book. She took all three orders and packed the bags into shopping bags, then stuck the orders on the bags. "These will be picked up Monday, and they should be done by the end of the week."

"That's wonderful," Jenny said. "They'll be ready to be wrapped and placed under the tree." After paying for the bags, everyone finished off their shopping with lunch at a local restaurant ten storeys up and overlooking the river.

"Having the boys' bags monogrammed was a brilliant idea, Jenny," Viv said over a warm vegetable salad. "And the blue will set off his eyes."

"That's why I picked it," Jenny replied, spearing a piece of salmon. "When in doubt, pick blue no matter what it is. For Pedro, pick black or white, and for Tomas, black, white or a dark brown. It all depends on what it is."

"You clearly know your sons well," Roger told her before inhaling a forkful of pasta.

"I've been doing it for nearly twenty-five years, so I've had some practice." Jenny laughed. "Have you finished off your lists?"

"Not quite." Angie finished off her linguine. "Just two more to go and that's it." She had been discussing with Pedro, her brothers, and Viv all week about what to get for Jenny and Spiros and Sarah and Matthew. Being a newcomer to the family, she had no idea what would be an appropriate gift for her new mother and father-in-law, or her new grandparents.

Viv had been having the same issue, and Carlos had been of no help. All the boys had ever given them was perfume and aftershave, the same ones year after year, right on cue as if like clockwork. But she'd suggested getting away from that now everyone had money. They could afford to spend a little more and buy something extravagant for their parents. That had left the boys perplexed, and the girls even more so.

"There are only two weeks left until Christmas Eve, so if you want to get it all out of the way and wrapped, then I'd suggest finishing it off today or next weekend." Jenny called for the bill. It had been quite a year with so much going on, and even she had been a little baffled as to what to buy her children and in-laws. But after a chat with her sons and thinking about what kind of life they were now leading, she'd come up with an easy solution, for this Christmas anyway. She had birthdays and next Christmas to think about, and by then the grandchildren would be along, and it would all be *very* different.

They gathered their things and went down to the car, stopping at a few boutiques and stores on the way home where everyone went their separate ways.

*****

Sheila walked into the office of Maurice Blackborn on Tuesday evening and sat down in front of his desk, waiting until he finished his phone call.

"Ah, Sheila...I have good news for you. I have located the heirs of the Papadopoulos and Poulos fortunes. And they are here in New York."

Sheila's brows rose. "I knew Andros's daughter was here, it was just a matter of finding her."

"Yes," the greasy slicked-back man across from her said. "But you might be shocked to find out *who* inherited the Papadopoulos estate and how the two are related, *and* where they are."

Her heartbeat sped up. "Are they both here in New York?" Leaning forward, she eagerly awaited his reply. She was closer to getting her payday.

"Yes...they are," Maurice hissed. "As you know, Angelina Poulos inherited Andros Poulos's estate. With your son dead, may his soul rest in peace, that left her the only heir to the fortune. Now," he licked his lips and leaned forward, "she is back in New York and is married to Pedro Stephanopoulos. They moved out of their old apartment and into a fancy new one on 5th Avenue."

Sheila felt her insides start to boil. "Little Miss Thing is living in a 5th Avenue apartment, and I have to live in a cruddy little hole in Harlem. How dare she."

"Yes," Maurice said. "How *dare* she. Except she's not renting it, she's just living in it, for you would not believe the fabulous twist I'm about to tell you."

Sheila leant forward. "Tell me, Mr Blackborn."

"Well," he went on. "It seems that while Stefano Papadopoulos was once Andros's stepfather, making him Luiz's ex-step-grandfather. Papadopoulos had long divorced Andros's mother. That means he was not, nor were his heirs, entitled to the Papadopoulos estate. However," he excitedly fidgeted in his seat, "Stefano Papadopoulos was the son-in-law of Giorgio Stephanopoulos…" He let the news sink in.

"Stephanopoulos?" Sheila frowned. "As in…"

"Yes," Maurice hissed louder. "Upon Stefano's death, his estate went to his legal heirs, since his wife had died and they had not divorced, that meant his father-in-law Giorgio Stephanopoulos, and his nephew Spiros Stephanopoulos, plus *his* wife and three sons inherited the estate. However…" He shifted through some papers. "All the papers I went through, and all the lawyers I talked to, said that the Papadopoulos estate went to one person. Would you like to guess who that is?"

"Well, obviously one of the Stephanopoulos family." Sheila was confused, trying to take in all the information.

"Yes, it was one member and one member only," Maurice continued. "A Mrs *Jenny* Stephanopoulos."

Jenny! The name alarmed Sheila. *Jenny* Stephanopoulos. Was she the Jenny that Giancarlo had called out for when they'd been together? She recalled the stories she'd kept about Andros's death and how Gardo had taken off in pursuit of Pedro's kidnapper, who turned out to be one of Stefano's men. So, had he met her while she was here?

"Wait, you said they were both in town. Jenny Stephanopoulos is here, in New York?"

"Oh, yes." Maurice greedily rang up the dollar signs in his head. "She flew the whole family over to New York weeks ago. Pedro and his new bride Angelina, who is back at school, Carlos and his lovely supermodel wife," he licked his lips creepily, "Vivian Villiers, and the fag son and his lover slash fake husband. She rented an apartment block for them, and as I also found out, just recently *bought it for the whole family.* The husband, Spiros, arrived last week. Plus, she has her parents with her."

"She *bought* an apartment building." Sheila was astounded. "On *5th Avenue!* But…that…must have cost…" She seethed deep down inside. Here was Jenny fucking Stephanopoulos spending *her* money, living in and buying a building on 5th-fucking-Avenue, and *she* was going without.

"Two and a half million." Maurice filled in the blanks.

"What?" Sheila's eyes went wide. "What!"

"She paid two and a half million for that whole building," Maurice repeated.

"But that could have been mine," Sheila yelled. "*That bitch* is spending *my money.*"

"Exactly." Maurice sat back in his seat. "That's why we must act now. I've already drafted up the paperwork demanding ten million dollars from each of them and the estates they inherited."

"Ten million each?" Sheila went quiet. "Twenty million?"

"Isn't that a nice round sum?" Maurice's smile was at its smarmiest. "Now, when do you want the papers delivered? This week, so they give in to our demands? Or right before Christmas, so they freak out all holiday season?" His fingers tapped against each other in delight.

"Serve them this week," Sheila told him. "I want that money now. I don't want to be slumming in my rat hole of an apartment when they're living it up on 5th-fucking-Avenue. Serve her first thing in the morning, Mr Blackborn. *I want my money.*"

The wheels turned in his head. "Your wish is my command, Ms Manning."

*****

On Wednesday morning, Jenny received a call from Brewster in the lobby. "Ma'am, there's a man here who says he needs to see you. Says he's a lawyer."

"A lawyer? Mmm, I'll be right down, Mr Brewster, thank you." She put the phone down and glanced at Spiros's curious face. "A lawyer is here to see me."

"I'll come down with you." Spiros stood up from a couch in the sitting area, and they went down to the lobby.

"Mr Brewster," Jenny called upon entering the lobby.

"Ah, Mr and Mrs Stephanopoulos. This is Maurice Blackborn, *the lawyer.*" He eyed the man suspiciously, and cast dubious glares back and forth between the lawyer and his boss.

Jenny faced the intruder. Tall, slim, greasy, with an even greasier smile. "Mr Blackborn, what can I do for you?"

"Well, for a start, I also need to see your daughter-in-law, Angelina Poulos."

"Angelina *Stephanopoulos* is at school. We can let her know about your visit later," Jenny firmly told him.

Maurice eyed the two of them, gauging their place in the relationship. Spiros stood quietly while Jenny did the talking. *She's definitely in charge of the family,* he thought. "I have some paperwork for the two of you." He pulled two envelopes from his inside coat pocket. "One for *Ms Poulos,* one for you." Handing them over, he watched Jenny take them slowly and suspiciously. "I have a client who believes they are due a part of the Papadopoulos and Poulos estates, so we have filed a claim for them." He watched Jenny's eyes narrow and Spiros frown. "Unless, of course, you're willing to settle out of court and pass on a chunk of those estates."

"I'm not willing to do *anything* you suggest, Mr Blackborn," Jenny said and saw his frown appear. "I will look at these papers and consult with a lawyer about them. Only *then* will you get a reply."

Maurice's face fell. "A lawyer?" His eye twitched. "I would have thought it was a reasonable request."

"It could well be, Mr Blackborn. But considering you've just foisted these papers upon me, and I haven't even read them yet, I'm not handing anything over. I'll make sure Angelina gets her papers. Good day, Mr Blackborn. Mr Brewster, show our guest out." They watched Brewster force Maurice through the door before the elevator doors closed.

"I didn't think anyone had a claim on the estates," Jenny said to Spiros.

"Neither did I," he replied.

They barely made it into the suite before Jenny ripped her envelope open. Reading the paper, she nodded her head a few times and then frowned. "Ten million dollars!" she exclaimed. "What the!"

"What! Who is it?" Spiros stood before her.

Jenny sighed in frustration. "Sheila Manning, mother of Luiz Manning, is suing the Papadopoulos estate for the death of her son. I can understand that," Jenny told him. "I would probably do the same, but she wants *ten million dollars* for it."

"Probably that greasy lawyer put that amount into her head."

Jenny ripped open Angie's envelope and read the paperwork. "Oh, listen to this," she huffed. "Sheila is *also* suing the Poulos estate for not only back child support from Andros, but *twenty-five years' worth* of it, plus money for herself all in the amount of…guess what? *Ten million dollars.*" She stalked around the penthouse. "I can understand that she lost her son and wants to be compensated for it, but *ten million dollars*…from *both* of us! That's just…" She slumped onto a couch. "That is *way* too much."

Spiros sat beside her. "What do you want to do?"

Sighing, Jenny thought about it. "I have no problem giving her money. Stefano's man did kill her son. But *not* ten million dollars."

"Fair enough." Spiros nodded. "What about Angelina?"

Jenny looked at him. "She's not going to be able to deal with this, especially the stress."

"But she's being sued too. She'll have to be told."

Jenny thought some more. "We *will* tell her and then *I'll* make the decision. But before that, there's some information we need."

"Like what?"

"Like *who* Sheila Manning is, *really*. And what happened with Andros."

"And how will you find out?"

Jenny went through a mental list of people she knew. "There's only one I can think of." She ran to the kitchen and looked through the tin she put bits and pieces in. After finding the business card, she ran back to the phone and made a call.

"Gardo."

"Detective Gardo, Jenny Stephanopoulos. How are you?"

He cleared his throat, surprised that she had called. "Good, good, and you?"

"Not so good I'm afraid. Something has happened, and I need to know if you can help me sort through it."

"Of course, if I can." Gardo warmed through to the cockles of his heart. Jenny with the blue eyes was calling him for help.

"I need to know exactly what happened with Andros and my son and daughter-in-law and, if possible, Tomas and Luiz."

"Ah, well." He cleared his throat again. "I'd have to ring Miami for that, but I could do that for you."

"Would I be able to see the files?" Jenny asked in her sweetest voice.

"Mmm, well...I couldn't allow you to *see* them, but...you could come to the station and I could answer all your questions."

"Okay, that would be wonderful. When would be the best time to come down?"

"Give me a half hour, and I should have the information from Miami."

"Excellent. I'll be there shortly to see you," Jenny told him and hung up.

Half an hour later, she was standing outside the police station feeling a little nervous. Entering the building, she saw officers hustling along corridors with people in cuffs. As she looked for the desk to ask directions, an officer stopped her. "Oh, Officer Burns, how nice to see you," Jenny greeted him.

"Mrs Stephanopoulos." Burns had been surprised to see her standing there looking frazzled, and his heart had warmed instantly. "It's very nice to see you. What are you doing here?"

"I've come to visit Detective Gardo about Andros Poulos and whether he could get me some information on Tomas's case."

"Oh." He deflated a little. "Well, he's up on the third floor."

"And how do I get there?" Jenny asked, glancing around for stairs or an elevator.

"I'll escort you," Burns offered and held an arm out in the direction of the stairs.

"Oh, that's very kind of you, Officer Burns," Jenny replied.

On the way up they chatted. "And how have you been Mrs Stephanopoulos?" he asked.

"Very well," Jenny said. "All of my children are together, my husband's here, everything is fantastic."

"That's good." Burns felt the warm feeling leave him. Of course, he knew there would never be anything between him and Jenny, but it hadn't stopped him finding her attractive and warm and welcoming. He stepped onto the third-floor landing outside the detective division. "Go through, his office is on the right side at the back."

"Thank you so much, Officer Burns," Jenny said and walked through the room to Gardo's office. "Detective." She found him staring out the window.

He spun around. "Mrs Stephanopoulos. Please have a seat." He waited for her to seat herself, taking in her red pantsuit and matching turtleneck with a jet-black fur coat. Sitting, he shuffled the paperwork in front of him. "You're looking well, Mrs Stephanopoulos."

"Oh, please, call me Jenny," she told him. "And I'm fine, thank you."

"Ah…" He stared into the blue eyes that had so captured him and blinked. "Um…" he faltered. "Now, you know I can't let you read the file, but I can tell you whatever you want to know Mrs…ah…Jenny…" He blushed.

"What I want to know is the timeline and the people involved in the case. And from Tomas's case, I want to know about Luiz."

Gardo arched a brow. "Why Luiz?"

"He was the illegitimate son of Andros Poulos, and so half-brother to my daughter-in-law Angelina. At one stage, they were related to Stefano Papadopoulos since he was Andros's stepfather at one time. I've inherited the Papadopoulos estate and Angelina the Poulos estate. So I want to know about Luiz."

"Mmm." He wondered why she was interested, but trolled through the paperwork. "Luiz Manning was twenty-five, born in New York to…Sheila Manning…" his voice trailed off. *She never told me she had a kid!* he thought, hesitating before reading on silently.

"Detective," Jenny called, wondering what he was thinking, or what was so bad.

"Huh!" Gardo snapped out of it. "Oh, sorry…Jenny…born to Sheila Manning. Kicked out of home at the age of seventeen, worked for *Seralift Productions* for a few years before hooking up with Bertha St John, ending up in Mykonos and obsessed with your son."

Jenny took a few deep breaths. "Yes, something I hated. Detective, you mentioned his mother, Sheila Manning, what do you know about her?"

His eyes narrowed. "Why would I know anything about her?"

Jenny was surprised by his sudden change of tone. "Well, you have the papers in front of you. Isn't there anything about her in them? Or maybe you've come across her before?"

He leant back in his seat. "What is she to you, Mrs…ah…Jenny? Have you been in contact with her? Has she done something to you?" If Sheila had been anywhere near his Jenny, he'd kill her.

Jenny thought for a moment, then pulled the papers from her bag. "Angelina and I received these today from a lawyer." She handed them over, and he read through them, shaking his head in disbelief.

What the fucking hell is she doing? he thought, seeing the ten million dollars written on the papers. "Jesus," he finally said. "Not making it easy."

"I understand she may want compensation," Jenny said. "And I understand she's upset at losing her son. But ten million for it is utterly ridiculous." She wrung her hands in her lap. "I told the lawyer I'd contact my own lawyer and look at my options, but in the meantime, I wanted to learn more about Luiz and find out what the chain of events was. I need to know more."

Gardo walked around his desk to lean against it next to Jenny. "Well…it seems you already know the family tree on the male side. You know Luiz is Andros's son, and I'm sorry your family was put through hell because of Andros and Papadopoulos. Ah…" he paused. "I don't have children, but…ah…if my youngest was set up by his girlfriend's father I'd have a problem too."

Jenny smiled up at him. "It's such a pity you never found love again, Detective. But maybe you still will. Now, about Luiz's mother… Do you know what sort of woman she is?"

He shifted uncomfortably, uncrossing and recrossing his legs. "No, but I'm sure if she kicked him out she had a reason."

"Yes, I suppose so," Jenny muttered. "I guess I shouldn't be surprised by being sued. Although we never thought it would be by anyone other than potential heirs."

"Well, to a degree, Luiz was."

"Yes, but he's also dead. I'm not sure what the legalities of the parents of potential heirs are, dead or otherwise." Glancing around the room, she thought. "Detective…"

"Please, if I can call you Jenny, then please call me Giancarlo," he said gruffly.

Jenny softened. "Giancarlo…would you be able to dig into Sheila Manning for me? Whether she's committed any crimes, or tried suing people before. Simple things like that. I don't need her whole life story, just if she's done anything illegal."

Her deep blue eyes implored him so, and her soft voice had washed over him like warm melted chocolate, heating him to all parts of his body. Of course, he would look into Sheila Manning. Of course, it would be easy as he knew her, and, of course, he could do it for his Jenny with the blue eyes.

*****

On Thursday morning, Jenny made an appointment to see a lawyer for that afternoon. They had decided not to tell Angelina until the weekend, so she would have time to digest it all without worrying about her studies, and because Jenny wanted to get legal advice first. After her meeting with the lawyer, she went back to the penthouse where Spiros was waiting.

"I wish you'd let me come with you," he told her, feeling a little put out. Jenny had been keeping things from him, and that wasn't normal. And he didn't like it.

She sighed and sat down next to him. "You wanted nothing to do with the Papadopoulos estate when I claimed it, remember. It's my responsibility to deal with whatever arises from it."

"And what has arisen?" he asked, looking at his wife's weary face.

Another sigh. "Well, she agreed that Sheila should get something for her son's murder, but isn't sure about back child support. I told her I felt Sheila was owed, but not to the extent of ten million dollars each. I have no problem handing over *some*, but nowhere near that much."

"Can you be taken to court?"

"If I refuse to pay, yes. If I offer a smaller sum, yes, but the court wouldn't necessarily agree because I'd offered something that would cover substantially, then they would have no problem throwing a ten million dollar court case out."

"So, either way, you can be sued?"

Jenny looked at her husband and put her hand over his. "Yes. But I don't plan on being sued."

"How much will you offer?"

"Certainly not ten million," Jenny muttered. "The lawyer's looking into the cost of payments and what not, and will let me know tomorrow how much it would all add up to. Plus, she'll look into compensation for murders and how much families get, so no discussing this around the kids. I don't want them knowing yet, okay."

"You'll have to tell Angelina."

"I know. I plan on doing that this weekend."

*****

On Friday, Jenny received the information from the lawyer and went to pick up the bags that had been monogrammed for the boys. She also received a call from Detective Gardo.

"Giancarlo, how nice to hear from you," Jenny answered.

"Mrs…Jenny," he said down the line. "I ah, have some information on Sheila Manning."

"Oh, good, tell me, is she a criminal?"

Giancarlo shuffled some papers. He'd gone all warm and fuzzy from the sound of her voice saying his name and had lost his train of thought. He finally found the papers on Sheila, surprised at how boring her life really was. "No. She's not."

"Oh." Disappointment rained down on Jenny. "Okay. Has she ever sued anybody?"

"No, she hasn't. She's lived in the same apartment for the last twenty-six years, had the same job for the last twenty-six years. Never caused any trouble, never been involved with anything dodgy. Doesn't own a car, so no tickets, always pays rent and utilities on time. Gets to work on time and knocks off on time."

"She's never been in trouble of *any* kind?"

"Never."

Jenny sighed. "It looks like I can't use anything against her."

"Why would you?" He was intrigued by the line she was taking.

"Well, if she was a criminal who was always suing people then I could use it against her if we went to court. But since there's nothing, I don't have anything to come back at her with. Not that I have a problem with giving her money. Just not *ten million dollars.*"

Giancarlo sighed. As much as he sided with Jenny over this case, he had been giving it to Sheila on the odd occasion and did know her lawyer was as dodgy as they came. "If it's any consolation, her lawyer, Maurice Blackborn, is a sleaze bag."

Jenny's delightful laugh fluttered down the line. "Yes, that's what my lawyer told me when she saw his name on the papers."

"Well…maybe I can dig up something on *him*," Gardo said. "It might help."

"Yes, thank you, Giancarlo, that would be so appreciated. Thank you for your help, goodbye."

The dial tone sounded, but all he heard was the sound of her silky-smooth voice say his name. *Giancarlo…*it whispered. *Giancarlo…*she breathed. Oh, God, he had fallen for a woman he could never have. If only he could, though, it would be beautiful. Her long legs would wrap around his, her arms around his body, her lips under his, and her full firm breasts flattened against his chest. It would be so warm inside of her. So warm and welcoming. Like home. He remembered her perfume and breathed deeply. It still lingered in his office two days later, and it made his mind wander with thoughts of her and how he would make love to her like no man ever had. *Even her husband,* he thought. *Spiros Stephanopoulos can't be that good a husband or father if he raised three arrogant assholes for sons.*

With a sigh, he finally looked down at the papers on his desk. How did he not know Sheila had a son? And how did he not know until he'd read the paperwork from Miami? How the hell did he not know that? *God, I hope Jenny wasn't suspicious when I stopped talking, but I had to get a hold of myself. To find out about the interwoven family tree in Chicago had been one thing, but to find out Luiz was Sheila's son, and to find out in front of Jenny.* "Jesus," he swore. "I need to stop thinking about her. She's married and not available." Chastising himself, he went back to work looking into Maurice Blackborn.

*****

After a chat with her lawyer, Marcy Bendinger, Jenny found out the general cost of child support and compensation for murder. While the cases were few and far between, there had been a few taken to court, but the sums were paltry.

"So the grand total of child support is $27,195 for twenty-one years. The basic rate of compensation for murder is about $25,000, and that's actually high."

"Okay, so together roughly $50,000. If we doubled that and gave her $100,000 each from the estates, would that be sufficient to ward her off, or from being taken to court?" Jenny asked.

"Well, if they turned down $200,000 and *still* sued, I'd say the judge would throw it out. Then they'd lose twice," Marcy said.

"So, offer it and see what happens?"

"You can only try."

"Okay, I'll think about it. Thank you so much, Marcy, bye." Hanging up the phone, she was thoughtful and thankful. Thankful that she had her children, whereas Sheila did not. *So I can understand why she's hurting and wanting compensation.*

Jenny sat back and crossed her legs. *I can't imagine losing my boys, not now, not ever.* It had driven her nuts when Carlos had disappeared and they'd heard nothing. Then Pedro. God, how it had hurt to lose her eldest and her youngest. Tomas hadn't hung around for long, but at least he'd told them of his decision to see the world, and as teary as it had been, she'd let her middle child go. And then to find out what trouble they'd been in and it was all because of bloody Stefano. "Ugh," she groaned. "Bloody bastard."

"Thinking about my ex-uncle again?" Spiros knew Jenny well and knew when things angered her. And always knew exactly what it was.

Another sigh. "If it wasn't for that bastard and his greed, my sons would *not* have gone through what they went through. And now we wouldn't be doing this."

"Well, this is just an after-effect. If Stefano didn't kill Luiz, she might have just sued the estate for back child payments. So, Angelina might still have this trouble. But you wouldn't." He folded the paper he'd been reading, having spent the day at home. For the last week, he had roamed the park and local neighbourhood with Tomas and Roger, getting to know his son-in-law and spending quality time with his son, making sure he knew he was loved and wanted. With Pedro sleeping all day he had no time with him, and Carlos was with Viv running around to her photo shoots, so it was Tomas that had gotten his quality time.

"That's true," Jenny said thoughtfully. "But it's both of us thanks to him, and as the adult, I need to take charge of it."

"And when are you telling Angelina?"

"Tomorrow," Jenny said. "I'm taking the boys shopping after lunch so Pedro can get some sleep, and then telling her after dinner. I'll sit her down and explain it all to her, plus what the lawyer said."

"Do you think she'll understand and go along?"

Jenny looked at her husband's expression. "I don't think she'll get all of the legal talk, but in plain English she'll understand that's she's being sued."

*****

That night, Gardo turned up at Sheila's steaming mad. "How the bloody hell could you do it?" He stormed through the doorway of her apartment after she'd opened the door. "How could you sue Jenny Stephanopoulos and Angelina Poulos for ten million each?" He thrust his hands onto his hips and swung his bulk around to face her. "Who the fucking hell do you think you are, Sheila?"

Scared, Sheila wrapped her robe around her. "A mother who wants compensation for the death of her son. Andros was his father; he's *owed* half of that estate. And they were both once related to Papadopoulos, and his man shot my boy right between the eyes. *So why can't I* sue them for money? My Luiz deserves compensation for what he went through."

"Luiz is dead by his own making," Gardo barked. "That little bastard son of yours killed four men to frame a man, *and* kidnapped Jenny's son from the hospital *after* poisoning him systematically over several weeks. And *you're* suing *her*? That's absolutely ludicrous!"

"Oh, really!" Sheila yelled back. "I don't think it is and Luiz would want me to. Besides, how do you even know I'm suing her?"

"Because she came to me about you." Gardo paced back and forth. "Wanted to know what sort of woman you were, whether you or your dodgy lawyer were criminals because you're suing her. She showed me the papers."

Sheila's jaw dropped. "She what?"

"She rang me up and asked if you were a criminal. Wanted to know more about the timeline with Luiz in Miami and what he did to her son. Wanted to know more about what *his* father did to her youngest and his daughter. Like father like son really." Gardo scowled, and it etched out all the lines on his battle-worn face. *"What the hell have you done, Sheila?* What *the hell* do you think you're doing suing an eighteen-year-old girl for ten million dollars? What *the hell* do you think you're doing suing her *mother-in-law* for ten million dollars?"

"Is *she* the Jenny you moan about in bed?" Sheila caught him out with her question.

"What?" A frown replaced the scowl. "What?"

"Is *she* the Jenny you've been moaning about in bed? The name you say when you're inside me?" Sheila was repulsed by the idea of it being the same Jenny, and yet strangely intrigued at the same time.

A thousand emotions flew over Gardo's face and through his mind. Yes, it was the same Jenny, but he wasn't going to tell Sheila that.

"It is, isn't it?" she asked, feeling her fear drain away and be replaced with anger. "It's Jenny Stephanopoulos's name that you call when you're fucking me, isn't it? Well, well, well. How ironic." A smirk came to her lips, and she saw the two emotions that landed full force on his face. Shame and anger. "How bloody ironic. You meet the *very* married Jenny Stephanopoulos and fall head over heels for her, and then I find out that she's the one who inherited the estate that I'm now suing."

"Sheila." Gardo swallowed.

"No, Giancarlo. Stefano Papadopoulos had my son killed like a dog and left his body in that scummy little hotel room where it lay," Sheila snarked. "He bloody well deserved better than that *regardless* of what sort of person he turned out to be. And *I* deserve compensation for it. *His* man killed *my* son. Jenny Stephanopoulos inherited the estate, so she owes me the money for the death of *my* son."

"And what does Angelina, an eighteen-year-old *girl*, and your son's *half-sister*, owe you?" Gardo muttered.

"Exactly what I *should* be owed," Sheila replied. "*Half of everything.* Because that's what Luiz would have inherited. Half of the Poulos estate."

"Except you're not suing for half," Gardo said.

"No." Sheila opened the door. "But maybe I should be. I think it's time for you to go."

He debated getting further into it, but knew she was serious about him leaving. Not that she'd ever kicked him out before, but considering what the topic of conversation had been, and the level of anger he was feeling, he thought it best to leave.

She closed the door behind him, felt her heart break for her son for the millionth time, and cried for the rest of the night.

*****

On Saturday, Jenny hauled Pedro out of bed and took the boys shopping. It was the last weekend before Christmas, and they had no idea what to get their partners.

"What do you boys want to get for the girls?" Jenny asked as they stepped off the escalator.

Pedro and Carlos grinned at each other. "Lingerie!"

"Oh, for heaven's sake!" Jenny exclaimed, seeing them burst out laughing. "You boys are too much alike. I *mean* something they wouldn't normally buy themselves. What about jewellery?"

"Viv's already got a whole bunch of that," Carlos said.

"And I don't know about buying Roger jewellery," Tomas added. "Maybe a bag or something manly like that."

"You'd need the luggage department for that," Jenny told him, coming to a stop. "What else besides that?" They looked around the floor full of clothing and accessories. "You have all the latest gadgets, you can buy records and books. We all bought perfumes and colognes weeks ago along with clothes and accessories, so what else is left but something personal from you to them to show how much you love them."

The boys shrugged. They'd never had girlfriends or boyfriends at Christmas before, let alone wives or husbands, and had no idea what to get them.

"Then I say jewellery for the girls." Jenny looked at each perplexed face. "And make it personal. Come on." Heading for the jewellery display, she helped the boys look for something that would be appropriate for Angelina and Viv and deftly found a pendant for both partners. "Those hearts." She pointed. "With the red stones."

The assistant pulled out one tray of silver, and one tray gold heart pendants with heart stones in the middle and hearts etched around the stone.

"What about these?" Jenny asked the boys, holding one of each.

Pedro and Carlos peered over her shoulder.

"Can they be engraved?" Jenny asked the girl, and turned them over to look at the backs.

"Of course," the girl replied, "but it might be late due to the rush."

Jenny eyed the pendants, set them down, and chose two others. "As long as we have them by Friday at the latest. Carlos, which metal?"

"Gold."

"Pedro?"

"Silver."

"We'll take these two on those chains." Jenny laid down the pendants and picked two medium-sized chains in gold and silver. She filled out the forms for the engravings, telling the boys what would be written on them, and then they paid. "I'll be back for them during the week." She thanked the girl, and on the way out they stopped at the luggage department and found a bag for Roger. "Now, who's in tonight?" Jenny asked as they headed for the door. "Because I have something to tell Angie, and you may or may not want to be there."

"What do you mean, Mama?" Pedro asked, loping alongside her.

Something caught Carlos's eye, and they all stopped while he examined it.

Jenny sighed. "We, Angie and I, were served during the week. Someone is suing the Poulos and Papadopoulos estates."

All three boys turned to stare incredulously.

"What?" Pedro's mouth moved. "What do you mean?" His head moved side to side. "What do you mean you're being sued, Mama?"

"It's nothing to worry about," she told him. "But I need to talk to her and explain the situation, so it's best if you're there while I do it."

"When..." Pedro trailed off.

"After dinner." She saw her son's face. "Don't worry. I'm dealing with this. Angie won't have to do anything."

"Guess we'll all be staying in then." Carlos looked at Tomas who agreed.

*****

That night, after dinner, they all gathered around the fireplace. Carlos had filled Viv in, and Tomas had told Roger. Now, it was time for Jenny to tell Angie.

"Angie, come and sit beside me, I have something to tell you." Jenny grabbed the papers from her bag and settled in on the couch.

"What is it, Mama?" Angie sat beside her parents with Pedro to her left.

"I received a visit from a lawyer this week, and he delivered these papers." She handed over Angie's who unfolded them.

"What is it?" She started reading. First, her eyes narrowed, then she frowned, and finally a gasp escaped her. "Ten million dollars."

"What!" Pedro exclaimed, and murmurs went around the family. "Ten million dollars! For what?"

Angie teared up. "I'm being sued by Sheila Manning for back child support for Luiz."

"What!" Tomas perked up from his spot between Roger and Viv. "Luiz! What's he got to do with this?"

Angie dropped the papers in despair. "What's going on, Mama? Why am I being sued?"

Jenny glanced from Tomas to Angie. "We both are." Indicating to the papers on her lap she continued. "Sheila Manning, Luiz's mother, has decided to sue you, as heir to the Andros Poulos estate, for back child support and compensation. She is suing the Papadopoulos estate for the murder of her son. Now, we know that one of Papadopoulos's men killed him, and I believe she needs to be compensated for that."

"You're giving her ten million dollars," Carlos blurted.

"Oh, for God's sake no," Jenny snapped, then sighed and shook her head. "As a mother that nearly lost her three sons this year, I know how she feels." Looking at each one for them she took in their features. "And if one of you were murdered in cold blood I'd bloody well want money too. But *not* necessarily ten million. I *do* believe she is owed, but not that much."

"So, what do I do then?" Angie's tears spilt over. "I've never been sued before."

"And you may not be now." Jenny wrapped her arm around Angie. "I've spoken to a lawyer. She said we could be sued if we don't give money and we could be sued if we do. But if they turn down a decent offer and still sue, then they may not win because they chose to be greedy. So, and this is just my thought, there are two things we can do." She looked at her daughter's teary face. "After adding up back child support and getting a general price for murder cases and what victims' families get in compensation, it comes to about $25,000 each. Now for me, I'm thinking of giving her a hundred grand. I thought either you could match that, or, I could just pay it all and you don't have to worry about it at all." She watched Angelina's reactions flitter across her face.

"A hundred grand. Mama, even that's too much." Pedro watched his mother.

"I know." Jenny reached out and held his face in her hand. "But I'd expect that or more if I lost you. Apparently, child support is about $27,000, compensation for murder is about $25,000. So I doubled that and thought a hundred thousand would be much better than ten million. And if they refused it and go to court, then it will, hopefully, look bad for them and they get nothing."

"So, we give her a hundred thousand each?" Angie asked in a small quivering voice.

"Yes. Or I pay the lot, and you keep your inheritance for you and your children."

Angie bit her bottom lip and thought about it. *Luiz was my brother. If he was alive, he'd be entitled to half, but after what he did to Tomas he doesn't deserve any of it. But this is his mother, and doesn't she deserve something? But what Daddy did was his choice, why should I have to pay?* "Oh I don't know," she finally said. "I'm sorry she lost her son, and he was my brother, but after what he did he doesn't deserve anything, and I'm not sure she does either."

"Okay, how about this. Since her time for suing over child support is probably gone, especially since she kicked him out at seventeen and he was twenty-five when he died, how about I up the amount and just give it to her from my money?" She didn't want Angelina to suffer any more than she had to. "And I doubt a court would really give her back child support anyway."

"How much more?" Spiros asked, knowing Jenny wouldn't want to put Angie through any more hell than she'd been through.

"I'll give her $250,000 from the Papadopoulos estate." She shrugged. "I have the money, and he was a bastard, and he did get his man to kill Luiz just to get Tomas away from him. It's not fair, either way, that she lost her son that way, so yes, I think Stefano owes her."

"But $250,000, Mama?" Tomas inquired. "That's even more than your original offer."

"And look what he did to you," Jenny said. "But at least he's dead and you don't have to worry about him anymore."

Tomas's face fell, as he remembered the sick feeling he'd had for weeks, only to discover he'd been poisoned by his former lover. He felt Roger's comforting arm slide around him.

"Look, Angie, if you don't want to worry about it let me deal with it. Maybe mother to mother I can get through to her and convince her that what I'm offering is all she'll get."

"What about the lawyer? He had dollar signs in his eyes," Spiros said.

Jenny chuckled. "Yes, but Marcy said I could try going one on one and I might get it over and done with. I'll just let her know it's my one and only offer..." She drifted off.

"Jenny..."

"Mama..."

Jenny had been thinking. "How about I offer her one million to walk away."

"What!" flew around the room.

"I'm trying to get around the scummy lawyer and not get taken to court," Jenny explained. "So, I'm thinking if I offer her *that* then she might take it and walk away. And she doesn't lose any to the lawyer, and the money is no skin off my nose."

"Yeah, but a million dollars, Mama?" Pedro said.

"Well, if that's what it takes then I'll do it to keep her out of our lives." Jenny looked at Angie. "You know what. Don't you worry about any of this. I'll deal with all of it and make it go away."

A deep breath shuddered through Angie's body. So many emotions all boiling away inside, fighting with each other. *After all Daddy did and all he stood for, now I have to deal with all of this shit.*

"Put it out of your mind," Jenny told her. "I'll deal with it. I wouldn't have told you, but legally you are being sued, and you needed to know about it so you could deal with it. But," she nodded, "at the end of the day you *are* only eighteen and shouldn't have to deal with any of this, so I will. I'm dealing with it, and you don't need to." She hugged her. "Don't worry about it."

Angie snuggled into Jenny's arms. It had been a long time since she'd been hugged by a mother, *had* a mother to tell her not to worry and that she'd deal with everything. It was nice to be held, and she'd gotten used to it over the last two months since meeting Jenny in Athens. Since getting married, she'd really been accepted into the family and treated like a daughter. She hadn't had motherly love in nearly a decade. She felt the warmth and love coming from Jenny. In her kisses on top of her head, in her embrace, in the way she spoke. She knew she was loved by an amazing man who had been raised by an amazing woman.

*****

Giancarlo grunted back and forth. After his visit and subsequent phone call from Jenny, and learning about Sheila, he'd vowed to forget about her. But here he was again, fucking her in her apartment. That's what Jenny did to him. Made him want to plant himself in a woman. And the only woman he knew of, outside of the prostitutes he had arrested, was Sheila. He felt the build-up; the pounding, ear bleeding, painful build-up of his seed and ploughed forth in release. Rocking to a panting stop, he pulled out and rolled over.

"Still thinking about Jenny?" Sheila asked, remembering her visit from the night before.

"No." Sitting on the side of the bed he grabbed his pants.

"Is that all I am to you?"

"What?"

"Is sex all I am to you?"

He stood and buttoned up his pants.

"You knock on my door, we have sex, you get dressed and go."

"Isn't that all you wanted?"

"It was. But since meeting Jenny Stephanopoulos you've changed." And he had changed in a big way. He'd been more passionate, caring, sexual, touching her in ways she hadn't experienced, and she'd liked it. A lot.

"Don't you ever speak her name," he bellowed, pulling his blazer on over his shirt. "You're suing her for ten million dollars even though *your* son committed a crime. She is *more woman* than you would ever hope to be."

Sheila shrank back, hurt by the comment. "I'm enough woman for you to come and ram your dick into," she spat. "I must be something for you to keep coming here. And as for Jenny, I *deserve* that money. After Andros ignored me and our son, I was left to scrimp and save and work a dead-end job in a supermarket to raise and support him. *And what does she get?* She gets millions and millions of dollars all because her husband used to be related to him."

"It was more than that," Gardo told her. "Papadopoulos had her sons kidnapped, he put her and her family through hell. If that means she gets the estate, then she gets the estate. It has *nothing* to do with you."

"*The hell it doesn't,*" she raged. "My son was Andros Poulos's blood. *He* was once Papadopoulos's stepson. *They* owe me."

Gardo stared down at the mousy brown overweight woman in the bed. "And what does Jenny Stephanopoulos owe you?"

The evil radiated from Sheila's eyes. "Everything!"

*****

On Monday morning, Jenny rang Gardo at work. "Giancarlo, Jenny

Stephanopoulos. I was wondering if you could give me Sheila Manning's address."

The alarm bells went off in his head. "And why do you want her address?"

"Well, since she's suing me, my lawyer suggested I go and see her mother to mother and try and convince her to take my offer instead of going to court and losing."

"And what's your offer?"

"One million."

His brows hit his hairline. "You're giving her…"

"Yes, well, she did ask for ten, from both of us. But I doubt the court would give her child support for a dead child that was twenty-five."

"True," he agreed, completely surprised by the twist of events.

"So, can you give me her address…please?"

Ah, the sound of sweet Jenny's voice pleading… "Do you really think it's a good idea? Going to see her without a lawyer?" He stalled for more time to hear her silky voice.

"My lawyer told me what to say, so I'm pretty sure I can handle myself. Spiros will be downstairs waiting. Once I'm done, we'll leave. May I have her address?"

"Ah…of course." He kept her talking for a few minutes more before she said goodbye. *I wish I could hear that conversation.* He'd told Jenny Sheila left work at seven so he knew not to pop around for a quickie, but he'd love to be a fly on the wall.

*****

At seven that night, Jenny and Spiros took the town car to Sheila's building, sat just down the road, and watched everyone who walked by. They spotted a person of Sheila's description waddle into the building at twenty past.

At half past, Jenny stepped out of the car and walked up to Sheila's apartment. She smoothed her outfit, took a deep breath, and knocked three times.

Sheila had just sat down with her rum and coke, and mail to watch

TV. "Whatever you got, I'm not buying," she yelled.

Jenny knocked again.

Sheila became annoyed, and hefting herself from her chair, threw open the door to see a middle-aged woman with straight brown hair and blue eyes, no make-up, and wearing a plain blue dress with stockings and shoes that looked to be ten seasons old under an old trench coat. "Ah, yes?"

"Ms Manning?"

"Yes."

"I'm Jenny Stephanopoulos."

Sheila stared in amazement. The woman Giancarlo had been moaning over was standing here at her door. The woman who had inherited the Papadopoulos estate was wearing old-fashioned clothes and standing before her. "You're…?"

"Pedro and Tomas's mother, and Angelina's mother-in-law. My lawyer suggested talking to you to try and come to a resolution that will make us both happy."

Sheila swallowed. *What the hell has Gardo been going on about with this woman? She's as plain and dowdy as me.*

"Can I come in?"

"Ah…sure…" Sheila was intrigued. How could she say no?

"Thank you. I wasn't sure what time to come." Jenny glanced around the tiny room. "I'm sorry if it's too late for you."

"No…ah…I just got home from work." Sheila waved to the couch, and Jenny took a seat.

"Well, ah, my lawyer told me about Maurice Blackborn and informed me about the legal side of things here in America. We did our sums, and I'm willing to offer you a cheque instead of us going to court. Especially against the Poulos estate."

"My son was a Poulos," Sheila hissed.

"That I'm told Andros disowned," Jenny said softly. "Which…I can see was a very unfortunate thing for you. I'm sorry he treated you that way. He didn't treat his daughter much better."

"I should have half that estate considering my Luiz was his son," Sheila countered.

"Ms Manning, according to the law, only Luiz was entitled to claim half, and since he has passed away due to Papadopoulos, that's why I'm here, because you're suing me. Now, after talking with my lawyer, she said the judge would no doubt kick out any claims against the Poulos estate for back child support and half the fortune since he is no longer here. She suggested I offer you a reasonable amount for compensation over his death, and in exchange you drop the lawsuits." Jenny dug around in her ten-year-old handbag and produced the papers from her lawyer. "Here. Here is my offer in exchange for dropping the cases."

Sheila took the paperwork and read the counter offer and legalese. Finally, she spoke. "My lawyer says I can get ten million from both of you."

"From what I've been told of your lawyer, Ms Manning, he has dollar signs in his eyes. How much is he going to take if you win anything? Ten, twenty, thirty percent? What if the judge throws out your claims and you end up with nothing? What will you owe him then?" She watched the emotions fly over Sheila's face as she re-read the papers offering one million dollars. "What if you take this offer to him, he turns it down and sues, and the judge declares you too greedy and throws it out? You end up with nothing. What if you take this offer to him and he takes it? How much does he get? How much will that leave you?"

She sighed. "Ms Manning, I don't know what it's like to lose a son. But I nearly lost three because of Luiz, and Stefano Papadopoulos. I'm offering you more money than you'd ever get out of the Poulos estate. Whatever you do, please consider your options. If you get rid of your lawyer, you can take my cheque straight out. Keep him, and you could lose everything and be right back where you are now." She dug a business card out from her bag. "Here's my lawyer's card. If you choose to deal with us personally, please call her. I can be more than accommodating, Ms Manning, because I believe you *should* be compensated for Luiz's death." Sheila looked at her in surprise. "But I don't believe you should sue an eighteen-year-old girl for something you'll never get. I don't believe ten million is appropriate, but I'm willing to work on it and discuss it when you're ready." Jenny stood up. "Thank you for listening, Ms Manning. Thank you for hearing me out. Goodbye. I hope to hear from you soon." Jenny moved to the door and opened it, but lingered. "I hope we can work this out, Ms Manning. Even in time for Christmas." Walking out, she left a stunned woman gaping at the doorway.

"How'd it go?" Spiros asked when Jenny settled into the car. He started it and drove down the street, trying to find his way home.

"Good. I think. She let me in, listened to me, and took the paperwork. Let's hope she dumps the lawyer and takes the money."

"Are you saying she won't?"

"I'm saying I hope she'll take it."

Sheila sat staring at the paper in her hand. *One million dollars. Jenny Stephanopoulos, owner of the Papadopoulos estate, is offering me one million dollars. And what was that get-up? For a woman with millions, oh, God, how many millions, she dressed like an old housewife. Why wasn't she dressed to the nines? With all that money, she should be. One million dollars. That's all she's offering me? When I asked for ten, from each estate. After everything Maurice told me, can I believe this woman? But she came here. She came to me and talked to me, personally. Woman to woman. What the hell was that? Asking me to drop the case against Angelina and the Poulos estate.*

She thought some more. *Should I take the money? Should I tell Maurice?* She hadn't signed anything yet, but he had told her time and time again he'd be taking thirty percent of everything and thirty percent of one million was three hundred thousand, leaving her with what, seven hundred thousand. And if they took it to court and won twenty million, thirty percent was six million. Why the hell would she want to give him that!

Maybe she could figure it out herself. Staring at the business card, she thought about it. She wasn't dumb, but Jenny Stephanopoulos had come to her. Come to her with a counteroffer, and if she took that offer, she wouldn't have to give Blackborn a huge chunk of it. *I wonder; she said she was willing to work with me on it. Maybe I could get ten million on my own? But wait, she did say she thought ten million wasn't appropriate. So…I wonder how much I could push for.*

*****

All day Tuesday, Sheila thought about the offer. One million would get her out of her apartment, but it wouldn't last the rest of her life. She was only forty-seven, and if she lived until her eighties or nineties, that money could be long gone. But…if she received more than that, and if she was careful with that money, she could still get a nice place, buy a car, and only work part-time.

All night Tuesday night, Sheila thought about the offer, and Wednesday at lunchtime she made the call. "Ms Bendinger, this is Sheila Manning. I would like to discuss your offer."

"Before you go further, Ms Manning, I must inform you, that if we broker this deal while you still have a lawyer, he will still be entitled to his percentage…"

"Ah…so…ah…what do I do?" Sheila asked.

"If you want to continue on your own and receive the whole payment, you need to discharge Mr Blackborn. Otherwise, he will take you to court for his due."

Sheila sat silent for a moment and looked at the clock ticking over in the manager's office in the supermarket. She didn't know what to do, so she decided to call the one person she knew would always be honest with her. Whether it hurt or not. "I'll call you back, Ms Bendinger."

"I look forward to your call."

Sheila rang another number.

"Gardo."

"Giancarlo, I need your advice."

"Sheila." He frowned. "What are you doing ringing me at work? You never call me at work. I told you to never call me at work."

"Calm down, I need your advice."

"About what?"

"Well, your pretty plain-looking Jenny Stephanopoulos came by to see me Monday night and offered me a settlement if I dealt with her lawyer. I have no idea what you see in her Giancarlo, for all the money she has she was dressed in ten-year-old clothes."

His frown deepened. Every time he'd seen Jenny she'd been dressed in the most stylish, updated clothing. It couldn't be his Jenny. "What do you want my advice on, Sheila?"

"I want advice on whether I should get rid of my lawyer and deal with the lawsuit myself, thus saving thirty percent, or keep him and try to go to court for ten million from each estate."

He laughed, sounding loud and manly. "You'll never get ten million no matter what lawyer you have. No judge will give you past child support, and probably nowhere near ten million for the death of your kid. Whatever she offered you, I suggest you take it and get rid of that dodgy ass lawyer of yours." He slammed the phone down. Oh, how she annoyed the hell out of him. Calling him at work of all places. But then she'd never done that before. Hefting his feet onto his desk, he thought about how different Jenny and Sheila were.

Sheila called Maurice Blackborn. "Mr Blackborn, I want to withdraw my lawsuits."

"You what?" he sputtered down the line.

"I want to withdraw my lawsuits. I no longer want to sue the estates, so won't be needing a lawyer."

"But I…but you…but I can get you ten million from each estate."

"I'm sorry, Mr Blackborn. After some heavy consideration and reading some books on law, I don't believe you can. And I'm afraid I'll walk away with nothing but lawyer's fees."

"Well, that's what you'll be walking away with now if you expect me not to charge for my time."

"I'm willing to cop that fee, Mr Blackborn. Please withdraw the lawsuits and send me your bill. Thank you."

"It will be in your mailbox today, hand-delivered. No wait, are you at work? I'll deliver it personally." He slammed down the phone. *How dare she* withdraw those lawsuits. What a payday they would be. How dare she! "Mandy," he yelled to his assistant.

A bubbly young blonde walked into his office. "Yes, Mr Blackborn."

"Type up my fee for Ms Manning. She is withdrawing her lawsuits and fired me as her lawyer. I'll be taking her bill around personally."

"Yes, Mr Blackborn."

Sheila rang Marcy Bendinger back. "He says he's bringing it around personally."

"Can you pay it?"

"I can withdraw the money from the bank. I don't have much, but I should be able to cover it."

"Good. Once you've paid, and he is no longer in your service, then you are free to come to me, and we can do a deal."

"When can I come?"

"How about after work? I can stay back while we hash this out."

"Okay, I'll be around after seven-thirty."

"That's fine. I'll be expecting you."

*****

Maurice burst into the supermarket where Sheila worked, demanding to see her. "Where is she? Where is Sheila Manning? I have urgent business to attend to with her."

Sheila wearily came forth. "I'm here, Mr Blackborn."

"Good. You can pay my bill since you don't want my help anymore." He thrust the paper at her.

Sheila took it and blanched at the price. *That will raid my bank account and leave me dry,* she thought. *But then I will have a bigger payday.*

"Is there a problem?" The manager came over.

"Yes, there is a problem," Maurice said. "I need my bill paid."

Sheila sighed. "I need to go to the bank to withdraw money. I'm at work now."

"I don't care," Maurice told her. "You dump me, you pay up." His greasy imposing figure stood before her, tapping his toe in an expensive Italian leather shoe.

"I need to take half hour off work to go to the bank," she said to her manager. "I'll make it up another time."

"I don't think it's appropriate for you to cut work," the thirty-something male manager said.

"I'm not cutting work," Sheila snapped. "I'm asking for a half hour so I can pay this guy off and get him out of *your* store and *my* life. Half an hour." She turned and walked off to the locker room to get her bag and coat. Walking out the door, with Maurice hot on her tail, she made her way into the bank down the street and made out a cheque to cover his expenses.

He snatched it out of her hand the moment she signed it. "Good. Now I hope you're broke and never get anywhere." He stormed out of the bank while she let out a huge sigh of relief. Hurrying back to work, she kept an eye on the clock and her boss. But come seven, she knocked off, took a taxi home, and quickly showered and changed before heading to the office of Marcy Bendinger.

Marcy welcomed her in. "Ms Manning, let's get on with it." She sat behind her desk. "Are you willing to accept the one million dollars Mrs Stephanopoulos is offering?"

Sheila took a deep breath. "No…I'm not."

Marcy didn't blink for they had foreshadowed this move. "Ten million is off the table, Ms Manning. So, what's your next offer?"

Sheila blinked. Just like that she'd lost her ten million dollar payday. "But I—"

"You can suggest an offer *under* ten million," Marcy told her.

"Oh." Sheila was momentarily sidetracked. "Nine million."

Marcy smiled. "Lower, Ms Manning."

Sheila became frustrated. "Well, what *are* you offering?"

"Less than ten."

"You already offered me one million. I want more than that. I deserve it."

"Then name your price."

Frustrated, Sheila popped out a number. "Five million then. If I can have less than ten."

Marcy picked up her phone and dialled a number. "She's asking five million…okay I'll tell her." Setting the phone back in its cradle, she turned to Sheila and laid her hands on the table. "You have a deal, Ms Manning."

"What?" Sheila didn't think she'd heard right.

"You have a deal. Five million is yours."

Sheila blinked. And just like that, she had five million dollars.

"You will need to sign a contract stating that you accept the offer of five million, and in return will not sue the Poulos or Papadopoulos estates for the rest of your life." Marcy slid the paper across the table. "It also says it is compensation for the murder of your son, so you shouldn't be paying any taxes."

Sheila blinked at the paper before her. "I sign this…and I have five million dollars?"

"Yes, Ms Manning. You will be a multi-millionaire."

Sheila breathed and picked up the pen, whipping her signature across the pages. "What now?"

Jenny walked through the door in her ten-year-old clothes and placed a briefcase on the desk in front of Sheila, opening it to show wads of cash. "It's $250,000. I thought you might like some to spend for Christmas. Every Wednesday, the bank will transfer two-hundred-and-fifty-thousand more until the five million is paid off. We will need your bank account details to set up the transfer. Be careful going home, Ms Manning; you could be robbed if people know you have it. It was nice doing business with you. Mother to mother." Jenny laid a hand on Sheila's shoulder, looked into her stunned face and left the room to go home to her family.

*****

On Thursday, two women did two very different things.

Jenny Stephanopoulos went to collect her sons' presents for their partners, bought some more food, and made plans to go after Christmas sale shopping with the girls.

Sheila Manning quit her job and booked herself into the salon at one of the city's fanciest department stores, where she pointed out a hairstyle that she wanted. After a cut, colour, and blow-dry, a luxurious facial and body scrub, she had make-up applied. Seeing herself in the mirror, she couldn't believe how different she looked. She stocked up on lotions, potions and make-up.

The next stop was ladies clothing, where she hired a personal shopper and was fitted for underwear, the latest style in clothes, and added shoes, bags and jewellery to the list. She was having so much fun that she stayed until closing time when she took a chauffeured car home. The driver even helped carry all of her shopping upstairs.

After triple locking the door behind her, she looked at all she'd bought. Oh, yes, Sheila Manning was in business. It being a Thursday night, she knew Giancarlo would more than likely be around. "Wait until he gets a load of me," she said to herself in the mirror. "He won't know what hit him." Deciding to be the one to call the shots for once, she called her favourite Italian restaurant and booked a table for two, *then* she called Gardo at the station.

"Gardo."

"It's Sheila. Are you free for dinner?"

"What?" The frown was back in place.

"I said, are you free for dinner? I have a table for two at *La Bellini* for seven. Can you get away?"

The frown depended. Here she was calling again, twice in one week, and now she was inviting him out for dinner. "Is that a trick question?"

"Are you hungry or not?" She was becoming exasperated.

"Well...yes..."

"Then meet me at *La Bellini* at seven. I'll see you there." After freshening up, she hailed a cab and went to the restaurant. Walking inside she inhaled the aromas of all things Italian.

"Ah, Ciao Bella. Do you have a reservation?" the maître d' asked.

"Ah, yes, a table for two under Manning. I know I'm a little early."

The maître d' scanned the list. "Ah, yes, Ms Manning. Do you mind waiting a moment while your table is set?"

"Of course not." She waited fifteen minutes before being escorted to her table. "I'm waiting on a gentleman friend, a Giancarlo Gardo. I'm hoping he'll turn up, but being as busy as he is this time of year, it's possible he won't be able to make it."

"Of course, I will direct him to your table." The maître d' held out her chair and helped her sit.

"Thank you." She smiled her thanks at him.

Another fifteen minutes rolled by, and at ten after seven, Giancarlo walked into the restaurant.

"Ah, Signore, what is the name?" the maître d' asked.

"Gardo. Giancarlo Gardo." His eyes searched the room for Sheila.

"Right this way, Signore, Signora is already waiting." He led Gardo to Sheila's table and pulled out the chair. "Signore."

Gardo stopped in disbelief. "Sheila?"

She smiled brightly. "Giancarlo, please, have a seat."

Not taking his eyes off the woman at the table, he sat, staring the whole time at the new hairstyle, make-up, clothes. "You're…"

"Rich!"

"Different." He frowned.

"Well, of course I am," she said. "I'm now the owner of five million dollars thanks to *your* Jenny Stephanopoulos."

"Five…" He continued staring as his voice trailed off. "She wouldn't…"

"*She did*," Sheila said smugly. "She upped the offer, and I took it. After all these years, I deserve it. So I quit my job and treated myself to a makeover. About time too."

Gardo was unblinking, staring. How could he not? While Sheila had always been a home to plant himself, the woman opposite him looked nothing like the old Sheila. She looked young and fresh and new. But still not his Jenny. And *how dare she* top her off at five million dollars! "Did you have to fight for it?"

"Not at all." Sheila picked up her menu. "I asked for ten, the lawyer said less. I picked nine, the lawyer said less than that, so I said five and we had a deal. And then you wouldn't believe it, Jenny herself came in with a briefcase with $250,000 in cash," she squealed as she leant across the table. "And I'll get the rest in instalments every week until the amount is paid. I'm rich, baby. R.I.C.H. Rich. Now, what do you want to eat?"

Gardo stared hard at Sheila. But it wasn't Sheila. It was a completely different woman to Sheila, and he wasn't sure if he liked her or not. Strangely, he found her attractive. She had her hair in that

Farrah Fawcett style and dyed a lighter shade of brown so that it wasn't mousy. Her skin glowed and was dewy, and her eyes were bright and sparkling and blue.

Blue!

Since when had they been blue?

The shade of lipstick made her lips look luscious, and the blue pantsuit fitted her fuller figure well and helped illuminate her eyes even more.

Her blue eyes.

Since when did she have blue eyes?

And why, oh, why, in God's name did she look like Jenny Stephanopoulos?

*****

It was Christmas Eve, and Jenny couldn't wait for her children to come. The penthouse was filled with aromas of roast chicken and vegetables, her mother was baking more cookies in the oven, and snow was falling outside.

Tomas and Roger came through the door bearing gifts, and after kisses all round, placed them under the tree.

"So many presents already here," Roger said, looking at name tags. "Ooh, this one's for you, T."

Tomas looked at the huge present and wondered what it was. "Whatever it is, I can't wait to open it."

Roger checked more tags. "Same size for Pedro and Carlos. I *am* intrigued."

"And that one's for you, Roger." Tomas pointed to the present beside his that was the same size. "Looks like Mama's got us all the same thing."

That warmed Roger's heart, and a soft smile came to his lips. To think his in-laws had thought enough of him to buy him a present as big as the ones they'd bought their blood sons.

Carlos came through the door with Viv right behind him. Both had armfuls of presents. "Carlos is here."

"You announce yourself when you enter a room, now?" Tomas

asked. "You're not important enough to announce yourself."

"The hell I'm not! My videos have just surpassed one million in sales. I'll do whatever the hell I want." He strutted around the tree looking at name tags.

"Really? That's great. We surpassed a million months ago," Roger told him. "Welcome to the club."

Carlos stopped and looked up in surprise. "You've…"

"Yep." Roger slapped him on the back. "We beat you to it." He and Tomas left Carlos standing there in shock. They exchanged glances and giggled.

Vivian laughed. "Aw, poor Carlos. Not number one anymore."

He blushed. "Of course I'm number one, Viv. My movies make millions, I write and star in them, *and* I've won the best cock award."

Pedro and Angie came through the door right at that moment. "What did you say? That you're a cock. We always knew that Carlos."

Angie giggled and laid out the presents they'd brought under the tree.

Carlos frowned. "No, I said—"

"We *heard* what you said, Carlos," Jenny told him, carrying a platter of hot biscuits over to the coffee table in front of the fire. "And I don't want to hear any more about your privates as it gives your father a big head."

Spiros guffawed from his spot on the couch. "Well, you know where my sons get it from."

"Ew, no," came three replies and Carlos, Pedro and Tomas covered their ears.

Roger laughed. "They had to come from somewhere, and it wouldn't be from your mother."

"Roger!" Jenny exclaimed in fake shock.

"Sorry, Mrs S, just stating a fact." He put his hands up in mock protest and grabbed a biscuit, biting the head off Rudolph as everyone grabbed one and sat.

"Don't eat too many, dinner's nearly ready," Jenny reminded them. "We have roast and pudding. Now, there's something I have to do." She went over to the tree and picked up three presents, presenting them to the boys.

"Presents? Already, Mama?" Pedro asked. "We don't normally open them yet."

"They're special," Jenny told her surprised son, watching them pull out Christmas jumpers. "Aren't they wonderful?" She watched each son's face fall and couldn't help laughing along with the others.

"Mama! What the hell!" Carlos threw his head back. "I am *not wearing* this."

Viv held up his red jumper with a fat Santa on the front. "Well, it's what you'll be if you keep eating the way you are."

Roger looked at Tomas's, a green one with a snowman on the front. "Oh, put it on. I can't wait to see you in it."

Tomas gave him a dirty look, but pulled it on for his mother.

"Mama, really? Rudolph?" Pedro whined, holding up a blue jumper with Rudolph pawing at the air.

Angie giggled. "The blue matches your eyes."

"Go on, all of you, put them on," Jenny urged them. She watched Carlos and Pedro pull them on reluctantly and clapped her hands. "Oh, my babies."

"Mama," came three groans.

Jenny headed for the tree again.

"Oh, Carlo Stefan, you look so hot." Viv grinned. "You're a *baaad* Santa."

"Oh, please," he grumbled. "You don't have to wear this monstrosity."

"Actually." Jenny handed a present to Angelina, then Roger, then Viv. "I didn't want the rest of you feeling left out.

"Ooh, I got one." Angie ripped open the paper and held up the jumper. "Oh, it matches." Pulling it on over her head, she flung her hair over her shoulder and looked down. "It's a girl reindeer." She snuggled next to Pedro.

"And they're facing each other." Jenny nodded at them.

They looked down to see that the two reindeer were indeed facing each other in what could only be described as flirting.

"And I got a snowman too." Roger pulled his jumper down and sat back next to Tomas, smiling at his lover's raised brows and throwing an arm around him. He kissed him on the temple which brought a smile to Tomas's face.

"And I'm Mrs Claus." Viv adjusted her red knit over her body. "A fat Mrs Claus."

"Well, if I'm fat Santa you're fat Mrs Santa," Carlos quipped.

"But I'm not fat!"

"No, but you will be full with child soon. That counts," Jenny joked.

Viv groaned. "Don't remind me. I hate the fact I'm giving birth during bikini season."

"Oh," Jenny remembered. "I didn't forget the rest of us." She produced two presents for her parents, white jumpers with gifts on them, and handed a brightly wrapped present to Spiros while she slid her own jumper over her head.

Spiros laughed when he saw his and received help from Jenny getting it on. Then he pulled his wife onto his lap and kissed her. "I love you, Jenny Stephanopoulos."

"I love you, Spiros Stephanopoulos." Laughing, and stroking her husband's face, she gazed deeply into his dark brown eyes.

"So, what did you two get?" Viv asked.

Jenny pulled back to show off her and Spiros's cheeky dancing elf jumpers. Cheeky because the elves were male and female and half naked.

"Aw," Carlos guffawed. "That should be Viv and me. We're the saucy elves, and you two should be the fat Santas as heads of the family."

Jenny raised a brow. "When you have a tribe of kids and give them these jumpers, *you* can be the saucy elves, *not* before. But right now, I want a picture of all of us." Hurrying over to the desk she grabbed the camera and set the timer. Placing it on the mantel over the fireplace she called for everyone to crowd around the couch that sat opposite. Pedro and Angie sat on the floor in front of his brothers and Viv, while Jenny, Spiros and her parents stood behind the couch.

"Smile," Jenny called and heard the little click. "I can't wait to see how that turned out. Let me take some more photos."

Groans were heard from the family. "Hush now, I want photos." Snapping Pedro and Angie, Roger and Tomas, Viv and Carlos, she went through the whole roll. "Darling, can you change the film for me?"

she asked Spiros, who obeyed his wife. "I need to check on the food." She rushed into the kitchen with her mother to inspect the chicken and pudding and declared them ready. "Everyone at the table." As Jenny laid out plates, her mother started cutting the chicken.

Carlos and Viv descended, as did Pedro and Angie. Spiros had refilled the camera and left it on the table by the phone. Only Tomas and Roger stayed where they were.

"Ah." Tomas winced in pain as he tried to stand.

"You okay, T?" Roger slid an arm around him.

"My bones…they're really aching." Tomas sat back and let out a gush of air as his body sagged. "They're worse today."

Jenny spied the boys and hurried over. "What's wrong?" She sat on the coffee table in front of them. "What's wrong?"

"Ugh, nothing Mama. I just have some aching bones," Tomas said.

"How long have they been aching and why didn't you tell me you're still sick?" She felt his forehead with the back of her hand.

"My bones have been aching for over a week." He gently moved her hand away. "And I had a headache for a few days. But it's gone."

"And I've got a sore throat now," Roger said. "It's probably just the cold. We're not used to it in Miami."

Jenny thought, allowing her motherly instincts to kick in. She knew something was wrong and knew it was a precursor to something worse. "I want you to write down a list of every ache and pain you've had, when you got it, and how long it lasted."

"Mama," Tomas protested.

"Do not defy me, Tomas," she said sternly. "*Something* is wrong with you, I know it. You've never fully recovered from the poisoning, and I want to make sure my baby's safe. The same goes for you, Roger. *Both* of you. Make a list, and if you're worse come next week, we *will* get that doctor in. Do you understand me?" She looked at both of them.

"Yes, Mama." Tomas glanced sheepishly from his mother to Roger.

"Yes, Mrs S." Roger sent a sheepish glance back to his lover.

"Right, now," she went on. "I'll give you some painkillers with dinner, and you can sit near the fire afterwards to keep warm. Did you turn your electric blanket on before you came up?”

“No. I was going to do it when we got home,” Roger said.

“Run down and do it now so it’s nice and hot when you go to bed. We’ll wait for you,” she told him, and watched him race off before turning to her son and gently rubbing his leg. “Hopefully it will relax your muscles and warm your bones.”

Everyone at the table had turned around at the door banging open, then turned their attention to Jenny and Tomas who were still sitting in the living room.

“I’ll help you, come on.” Tucking herself under his arm, she helped him to his feet.

“Ugh,” he winced, bending over. “God, everything hurts.” His face was screwed up in pain as Spiros came to his side, taking his other arm.

“What is it?” Spiros asked his son and wife.

“His bones are killing him,” Jenny told him. “We need to get some painkillers into him. Help me get him to the table.” They helped Tomas across the room to the dining table and saw Pedro and Carlos stand in concern, ready to help if necessary.

Roger came flying back into the penthouse and closed the door behind him.

“Maybe we shouldn’t have been out every day,” Spiros told his son. “The cold has not done your bones any good. Even mine are a little achy.”

“You didn’t say anything,” Jenny said to him as they sat Tomas in his seat.

“Well, it could also be old age,” Spiros quipped with a wink.

Jenny snorted. “You’re hardly old.”

“No, but this weather is cold and looks like it’s gotten into our bones. Like father like son.” He kissed Tomas’s head and resumed his seat, motioning for the boys to sit as well.

“You okay, little bro?” Carlos asked, concerned at how sick his brother had been over the last few months.

“Bone ache, headache. I’ve probably come down with something,” Tomas told him.

“He’s weak from the poisoning.” Roger took his seat beside his husband. "I suggest seeing a poison expert again and finding out what the side-effects are and how long they last for."

Jenny had grabbed a blanket from the couch, laid it over her son's lap, and wrapped it around his back to keep out the cold. "We saw one in Athens, and he said Tomas was fine. But if you're still suffering from not getting proper care, then we'd better find out what's going on inside of you." She finally took her place at the end of the table next to her ill son and looked around at her family. "Everyone have their meals? Good, let's eat."

The conversation stayed on Tomas and Roger. If Tomas was still sick then maybe they'd all come down with something. With immune systems low, it wouldn't be hard for any of her children to catch a cold or flu.

"Pedro, do you keep warm when you're working?" Jenny asked as she tucked Tomas in near the fire after dinner. The boys laughed.

"Mama. I dance under hot lights on a stage. There ain't no way I get cold," he replied, sitting next to Viv and Carlos on the couch. "But I don't wanna get sick, so stay away from me, bro."

"But do you at least rug up when you're out and about? Same goes for the rest of you. The girls are pregnant, they can't be getting sick now."

Angie pulled her hair over her shoulder and snuggled under the blanket between Viv and Pedro. "I rug up, Mama. It's cold out there."

"Good." Jenny passed the tray of biscuits around. "Being sick and pregnant is not fun, *believe* me. Remember morning sickness?"

Viv and Angie groaned.

"It's that times a hundred," Jenny informed them. "And all you do is worry about losing the baby because you're throwing up and on the toilet all day."

"Ew, gross, Mama." Pedro screwed his face up.

"It's a fact of life, my baby. That's why you need to take care of yourselves and your pregnant wives."

Tomas sighed, feeling worn out down to the bone. "Can we change the subject?"

"How about some Christmas Eve TV?" Jenny suggested, turning

the TV on. "Or we can sit and sing carols, listen to more music." They'd had an album of Christmas music playing throughout dinner.

"Oh, no, not carols, Mama," Pedro whined. "You always make us sing carols."

"And what's wrong with that? It *is* Christmas," she retorted.

"Can't we just sit here and watch TV and chat and eat biscuits?" Carlos asked.

Jenny glanced at Tomas, whose eyelids were drooping. "If you need to rest then rest," she murmured, laying her hand on his.

He nodded and closed his eyes, laying his head on Roger's shoulder as Roger put his arms around his sick lover.

"Let's see what's on TV. Pedro, get up and change the channel."

"Aw, Mama!"

*****

Sheila looked around her sparsely furnished apartment. The day before she'd cleared out her old stuff, had the apartment cleaned and fumigated, and had new furniture brought in. Not a lot, just a lounge suite, bedroom suite, new TV, fridge and washer. Things that she could take with her to her new apartment. When she found one that was. She knew she wouldn't have time to find anything by Christmas, so planned on looking come Monday. *Nothing too expensive*, she thought. *But a nice apartment or house in a nice area that I can afford. Gotta keep those pennies saved.*

Sheila planned on blowing the first $250,000 and then saving the rest. She may have had a low paying job for the last twenty-six years, but she wasn't stupid, having finished school and college before getting pregnant with Luiz. She'd scrimped and saved since, knew how to budget, and had done her sums. She was able to afford up to $500 a week on rent or a mortgage, but if she bought a house she'd have insurance and taxes as well, and that could triple the cost. She had to decide whether she wanted to stay in the city, or go out to the suburbs and either buy a car, or waste money on transport for the rest of her life.

Sitting in her recliner, she lounged in her silk negligee and matching dressing gown, wondering if Giancarlo would be over. Being Christmas Eve, he could be busy, but maybe not. From the way he had stared at her during their dinner Thursday night, she'd wondered if he was seeing her in a whole new light. Not that he had liked what she'd done. She remembered back.

"I can't believe you took her for five million." His gruffness was in place as he stared at the woman sitting across from him. Sheila looked so different to the last time he'd seen her, and that was only a few days ago.

She huffed, tired of him talking about it. "Look. My son was killed, and I was entitled to compensation. Even your Jenny thought so. She told me."

He flinched. "She's not my Jenny."

"Really?" She sipped her wine, studying the man on the other side of the table. "From the way you moan her name every time we're together, one would think you were in love with her."

He looked up sharply. "I'm not. I just happen to think she's an incredible woman dealing with a lot."

"And I'm not," she hissed. "I lost a son, she didn't."

He stared hard. Having never had children he didn't know what it was like to lose a son, or even nearly lose three. But he wasn't sure Sheila was too overly emotional about it. "Did you ever love your son?"

Her gaze flickered away.

"You didn't," he pushed.

"Of course I didn't," she spat. "His father denied him, and I resented him. Both of them. Andros ruined my life, and Luiz ruined my figure. I had to work hard and scrimp and save to send him to school. I was glad when he left."

"So why does anyone owe you?"

"Because someone took it upon themselves to kill him." She stared hot daggers across the table at him."

Gardo sighed. He couldn't really disagree with that.

Sheila watched the Christmas proceedings on the TV and relished the fact she could now afford to crank up the heat. Her fridge was full of her favourite food, and she had her rum and coke beside her. "Ah yes…a very merry Christmas to me," she cheered to herself.

*****

Giancarlo ran hard after a thieving criminal. He tackled him to the ground, hauled him up, and slammed him against the car parked at the curb. "You, are under arrest, you little toerag," he breathed in the perp's ear. "Take him away." He threw him at the officers who came running up and turned and leant on the car. It was a rough night. Christmas and New Year's always were, with more thefts than any other time of the year. He hefted his bulk up and made his way back to his car three streets away.

"I'm getting way too old for this shit," he muttered, feeling the ache in his calf muscles. "Way too old." But retirement for him was two year years away, and he wanted to try and make it to a decent pension so he at least had something to live on for the rest of his life. He was only fifty-three, and a cop's salary didn't go far. At least he had his little house in Forest Hills, and it was paid for after all these years.

He sat in his car, slammed the door, and looked at his watch. It was nearly eleven. He still had paperwork to do, but also wanted to make it to Sheila's. *God, why can't I get enough of her? Why have I needed to see her so much lately?* The sex was good, as it always was, but that's all it was. Sheila had asked him why he always left afterwards, and the truth was, he didn't find her attractive. Just willing to have sex occasionally with no strings attached. And since he hadn't found anyone else, he'd stuck to her for the last couple of years. But now…now that Jenny Stephanopoulos had come into his life with her blue eyes and silky voice, he'd wanted better. He'd wanted Jenny.

"And then bloody Sheila did herself up and now she looks like Jenny. When the hell did Sheila have blue eyes?" He thought back to dinner two nights ago and gunned it to the precinct.

He stared at her. Her blue eyes, her new hairdo that made her look like Jenny. His Jenny. Why the hell did Sheila look like Jenny? She never had blue eyes before, did she? He couldn't remember, but did recall mousy brown hair in a drab hairstyle and a homely yet unattractive figure. But in that pantsuit, one so much like Jenny's, she looked quite curvaceous and sexy.

Sexy!

Get the fuck out Giancarlo. Sheila Manning, sexy? She's never been sexy. He detailed her body in his mind. Remembering what he could as he'd never really taken notice of her naked. Large full breasts he loved to get his mouth on. Her nipples took up most of the space, and he loved sucking on them. Full womanly hips, not much in the curve department. Her legs had been strong, he knew from all the times she clamped them around him. Her lips were dry and cracked, but her mouth was inviting. Definitely not the woman sitting across from him now. This woman looked alive. Her eyes sparkled with the brilliance of sapphires, her lips were full and inviting, her skin looked soft enough to touch. So, why the hell had he never noticed her?

Because she had never been noticed. She looked dowdy and bland, maybe for a reason. Maybe to keep men away. Maybe because after what Andros did she didn't think she was worthy of love, or worthy of a man. Raising a son she didn't want or love, feeling hard done by, Sheila Manning had shut herself away from the world physically. But now that she had money to do herself up, she was coming to the fore. And she was clearly enjoying her new life already.

She'll probably blow through the money by this time next year and be crying poor again. Better not come to me whining about it.

Pulling into the station, he left the car running as he sat thinking. It was Christmas Eve, after eleven, and he didn't feel like dealing with paperwork and crims. Blowing it off, he reversed and headed for Sheila's, banging on her door fifteen minutes later.

She knew he'd come. *Hoped* he'd come. Adjusting her dressing gown so it lazily fell off one shoulder, she opened the door and spoke calmly. "Giancarlo. Not working tonight?"

He took her in. Fluffy hair, dewy skin, and a sexy curvaceous body in a silk concoction that hardened him in an instant.

"Come in." She held the door open and waved him in.

He spied the new TV, couch and two chairs. The apartment smelt clean, was tidy, and he noted the new fridge in the adjoining kitchen. "Bought some furniture as well, have we?"

She locked the door behind him. "Why not," she said, rubbing against him as she passed by. Taking her place in her recliner, she displayed her legs to lure him in.

He stared down, the soft, dewy skin on her face extended down to her legs that were now enticing him. He hardened further. Her scent wafted around him, inflaming him even more.

"I also have a new bedroom set," she said as sexily as she could. Ever since her makeover, she was feeling different. Alive, sexy, flirty and full of life.

His erection plunged forward, straining for release.

She watched it for a few seconds then said, "how about I show you my new bed and take care of that in the meantime?"

He surprised her by throwing down the trench coat he'd been holding, picking her up by the waist, crushing her to him and carrying her into the bedroom. He threw her down, ripped off his clothes, and set his erection free. His hands slid up her legs to pull her knickers down, and moved back up to push the nightie out of the way. He smothered himself in her breasts, feeding on her nipples.

She groaned and bucked up under him, giving him what he wanted.

And he took what he wanted, all the way to morning.

*****

None of the Stephanopoulos households was up early. The boys were adults and didn't run for the tree anymore, trying to outdo each other by seeing who could get there first and rip all their presents open. Instead, they all slept in, languishing in their own apartment, their own lover.

Carlos yawned and stretched, his eyes opening to a bleary day. "Mmm," he moaned, feeling Viv move beside him. "Merry Christmas, my darling wife."

She slid on top of him and their mouths met. "Merry Christmas, my darling husband." Sitting up, she encased him within her, feeling the hardness of his morning erection. Pulling the covers up to keep herself warm, she rode him until she was done. Groaning, falling on top of him, and stretching out. "Mmm, Merry Christmas to *me*!"

Carlos laughed and wrapped his arms around her. "Mmm, more like Merry Christmas to *me*. How come we don't wake up like that every morning?"

"What? All night sex isn't enough for you?" Leaving kisses across his chest, her lips trailed down.

"Well, not always. I am a porn star, you know. I need sex all day every day."

She snorted and came back up. "Just you wait until the baby comes. You won't be getting *any* unless you give it to yourself."

*****

In Apartment 2, Roger was waking after a fitful sleep. Tomas had been waking all night groaning about bone ache. Roger had rubbed his muscles down, trying to help in some way, but except for more painkillers during the night, nothing had helped. He breathed in, smelling his lover's scent as he lay curled in his arms. His lips turned up in a soft smile, and he gently kissed his husband's shoulder as he spooned him.

"Mmm," Tomas made fitful sounds.

"Shh," Roger whispered raspily, feeling his own throat burn. "Keep sleeping, you need your rest."

"Mmm." Tomas opened one gritty eye and shifted his leg slightly. "Your throat?" he rasped.

"Yeah," Roger tried again, peering over Tomas's shoulder. "Looks like I'm sick now too. How are you?"

Tomas breathed in and opened both eyes. "Okay, so far. Sore throat, stuffed head. It will probably get worse when I get up."

Roger rolled back and checked the bedside clock. "It's only eight. Your mother said not to come up until lunchtime. We can rest some more."

"Mmm." Tomas closed his eyes and drifted back to sleep.

*****

Angie opened her eyes to her first Christmas with a new family. And not just a new family, but a new husband. She snuggled into his bare chest and felt his arms automatically tighten around her. She felt safe with Pedro. Safe in his arms, safe with his family, safe here in the apartment. Well, after that first week of sleeping on the couch in the penthouse. Once Papa had come she'd needed to get out, but she'd been okay. Nightmares still popped in occasionally to say hello, but they didn't bother her much anymore. That's because she was safe. But now it was Christmas, and she couldn't wait. "Pedro." She nudged him. "Pedro."

"Mmm?" He raised a brow. "What?"

"What time can we go up to Mama's?"

Shifting slightly, he murmured, "lunchtime."

"Can we go now?"

"What?" His brows slid down. "Now?"

"Yes."

"What time is it?"

"I don't know, check your clock."

"Ugh, Angie." His arm snaked out to grab the clock on the bedside cupboard and he brought it to his eyes, which he opened. "It's eight-thirty. Go back to sleep, it's Sunday."

"It's Christmas," she replied excitedly. "I haven't spent a Christmas with a family since my mother was alive. I want to go up now."

"No one will be there. Mama told us all to sleep in and enjoy our time together as it's our first Christmas married…" He drifted off, but came back to the sound of the TV going. "What *are* you doing?"

"Seeing what's on TV." She jumped back in bed after flicking through the channels. They had all been lucky enough to have TV sets in their bedrooms as well as their living rooms.

"God, Angie." Pedro rolled away from the sound and buried his head under his pillow. "It's Sunday and way too early."

"Party pooper." She pouted, kissing her husband on the shoulder. "It's our first Christmas together and do you think Carlos and Viv are sleeping? *No.* They're probably proving why he's sold more videos than you."

Pedro raised his head. "Excuse me?" he asked with a jaunty grin. "How about I show *you* who's the best porn star around?"

*****

Giancarlo had hauled his masculine frame from Sheila's bed at seven-thirty, gone home, showered, changed, and been at work by quarter to nine. It was Sunday. Christmas Day, and he had to work. Not that he minded. He had no wife or family to be with, and it was lonely at home. But last night he'd had Sheila, and now a part of him was feeling lonely and a little cold.

What the hell has she done to me? he thought. Went and made herself like his Jenny and took him to her big, bountiful bosoms, so warm and welcoming. And she had welcomed him all right. Meeting him at the door in that silky thing all sexy and smooth. He couldn't help himself. He'd needed release, and relief, and had all but thrown her on the bed, ripping at his clothes, her clothes, and taking her warm, welcoming body for the rest of the night.

*You're a guilty sinner...*drifted through his mind.

What am I guilty of?

Cheating on the woman you love...

Jenny?

Yes...your Jenny...

Except she's not mine and so I'm not sinning!

You're not married either...

I don't need to be married to have sex. Just stop it.

He slammed a file of papers down on the desk, feeling a rage he couldn't describe building inside of him. He wanted Jenny, but he was with Sheila. He wanted Jenny, but he had sex with Sheila. He wanted Jenny, but he couldn't have her, so he had Sheila instead.

So, Sheila's a substitute? For a wife I don't have...and now...I can't have Jenny. So, Sheila's still a substitute?

The fact that he couldn't really grasp on to why Sheila frustrated him, and Jenny made him love her, pissed him off even more.

*****

Sheila drifted in and out of sleep. Her pliant body lay naked under the satin sheets and down comforter, brand new two days before. She was a little sore, but thoroughly fucked by the very virile Giancarlo Gardo who went at it all night. Her body still burned from his hands searing their way across every inch. Her breasts and nipples still tender from the sucking his huge manly mouth had given them.

Stretching her hands above her head, she arched upward, stretching her back muscles before collapsing with a contented sigh. Ever since Jenny had come into his life, he'd been a better lover, and ever since Jenny had come into *her* life she'd been a better woman. No more mousy doormat along for the occasional fuck. Since her makeover, he'd looked at her differently, made love to her differently, and she couldn't figure it out. Except for still being called Jenny in the odd moment, she didn't think it was all about Mrs Jenny Stephanopoulos anymore. There was something else. Something else he was battling with, and she'd love to know what.

But as long as he comes around and does what he did last night, I don't care, she thought. *Because I want more of that. And if I have Jenny from Mykonos to thank, then I will.*

*****

Jenny slid her fingers across Spiros's chest, sighed in contentment, and smiled. She couldn't wait for him to open his present. To see the look on his face when he saw what she had bought him and their sons, although he'd already argued that her buying him new clothes was enough. She'd argued that he hadn't had new clothes for the last ten years since before they'd moved to Mykonos, and neither had she for that matter, except for some new dresses to wear to church. Now, she had a whole new wardrobe of the latest fashions and so did he.

Spiros clamped down on her hand. "How you tease me so, my love." Taking her hand to his lips, he held it there as she wiggled her fingers.

"I'm not teasing," she breathed, looking up into his eyes as she lay in his arms. "I want my husband."

With a fire in his belly, he took his wife into his arms and wished her a very Merry Christmas indeed.

Normally, on Mykonos, they'd be at church Christmas morning. But times were different, and Jenny welcomed her husband and writhed under him while he did his job.

The moustache he had grown erected her nipples, bringing them to attention as it teased. His lips tormented, his tongue tortured.

Flinging her arms above her head, she moved her legs apart to accommodate him fully. And he did what he knew she wanted him to. Something that came so easily to him.

Please and pleasure his wife.

An hour later, they reluctantly rolled out of bed, showered together, something they rarely did, and made it downstairs to start lunch before the kids arrived.

Angie and Pedro turned up first. "Merry Christmas, Mama. Merry Christmas, Papa," she cried, excitedly jumping over to her parents for hugs and kisses.

Spiros took her and Pedro into his arms. "Merry Christmas you two. Your first together as husband and wife." He took their faces in his hands. "And still babies. Still so young."

"But we are learning to be adults, Papa," Pedro told him, kissing his mother. "Mama."

"But you're still so far from being legal adults." Jenny fiercely hugged Angie. "My baby," she murmured against her head as she rocked back and forth.

"Mama." Angie sighed happily.

Carlos and Viv strolled through the door. "Carlos is here."

"Again with the announcement." Pedro rolled his eyes and looked at his brother.

"Carlos may be here, but he is *not* in charge," Spiros told his eldest, taking him into his embrace. "Not until I am dead are you in charge."

"So…how long do I have to wait then?" Carlos cheekily asked.

"Carlos!" Jenny chastised, pulling Viv into her arms as Angie wouldn't let go. "Merry Christmas," they said, and all hugged together.

"Anyone seen Roger and Tomas?" Jenny asked.

The door banged open, and her father helped Roger get Tomas into the room.

"Tomas, oh, my God," Jenny cried out, pushing a stunned Angie away and running for her son. She felt his forehead and saw his red eyes. "You're sick, come and put him on the couch. Oh, my poor baby."

Roger and Matthew gently set him down, and Jenny laid a blanket over him. "Oh, my baby. You *are* sick." His cheeks were sunken, his colour grey.

"We both are, Mrs S," Roger rasped through his swollen throat. "We must have caught something. With all the winter bugs that would be flying around, it wouldn't be hard." He sat beside Tomas.

"Oh, of course not." Feeling his face, she poked at his glands, noticing they were enlarged. "Have you had painkillers? Do you feel like you're going to be sick?"

"We had them with some toast. T was aching all night, and the electric blanket didn't help. I had to rub his muscles to loosen them up."

"I bet he did," Pedro sniggered to Carlos. Both stood behind another couch, watching.

"Pedro! Not funny," Jenny scowled at her sons.

He blushed. "Sorry, Mama."

Jenny turned back to Tomas. "All right, you two, this has gone on long enough. I'm getting the doctor in tomorrow, and we're going to find out what's wrong. No arguments. Since it's nearly lunchtime, why don't you both rest because you look ghastly and I'll see to lunch. We'll wait to open presents later. Okay?" She received nods in return and went to look in on the special Greek Christmas recipe pork and baklava dishes that she made every second year. She'd wanted to bring a little bit of Mykonos to New York and hoped she'd achieved it.

"So…do you know what's wrong?" Carlos asked, sitting on the arm of the couch he'd been standing behind. "Coz if it's contagious, we can't be getting it."

"Yeah, I'm working New Year's, I can't be sick," Pedro added. "Although…if it's just a gay thing…" He cheekily wagged a finger at them. "Then we don't need to worry."

"Pedro." Spiros pulled his son up. "It could be a simple case of the flu or pneumonia."

"And it *could* be a simple case of a gay thing," Pedro went on. "I'm surrounded by it at work. Half my co-workers are gay, and so are many of the customers."

Tomas rolled his eyes, as painful as that was.

Roger shifted uncomfortably. "Being gay doesn't mean we can't catch colds and flus, you know."

Pedro shrugged. "I know, just joking…kinda. It *could* be a gay thing? Do *you* know for a fact that all gays get the same health issues the rest of us do? What if there's something *only* gay men or women get that straight people don't? Would *you* know about that?"

Roger thought about his questions and finally conceded that he was possibly right. He traded glances with a frowning Tomas.

Tomas had been considering his brother's comments and worried about them. He hadn't been out for long, only since August when he'd had his first experience with Luiz, and then Roger who was only his second lover and husband. Not that he knew what being with a woman was like, and who knew how different his life would be if his first sexual experience had been with a woman instead of a man and he was living a straight life like his two brothers. Being gay meant a lot of things in 1977, and the plain old truth was, gay people didn't know what was out there for them, legally *or* health wise, regardless of how much they tried to fight the systems in place. And that was something he hadn't even bothered to stop and consider outside of the legality of marriage and the fact they, as gay men, could not get married. What other legalities were there concerning him and his husband that they needed to know about, and what did the world *really* have to offer gays? He stared into Roger's eyes. *We really need to go over every detail of what our lifestyle means and put all our thoughts and wants down on paper in case anything does happen to us. Like illness and death,* he thought.

Roger sensed something serious was going through Tomas's mind and squeezed his hand reassuringly.

"Lunch is ready. Do you boys want to carry Tomas over?" Jenny called out.

"Nope, not me." Carlos fled for the table, a laughing Viv trailing behind him.

"Not me. I gotta work next weekend." Pedro grabbed Angie's hand and led her to the table. "Don't wanna get sick, babe."

"I'm disappointed in you two," Jenny scolded them, getting guilty looks in return.

"I'll help," Spiros said. "Let's get you up first." He helped his son stand, and in one powerful movement, he lifted him into his arms.

"Wow, could you do that for me too," Roger joked as he followed them to the table. "I'm flagging in energy."

"Then sit and get some food into you," Jenny said as Spiros put Tomas into his chair. "Do you want a blanket?" She received a shake of his head in return.

Spiros kissed his son's head before pulling out his wife's chair and then seating himself.

Jenny dished out the Greek roast pork and vegetables and passed plates around the table. "Do you just want vegetables, Tomas?" He nodded, and she gave him potatoes, carrots, peas and beans and poured a small amount of gravy on top. But he even turned his nose up at that. "The smell?" she asked and he gave another nod. "Can't you talk at all?"

He looked up, breathed in, and in an almost unintelligible rasp came, "Not really."

"Ooohhh, that's bad." Jenny's face screwed up. "Worse than Roger."

"Well…considering what they do," Pedro cheekily murmured.

"Pedro!" Jenny stopped him. "Enough of that."

"That was only funny the *first* time you said it," Roger told him while Tomas frowned in disappointment.

Pedro looked at his brother's face and saw the hurt. "Sorry, bro, just joking. I don't mean anything by it." He felt bad as his brother looked really sick.

Tomas nodded in return and ate a piece of roast carrot, barely managing to swallow it. He ate what he could, took painkillers, and ate a mouthful of dessert, listening to his family talk about their day. It was their first Christmas together in New York and as married couples, and he was miserable at the fact he was sick, wishing he had been as healthy as he was *before* he met Luiz. Even though he'd seen a doctor in Athens and felt okay, the last few weeks he hadn't. And he'd made Roger sick as well.

Roger sensed Tomas's emotions and glanced at his husband. Seeing the sadness in his eyes, he squeezed his hand and smiled, receiving a sad smile in return.

After lunch, Spiros carried Tomas back to the couch, bringing another smile to his face. "I haven't done this since you were little and broke your leg," he told his son as he gently set him down. "You kept coming up with all sorts of excuses for me to carry you."

A silent laugh came from Tomas, the smile lighting up his face. He remembered that. He was ten and had busted his leg when he'd fallen off his bike and rolled down a hill in the park. His father had carried him everywhere until he had the plaster off, and it had been one of the best times of his life. His father, tall and strong, would lift him high in the air and swing him around. Being in his father's arms had been the best thing ever. The love, the happiness, the times together, just the two of them…he remembered it all.

"Good memories, T?" Roger sat beside his sick husband.

Tomas happily nodded, a huge grin on his face.

"Good," his father said from the other side as he gripped his son's hand and looked at him with love.

Tomas grasped it in return, radiating his happiness at his father.

"Present time. Who wants to go first?" Jenny called, sitting on the ottoman and smiling at her husband and son.

"We will." Angie bounced over to the tree and picked up Pedro's present. "For my *husband*." She gave it to him with a kiss.

"Thanks, babe." He lifted the lid on the box and pulled out the monogrammed bag Angie had bought him. "Oh, this is gorgeous, babe." His fingers traced the silver initials PMS on the flap. The buckles and hardware were silver as well. Opening the flap, he found more presents. Pulling out a large square object he ripped off the paper and found three of the latest albums. "Cool. I was after these."

"I know," Angie said from her spot on the sofa arm next to him. "One more."

He looked inside and removed another present, finding the latest book on music and DJing.

"Thought you could brush up on your skills," she said, flicking her hair over her shoulder.

"Hey," he protested. "I'm the best there is."

"Or so you think," Carlos grumbled. "Can we get on with it?"

Jenny jumped up and distributed gifts. "Carlos from Vivian, Vivian from Carlos." She handed them over then went back for more. "Angelina from Pedro,"

"Yay," Angie squealed, clapping her hands. She was wearing the Christmas jumper from Jenny and would treasure it always. She'd never had a family tradition, and if this was one of them, she would grab it with both hands and run with it.

"Mum and Dad from each other and from Spiros and me." Jenny handed over presents.

"Oh, thank you, darling," Sarah said, taking the brightly coloured gifts.

"Roger to Tomas and Tomas to Roger." Jenny sat and watched everyone open presents, reminiscing about the days when the boys were little.

"Cool, I got a bag too. Thanks, Viv." Carlos quickly kissed her and examined his bag.

"Thank your mother. She helped pick it out." Viv laughed, opening her gift. "Oh, Carlos, it's beautiful." She pulled the heart pendant from the box and held it up. It dazzled in the light.

"Well, you can thank Mama, she helped pick it out." Carlos laughed and clasped the chain around her neck.

"I got one too," Angie squealed and quickly put it around her neck. "Oh, I love it." She kissed her husband. "I love it, but what will you get me for Valentine's Day?"

Pedro groaned. "Can't we just get through Christmas first?"

Tomas opened his present to find a matching bag to his brothers. *Thank you,* he mouthed to Roger, kissing him before sneaking a look at his mother and mouthing thank you to her too, getting a smile in return.

"I got a bag too!" Roger exclaimed, pulling the brown leather bag that matched Tomas's out of the box. "Thanks, T." He kissed his husband who was smiling despite his illness.

"Hey, mine's engraved." Angie read the back of her pendant. *"A, I heart U, P, Christmas 1977."*

"Oh, mine is too." Viv read the back of hers.

"And mine's monogrammed," Roger added. "Just like the boys' bags are monogrammed." They all looked at Jenny who raised her brows and looked away as if to say, *it wasn't me.*

Smiling, she went to collect the presents for her children. "Don't open them until you all have them," she warned. "Spiros, help me."

He hefted two large presents over to Carlos and Viv, two more to Pedro and Angie, and the last two to Roger and Tomas.

Jenny sat back down to watch her six children watching her. "Go on, open them."

They all attacked to reveal monogrammed matching suitcases for each couple.

"A suitcase, Mama?" Carlos asked, a little disappointed at the gift.

"Open it, keep looking," was all Jenny said.

Getting onto the floor, they unlocked their cases to reveal smaller ones inside.

"A set," Angie cried. "In black leather, cool."

"Keep going," Jenny told them.

They pulled out the smaller case and opened them to find cabin bags.

"A full luggage set," Carlos said. "With our initials." His and Viv's sets were dark blue leather with gold initials and hardware.

"With all the flying you've done this year, and you'll be doing next year, I thought it was high time you had decent luggage sets so you could travel in style," Jenny told them.

Roger and Tomas had dark brown leather with gold hardware, and

Tomas held up his bag from Roger, glancing from his mother to Roger.

"Hey, our bags match," Roger said, looking from the bags to Jenny. "No wonder you suggested them." He checked the others. "They *all* match."

"I'm good at that." Jenny nodded in agreement with herself. "And I happen to see another large present under the tree." She went to collect it and gave it to Spiros. "For you, my darling husband."

"Jenny, you didn't." He pulled the paper back to reveal a dark green leather suitcase.

"I have a new set, so why should you miss out." She watched her husband open each case to reveal the one inside.

"It is beautiful workmanship." He examined the bag. "Just beautiful."

"And I have some more presents." She retrieved a box of small gifts from under the tree and handed one to Spiros. "This one first." Watching him open it, she saw him remove a silver metal watch. "It's for everyday use, wearing to the shop and what not."

"It's lovely." Spiros looked from the watch to her. "I did *need* a new watch."

"I know, that's why I also bought everyone one of these." She handed her husband, parents, and six children small brightly wrapped gifts.

They opened them to reveal gold or silver metal watches with diamonds around the face and black leather bands. The girls were slightly smaller than the men's.

"Jenny, you shouldn't have, one was enough." Spiros was slightly annoyed. His wife was spending way too extravagantly, and even though he knew it was what she wanted to do, it made him uncomfortable with all the gifts.

"Mama." Carlos was astounded. "Awesome."

She watched her children put their watches on. "And they're inscribed with your name and year," she added, seeing the amazement on everyone's faces except for Spiros who had placed his gold watch back in the box. "Don't you like it?"

He sighed. "You're going overboard, my love. I don't need two watches, one is more than enough. I can understand spending on the children, but I do not need so much."

She spun around on the ottoman to face him. "Ever since I met you, you worked hard to provide for yourself, then me, then the boys. After you turned down Giorgio's estate, which was *your* choice, I thought you backed me up on taking Stefano's? I want to look after our boys. I want to spoil them rotten even if it's just for this Christmas or next birthday. I want to spoil my parents and my husband. Why is that wrong after everything we've been through?"

A sigh escaped him. "Because it all seems like too much. Especially these watches."

"Am I not allowed to spoil my husband?" Jenny asked. "You're in your fifties now, Spiros, I'm nearly there, and we deserve nice things at this age. And I want to set my boys up for the rest of their lives and make sure they are well taken care of. You've done that for twenty-five years, now let me take care of them, *continue* to take care of them, *and you*, for the rest of their lives and yours. It's my job as your wife and their mother to take care of all of you. And now that includes Vivian, Angelina, and Roger, plus two unborn grandbabies. *They're* going to need looking after too. So let me do my job and look after *all of you*." She implored her husband.

He nearly relented. "It's *my* job to look after everyone."

"And you've done it. Now that the boys are adults *let me* do it and repay you for all the years you've looked after me," she said. "Besides, I can't take the watch back if you don't like it because it's engraved."

He laughed lightly. "That's my Jenny. First, a fine apartment to stay in, and then expensive presents."

"All part of the plan," she told him. "The apartment building is ours for our family. For Pedro and Angie to live in safely. For Carlos and Viv, and Tomas and Roger to stay in when they're here. It's our home here in New York," she told them all. "No more finding hotels to stay in. No more worrying about where you'll stay. *This* is your home."

"We get to stay here permanently, Mama?" Angie was wide-eyed at the thought of living somewhere so grand.

"Yes," Jenny said. "This is our home here in New York because I bought the building." She turned her attention from wide-eyed children back to Spiros who had an array of emotions sweeping over his face amidst the gasps from the family. "I want a safe place for my baby and grandbaby to stay while they're working and going to school here. And I will *not* argue with you over this Spiros. We can provide them with homes and make sure our children and grandchildren are safe. Doesn't that matter?"

A deep frown spread across his face. "Of course, it is important that we take care of our family, but an *entire* apartment building, Jenny?"

"It's not like we can't afford it?" she replied.

With a groan and a sigh, he shifted in his seat. He knew she was right, but it was all too extravagant. And it was all too much…too much. *Stefano, my only hope is that you are turning in your grave,* he thought. *Jenny did say she wanted to blow it on the boys and here she is doing just that.* But as much as he didn't like it, he knew she was right. The family needed to be looked after because it was growing, and if an apartment building was the way to go to keep them all safe and in one place, then so be it.

"Okay, my love." He took Jenny's hand. "The family owns an apartment building." Not that he liked it.

"Are you two done?" Carlos asked, secretly ecstatic at his family owning an apartment building in New York. "Because we have presents for you, and Grandma and Grandpa." He jumped up and found the two small boxes he'd placed under the tree. He'd been in charge of them since Athens, and it had been killing him holding onto them. Handing them over to his parents, he sat back beside Viv and perched on the edge of the couch in excitement.

"Are these the presents you mentioned that day in the department store?" Jenny asked as she and Spiros opened up their boxes.

"Yes, they are," Carlos said.

Jenny saw her present sparkling in the satin bed of the box. "Oh, I love it!" She lifted up a medium-sized silver charm bracelet with diamond covered initials dangling from it. S, J, C, V, T, R, P, A, all in a row.

"And the store has more, so when another Stephanopoulos comes along you can order one anytime to add to it," Carlos told her. "We couldn't leave the two of you out of this initial thing we all have going on."

"The Stephanopoulos tradition is not just about cufflinks," Pedro added. "Even though that's what we got Papa." He grinned and watched his father clasp his cufflinks to his shirt cuffs.

"And now I've added to it with the monogramming of your bags," Jenny said. "Who knew! Looks like we'll continue this with the grandchildren when they come along. It will be our tradition that we pass down through the generations. Parents to children, brothers to brothers."

"I am very honoured, my sons, that you would buy me a pair as well." Spiros admired the handiwork of the Greek artisan who had made the boys' cufflinks.

"We weren't about to let you go without, any more than we were going to let Tomas and Roger go without." Carlos glanced at the matching pair of his father and brother beside each other. Their smiles beamed back at him. He knew how important it had been to his brother and brother-in-law, just the tears and smiles had been enough to show him. He wasn't about to let his father miss out as well.

Viv excitedly jumped up and retrieved the rest of the presents from under the tree, handing them to Jenny and her parents.

"Oh, another one?" Intrigued by the second present, Jenny pulled the ribbon and removed the lid with Spiros leaning over her shoulder. Folding back the tissue paper she revealed a photo frame. "Oh, boys, oh," Jenny cried, picking the frame up. Inside was an 8x10 photo of her boys dressed up and standing behind a couch while the in-laws were seated on it.

Viv sat in front of Carlos to the right of the picture. Roger sat in the middle with Tomas behind him. And Angie sat to the left with Pedro behind her. He had his right hand on her shoulder which she clasped, and his left arm around Tomas's shoulder. Carlos was doing the same thing, while Tomas had both hands on Roger's shoulders.

"Oh." Tears welled in Jenny's eyes. "My babies. When did you do this?" She glanced at her parents to see they had received the same present.

"Just last week," Carlos said. "We left it a bit late coz we couldn't think of anything else. It was Viv who came up with a family photo."

"Cabot Conroy, my photographer friend, was able to do it. We had a Christmas set made up and went for it," Viv informed them.

Jenny studied the photo, seeing the tree in the background, and the bowls of balls on the coffee table in front of her children. Looking at each one, she said, "My babies. Thank you so much." She held it out for Spiros to see. "Our children."

He smiled and took it from her, setting it in the middle of the mantel above the family's stockings for all to see, for the rest of eternity.

*****

On Monday afternoon, the doctor came to examine Tomas and Roger. Jenny had kept them in the penthouse in one of the smaller bedrooms, shivering and sweating, aching and moaning, so she could look after them both without having to run down to their apartment.

"I'm so glad you could come. My son saw a doctor a month ago for something else, but now he's so sick." Jenny led the way upstairs.

"There have been a lot of colds and flus going around this year." Dr Hubbard trailed after her. "A lot of my patients at my practice have all come down with something."

They arrived in the bedroom to find the boys shivering.

"I put them together so it didn't spread, but since the family's been together over Christmas, I'm worried my daughters-in-law might catch it. These are my sons, Tomas and Roger."

Tomas looked at them through hooded eyes. "Hurts…" he rasped.

Dr Hubbard set his bag on the bed and removed his stethoscope to listen to the boys' chests. "Tell me, sore throat?" He got two nods. "Aching bones?" A second set of nods. "Headaches?" A third set of nods. He felt their glands and took their temperatures. "I'd say you both have a nasty case of the flu." He looked at the pallor of their skin and sunken eyes. "Is this the worst it's been so far?" They nodded once more. "Tell me, Mrs Stephanopoulos, what timeline has it been and what have you done?"

"Well," Jenny started, thinking back. "Tomas had a sore throat two weeks ago, but that went after a couple of days of painkillers and old-fashioned home-cooked chicken soup. Then last week, just before Christmas, we found out he'd had a headache for a couple of days, plus bone ache. On Saturday, then yesterday, it was worse for both of them. Barely able to talk, they moaned and groaned all night, and now you see how they are, they look like death." She waved a hand at her sons.

"Yes, well, it looks like this one picked something up and couldn't quite shake it off because he's worse." He pointed to Tomas. "And then he passed it on to the other one. Are you boys together all the time?"

"Yes," Jenny jumped in. "They share an apartment and are together all day every day. They're like twins." Jenny narrowed her eyes at her sons hoping they'd pick up on her *don't mention you're gay or a couple* vibe.

"Not working then?" The doctor scribbled something on his pad.

"They had some time off for a family holiday, but now with being sick, their bosses don't want them back until they're well again." Jenny supplied the information which was partly true.

"I'd definitely say they have the flu and a bad case of it. Keep up with the fluids, but give them these instead of plain painkillers." He handed over the prescriptions. "It will help attack the germs, and the other will help the system get better. Plus, you could give them vitamins c and d, that should help."

Jenny took the prescriptions. "Is there anything else? Like cold compressions, or heat packs for their aching muscles?"

"It might help." Hubbard snapped his bag closed. "But when it comes to the flu, it can be a hard thing to get rid of. It's a matter of trying everything to see what works. Other than that, I can't suggest anything. If it gets worse, get them to the hospital, but from the look of them I'd say they're at their worst." He looked back at the boys huddling together under the covers. "I think it can only get better from here."

"How much longer will it take?" Jenny asked anxiously.

"Well, since the symptoms started showing up two weeks ago, and now you have everything together, it may take a week before it's abated enough for them to feel human again. But give it a few more weeks after that to really kick it out of their system. The vitamins will help. Other than that, there's nothing I can do."

"Thank you, doctor. I'll walk you out."

While Jenny led the doctor out Roger snuggled closer. "We need to keep warm, T."

"But I'm hot," Tomas rasped. "So hot."

"That's the flu," Roger said. "Hot one minute, cold the next. It's the fever."

"So sore," Tomas mumbled, his muscles shivering and shaking. "Hurts so much."

Jenny came back. "Your father's going to watch you while I run down to the pharmacy. I should have been giving you vitamins weeks ago. Oh, I feel so foolish not doing my motherly duties. I thought the doctor in Athens was enough, but clearly not. And now you're both suffering because I didn't do enough." She tucked the comforter around them. "Hopefully the pills will help, and the vitamins will boost your immune systems back up. You boys rest." She gazed into their yellow tinged sunken eyes and felt their foreheads.

Oh, dear, she thought. *Why do I have such a bad feeling about this? All because of bloody Luiz.* "I'll be back soon."

Leaving Spiros in charge, she dashed down to the corner store where she consulted the pharmacists about vitamins while waiting for the prescriptions to be done. Thinking her whole family could do with a boost, she bought vitamins for Viv and Angie for their pregnancies, and added bottles of vitamins for Carlos and Pedro. She also remembered to pop the rolls of Christmas film in before dashing back home to administer her sons the first lot of pills and fill them with chicken soup. She'd made more with the leftovers of Christmas Eve dinner.

Sitting down in the easy chair beside the bed, she watched them sleep fitfully. Soft moans escaped here and there, a shift of a leg, an arch of the back to get out stiffness. She left cold compresses on their foreheads and opened the window a little to keep the room cool. Sitting by the bed, she fretted about her son and his husband.

Why do I get the feeling this is more than the flu? Why do I get the feeling this has to do with Luiz? What sort of germs could he have passed on to my baby? What effects could the poisoning have had? Frowning, she settled back into the chair and kept an eye on them, only to be woken by Spiros laying a blanket over her.

"You were shivering yourself," he murmured. "I hope *you're* not coming down with the same thing."

Smiling, she said, "No, just chilly. I thought fresh air would help clear the germs away and keep them cool." She moved to check on them, but Spiros stopped her.

"Let me."

Relenting, she watched him inspect their temperatures and dab their faces with the wet cloth. "What about you? You might get sick yourself."

He shrugged and turned his head to look at his wife snuggling under the blanket. "If I get sick then you can look after me like you always have."

Remembering back, she could not think of a time when Spiros had been sick. At least not as long as she'd known him. He had always been strong and virile and healthy as an ox, while the boys had picked up everything. Mumps, measles, chicken pox, colds and flus. You name it, they probably had it, right along with their cousins. But after moving to Mykonos they'd calmed down, become healthier, worried more about what they ate and worked out. Tomas had thrived on sea air and exercise, but now…

Maybe I should take him back to Mykonos for that sea air, Jenny thought. *Or maybe I should go to Miami with them and take care of them until he's well.* The thought of Miami intrigued her, but she also knew that's where the Seralifts were, and the thought of them made her sick. She desperately wanted to get her kids out of that business, and maybe the Papadopoulos fortune could do just that, especially for Tomas and Roger since they didn't have kids on the way. They could do whatever they wanted. Go wherever they wanted and not have to work in porn movies. Sighing, she laid her head against Spiros who sat on the arm of her chair.

"What is it, my love?" He was concerned for his son, having not seen him so sick since he was a child, and for his wife who was burdened by something.

"I don't know," she said with a shake of her head. "I can't put my finger on it."

"What do *you* think it is?"

"Something bad. Something other than the flu. It's just a feeling deep down in my gut. My soul. That what Luiz did was bad, and the after-effects are going to last the rest of Tomas's life."

"Have you ever felt that way before?" he asked.

A sigh from deep within her gut came out. "No."

*****

Jenny had warned the family to stay away for the rest of the week while she nursed her babies back to health, which was fine for Carlos and Viv as Viv had photo shoots to do, and Carlos was busy writing movie scripts for the actors and actresses of the DeVille stable. If he was finishing up after his stint as an actor, then he wanted to show Harry he had it in him to continue as a script writer for future movies. He'd even taken the *Golden Gods* idea and turned it into something spectacular.

"What did *you* think of it?" he asked Viv the next day between photo shoots.

"It was good," she mumbled around getting her make-up touched up. "I liked the fact it wouldn't be just you."

"They did keep mentioning something in Greece about all doing a movie, so I thought I'd write some new stuff and that's what I came up with. It would be longer than normal. Think Harry and the others will like it?"

"I think at this stage, anything Harry can make money out of where you're concerned will be a bonus." Viv stood and disrobed. "How do I look?" She modelled the latest European trends in swimwear that was coming to the states early May. She patted her stomach. "At least I'm still flat."

Carlos looked up from the writing pad in his lap to survey his gorgeous wife in her iridescent blue bikini with pink sequins and matching sarong. "Hot babe. Can't wait to see you wear that this summer."

She snorted. "With a baby to give birth to, I'll be lucky to fit into a kaftan."

*****

At four o'clock on Friday afternoon, Angelina walked through her door after spending the day shopping with Maggie, dumped her bags on the couch in the living room, went into the bedroom, and bounced onto the bed to smother her husband in kisses.

"Ah, Angie. I need my rest," Pedro groaned.

"I know," she said. "But I want to show my husband how much I love him. We haven't had sex in the afternoon for ages." She spread out on top of him. "I miss it."

"We don't have sex because you don't feel like it," Pedro muttered, trapped under the blankets.

"True," she replied, her face next to his. "I like it at night, on the weekends. Maybe I'm just not that horny now I'm pregnant."

Pedro half snorted, half laughed. "At least I've gotten more sleep out of it. I don't have you waking me up by bouncing up and down on my cock anymore. How many names did you end up giving it?"

She giggled. "I lost count. Do you think we can go upstairs tonight? It's New Year's Eve Eve, and I've missed Mama and Papa."

"Mmm, don't know. Depends if Tomas and Roger are still sick."

"I want to see Mama." Angie frowned, missing her desperately. "I miss Mama so much."

"Mmm, well that's something you'll have to get used to once they go home."

"I don't want them to go home," she cried, sitting up next to him. "I want Mama and Papa to stay forever."

Pedro finally opened his eyes to look at his wife. Young, pregnant and married, and she was pouting like a petulant child. "We don't even know if *we're* staying here forever. You have school, what happens after that? Will we still be here? And I don't know how long my gig at 69 will last. What then?"

Angie bit her lip and shrugged. "I don't know. I just want my Mama and Papa to stay here with us. Mama bought the building so we'd have somewhere to live and everyone else can stay, so why can't they?" Tears welled in her eyes.

"Because Papa has the meat shop and they live on Mykonos." Pedro leant against a pile of pillows and wiped away Angie's tears. "Don't cry, babe. They'll be back for birthdays and the birth of our baby."

With a quivering bottom lip, she finally burst out, "But I want my Mama and Papa. I miss them."

Pedro took her into his arms. "Oh, Angie. They love you like a daughter, and to them, you and Viv probably are, but they have their lives too. And you have school, and I have 69. We can't expect them to up and move to suit us."

After sobbing into her husband's chest for a few minutes, she couldn't take it much longer. "I want my Mama." Leaning across Pedro, she grabbed the phone and rang the penthouse.

After five rings, Spiros answered. "Hello."

"Papa, I miss you and Mama. I want to see you. Is Tomas well enough for us to come up?"

Spiros laughed. "Ah, my little Angelina, just let me check with Jenny." He left her hanging on the phone before coming back. "You can all come up for dinner tonight. The boys are better and—"

Angie slammed the phone down, raced out the door and upstairs to burst through the door just as Spiros was putting the phone down. "Papa, I missed you." She leapt into his arms for a big hug and received one in return.

"Oh, we've missed you too, Angelina." Spiros kissed her cheek and put her down.

"Where's Mama?" Angie looked around to see Jenny tucking Tomas and Roger into one of the couches. "Hey, you're out of bed," she said, racing over to them. "Mama! I missed you." She flung herself into Jenny's arms.

"Oh, sweetie, I missed you, too." Jenny hugged her fiercely then let go to finish up with the boys. "Where's Pedro?"

"Who?" Angie asked.

"Who?" Pedro repeated, rambling into the penthouse in pyjamas, a robe, and tousled hair. "You saw me less than a minute ago before you flew out of the bedroom."

Angie giggled. "Of course I know *who* you are, I just forgot."

"Nice!" Pedro said to his father. "My wife forgot who I am. Hey bro, how are you?" He sat down on one of the couches and Angie sat beside him, happy to be back in the penthouse with her parents.

"Better," Tomas said, the worst being behind them. "My throat's better. I can talk again, and I'm not having hot and cold flushes."

"The pills have done their work," Jenny said, coming back with glasses of cold juice for the boys. "The fever is gone, and so have most of the aches and pains."

"So, you'll be okay to come to 69 tomorrow night?" Pedro munched on a biscuit from a plate that Jenny handed around.

"Ugh, I don't know." Tomas took a bite out of Rudolph.

"I think at least an hour or two." Jenny sat on the ottoman. "We're always together at Christmas and New Year's, and this should be no different. You're well enough to pop out for a few hours, and it might do you good," she told Tomas and Roger. "We'll just sit on the sidelines. Is there a place to sit and watch?" she asked Pedro.

"Sure, there are small lounge areas off to the side where you can sit and watch the action. I asked Eddie to keep one reserved just in case," Pedro replied.

"Good. Then we can start the night off here, maybe go out and roam the streets, see what happens in New York at New Year's."

"They have that big ball drop every year," Angie said. "Maggie told me her and her parents are going to it."

"What happens with that?" Jenny asked, interested to hear more about the glass ball and what it had to do with New Year's celebrations.

"It's been happening since 1907, and it's hosted by Dick Clark. Plus, it's live on TV. The ball's made of glass and light globes, and slowly comes down a pole to the countdown, and then lights up at midnight."

"That sounds exciting. I vaguely remember something about it over the last few years, but we don't get to see much in Mykonos. What about this? We watch some TV, then go out about eight, roam around, then go to the club about eleven. Stay for an hour or two, and come home. How does that sound? Will that be too much for you?" Jenny laid a hand on Tomas's knee.

"Ugh," he groaned. "I don't know, Mama. I have just enough strength to walk downstairs and sit on the couch."

"Nonsense," Jenny said. "If I have to go and get you a wheelchair then I will. Or, we can just drive around and look at the city until it's time to go to 69. We haven't seen Pedro play since last year on Mykonos. I can't wait. What sort of club is it?"

"Ah." Tomas's eyes widened as Angie giggled.

"A very free and easy one," Roger finally said, watching everyone pull faces.

"In what way?" Jenny asked, intrigued as to what her children were keeping from her.

Roger looked from Pedro to Tomas. "It's very loud, very colourful, and very disco. They welcome all sorts. Like us..." He laid his hand over his husband's.

"Oh...*that* free and easy." Jenny glanced at Spiros. "Anything we need to watch out for?"

"Ah..." Tomas and Roger exchanged amused glances.

"What?" Jenny looked from one to the other.

Tomas grinned and cast a glance at his brother. "Pedro's outfit."

Pedro groaned. "Don't tell her."

"She's gonna see it," Angie said, her giggles growing into laughter.

"What's wrong with it?" Spiros entered the conversation.

"Well..." Pedro pulled a face. "It's not like what I wore on Mykonos."

"That doesn't matter," Jenny told him.

"Exactly," Roger added. "It's what you do that counts, and he's the best I've seen, Mrs S. And I've seen a lot of DJs over the last few years."

"Thanks, bro." Pedro grinned. "Look, Mama, I don't wear much on stage, it's too hot and too much of a burden when I dance. So you might not like it, but then," he screwed up his face, "neither do I."

"I can't wait to see it then," Jenny said. "I'm going to ring Mum and Dad and see if Carlos and Viv are in."

Forty-five minutes later everyone was seated around the dining table.

"What plans do you have for tomorrow besides spending it with us?" Jenny asked Carlos and Viv.

"Drop in to see some friends early on," Viv replied. "We could all meet up later at 69. You play for twenty-four hours don't you, Pedro?"

Pedro swallowed a mouthful of mashed potato. "Yep. I work until one tomorrow morning then home for sleep then back to start all over. Master Z and I will be taking turns for a whole day."

"We were planning on dropping by around eleven and staying for a couple of hours. Will that fit in with your plans?" Jenny asked, scooping up a forkful of peas.

"That's fine, Mama. Viv's friends were heading for 69 at some point anyway," Carlos said.

"Good. It's settled then. We'll spend it together," Jenny said.

"You fit enough to come out tomorrow night, bro?" Carlos asked Tomas before shovelling another mouthful of food in.

Tomas looked sideways at Carlos as he realised what his brother had just said. "I *already* came out, bro."

Carlos glanced up from his plate. "What? Nah, I meant come outside after being sick all week. You fit enough?"

Roger laughed under his breath. "We knew what you meant."

"Well?" Carlos repeated, completely unaware of what was happening.

"That's Carlos," Pedro said. "His ego's become so big he doesn't even realise what he's saying." Everyone but Carlos laughed.

"I might be well enough to *come out* for a few hours to celebrate New Year's," Tomas told Carlos.

"Cool," Carlos replied. "So, we'll see you tomorrow night."

*****

They rolled to a slow stop outside of *Studio 69*, to see a long and freezing, but excited line of partygoers waiting to get in.

"Are we able to just walk in or do we have to wait in line?" Jenny asked, glancing out the window of their car. They had driven around for the last two hours after watching New Year's Eve celebrations on TV, and now they were there to see Pedro.

"I have our tickets, Mama. We had to buy them for tonight." Angie pulled them out of her purse. She wore her long black fur coat over a tight sparkly lycra bodysuit with studded boots and a silver knitted top over it. Her heart necklace from Pedro hung around her neck.

"Oh, good, let's go then," Jenny said, excited at what lay ahead.

They alighted one by one from the car, and the people in line turned to stare, screaming when they saw Tomas and Roger step out of the car.

"Oh, my God, it's Tomas Stefan and Roger Dencott," someone yelled before starting the chant of 'porn stars' that spread through the crowd.

Tomas blushed and shied away, so Roger put a protective arm around him while Spiros stood on the other side. Angie led the way in, flashing the tickets and introducing her family to the bouncers who let them in.

Once in the club, Jenny stopped and stared. A massive disco ball hung from the ceiling and sent shards of coloured light in all directions, glitter bombs were going off, champagne flowed, and balloons floated through the air.

Craning her neck to look for Pedro, she found him on stage in his short shorts and boots. Her brows rose. "So *that's* what he wears?" She exchanged an amused glance with Spiros.

Angie giggled. "And he *hates* it. Come on, let's find our booth." She led them to the side of the club to the private lounge areas. "Here we are." She stripped off her coat and dumped it on the lounge, then her bag landed on top of it. When she turned around, she spied Maggie. "Hey, Maggie's here." With a wave of her hand, she ran for her friend at the front of the stage and waved up to Pedro, pointing in the direction of the lounging area.

He turned to see his parents and grandparents waving back and blushed.

"What are you doing here?" Angie asked Maggie. "I thought you were going to the ball drop." She shook her groove thing to the music.

"I was, but told my parents I'd rather spend it with my bestie, so here I am," she replied. "Besides, they had all their friends to party with, and who wants to spend New Year's with old people?"

Angie giggled. "I'm spending it with my in-laws, what's wrong with that?"

Maggie blushed. "Yeah, but…that's different."

Spiros helped Jenny out of her coat to reveal a lamé party dress and chic black stockings and heels. "Look at you all dolled up." He laid the coats over the back of the couch.

"And look at you." She straightened the collars of his black suit and shirt. They were new, and she'd told him how devastatingly handsome he looked in them.

Roger and Tomas helped each other out of their coats, and they looked equally as handsome in their Tony Manero suits. And more than a few people were watching the porn stars closely.

"Will you two be dancing?" Jenny asked them as she scanned the crowd.

"No, I don't—" Tomas started

"Why not?" Roger finished.

Tomas looked at Roger. "I don't know if I have the energy."

"One dance, or two, it's New Year's. We *have* come to dance the new year in you know," Roger told him.

Sitting down, Tomas sighed wearily. "I don't know, maybe."

"Well, I for one love this song, so we're going to dance." Jenny pulled Spiros onto the dance floor.

"Ah…what are we doing?" he asked as he followed Jenny.

"We're going to dance." Jenny started moving. "We haven't danced since the weddings, and before that, it was probably their birthdays, so a long time coming." She slithered up and down in her slinky blue party dress, bumping and grinding against her husband.

"Jenny," Spiros hissed. "We don't dance like this." He was embarrassed by their surroundings, having never been in such an open club before.

"First time for everything. You know what they say…when in New York at 69…" Spinning around she clicked her fingers and waved her hands in the air. "Come on, party pooper." Taking his hand, she spun him around. *"Come on."* She saw his face. "Loosen up, Spiros Stefan, you're the father of the porn star brothers, and it's New Year's Eve 1977. We're in New York, it's hot, the disco's jumping, and you're gonna get some more of what I've been giving you since you arrived in New York." She turned around so her back was to him and bumped and ground up and down. "It's New Year's, get in the groove, man."

Unable to contain himself, he laughed. "Good grief. What's gotten into you?"

"It's going to be a new year in," she looked up at the big clock above Pedro on the stage, "forty-five minutes and I'm hoping it's better than this one."

Spiros spun her around into a dip then lifted her back up. "Cheers to that."

They danced for another fifteen minutes before seeing Pedro come off stage after putting a twelve inch on. They met up with him at their lounge.

"My baby, you are good." Jenny kissed both cheeks. "But that outfit…" She looked him up and down.

"I know, I hate it," he moaned. "But everyone here wears the same thing."

"Well, it's not like I haven't seen you without clothes on," Jenny went on, eyeing how tiny the shorts were. "You *were born naked* and ran around a lot as a kid without clothes on, so it's not like we haven't seen what you have." She nudged Spiros and winked. "You know you all take after your father."

"Mama," Pedro moaned again. "Can you *not* say stuff like that?" He covered his face for a few moments.

"Why? You were naked in my stomach for nine months, then you popped out like an eel. *A naked eel.*" Jenny laughed at his discomfort and the face he pulled.

"Mama, enough!" Pedro spied his boss over their shoulders. "Ah, Mama, Papa, this is Eddie Monteif, owner of 69." He pointed behind them, and they turned around.

"Ah, Mr Monteif." Jenny shook hands. "Are you responsible for these ridiculous costumes the staff have to wear?" She saw Tomas and Roger giggle behind their champagne glasses.

"Well…" Eddie had never met a staff member's parent before and didn't know quite what to say. "Sex sells, Mrs Stephanopoulos, and your son has what it takes. Only beautiful people work here, and your son is one of them."

"*I* know that." Jenny laughed. "I helped make him, of course he's gorgeous."

"Hey, Mama." Carlos and Viv rushed up to them. "We made it." He kissed everyone before being introduced to Eddie.

Eddie's eyes widened to saucer size. "Whoa, all three porn star brothers…in my club…on New Year's…Pedro, you should have told me your brothers were coming. And it's time you got back on stage."

"Yes, boss." Pedro saluted.

Jenny turned to him. "Make sure you eat and keep your fluids up." She gave him a quick kiss.

"Yes, Mama," he replied and ran back to the stage.

"So, what do you think of his outfit?" Viv asked, sipping a glass of sparkling water.

"Scant." Jenny laughed. "But I've seen him naked, so what can anyone do? At least it covers what it's meant to."

"Barely." Viv giggled.

"How ya feelin', bro?" Carlos slapped Tomas on the back as he sat beside him, sipping a beer he'd grabbed from one of the roller-skating waiters.

"Good. Better than expected," Tomas said. "The city has given me some energy back, and the club is giving me a vibe."

"A vibe huh?" Carlos grinned. "Considering what's going on, I'm surprised you haven't joined in." He pointed to a male on male couple making out by the bar, about twenty feet to their left.

"Who knows, we might be saving it for the new year." Roger raised a jaunty brow after checking the couple out.

"I bet," Carlos said. "So, what do you think of this dude?" He nodded at Eddie who was still talking to their parents. "Gay or what?"

"Definitely," Roger replied, grabbing the beer he'd ordered from Leon, who rolled away, but kept looking over his shoulder.

"Think he's after our little bro?" Carlos asked, peering closely at Eddie.

Tomas snorted. "Isn't everyone?"

Carlos pretended to be hurt. "Ah, no, some people *are* after me. I'm a porn star *too,* you know."

"Yeah." Tomas took a swig of Roger's beer. "Only in your head do people want you."

"Fun-nee," Carlos quipped. "Come on, Viv, let's dance." They hit the floor and partied next to Angie and Maggie, and were joined by his parents after a few more moments with Eddie.

He spied the two love birds on the couch. "So, Mr Stefan and Mr Dencott. The gay porn stars are in my club. Once again, welcome back. I hope you're having a good time?" He eyed the delicious morsels that were Tomas and Roger and couldn't stop himself from getting a hard-on.

"Having a good time, thank you," Roger replied.

"Not dancing at all?" Eddie asked.

"We've been ill the last few weeks, so we're saving our energy for the countdown," Tomas explained, hoping he'd go.

"Ah, well if you need a little pick me up," Eddie said. "You just need to ask."

"No, thanks, drink is all we need." Roger raised his beer. "Thanks anyway."

"Okay, if you change your mind." Eddie sauntered off into the crowd, schmoozing with everyone he came across. Halston, Diane Von Furstenberg, the Hemingways, Mick Jagger. The celebrity list was endless.

"Jesus," Tomas muttered. "Some people pile it on thick, don't they?" He glanced around at all the celebrities, a little overwhelmed at being in the same room as people he saw in magazines and on TV.

"Yeah, they do," Roger answered. "But we're big in the porn industry, and people are going to notice."

"Yeah…about that…" Tomas's voice trailed off.

Roger studied his lover's face as Tomas glanced down at his lap where his fingers played with the champagne glass. He sensed it and knew it was coming. *And* he didn't have a problem with it. "You want out of the business."

Tomas looked up in surprise. "Are you a mind reader now?"

Roger laughed. "No. But with you being so reluctant to join it, and with everything that's happened, plus being sick and your mother wanting you to quit, it was a safe bet that's what you were thinking."

A sad smile crossed Tomas's face. "Yeah, you're right. I never really wanted to do it. I just did it to be with you. But now that we're married…" He shrugged excitedly. "*We're married.* We're *together*, we can do whatever we want, and I *love* training."

"Get back to it then," Roger said, sliding an arm around his husband. "If you love it that much go back to it, and either I can keep on helping out at the studio, or maybe I can join you as a trainer and we can start a business together. How about Stefan and Dencott, *Personal* Trainers?"

The grin spread across Tomas's face. "I love it, and it's a good thing you put my name first."

"Yeah, and why's that?"

"Coz I woulda thumped you."

"Really! What about kissed me instead?" Roger tried to get a kiss out of him.

"Oh, you want a kiss, do you?" Tomas planted his lips to Roger's and let them softly linger for a few moments before pulling away. "How's that?"

"Good. But how about some more?" Roger went back for seconds.

"How about we save it for New Year's? We only have," Tomas glanced at the clock, "ten minutes to go."

"How about we dance, then? Come on." He hauled a protesting Tomas to his feet and over to the dance floor.

"Roger, I don't want to."

"Hush! We have ten minutes until New Year's, let's enjoy it." Roger pulled Tomas close and they slow danced despite the disco song being the latest hit by Heatwave.

"Come on, people," Pedro called. "We have ten minutes until it's 1978. Let's party like it's the year 2000." Waving his arms in the air, he got the crowd jumping. The regulars were there, Bev, Sara, Martine and Stan. Even Greta, Stephanie, Thomas, and Carson had turned up to see their star performer play, but steered well clear of his family, especially the parents.

No, Greta did not want a rematch with Jenny Stephanopoulos after the right royal dressing down she'd received in Athens. No, there was no way in hell she'd be on the end of that again.

"Oh, *my God*, doesn't he look divine," Thomas cried, swirling his straw around in his drink. He had been drooling over Pedro since they'd arrived at eight.

"He does," Greta replied. "I spoke to him during a break, he promised to be back at work the second week of January, and I promised to have the movies ready to go. He's only doing one a week to have them done and out of the way before Angie and he become parents."

"Lucky bitch!" Stephanie fumed, downing her tenth champagne for the night. It only added to the fifty other drinks she had consumed since they'd arrived. Basically, she hadn't stopped drinking.

"So, you're the one who captured Pedro," Bev slurred over Angie. "You lucky bitch!"

Angie gave her the cool once over. "Yes, I am." She turned her back.

Bev turned to Sara and Martine and mocked her. "Yes, I am," she repeated. "Who the fuck does she think she is?"

"My daughter-in-law!"

They turned to see Jenny with her arms crossed and giving them the eagle eye. "I've heard all about you, *Bev Marie*," she spat. "You stay the hell away from my son *and* my daughter, do you understand me?"

Bev shrank under Jenny's scrutinising gaze. "Um...yes..."

"Good. Now move over to the other side of the room and stay there." Jenny pointed, extending her arm all the way.

Bev skulked across the room while Sara and Martine pissed

themselves laughing and stayed where they were.

"Only five minutes to go people. Make sure you have your drinks, you have your partners to kiss, and you have your dancing shoes on. We've got five minutes left." He waved Angie over and leant down to tell her something.

She nodded and looked around the club, heading for Jenny and Spiros before getting Carlos and Viv, and Tomas and Roger, and getting them all up on stage.

"No." Spiros pulled back. "I don't want to go on stage."

"Oh, for goodness sake, Spiros, you're their father, be proud of it." Jenny laughed and dragged him up the stairs.

Pedro pulled his brothers close and spoke into the mic. "You all know my brothers Carlo and Tomas Stefan, and you've seen us the way we were naturally made, well, now meet the people who made *us*, our parents, Spiros and Jenny Stephanopoulos."

A screaming cheer went through the room as Jenny pulled Spiros up to the decks beside their children. Waving as if she was a queen and everyone was there to see her, she lapped it up.

"Stefan, Stefan, Stefan," the crowd chanted.

Jenny nudged Spiros. "Smile and wave," she hissed.

With an embarrassed wave, Spiros half hid behind his wife while the boys gathered round.

"We have three new additions to the family as you know. Vivian Villiers, the amazingly gorgeous supermodel, is married to my oldest brother Carlo Stefan."

Viv stepped up beside Carlos and waved. Screams moved around the room in waves.

"And Roger Dencott is married to my other brother, Tomas Stefan." The screams grew louder.

They both waved, although Tomas was not liking being on stage.

"And, of course, my beautiful Angelina who became my wife." She sneaked under his arm to be by his side. "And even my grandparents are here. Mama's parents are in our lounge area over there."

They had refused to come on stage, and while they weren't openly open about the gay lifestyle that 69 embraced, they were there to support their grandson and celebrate the New Year with the family.

"We have one minute left. Everybody get drinks, get partners, get ready. We're going to be counting down any second."

Eddie brought a tray of drinks on stage for everyone, and they waved Sarah and Matthew over to the side of the stage so they were at least near family. They stood on the stairs.

Sheila stood down in the crowd. *So, that's Spiros Stephanopoulos,* she thought, eyeing off the good-looking Greek that was the spitting image of Tomas. *And there's Jenny Stephanopoulos, not a mousy looking figure now, is she.* She'd watched them wave to the crowd at 69 as Pedro introduced them and the rest of the Stephanopoulos family.

Well, well, well. How she conned me. I see what Giancarlo was on about now. All the things he said about her. But why would she come to me like a dowdy housewife and yet be all dressed up like that? She studied the upswept hairdo and blue lamé dress with the chic black heels. *Huh, the latest style and probably costs hundreds of dollars.* Definitely *not the mousy housewife.* Her attention turned to the boys and their partners. *Ooh, got a fag for a son, wonder if Giancarlo knows that? Probably, since he was involved in the kidnappings.* She went back to Spiros. *I can definitely see where the boys get their looks. Except for Carlos who's the spitting image of her.*

Her. Jenny bloody Stephanopoulos. The woman who'd captured Giancarlo's heart. *Intriguing.*

She watched the slim figure wind herself around the Greek god beside her. *He* is *a tasty morsel. I can see why she latched onto him.* And since she'd dared to sneak a peek at the boys' movies, she wondered what the patriarch of the family looked like in the manhood department. *They're all large boys, I'd love to see what daddy dearest looks like.*

"Fifteen seconds left. Okay, everybody, get ready." Pedro turned the music down. "Here we go. 10, 9, 8, 7," the crowd screamed in unison, "6, 5, 4, 3," everyone raised their glasses, "2, 1, Happy New Year! Say hello to 1978 everyone."

Sheila grabbed a glass of champagne just as the clock struck midnight and wished she had Giancarlo to kiss. The masculine mouth, the fire in his eyes, the strong grasp. Hell, even his tongue was strong and knew how to pleasure a woman.

She was on her own, had no one to welcome in the new year with, but she'd refused to sit at home this year and had decided to get out and party for once. Well, once since her holiday to Santorini twenty-six years ago.

I wish Giancarlo was here and then he could see his beloved Jenny kissing her husband. I wonder if he's met Spiros yet? Seen him up close, seen the delectable Greek baklava he is.

Glitter bombs went off, and balloons and streamers came tumbling down as Pedro played *Auld Lang Syne*. He took Angie into his arms for a passionate kiss.

Carlos and Viv were in each other's arms locking lips, Tomas and Roger were playing tonsil hockey, and Jenny was making the most of her husband.

Sheila sipped her drink and watched Jenny and Spiros kiss passionately, imagining it was her he was kissing. *Whoa, where did that come from? Me...kissing Spiros Stephanopoulos? Why would I think such a thing? Well...because just look at his three sons...they're gorgeous and well hung, so why wouldn't I want to get some of the action?*

There wasn't a dry eye in the house, and even the staff was getting it on with someone. Maggie had popped behind the bar to greet in the new year with Mike, and Sarah and Matthew went back to their seats.

Once the song was over, Pedro played *Stayin' Alive* by the Bee Gees and the night went on.

"Whoo," Jenny screamed over the frenzied noise. "Oh, my God. I can't believe we've done this. Oh, my God, I love you." She flung her arms around her husband's neck, and he spun her around.

"I love you too, my Jenny." He pulled her to his lips and kissed her again.

Watching the night go on, Sheila couldn't wait for Giancarlo to see her in her dark green lamé party dress and upswept hairdo. Ironically, she looked similar to Jenny. Same style lamé dress, same stylish updo.

Well, well, well, no wonder he's been having such a problem getting used to the new me. I look like Jenny Stephanopoulos. Fancy that.

*****

Giancarlo glanced at the clock and watched the last ten seconds tick over from 1977 to 1978.

Nothing happened.

No fireworks.

No cheering.

No beers clinking at the bar.

Nope, none of that.

There was some noise happening on a floor below that was drifting up toward him, but as for the detective section, he was it.

He was sitting at his desk on New Year's Eve, his elbows planted on the battered old wood, hands crossed in front of him, with his thumbnail sliding in and out between his teeth except when he occasionally bit down on it to stop it. His eyes never left the clock. Never left the minute hand ticking over to one minute past.

He sat there trying not to think of Jenny. No doubt she was with her family, kissing her husband, whom he was yet to meet. No doubt they were having a good time ringing in the new year. Was she at home, or was she out celebrating? Was she enjoying the night, her husband…?

Get out of my head!

Tearing his eyes from the clock, he turned his attention to Sheila, wondering if he should drop by. She'd probably be home alone as she'd been at Christmas, and would be warm and comforting. Leaning back in his seat, he thought about how he'd been at her place every night he was free, or every time he knocked off, and how he couldn't wait to get around there. Couldn't wait to feel her underneath him, around him, beside him.

Oh, God, what's happening to me? What has this woman done to me? Why has she made herself look like my Jenny? Jenny with the blue eyes, Sheila with the blue eyes. Why does she suddenly make me stay until morning when I go home spent and empty and counting the minutes until I see her again? Why does she do that?

Leaning back, he was glad he had the next three days off. He just had to get through the next six hours before he could go home to Sheila.

January 1978

As it turned out, everyone had stayed at 69 until midday when Pedro finished. Every celebrity in the club, every party goer, except for Sheila who had left hours before, and Sarah and Matthew, who had gone home around one that morning.

"Okay, everyone, it's midday on January 1st, 1978. My time is done. Go out, enjoy the rest of the day, and I'll see you back here tomorrow night," Pedro yelled.

"Whoo." Angie and Maggie threw their arms up at the front of the stage.

Pedro tumbled off stage and over to his family who stood in the lounge area. *"I am exhausted!"*

"It's no wonder, my poor baby, working twenty-four hours." Jenny pinched his cheeks "You were fantastic."

Pedro blushed. "Thanks, Mama. But now I'm ready to go home, so I'm going to grab a quick shower and change and be back." He hurried off to the changeroom while the family chatted.

"Can we drop Maggie off on the way home?" Angie asked as Maggie stood chatting to Mike.

"Or will she be going home with her boyfriend?" Jenny asked in return, watching the two weaving their fingers through each other's as they stood face to face. "Lovestruck, your friend Maggie is."

Angie glanced at them. "She is, but doesn't want to get serious yet. Doesn't want to end up *pregnant and eighteen* like me." Her hand moved to her flat stomach.

Jenny slid an arm around Angie's shoulders. "You shouldn't be eighteen and pregnant either. You're too young. You and Pedro participated in a very adult act, and now you're dealing with the very adult consequences. No eighteen, or twenty-year-olds should be doing that."

Angie looked up at her, knowing she was right, but also knowing she had her support.

"Maggie's making the right decision for her, and that's what matters," Jenny finished. "And yes, we can take her home. I'd be an even bigger irresponsible parent if I allowed an eighteen-year-old to get around on her own."

Tomas was resting in Roger's arms on the couch, his eyes closed, his energy gone.

"You okay, T?" Roger asked, feeling his lover's body sag in his arms.

"Tired…worn out…happy," Tomas murmured.

Roger kissed his forehead. "Good. We'll have a long sleep when we get home. I'll tuck you into bed and keep you warm while you sleep."

A small smile came to Tomas's lips as he opened his eyes to look at his husband. "Mmm, sounds so good. Can we make love first?"

Roger gazed into his lover's eyes and said one word. "Always."

Carlos and Viv finished chatting to her friends, who had also gone the distance, and waved goodbye. Coming over to the lounge, they grabbed their coats. "Are we going or what?" Carlos asked, helping Viv with her coat.

"Just as soon as Pedro's back." Jenny picked up her own coat and slid it on. "Who's hungry? Do we want to stop for food on the way home?"

"I am," Tomas and Roger answered.

"Starving," Angie added as Pedro came up. "Hungry, babe?"

"Starving," he replied, making her giggle because they had said the same thing. "What are we eating?"

"What's open on New Year's Day?" Jenny asked as they made their way to the door.

Pedro and Angie looked at each other and laughed. "Everything."

After stopping at a local fast food restaurant for sustenance, they made their way home and up to their own apartments.

Except for Jenny, who stood on the pavement looking at Central Park. She breathed in, wrapped her fur coat tighter around her, and looked up at the sky.

"Jenny?" Spiros stood beside her. "Everyone's gone up."

"Isn't it crisp," she said, gazing at the snow-covered tree-lined streets for as far as she could see. "It's so crisp and cool, and it's a new year."

"It is. And now we're 1978. A new year, a new start, a new place."

"Yes." Jenny's mind wandered. "A new place…it's so nice here. I'd love to see it in summer and spring."

"You will. When we come back for the babies," Spiros said. "But now we must think about getting back."

She frowned and briefly closed her eyes. "Did you *have* to bring that up now? It's New Year's Day. The first day of a new year. *And it's Sunday.* You *had* to bring up going home."

"Well, that was the plan," he reminded her. "You were here to settle them in and help them get ready for being parents. We've spent Christmas and New Year's together and now it's time to go home."

Jenny finally turned to him. "No! I'm not going home." She strode inside and left him standing on the pavement.

*****

Giancarlo woke, grunted, and rolled over to come face to face with a sleeping Sheila, having forgotten he was still at her place. He'd decided to go there once he'd left work. Go to Sheila. The only place he'd been regularly going.

He'd turned up out the front of her building at ten past six. As he was getting out of his car, a taxi pulled up and out stepped a woman in a fur coat and black heels with a stylish updo. At first, he thought it was Jenny, but when she turned he'd seen it was not.

"Sheila?" he'd said in disbelief, not even considering she'd be out.

"*Giancarlo!*" *Glancing up in surprise, Sheila halted. "I wasn't sure if you'd be coming let alone what time you'd get here."*

"Ah, well, I just got off at six. I have three days off." His hands were in his pockets as he stared at the woman before him.

"Well…are you coming up?" she asked, moving toward the front door.

"Might as well." On the way up the stairs, he asked where she was coming home from.

"Oh, I had a fabulous time at a little party," she babbled. "There was no way I was going to sit home for New Year's this year." She unlocked her door and held it open for him.

"Huh. I thought you would have been at home." He stepped inside and removed his coat.

"Not this year. I went to Studio 69." She waited for his reaction as she slid off her coat.

"You went to 69? Why would you…?" He stared at her green lamé party frock.

"Why would I what?" she asked, moving to him, undoing his tie, unbuttoning his shirt.

"Why would you go to 69?" he muttered, instantly hard at the touch of her hands.

"Well, I heard the DJ was good," she said slyly, unbuckling his belt.

"And…is…he…" Giancarlo breathed hard, just as he did when running after a perp. "The Stephanopoulos kid…" The groan escaped from between his lips as her hand went around his cock. His eyes closed at the warmth, and his head fell back.

"Oh…he was so good," she murmured, massaging him. "So good he brought the whole family with him, and I got to see where those boys get their genes from."

"Oh, God…" He groaned, his cock as hard as a rock.

"And guess who was in the same outfit as me…" she paused, "Jenny Stephanopoulos."

His eyes flew open and he focussed. "Jenny? Jenny was there?"

"Yes." Sheila kept her voice low. "The whole family was. Including Spiros Stephanopoulos himself."

Gardo's eyes narrowed despite the hand around him. "He was there?"

"Yes," Sheila continued. "And I can definitely see where those boys get their looks from."

"So…what's he like?" A part of him desperately wanted to know, having never met the man. And a part of him wanted him dead so he could have Jenny all to himself.

"The spitting image of the fag son. Except with a very sexy moustache. Very sexy," Sheila murmured, imagining it was Spiros she was holding. "So, sexy. So, hot. So…Greek. And they kissed so passionately on stage that it was hot…" Sheila got the reaction. "I can see why you call me Jenny. We look so much alike. I see what you saw. Definitely not the mousy housewife that came to me. All dressed up and the receiver of Spiros's tongue."

Gardo had enough. He didn't want to hear about Spiros fucking Stephanopoulos. He yanked her hand from his pants in a vice-like grip, and hauled her into the bedroom. Throwing her down on the bed, he pulled himself out as she pulled her knickers down, and he had her with the ferocity of a mating lion.

Hard, fast, and ferociously.

She felt him and cried out. "Harder, oh, God." She tried to imagine it was Spiros, but couldn't grasp onto that thought, for whenever Giancarlo was inside her, it was always him that had her attention.

He lay facing her, having woken since to plough into her, and now watched her, make-up smudged, hair awry, breathing beside him. Pulling his arm out from under his pillow, he checked his watch. Nearly one in the afternoon. He had two and a half more days off, and all he wanted to do was spend them with Sheila. Fucking her until she hurt and he was spent. Fucking her because she wasn't Jenny. Fucking her because she was the only woman who wanted him and Jenny didn't. Fucking her because he couldn't fuck Jenny.

*****

"What do you mean you're not coming home?" Spiros ran into the building behind her, getting into the elevator before the door shut. "That was the plan, Jenny."

"I don't want to talk about it today." Her eyes watered. "It's Sunday, I don't want to talk about it." They reached the penthouse and entered.

"Jenny." Spiros spun her around. "The plan was to go home come New Year. We *are* in the new year." He didn't like where this was going.

"Why did you have to bring it up?" she cried. "Why did you have to bring up leaving my babies? It's Sunday, it's the first day of the year, and you already want to go home? After the awesome night we've just had, *you* want to ruin it." Tears flowed down her face. "All I wanted to do was come home and make love to my husband and fall asleep in his arms. And all *he* wanted to do was talk about going home to bloody Mykonos." She wiped her face. "You want me to leave my babies. Well, I don't want to. Tomas and Roger are still sick, and Viv and Angie have their first ultrasounds soon, not to mention their birthdays are six weeks away, and you want me to tear myself away from my babies and go back to lonely little Mykonos just to please you? Why did you have to ruin this moment, Spiros? Why couldn't you have left it for during the week?" She turned and ran up the stairs to the bedroom, leaving Spiros angry and heartbroken at the same time.

Angry that he had hurt his beloved. Angry that he couldn't wait to get home and hadn't even considered her feelings. Heartbroken because she was no longer the Jenny he'd married. She had changed, and he didn't like it. She had changed, and he had not. Following her up the stairs, he found her crying in the shower.

"I'm sorry." He took her into his arms. "My timing was horrible. It isn't the day to talk about leaving."

"I don't want to leave my babies," she sobbed, wrapping her arms around him. "I lost them once, I don't want to lose them again. They're all here now. I have nothing at home."

"You have me."

"But what do we do? We wouldn't see the boys, or the grandbabies. I won't have my boys to worry about and feed."

He pulled back and took her face in his hands. "I'm sorry. I'm sorry I brought it up yet. I don't want you to be alone, Jenny. I love you. I don't want you to be without your boys."

"Their birthdays are next month. What's the point in me going home for four weeks and then coming back? That seems silly to me."

"Yes. I guess it would be." Spiros knew travelling every month would be an inconvenience.

"I need to stay," Jenny said into his chest. "And then when their birthdays are over we'll talk again."

Spiros gently rubbed her back. "I don't know if I can stay until then. I might have to go home to monitor the shop and house."

"Can't you call Christo? He's been managing the shop for the last month. You've only been here a month, Spiros. Have you not been calling him?"

"I have. And everything seems to be fine."

"Well, then?"

Sighing, he knew he didn't want to disappoint her. She had given up so much for him, but New York was not his town. Not his city.

"Stay for me, until their birthdays at least," Jenny pleaded. "It's only six weeks away."

"And what of the boys? Will Tomas and Roger, or Carlos and Viv be staying?"

She sighed. "I'm hoping to get Tomas and Roger back after they finish their movies, and I'm hoping I can convince Carlos and Viv to move here as well."

"And why can we not all be in Miami or L.A.?" he asked.

"Because Angie's going to school here, and everyone else works in porn. Tomas can set up a gym anywhere, Viv can model anywhere. I really hope I can get them here for the birthdays in June. At least it will be summer."

"And you will be in your element," he told her.

She finally smiled. "My babies are having babies."

"Yes." Spiros matched her smile. "Our babies are having our grandbabies."

*****

"Oh, God." Viv collapsed onto her lover. "Oh, God, you're so good."

"And you're so horny," Carlos puffed, wrapping his arms around her.

"Can't help it. Pregnant women want more sex." She stretched out. "But then when you're married to a porn star you can't help but want sex."

He laughed. "Except we had explosive sex before I got into the industry."

"And now we'll continue to have explosive sex once you get out of it."

He put a hand behind his head. "You really want me out of it?"

"Absolutely." She rested her chin on his chest so she could look at him. "I get that you have more movies you're contracted to do. But once they're done, that's it, Mr Vivian Villiers. No more porn for you."

A chuckle slipped out of his throat. "*Mr Vivian Villiers?* Nah, nah, not happening *Mrs Carlos Stephanopoulos.*"

*****

Angie sighed in contentment. Her husband had just thoroughly made love to her, and she was feeling good. Relaxed. Happy.

"Ugh, babe." Pedro groaned and stretched out his six-foot frame. "Still so good."

"And why wouldn't it be?" She rolled into his arms and kissed his chest.

"You're pregnant. It might affect our sex life at some point."

"True." She snuggled in and his arms closed around her. "But right now, I still love making love with you any time of the day."

"Mmm," Pedro moaned. "It's Sunday. Let's get some sleep."

*****

"Oh, Tomas," Roger muttered against his lips. "Mmm, I love you."

Wrapped in each other's arms after a hot relaxing shower, they showed each other how they felt. Hands explored, mouths kissed, tongues caressed.

Tomas moaned as Roger's mouth found its way across his chest to latch on to a nipple. "I love you, too. Oh, God, I've missed this."

Due to being sick and staying in the penthouse, they hadn't been intimate for over a week.

Roger rolled on top of his lover who lifted his legs for him to gain entrance.

"Oh, God," Tomas moaned as Roger's hand closed around his cock. "Oh, God." He came. "Oh, God, I couldn't wait. I'm sorry."

"Don't be, my love," Roger panted. "I'm about to come too." He emptied himself into his husband. "It's been so long, we're both overexcited." He stayed on top of Tomas, his hand stroking and kneading his lover's body. "I love you. Oh, God, I love you."

"I love you, too," Tomas murmured against his lips. "I love you, too."

*****

"Ah, oh, Spiros!" Jenny clung to her husband, as his twelve-inch Greek sword took her with its masculinity. "Oh, God," she cried, feeling it push against her uterus.

He was long, strong and filled her all the way and then some, never able to be fully inside of her, but knowing he could still fill her completely.

"Jenny," he murmured. "Oh, Jenny." How he loved his wife so much. She was the only woman he had ever been with. The only woman he ever *wanted* to be with. But while she had changed on the outside with her makeover, and had changed her attitude, she was still his Jenny Stephanopoulos in bed. Compliant, giving, and willing to do his bidding. Three hard thrusts gave forth his seed, and he was done. "Ah." He captured her mouth and kissed her passionately, showing her how much he loved her and what she meant to him.

*****

Sheila awoke and needed a pee. With Giancarlo sleeping, she quietly slipped out of bed and made her way into the bathroom. Seeing the state she was in, she showered and dried her hair, making herself presentable. Heading into the kitchen to make food, she found it was three in the afternoon.

Whipping up eggs and bacon with toast, she heard Gardo thump into the bathroom before coming into the apartment. "Hungry?" She glanced up to see him in his boxers and singlet, hair mussed, socks still on.

He stood staring at her as she pattered around his kitchen. Not since his wife had left him just over thirty years ago had another woman been in his kitchen, making him breakfast in her dressing gown. It was silky and clung to her curvy body, swishing around her legs as she moved.

But then, it also wasn't his kitchen.

"We can wash your clothes if you plan on staying for all three days. I'm sure I can find you something to put on in the meantime," she was saying as he watched. Carrying two plates to the small two-person table at the window she told him to sit.

Realising he'd been frowning, he stopped and took a seat at the table, all but devouring the hearty breakfast, or in this case, late lunch, before him.

"You were hungry." She poured him a second cup of coffee.

"Haven't eaten since," he thought back, "probably this time yesterday." He bit into his last slice of toast, feeling weird at having breakfast in his shorts with a woman. A woman who was not his wife. That hadn't happened in over thirty years.

"More? I can make more toast, more eggs and bacon if you want?" Sheila watched her lover think things through. It was strange for her too. Andros had been the only man she'd given herself to and look how that turned out. Gardo was only her second, and as far as apples and oranges go, the two were as different as night and day. But then so was she. And times had changed. Being a twenty-two-year-old in 1951, sex was not permitted outside of marriage, and if you ended up having sex and were with child, then you were shunned and kicked out of home. Which she was, and it's exactly what she had done with Luiz.

But it was a new year. 1978. And she was forty-seven. He was fifty-three, only six years' difference, but what a different man to Andros. Andros was young, already experienced, at least she had thought due to *her* inexperience. He had wooed her and courted her to get her into bed, and while he was her first, she soon lightened up and got into it, becoming a wild woman in bed. She enjoyed sex with him immensely. But Giancarlo was different. *Maybe it's the fact we're both mature adults who have gone without for so long that we've somehow made our way to each other. I'm different, my body's different, the times are different. Talk about free love.*

"No, no, that's more than enough." He finished his coffee and sat a little awkwardly. *God, I'm wearing shorts, a singlet, and socks at the breakfast table and it isn't even my table. So…what the hell do I do now?*

"Would you like a shower? I can throw your clothes in the wash."

"What?" He came back to the situation after being lost in his own head for a few moments.

"Would you like a shower?" A slight smile sild across her lips. "I have new towels, man-sized, and I think I have a robe that will fit you."

"Um…" He looked around everywhere but at her. "I guess."

"Okay then, come on." She led him to the bathroom, gave him a towel and new soap, and grabbed the dark blue velvet robe she'd bought just in case he stayed. "Here, put this on." She handed it over, and he looked at it before closing the door. "Drop your stuff outside the door and I'll get it washed." She gathered his shirt and pants then picked up his undergarments from the hallway floor, giving them a wash in her new washer before shoving them in the dryer and setting up the ironing board and iron.

Giancarlo came out wrapped in the blue robe, glad it covered his bits. Not that it mattered. Sheila knew his bits intimately anyway.

With a few minutes left on the dryer, Sheila poured two more cups of coffee and urged him onto the couch. "Here." She handed a cup over and sat beside him. "Let's watch the new year's festivities."

*****

Jenny languished in her husband's arms. He knew how to love her and loved her with every fibre of the being God made him. But, by God, he could be stubborn! She thought about what going home would mean. Not seeing her babies. Not hearing about their work days at dinnertime. Not taking care of them when they were sick. Not seeing their in-laws, and being *nowhere near* their grandchildren when they were born. What was in Mykonos now? Their empty house. And the meat shop? She didn't want to work in the meat shop and never had. It was not hers, and she didn't want it. It was Spiros's inheritance from his father. There was no family left there, so what sort of lonely existence would she have? She had a couple of friends, but had never really been accepted into Greek life, although two of her boys had. Tomas and Pedro. Carlos had been an outsider like her, but a girl magnet because he was so different. And all *she* had been was the dutiful housewife keeping the house running while her husband was at work.

Well, not anymore, she thought. *My babies have all left, and there is nothing there now except for their things in their rooms. And I don't have much anyway. All the good things I have I brought with me so I'd have them around.*

She shifted her head slightly, listening to his even breathing, hearing his heart beat under her ear. She loved Spiros more than anything in this world, but she also knew that her babies came first. Always had, always would. And there was no way in hell she'd let him stop her from being with them. Even if it was in another country. She'd already forsaken her own family for him when she packed up the boys and moved from Australia to Greece, living with her mother-in-law until she died two years later. At least she'd had a house then to call her own. And it had been added to so the boys had their own rooms and bathroom. And her in-laws' old room was now the guest room with ensuite. But still. She knew there would always be a day when they married and started families. She just never imagined it would be in another country, and not even that of their birthplace.

Why couldn't they have moved to Australia? At least they would be with family. But no, they chose America, and now Jenny had to choose between her babies and her life in Mykonos. Her boys or her husband. *Well, I won't have to if I can get him to stay. I need to convince him to stay now our babies are here and having babies. There's no way in hell I'm going to stay in Mykonos and not see my grandbabies. No way in hell at all. Come hell or high water, my babies will always come first.*

*****

"Oh, my baby, do you really have to go?" Jenny cried the following Saturday.

"Mama, we need to get back to work," Carlos told her. "I have to finish off my contract, and Viv has a few jobs to finish before she gets too big." He dropped his new luggage set by the door.

"Hey, I heard that." Viv rolled her own luggage into the living room of their apartment.

"But you'll be coming back for your birthday in February," Jenny went on and wrung her hands fretfully.

"Of course we will," Carlos told her, seeing the fear in her eyes.

"We'll be back on the Sunday before, but will have to leave again on the 16th." Viv set her handbag down to slide into her fur coat.

"And then I want you back here for the birth of the baby in June," Jenny said. "No excuses, you'll need all the help you can get, and you can take a few months off to get used to being a new mother."

"It will be nice to have the summer off," Viv said. "That will be the first anniversary of us meeting." She poked Carlos in the arm.

Carlos thought back. "Yeah, babe, it will. You don't expect a present, do you?"

Viv rolled her eyes. "No, darling, I'll be too busy popping out your child."

"Hey, yeah," Carlos said, pulling on his coat.

"Ugh." Pedro and Tomas groaned. The whole family was in their lounge room to see them off. "Seriously, dude. You're worrying about having to buy a present and had completely forgotten about your wife having your baby?" Pedro said.

"Of course he did." Tomas crossed his arms. "You know he only thinks about himself."

"Not true," Carlos protested, waving them out of the apartment. "I think about Viv too."

"Well, whatever you do, promise me you'll be here for your birthday and summer. I want to spend lots of time with my daughters teaching them how to handle babies," Jenny said.

"I think they already have that down pat," Tomas replied in all seriousness. "Look at what they're married to."

"Hey, bro," Pedro protested. "I happen to be very intelligent for my age. Aren't I, babe?" He turned to Angie for support.

"Um…" She glanced away. "Sure, babe."

"Ha! Not even your wife agrees." Tomas laughed.

"Mmm, she'll get hers," Pedro murmured, watching Angie grin as they went down in the elevator.

"The car will take you to the airport, and I rented a private plane to fly you home so you can spend time not worrying about being noticed," Jenny told them.

"Aw, you took away his fun, Mama," Tomas mocked as they walked onto the pavement to say goodbye. He noticed Carlos frowning. "See, he hates the fact he won't be recognised on the plane."

Jenny laughed and hugged Carlos. "You're famous enough, Carlos, so pull that ego in check. It's not about *you* anymore; you need to be the man and step up for your family." She pulled back with a serious expression. "Do you understand?"

He nodded, noting the concern. "Yes, Mama. It's not about Carlos until the baby comes."

The boys groaned and rolled their eyes.

"What?" he cheekily asked. "Joking." After giving everyone hugs and kisses, they climbed into the limo and drove off, waving out the back window.

The others went in, but Jenny stood watching the car, pulling her coat tighter around her. Her baby was leaving again, and she *hated it.*

Spiros went to her side and put his arm around her shoulders. "My love, let's go in, it's cold."

Reluctantly, she moved, tearing her eyes away from the road, allowing Spiros to lead her back inside into the warmth of their penthouse.

"One down, one to go," Spiros said quietly, hanging his coat in the small coat closet under the stairs.

"Don't say that," Jenny cried, handing over her coat, a forlorn expression on her face. "Don't say that." She went over to the fireplace to warm herself and stood facing the photographs of the family in their Christmas jumpers, and the one of the six of them that they had given her for Christmas. She felt tears well, and the emotions threatened to overflow. Her eldest had flown the coup once more, and she hated it.

"So, what are you kids doing for the weekend?" Spiros sat down, watching his wife.

"Just hanging out." Angie shrugged. "It's freezing out, so not much *to* do."

"Sleeping," Pedro added from his spot beside her.

"We'll be sorting through our stuff to see what we take back to Miami," Roger said, and Jenny's head turned sharply. "Won't really need fur coats, or leather jackets down there," he finished.

"And when will you be back?" Spiros asked, aware of his wife's head movements.

"We'll fly in on the 11th and stay for a week," Roger continued. "We'll be taking it easy from now on."

"Finishing up your work with the Seralifts?" Jenny said more as a comment.

"Yes, Mrs S," Roger said. "Once we get our last two movies out of the way that will be it. For both of us."

"And what will you do then?" She stared hard at the photos, trying to keep a lid on her emotions.

"I hope Marcus will let me stay on as a stagehand, so I at least have a job. And if Tomas is healthy enough to get back to work, he can do that."

"And what about getting out of the business entirely?" Jenny pressed. "Completely?"

"I did suggest to Tomas that maybe I could become a personal trainer too, and then we could set up our own gym," Roger said.

"I actually can't wait to get back and hit the beach and get back to training," Tomas said, linking his fingers through Roger's. "I'm feeling good, not a hundred percent, but good. So maybe the sea air will do me good too."

"I thought of taking you back to Mykonos with me," Jenny murmured, still staring at the photos. "I thought the sea air and being back in your old room might help you get better."

"Mmm…" Tomas sighed. "That *does* sound good. But I left Mykonos to see the world Mama, have new adventures, see new places."

"I know." She walked toward the window and stared at the park.

They looked from her to Spiros who shook his head slightly.

Thinking about what could be going on; Tomas walked over to his mother, sliding his arms around her, resting his chin on her shoulder. "It won't be for long, Mama. We'll go home, finish off work, and get it over with. Then we'll be back for our birthdays."

"I know." She sighed and kissed his cheek. "It's just…my babies are leaving again." Looking at his big brown eyes and black hair, she smiled. "You look so much like your father."

Tomas grinned. "So I'm told."

"And is that such a bad thing?" Spiros asked, taking them both into his arms.

Jenny smiled. "Of course not." She kissed her son and husband then asked everyone what they wanted for lunch, and drying her tears, went to prepare it.

*****

Carlos rocked up at Harry DeVille's mansion first thing Monday morning. "Harry, got an idea for you!"

"Carlos, my boy." Harry rose from behind his desk and gave him a fatherly hug and slap on the back. "When did you get in to town?"

"Saturday." Carlos put his blue leather bag on Harry's desk. "But

I've been working on ideas and scripts for the last few weeks and want to know what you think." He pulled a huge pile of paper out. "This is a script for Neesa, and this one's for Mariska. One for Giselle, here's a few more, and this one's... *The Greek Gods.*" Handing over a thick script he watched Harry raise a brow and puff on his cigar.

Harry looked down at the script in his hand. "*Greek Gods* huh?"

"I vaguely remember a mention of all of us doing a movie together," Carlos reminded him, throwing himself on Harry's couch. "Not that I can speak for my brothers, but Pedro wants out of his contract after his eight movies. Tomas and Roger have two left, and I have the rest of the *Meat Shop* movies. With Viv having our baby, this is not a profession I want to be in anymore. In *front* of the camera anyway. I'd rather write scripts."

"Really?" Harry hadn't been expecting this turn of events, even with all the badgering from Carlos about writing and set management. "You have your *Meat Shop* movies to film, and that was all you were contracted for. But I'll give these scripts a read and see what they're like. If they're as good as the others, you might have a new career, kid."

"I know it means you won't earn all that money from me anymore, but I have a feeling *The Greek Gods* will more than make up for it if I can get my brothers on board."

Harry nodded and sat behind his desk. "How *are* your brothers?"

"Pedro's good. Tomas and Roger are getting over their flu. Angie and Viv are dealing with being pregnant."

"Is Viv giving up work?"

"Probably over summer while she gets back in shape. That reminds me, Mama wants us back in New York for Valentine's Day, and then for summer for the births, so unless we filmed at that time..."

"Everyone will be in New York?" Harry asked, casually flicking through *The Greek Gods* script.

"Yes. Mama and Papa are staying until our birthdays, then everyone converges for summer to see the babies born."

Harry glanced up, amused. "You're going to be a father."

Carlos grinned. "Yep."

"How does it feel?"

Carlos sighed, his eyes wandering as he tried to put his thoughts together. "Exciting, scary, amazing, scary…I can't wait. Seriously." He looked at Harry. "I can't wait to meet the human Viv and I made. To be a dad."

"You're still young, though, it's a big responsibility." Harry went back to perusing the movie.

"I know. But I'll be twenty-five next month, so not as young as Pedro who'll be twenty-one. And poor Angie, she's only eighteen now, nineteen at the birth. It's going to be a hell of a lot harder for them than Viv and me. We have the maturity, we have a home. Oh, did you hear what Mama did?"

"Mmm? Besides tearing me a new one in Athens, no." Harry grinned.

Carlos laughed. "No, she bought an entire apartment building on 5th Avenue in New York for the whole family to live in when we're there. She decked out nurseries and everything."

"Your mother's staying in New York?"

"Just until our birthdays for definite and then we'll see. Papa wants to go back home, but Mama wants to be with her babies, so who knows."

"How do you feel about finishing off these movies of yours? This week good enough? And I'll get those scripts finished."

"If we can finish them off in one day, you're on."

*****

"Ready on set?" Andy Merkin, director extraordinaire called out at the DeVille mansion two days later. "Carlo, Anastacia, on set."

Carlos strode onto the *Meat Shop* set ready to go. He only had two more, and he was done with his contract as he'd only been signed for ten. Taking his place behind the counter, he waited for his cue and watched as Anastacia, an Italian Greek wannabe porn actress, strutted on stage in her tiny white dress and big head of curls. She wore no bra, and her voluptuous breasts filled the bodice to bursting. Three of her buttons had already popped off and opened the dress to reveal those breasts, stopping short at showing her nipples.

Carlos stared at her nearly bare chest and felt nothing. Inside anyway. His cock hardened, but he felt no attraction, no sexual thrill as he had in the past. Now, there was nothing. Before, there was everything; a spark that he had with every woman. But marrying Viv had changed that. Marrying Viv had changed *him*.

"Ready on set…in three, two, one…and *action*," Andy called.

Carlos went through the motions, showing Anastacia different cuts of meat, showing her his sausage, giving her his sausage, having her against the cabinet *and* the meat. And then it was over, and he was dumping the condom in the bin.

That's what Viv had asked. The one thing she'd asked. Besides siding with his mother about quitting after marriage, she asked that he continue to wear condoms while fucking every woman at the mansion. And he abided by it, taking the ten seconds to roll it on before continuing the act as he always had. It would be cut out later in production, as it always was. It was also a rule Carlos had told Harry at the beginning of his contract. No free sex, only *safe* sex. And he had only one movie to go that afternoon before his contract was over.

He was filming them on the same day so they were done and dusted. Then all he had was *The Greek Gods* movie, and even that wasn't a goer at the moment. He needed to talk to his brothers about that one, and Harry needed to talk to Greta and Marcus. But if they could get it all together, Carlos had no doubt it would be a massive best seller. It just needed to be made.

They took a break and set up for the next movie.

*****

On Saturday morning, Pedro said goodbye to his brother and brother-in-law before leaving for his movie. It was the first of eight he had left and wanted to get them out of the way fast.

Jenny hugged Tomas and didn't want to let go. "My baby," she crooned. "All my babies are leaving again."

He patted her back and smiled. "Mama, I'm going back to Miami, it's our home now."

"No!" she said sharply, pushing him away. "Miami is *not* your home. Home is wherever I am, and I am *not* in Miami. Is *Seralift that* important?" she asked a stunned Roger.

"Ah, no." He shook his head and glanced at a confused Tomas.

"And your apartment, can you give that up? Ever considered leaving Miami?"

"Mama, what's going on?" Tomas had never seen the look in his mother's eyes before, and it was worrying him.

"Is Miami necessary, or can you live anywhere?" Jenny pressed on.

"Ah..." Roger looked from his mother-in-law to Tomas and back. "I guess if we're quitting *Seralift* we can live anywhere."

"Good, good." Jenny calmed down. "Because there's something I want the two of you to do." Taking a deep breath, she continued. "I want you to finish up at *Seralift*, pack your belongings, and move here to New York when you come back next month."

"Mama!" Tomas was shocked. His head moved back and forth, his jaw up and down. "Why?"

"Jenny," Spiros said from his place on the couch beside a surprised Angelina.

"I want the two of you here in New York. Purely as a base. As I said, I bought this building as a home for my family to live in and stay at whenever they were in town. I want you to pack up your belongings and move them here to New York because I have plans for you after that."

"What plans, Mama?" Tomas was frowning. His mother was freaking him out, and he was starting to panic.

"Good plans, my baby." She touched her hand to his face and smiled. "I have such big plans for the both of you, and it's important for your base to be here so you can come home and see the kids, *and* your family."

Tomas and Roger exchanged another look and saw Spiros's confused frown.

"Please promise me you'll be done with *Seralift* and be packed to come back by your birthday."

With a slight shrug, Tomas said, "Uh, okay Mama."

"Roger." She turned to her son-in-law. "The time for porn is over. The time for you two to have a life is upon you. Please, promise me."

Roger knew something was going on, but as he hadn't been in the family long didn't know what it was. It had to be something important for Jenny to be saying what she was with a look like that on her face. And while he'd been at *Seralift* for a while, he also knew after marrying Tomas in Greece, that the porn industry didn't excite him anymore. Maybe Jenny was offering an alternate route.

"You've been through so much and have been so sick because of damn Luiz and *Seralift*. It's time for you to leave Miami and start a new life. And I have big plans for you, Tomas Stephanopoulos. Big, big plans," she told her son. "So, you go back and finish up, and come home as soon as possible. Even sooner than your birthday if you can manage it."

Tomas dazedly nodded, dumbfounded by his mother's words. "Okay, Mama."

"We gotta go, Mrs S." Roger grabbed their coats and handed Tomas his. "Mr S, Angie, Mr and Mrs M." He involved Sarah and Matthew who were staying until the boys' birthdays.

"Okay. We'll come down with you." Jenny took her son's arm, and they went downstairs. "You have the car and the plane too. I want my babies getting back safe and sound." She kissed them both on the cheeks. "I want you to be safe, Tomas, because you've been in such danger these last few months."

He stared at her with his big brown eyes. "I will, Mama. It's all behind me now." With last kisses, he and Roger drove off to the airport.

"Oh, my baby, I don't like this," she muttered, watching the car until it disappeared.

"That was weird," Roger said. "What is up with your mother?"

Tomas had been staring out the back window, his hand spread out on the glass until he couldn't see them anymore. "I don't know." His face was obscured by a frown. "She's always been my supporter; look what she did for us in Mykonos. I have a *really* bad feeling about it."

"About what?" Roger was intrigued and worried about the whole thing.

"I don't know." Tomas's frown deepened. "I can't put my finger on it."

Spiros led the others up to the penthouse, and Jenny sat staring out the window while the others watched TV. Thoughts flew through her mind, and finally, she grabbed a pad and pen from the phone table and began to make a plan.

*****

"Pedro." Stephanie rushed over to him. "Oh, I'm so glad you're back." Flying into his arms, she held him until he untangled her and set her straight.

"No more of that. I'm married, and it's inappropriate. Where's Greta?"

"Here, darling." She came tottering over. "Ready for movie number one?"

"As long as I only have eight left and you haven't added another number in front of it," Pedro told her. "Same concept as always?" He looked across the roof of the building, done up like the others as a party. DJ booth at one end, bar at the other, and dance floor in the middle. Flowing curtains, disco lights, and light up dance floor completed the ambience.

"Same concept, except with a winter theme." Greta followed him as he gazed across the New York skyline. It was a snowy, wintry day with little white dots floating through the air. "We'll be bringing in a snow machine to add to the atmosphere."

Pedro nodded. "It's a hell of a view."

"It is, and now you need to make a movie." She led him backstage to get dressed in his white fur DJ outfit, and an hour later the game was on.

The music blasted through the air, the disco ball twirled, the girls danced, and Pedro did his thing until he was done.

"Great show," Greta called afterwards. "Pedro." She walked him back to the dressing room. "Is everything all right? You weren't your usual self."

"What do you mean?" He slid his pants on.

"Well, the smile wasn't really there when you were fucking the girls. You had a different look about you. Like you were…" She shrugged. "Not really interested."

Pausing, he considered his actions. "Do I need to do it again?"

"No…but…what's going on?"

He sighed. "Maybe it's that I'm married now with a baby on the way." He hefted his bag over his shoulder. "And I don't want to be doing this after the baby comes along. I'll be done with it."

"You'll really finish doing movies?" Greta remembered the last conversation with him at New Years.

"Absolutely." He nodded. "I gotta worry about my wife and baby from now on. I can't do this…" He waved a hand across the set. "Get naked and have sex when I'm raising a baby."

"I guess not," Greta conceded. "I've had a call from Harry about a movie for the three of you. Would you be interested in that?"

"I don't know." He shook his head. "I don't know. I'm gonna go. Send me the details for next week's movie and I'll see you next Saturday."

"Okay." She watched him go, knowing his heart wasn't in it anymore.

If it ever was.

*****

"God it's good to be home." Roger closed the door behind them and looked at his apartment. "I can't believe we're home after what, two months?"

"Nearly three." Tomas flung open the curtains and looked at the sunny Miami day.

"Jesus. We haven't been home in nearly three months?" Roger stood behind his lover and wrapped his arms around him. "Ah, it's good to be back where we first moved in together."

Tomas rejoiced in his husband's arms for a moment, but glancing towards the bedroom the smile left his face. He remembered Luiz stalking them and entering their home, taking their photos, poisoning his milk, and kidnapping him from the hospital.

"T?" Roger sensed something.

"I think I finally get what Mama was talking about." Tomas looked from the bedroom to Roger as he moved out of his arms. "Luiz was *here*, he *poisoned me here*. He broke in and took photos of us. I'm not sure I can be here, stay here, *live* here knowing our privacy was invaded. Not to mention he left a dead body downstairs and tried to frame you for all of the murders *he* committed." He shook his head, feeling a panic rise. "I don't want to be here anymore, Roger. I don't want to live in a home that was violated like that. *I* was violated physically. I was poisoned and have been sick ever since. I don't know if I can be here…even until we go back to New York." His head moved side to side, and he grabbed his face. "I can't live here, Roger. I'd rather stay in a hotel until we finish at *Seralift* and then leave here. Leave Miami. There's nothing here for us now, just bad memories, bad things, bad people." His breath came in short, sharp bursts.

"Okay, it's okay," Roger soothed him. "We'll…" He looked around. "Pack our clothes and personal belongings and move into a hotel for the next few weeks. It's okay. We'll get out of here. I emptied the fridge before we left, so we just have our stuff to pack. And we'll let the estate agent know we're moving out and he can have it back."

Tomas calmed down. "Good…good…let's go today."

"Okay, my love. We'll go today."

*****

"When did you two get back?" Marcus Seralift looked up in surprise from his chair in the *Seralift* studio where they made their movies.

"Saturday." Roger stood beside him, hands on hips, looking at the set they were getting into position.

"It took you long enough," Marcus said, watching Tomas who looked as if he didn't want to be there.

"Well, we have been sick the last four weeks, so not much point coming back and giving everyone our germs," Roger told him.

Tomas huddled next to Roger, his arms around his own torso, slightly hunched over. He wasn't sick, but had a sick feeling about being there. *Mama was right,* he thought as he looked around. *This isn't for me. It never was and never will be.*

"How about those movies you owe me then?" Marcus knew body language, and Tomas's said, 'no way in hell'.

"That's what we came to talk to you about," Roger said and crossed his arms. "We have two more to do and want to get them done this week. Now, there was no concept chosen for them, so I'm wondering if we could do a doctor-patient kind of thing. Besides the fact we actually *have* been sick, we haven't done that kind of movie for ages, and Tomas and I haven't done one at all. What do you think?"

Marcus gazed from him to Tomas. "Considering the kid still *looks* sick I'd say it's a good idea. I'll get a couple of scripts done up, and we'll get a set together. I'll give you a call in a couple of days."

"Great," Roger replied. "Oh, wait." He dug a card from his jeans pocket. "We're staying at the Sunset Motel now. We realised when we arrived home that it wasn't home anymore and moved out. With everything Luiz did…it just isn't the place to be now."

"Fair enough." Marcus took the card. Room 23 had been written on it. "I'll call in a couple of days."

"Great. We'll see you then." Roger led Tomas back out into the sunshine.

"Well, well, well, Mr Dencott, Mr Steph-an-op-oulos. You're finally back in Miami." Detective Jeremiah Barden was leaning against their car.

"Detective." Roger sighed. "Hadn't we finished with you?"

"With me yes, with paperwork no," Barden said. "Gardo from New York had faxed me for some info…said you were all there." He eyed Tomas. "You *still* don't look good."

"We've had a bad case of the flu for the last four weeks," Tomas replied. "We're still getting our strength back."

"How did you know we were back, Detective?" Roger unlocked the car.

"I had the estate agent give me a bell when you were back, and he told me you'd come home and moved out to a hotel."

"Yes, well, with everything that happened in that apartment building it wasn't a good idea to stay. Besides, we'll be going back to New York soon, so not much point staying there. Did you want something?" He opened the door and helped Tomas in.

"I just need you to sign the paperwork concerning your case, and that will be it." He produced a thick wad of folded paper from his trench coat pocket, along with a pen. Laying them out on the hood, he pointed to where Roger needed to sign. "Here, here and here. Mr Stephanopoulos signs the same spots."

Roger signed and passed the paper to Tomas who leant against the dashboard to scribble his name.

"Is that it?" Tomas asked, handing the papers back.

"That's it unless you have other things you need to deal with?" Barden told him.

"Not legally, we don't." Roger shut Tomas's door. "I hope this is the last time we ever see you, Detective."

"Mmm." Barden frowned as Roger walked around to the other side of the car. "Maybe. Everything has either been wrapped up or is in the process of." He thought about their upstairs neighbour, George Cauldwell, the raving necrophiliac who'd been sentenced to jail for fucking a dead body. A body that belonged to the very dead Aiden Head, the last *Seralift* porn star that Luiz had killed and dumped in the undercover garage of Roger's apartment building. Except George had gotten to it first, and contaminated the crime scene by having sex with it. Barden had caught him in the process. "Four dead porn stars, a former porn star killed for kidnapping a current porn star, and the boyfriend is accused of the murders. Quite a story to wrap up and finish."

"And *is it* finished?" Roger opened his door.

Barden glanced down at the paperwork. "I just need to file these, and it will be."

"Good. Goodbye Detective." Roger climbed in, gunned the engine, and left the car park, heading for the beach for some sea air.

"Mmm." Another frown. "Somehow I don't think it will ever be completely over for you two. Luiz Manning played a big part in ruining what you had, and he will be the death of you both." Jeremiah wasn't an overly religious man in his old age, but his gut was never wrong. He made a promise to himself to look out for them in future, because something told him they just didn't have one.

*****

Sheila stood in the living room of her new apartment located in Morningside Heights, a good neighbourhood that wasn't far from all the exciting aspects of the city that she could easily walk or take public transport to. It was bright, light, and airy, on the fifth floor, which was also the top floor, and had an elevator so she wouldn't have to walk all the way up with her groceries anymore.

Her furniture had been set up, as she'd ordered more from the store, a nice dining table and chairs, a few cupboards for knick-knacks, and a bookcase for books. Her fridge fitted in the kitchen, and she actually had a small laundry room instead of having her washer and dryer in the kitchen. Her bedroom suite fitted in the bedroom perfectly, and brand-new curtains hung at the windows.

Wearing a fitted white pantsuit and low heels, she turned slowly, taking in the sun that poured through every window. She had a corner apartment, and it overlooked green trees in the park across the road. There was heating and cooling, and the rent was *very* affordable. She could definitely afford the comforts of a nice home now.

The phone, gas, and electricity had been connected the day before, and deleted from her old apartment. All she needed to do was ring Giancarlo to let him know her new address and phone number. Picking up the phone, she dialled the number on his business card.

"Gardo."

"Giancarlo, it's Sheila. I'm just ringing to let you know I've moved into my new apartment today and have a new phone number. Have you got a pen?"

Grumbling, he searched for one and grabbed a notepad. "Go ahead." He scribbled the information down, noting the nice neighbourhood.

"Got it."

"Great. Are you coming around tonight?"

"Mmm, probably not. Got a stakeout to deal with and a shit-ton of paperwork to go with it."

"Okay. I'll see you when you're free then."

"Okay."

She replaced the phone, disappointed that he was busy and wouldn't be coming over for her first night there. It had been a few weeks in the making. Having found an apartment between Christmas and New Year's, she had to wait for the former tenants to move out and have the place cleaned before she could move in. The carpet was pale cream, the walls white, and the kitchen and laundry had sand-coloured linoleum, lots of storage, and a nice window.

She sighed. *The one thing it lacks is a man.* She'd had extra wardrobes put in the bedroom, and there was a second smaller bedroom that she'd turned into a walk-in closet to fit all of her clothes, shoes and bags she'd splurged on before Christmas and in the post-Christmas sales.

Wandering through the place, she imagined Giancarlo there every day, dressing for work, coming home to a good hot meal. Flopping down on her leather couch, she thought about Jenny Stephanopoulos and how she'd had Spiros to come home to her at the end of a long day with three boys to raise, and a home on an island. It must have been bliss, and yet she had gone without.

Her anger boiled inside of her. *She had everything I didn't. A husband, kids, a home on an island, and what did I get? Andros fucking Poulos taking advantage of me and getting me pregnant just to deny I was having his baby. Maybe I should have aborted him and then none of this would have happened. I could have found another man, married, and had kids that I loved, instead of one I didn't. One that I hated.*

She wondered why Giancarlo hadn't remarried and had kids. But then he'd never mentioned his past much. Just that he'd been married and divorced and that was it. Yet he knew a lot about her and her past. That she had a bastard son by Andros, who had tried to kill Pedro, and that bastard son had tried to kill Tomas. Father and son tried to kill two brothers, and their ex-stepfather and grandfather were behind even worse. And it all led back to the Stephanopoulos family. How ironic.

"Oh, the tangled web we weave," she murmured.

*****

Roger and Tomas turned up at work two days later ready to finish off their last two movies. Their contract was for thirty, and they'd completed all but two.

The set was a hospital room. A bed and machine stood against one wall, a fake window on another, a door on another.

"Here's the script. Not a lot of words as usual, so when you're ready." Marcus handed over a piece of paper to each of them.

"Only one page?" Roger asked staring down at it. "Is that it?"

"Well, you boys aren't known for your words, just your actions." Marcus grinned. "Get on set and have a run-through."

After an hour of run-throughs, with the lighting guys setting everything just right, they changed into their outfits and took their places.

Tomas was the white gowned patient in the bed, a little freaked out at being back in the hospital, fake set or not.

Roger was the doctor with his stethoscope around his neck, and not a whole lot under his white lab coat.

"Ready on set," Marcus bellowed as Violet came hurrying to his side.

"Oh, I can't believe we're back in production," she excitedly whispered, her grey pearls matching her grey pearl-coloured suit.

Marcus settled into his seat. "Don't get your hopes up," he said quietly. "I think once they're done they're really done."

"What do you mean?"

"It means no more porn stars," he said and looked at her. "All right everybody, let's go in three, two, one…and action."

Tomas languished in the bed, eyes closed, moaning softly. His hand lay on his top of the covers over his stomach.

Roger came in, looking at his clipboard, to examine the patient. He set the clipboard down on the side cupboard and checked the machine before looking into the patient's eyes, pretending to fall in love at first sight. This wasn't hard since that's the way it pretty much happened for the two of them.

Tomas pretended to wake and stared into Roger's eyes. "Doctor, what's wrong with me?"

"A severe case of heartache I'm afraid," Roger said. "Sit up and let me listen to your heart." He helped Tomas sit and used his stethoscope before realising what smooth skin the patient had. Pulling the gown forward, he pushed Tomas back onto the pillows. "I'll just examine your chest." Folding the gown down, he revealed the muscular chest with its spattering of black hair. Gently listening to his heartbeat, Roger's character started using his ears and lips and mouth to listen. "Oh, my God," he moaned. "You're so beautiful." He sucked softly on a nipple.

"Doctor?" Tomas groaned. "Is this what you're prescribing to make me better?"

"Oh, yes," Roger moaned, his hand sliding up and down. "Let me make you better."

"Oh, Doctor." Tomas arched. "Make me better."

Roger pushed the covers all the way down, sliding his hands over the patient's naked body. "Oh, I will make you better," he said, slowly stroking Tomas's manhood into an erection. "I will make you feel so good."

In a tangle of arms and legs, they joined until the deed was done and Roger was dismounting. After covering the patient, he picked up his clipboard, straightened his jacket, and asked the patient how he felt.

"So much better," Tomas murmured.

"Good," Roger said, marking something on the clipboard. "I think a follow-up visit at home will be just what the doctor ordered. I will see you in a few days."

"And cut," Marcus bellowed. "Get the next scene ready."

Roger helped Tomas from the bed while the hospital was turned into a small apartment with a raging fireplace and a king-size bed covered in fur.

"You okay, T?" Roger wrapped a fur blanket around him.

He smiled. "I'm okay. I feel good. I have some energy, and I could definitely do that again." He pulled Roger close. "I definitely *want* to do that again."

Roger grinned. "Awesome. Let's get ready."

At the side of the stage, they had a drink and some food to keep up their strength, and then did a walk-through of the new movie before starting.

"Ready to go again," Marcus yelled. "In three, two, one…action."

There was a knock at the door, and Tomas slid out from under the bed covers, threw on a robe, and answered it. "Hello, Doctor, I wasn't expecting you, please, *come* in." He held the door open for Doctor Roger who came into the room making a note of everything.

"I came to give you a check-up." Roger set his bag on the fur-covered bed.

"Oh, great." Tomas stood in front of him. "How do you want me?"

Roger cocked a brow and looked at the camera. "Every which way I can," he said.

"Pardon?" Tomas replied. "I didn't catch that."

"How about if I examine your heart and lungs." Roger removed his stethoscope from around his neck as Tomas undid his gown to display his package.

"Oh, my," Roger said, holding the cold disc of the stethoscope to Tomas's chest, yet looking down at the patient's privates. "You're very long and strong indeed. The longest I've ever seen."

"I try to stay in shape," Tomas said as the cold disc moved lower and lower.

"Turn around." Roger turned him and removed the robe. "I need to check your lungs." His fingers slid down Tomas's back to his ass. "My, what strong muscles you have," he whispered as his hands moved to the front and closed around Tomas's hard shaft.

"Oh, Doctor, that feels so good." Tomas let his head fall back as Roger massaged him.

"Yes, yes it does." Roger breathed. "Sit while I take your temperature."

He sat the patient on the end of the bed, the fur beneath him.

Tomas leaned back, legs spread. "How do you want me to do it?"

"Let me show you." Roger sat beside him on the bed, his left leg under him so he could face Tomas. Under his lab coat, he was naked and on full display. His right hand massaged Tomas more roughly, eliciting groans from deep inside. His left hand moved the patient's hand to his own cock, making it grope it and his ball sack.

"What's my temperature doctor?"

"Hot, oh very hot. Hot like me, can you feel it?" Roger asked.

"Is that good?" Tomas murmured seductively.

"No. It's very, very bad," Roger replied. "I need to make sure." His hand slid up Tomas's torso as he breathed close to him. "I need you to lie back on the bed and roll over."

Tomas slid backwards and lay down, arms above his head. "Like this?"

Roger groaned, and his hand slid all over him. "Now, roll over."

Tomas slowly rolled over, stretching out on the fur and arching his back. "Like this?"

"Oh, yes." Roger lay beside him. "Now, I have to take your temperature." He entered, and they groaned in unison. Hands slid all over the patient as Tomas bucked up and Roger met his needs.

"Oh, God, Doctor, oh, God," Tomas groaned as Roger hit his peak. "Oh, Doctor."

They lay panting for a few moments. "Doctor, how's my temperature?"

"Hot, very hot," Roger murmured against Tomas's shoulder. "I think you might have to come back to the hospital."

Tomas seductively glanced over his shoulder. "Can't you just look after me here?"

"Oh, it will be my pleasure." Roger thrust and they were off again.

Marcus let the cameras roll while they fucked again and then yelled cut. "And that's a wrap, boys. You've fulfilled your contract, and you are done."

"Finally." Tomas sighed in relief and pulled the blanket around him.

Roger stood and wrapped the lab coat around him until he could dress. "Good working with you, Marcus." He shook his hand when he came over. "But after Luiz killed off four of our castmates, it's time to retire."

"You sure?" Marcus stuck his thumbs in his belt as he puffed on his cigar. "There was talk of a threesome with the kid's brothers?"

"Not that we heard," Roger replied.

"Would you do it if you were asked?" Marcus went on.

"No," came out of Tomas.

Roger laughed at how quickly he'd said it. "Probably not, Marcus. We'll get dressed and go unless you have some paperwork."

"No, no, you two love birds go. I can understand if this isn't the place for you anymore. Luiz bloody nearly ruined me, the little bastard."

"Yeah well, looks like we all need to recover from Luiz and what he did," Roger said.

"Yeah, yeah." Marcus puffed smoke over them causing Tomas to wave his hand in front of his face. "Looks like I'll have to hire a couple of new guys to replace you two."

"I'm sure you'll find plenty of gay men in Miami to take our places," Roger said. "Meantime, we're gonna get changed. Come on, T." He led him to the changeroom, then walked out into the Miami sun for the last time.

*****

"Have you got around to *The Greek Gods* script yet?" Carlos asked Harry on Friday morning. It was already the twentieth day of 1978 and Carlos couldn't believe he'd been back for nearly two weeks. But they had been a busy two weeks, with Carlos cleaning up and renting his place out so he could move into Viv's luxurious home. He'd filmed his two movies and watched one of his scripts being filmed. A lot had happened in two weeks. It was crazy what could be achieved in such a short time.

"Yep. I've finally got around to it." Harry rocked back in his chair.

"And?" Carlos planted himself on the desk.

Harry studied the kid sitting on his desk. Young, fresh and prime meat. But not anymore. "You have a hell of a way with writing kid. You ever thought about being a professional writer? Novels, books, newspaper columns?"

Carlos laughed. "Never thought about it, Harry. I love women too much to waste my talents sitting down with a typewriter."

"Yet, that's where you've ended up. Stop loving women, did you?" Harry grinned.

"Nope." Carlos grinned back. "Just married one."

"Has marriage changed you that much?"

The grin turned into a soft smile as Carlos thought about it. "Yeah, yeah it has. Viv is all I think about. I love her like I've never loved any woman, and *believe me*, I've never actually loved any of them until Viv." He sighed in content. "I still can't believe I scored Vivian Villiers."

"Neither can I," Harry guffawed. "Out of all the men who have thrown themselves at her, she picks a kid sixteen years her junior."

"Hardly a kid, Harry." Carlos picked up a paperweight and moved it from hand to hand.

"Hardly a man," Harry replied. "You may have a ten-inch cock, my boy, but with everything you've gotten yourself into in the last what, seven months, you've done nothing but show you're still a kid."

"If a ten-inch cock is all it takes to be a man then I've got it. But *none* of that was *my* fault, Harry. I didn't do anything. It was done *to* my brothers and me."

"Yeah, yeah." Harry waved a cigar filled hand. "You didn't do it. But I doubt that means you're a man."

"This conversation is going around in circles." Carlos stood up and paced. "What did you think of *The Greek Gods* script?"

Harry's face lit up, and his eyes turned into dollar signs. "It's good. All the words are perfect, nothing more, nothing less. The direction is good, your notes on the staging are excellent. I can't wait to see it in person."

"Yeah." Carlos sighed. "Just gotta get my brothers into it."

"Think they'll go for it?" He watched Carlos pacing back and forth in front of his desk.

"Mmm, I don't know. Mama wants us all out of the business. I'd love to keep writing, Pedro will still DJ, Tomas was never really interested."

"All finished with your contracts?"

"Pedro has a few more, but I'm done, and so are Tomas and Roger."

"So how will this movie happen?"

Carlos stopped, a thought going through his head. "Maybe…no… they wouldn't be able to…"

"What?" Harry was wondering about the process going through Carlos's mind.

"No…"

"What!" Harry eagerly leant forward in his seat.

Carlos turned around. "I just had an idea, but it's too far out there to even contemplate now."

*****

Detective Star was pounding away at his typewriter when his partner, Drew, came barging up to his desk.

"Guess who's back in town." Drew slapped the paperwork down in front of Star on his desk.

Star looked from his messy, mistake-riddled report, to the thick stack of papers Drew had thrown down. One word stood out from any other. One word that was a name he hated.

Stephan-freakin'-opoulos!

"What do you want with that punk?" Star asked, going back to his typing.

"Didn't you hear what I said?" Drew took his seat and tapped his fingers on the desk. "*He's back in town.*"

Star glanced up sharply. "When did he get back?"

"Two weeks ago."

"Why the hell didn't you tell me," Star yelled, springing up from his chair and grabbing his jacket from the back of it.

"Because I didn't know until just now when a cop told me he'd seen him in town," Drew replied.

"Let's go." Star was already halfway across the floor.

"Do you know where he is?" Drew caught up with him.

Star stopped. "Do you?"

"No."

"Then where the hell are we going?" Star was pissed that he hadn't heard sooner.

Drew sighed at his partner's impatience. "Let's try Harry DeVille's first."

"Right," Star said. "Let's go."

Twenty minutes later they banged on Harry's door, and a maid let them in. She directed them to Harry's office where they came across Harry and Carlos.

"Who the hell let you in?" Harry bellowed, surrounded by smoke.

Carlos turned to see who was there and nearly ran.

"The maid," Star said and zoned in on Carlos. "Stephan-freakin'-opoulos. We've got some paperwork for you."

Carlos sighed. "Yeah? You, too, huh? Gardo had some for Pedro."

"Yeah, well..." Star put his hands on his hips and looked around. "Don't know anything about that."

"Well, whatever you want, let's get it over with," Carlos grudgingly told them.

Star produced the papers and shoved them at him. "Here." He strutted around Harry's office. "Nice digs."

"I like them," Harry said, watching the detectives closely as Carlos signed the paperwork.

"Yeah." Star looked at all of the photos on the wall. Celebrities with Harry, all smiling and happy to have a photo taken with a porn king. "Pay well, does it?"

"Yes, it does," Harry said smugly. "Weren't you demoted after that kidnapping debacle you screwed up?"

Star flashed him a pissed off look.

"Is that all?" Carlos handed the papers to Drew. "I just had paperwork to sign?"

"That's it." Drew tucked the papers away. "Our captain sorted out the rest after the FBI contacted him." He shrugged. "They'd taken over, so it wasn't our case anymore." He watched Star prowl around the room, edgy, like a tiger hunting prey.

Carlos followed Drew's eyes and saw Star. "Yeah, Payday said he'd sort it all out."

"It turned out well, then?" Star asked, still looking at photos.

"Papadopoulos is dead, I got married and have a baby on the way, so, yeah, I guess you could say it turned out well," Carlos told him.

"So, who was Papadopoulos to you?" Star finally turned to him, hands on hips.

Carlos sighed. "My grandfather's ex-brother-in-law."

Stars brows rose, and he laughed, deep and throaty. "You're shitting me? Your *ex-great-uncle* wanted *you* dead. He kidnapped you *and* your brothers, and he was *your grandfather's ex-brother-in-law?* Oh, that's freakin' hilarious."

"Glad *you* find it so funny," Carlos spat, his anger boiling and his resolve to stay calm wearing thin. "*We* didn't."

Star stalked over to him. "So what happened then? You kill him?"

Carlos glanced at Harry and Drew. "No. My great-grandfather did."

Star's laugh grew louder and bounced off the walls and closed windows. "Oh, my God, it just keeps getting better," he said to Drew who raised his brows in return. "What else? What happened to your great-grandfather? Payday arrest him?"

Carlos became stony-faced. "Payday did nothing, and my great-grandfather died in November from old age."

The laughter stopped and the light left Star's eyes. "He did nothing?"

"My great-grandfather was a hundred and one, Detective Star," Carlos said icily. "He died of old age."

"You get all the money, then?" Star breathed over him.

Carlos cocked a brow and took a step back. "No, we didn't. My father didn't want his grandfather's fortune, so it all went to charity upon his death."

Star sneered. "Poor diddums, still broke."

"Still making more in one week than you make in one year," Carlos bit back.

Star darkened. "What about this Papadopoulos and his money?"

"Oh!" Carlos's mood lightened for what was to come. "Didn't you hear?"

Star frowned. "No, what?"

"We inherited that by default. Mama took that fortune as revenge on what he did to us. *She bought the family a huge apartment building in New York.*" Carlos smiled sweetly and saw Drew hide his grin.

Star's eyes burned bright with fury. *How the fuck could this kid still have so much after everything he'd gone through? Everything that had been done to him. How the fuck did he have it all after all of that, and I still have the shit life I've always had.*

Stephan-freakin'-opoulos!

February 1978

Sheila slid into the fire engine red silk negligée and matching dressing gown as she stood in her dressing room. It was Valentine's Day, and she was hoping Giancarlo was coming over. He'd been busy all week, and she'd missed him. She had red and white satin sheets and a matching bedspread on the bed, and champagne and chocolate-covered strawberries in the fridge, ready and waiting.

Taking a last look in the mirror, she padded into the bedroom to make sure everything was perfect. The bed was turned down, the pillows were just so. A red lamp shade made the room glow red.

Making her way into the living room, she arranged cushions on the couch and continued into the kitchen. Her kitten slipper heels tapped on the linoleum as she checked the food, and grabbed a box of matches to light the red and white candles on the coffee table. Once they were lit, she sat and awaited his arrival.

Since Christmas, he'd been staying longer, all night, and New Year's he'd stayed for three days where they barely made it out of bed. But then work had beckoned, and he was back to late nights and early mornings. She'd seen him only every few days and missed him.

Yes, she missed him.

Sighing, she flicked through a magazine. He'd been so often, and stayed through the night, that she'd gotten used to it. Used to a man in her bed. Used to being beside a warm body most nights. Used to a man inside her. And when he wasn't, she missed it. Missed *him*. And she wanted it permanently.

Permanently?

As in…full-time?

The knocking on the door brought her out of her stunned silence, and she found Giancarlo wearily leaning against the doorjamb. "Hard day?" She waved him inside and settled him into one of the recliners before getting an ice-cold beer from the fridge. "Here." Handing it over, she stood behind the chair and massaged his broad shoulders as he knocked back the bottle. "Another?"

He sighed. "Sure."

She got him another and went back to massaging his shoulders. "Why don't you have a hot shower and we'll go to bed."

Another sigh. "Sure."

Since he'd stayed at New Year's, she'd gotten some things for him. Toothbrush, shaver, masculine shower products, and all had their place in her new bathroom. She'd also bought boxers, singlets and socks, and put them in the wardrobe in the bedroom, having taken note of his size when he'd stayed. She'd bought him some shirts and matching ties as well. He'd protested, she'd put her foot down. It was easier for him to have stuff there than to keep going back to his house.

Getting the strawberries and champagne from the kitchen, she set them on the bedside cupboard, displayed herself on the bed, and waited for him. Not that she had to wait long.

He came into the bedroom naked and standing to attention.

He hadn't brought her flowers, which would have been nice, but considering the man he was, and he was standing naked in front of her, he was all she needed. All she wanted.

She slid down the bed as he crawled on top of her to find she had no underwear on, and with one manly thrust entered, giving her the best Valentine's Day of her entire life.

*****

"Welcome to *Studio 69*," Pedro said into the microphone. "It's Valentine's Day, and you know why it's a good day?" He waved at the crowd to join in. "Because it's not only Valentine's Day, it's *my* 21st birthday." A cheer screamed through the club. "And not only it is *my* 21st birthday, it's my brother Tomas's *23rd* birthday."

Tomas grinned from ear to ear as Roger grabbed hold of his shoulders. The club was full of lovers for Valentine's Day, and his whole family was there.

"And," Pedro went on. "Not only is it my brother Tomas's 23rd birthday, but it's my brother Carlos's *25th* birthday."

The cheering grew so loud Jenny covered her ears. She was standing with her family on the dance floor looking up at the stage.

"So that means we are all born on the same day, two years apart. Three incredible Valentine's presents our mama gave our papa," Pedro told everyone.

Jenny laughed and turned to her husband who was smiling. She gave him a nudge and a saucy wink.

"Certainly were," Spiros said above the roar of the crowd. His arm was around his wife, and he felt the excitement flow from her through to him. He saw Tomas and Roger beside her, Carlos and Viv a few feet away, and Angelina was in front of them beaming with her pregnancy glow.

Angie was cheering when she felt something move in her stomach, and she grasped her five-month bulging belly. Looking down, she felt it again, unsure of what it was. In a panic, she looked up at Pedro who couldn't see her, and then turned to her in-laws, eyes as wide as saucers in fear.

Jenny saw her panicked expression and the hands splayed across her belly and slid her own hand over it. She felt the kick and a smile lit up her face. *It's moving,* she mouthed, seeing Angie's panic continue. "It's all right. The baby moved," Jenny all but yelled.

"It moved?" Angie hadn't felt it before. Just knew there was a child growing within her, but had not felt it move or kick like that, and it was weird.

Jenny nodded as the rest of the family noticed. "It moved."

Angie's head slowly moved up and down. All sound had ceased, and all she heard was Jenny's voice coming through. "It moved."

Jenny smiled and nodded, pulling her daughter into her arms. "Everything's okay, it's kicking." She held on for a moment longer before releasing her and brushing her hair from her face. "You're having a baby."

A nervous giggling laugh escaped from Angie. "I'm having a baby."

Jenny spun her around to face the stage and wrapped her arms around her, remembering back to the times she had been pregnant.

"So, you get all three porn stars here at *Studio 69* for Valentine's Day. Plus, an added bonus of Tomas's real-life *and* movie partner, Roger Dencott."

Roger laughed at the screaming they received. "I think I received a bigger cheer than Carlos."

"Don't let him hear you say that. He'd argue until he's blue in the face that he got the bigger cheer," Tomas told him above the din.

They danced and partied until ten o'clock when Eddie hauled out a huge birthday cake on a trolley. He waved Pedro down from the stage and waited until all the boys crowded around.

"When the porn stars' mother, the lovely Jenny Stephanopoulos, asked if I could do a cake for her boys' birthdays, I thought why the hell not. And so I had an artist friend of mine come up with this." A huge spotlight lit up the cake. It was five figures writhing on the floor having sex. Basically, an orgy of a cake. "I figured it should be something to do with their career choice."

Jenny's brows hit her hairline as she stared in shock. "I was just thinking a normal rectangular chocolate cake," she told Eddie when he shoved the microphone in her face.

"I thought you might," Eddie said. "But I thought since this might be the only birthday they celebrate here all together, that it should be something memorable that they'll never forget."

The boys were lined up behind the trolley already digging into the cake.

"You boys were supposed to wait until we sang happy birthday," Eddie complained. He received three shrugs in return before leading the crowd in a resounding rendition of happy birthday. "Once you boys have finished eating it will be taken over to the bar and cut up.

Cake for everyone."

The girls had been taking photos of the cake, but now the boys got to feed it to them.

"Oh, my God, that's so good," Angie mumbled around a piece.

Tomas fed Roger a penis. "Not the first time you've had a black cock in your mouth," he joked as Roger wrapped his lips around the chocolate cake.

Roger chewed and swallowed. "No, but I prefer tanned Greek cock now."

Tomas blushed and picked up another piece.

Carlos swallowed. "This is awesome cake. Have some more Viv." He held another huge chunk up for her.

"Ew, no." She put her hand up and stepped away. "No more cake for me. One piece was enough." Patting her bulging stomach, she added, "Sugar's no good for the baby."

"You boys finished?" Eddie asked. "I'll take it to get cut up for everyone else." He noticed the breasts and penises were gone. "Well, we all know what you lot like!" He wheeled the trolley away, and Pedro walked back behind his decks.

Jenny and Spiros moved to the sidelines to watch their babies celebrate their birthdays. Her smile lit up her face, happy that *they* were ecstatically happy. Tomas and Roger were dancing in each other's arms. Carlos and Viv were trying to dirty dance, but her stomach was getting in the way. Angie was throwing her hair around while she danced with Maggie. But tears lit up her eyes as well and threatened to burst forth in a torrent down her cheeks.

Spiros sensed the change and comforted his wife. "Pedro's a man now, he has reached adulthood like his brothers. They are *all* men now."

The tears flowed forth. "They will always be my babies," she sobbed, not believing that all three of her sons were now legal adults.

"I know they will always be your babies. But it's time to let them be the men they were meant to be."

Jenny looked up at her husband. He had stayed the extra six weeks for her, and they'd had a wonderful time exploring the city, eating at restaurants, and spending time together which they hadn't done since Carlos had come along. But she knew what was coming. Her head moved left to right. "No. They will *always* be my babies." Casting her eyes over them, she watched them enjoy themselves until Pedro finished for the night at six the next morning. Driving them home, she told Tomas and Roger, and Carlos and Viv, to come to the penthouse at four that afternoon.

*****

Tomas and Roger, Carlos and Viv, turned up at four on the dot to find Jenny pacing and Spiros watching her with a frown.

"Mama, what's for dinner?" Carlos yawned as he took a seat on the couch.

Viv sat next to him. "I hope it's not meat. I can't stand meat at the moment."

"Mama?" Tomas and Roger sat in their usual places. They'd driven back two weeks earlier in Roger's car as he wanted to keep it, while Tomas had quickly sold his to a co-worker at *Seralift* as he didn't need it any longer. They took Jenny up on her offer of a place to stay in New York as Miami wasn't their home anymore, but they weren't sure the Big Apple was either.

Jenny finally stopped pacing and faced her children. "I've made no secret of the fact that I want my babies around me. Now, Viv, I know you've lived in Hollywood for years, but I'd like you to consider living here once the baby comes."

Viv was stunned. "Live here…in New York…you mean move?"

"Yes," Jenny said. "I want you and Carlos to move here, live in this building and work from here. He can write his scripts, and you can do modelling shoots, or fly off to one."

"Well…" Viv looked at Carlos with an unreadable expression. "I hadn't given living here permanently any thought."

"Well, I'd like you to, for now anyway. But what I really want to do is…" She moved to Tomas's side. "Is give you and Roger the opportunity of a lifetime."

"What?" Tomas exchanged a glance with his husband. "What kind of opportunity?"

Jenny bit her lip. "One that means you will never have to worry about working again. *Especially* in porn. One that means you get to see the world like you wanted to do. What you left Mykonos for."

Carlos exchanged a glance with Viv, curiosity arousing his senses.

"What do you mean, Mrs S?" Roger asked, intrigued by the turn of events.

Jenny sighed. "As my husband pointed out last night, my youngest is no longer a baby, but a man. And because my sons are all men now, I want to do what I can for them, so they have every opportunity they can have. So," she took a breath, "I have set up a bank account for you both to travel."

"What?" four voices said at the same time.

"Mama…what?" Tomas was shocked. "I don't understand."

"Yeah, why does he get a bank account and I don't?" Carlos demanded.

"How much money do you earn from your movies?" Jenny snapped back.

He blanched at her tone. "A lot."

"Then you don't need a bank account, do you?" She frowned at him in anger.

Reluctantly, he knew she was right, and that something was wrong. "No, Mama." Looking at his father, he raised a brow, but received a slight shake of the head in return.

"I'm sorry." Jenny relented, and her tone softened. "But you can be so goddamn selfish sometimes Carlos, and life is not always about you."

He blushed, embarrassed at having been called out. "Sorry, Mama."

Jenny turned back to a confused and worried Tomas. "Ever since you told me you had fallen for a guy that was engaged to one of your clients, I worried for you. Not that you had found something with a man, but because he was already so complicated and you didn't need that." She saw his frown and patted his hand. "I worry about you, Tomas. Luiz was a problem that grew into a monster and he all but ruined your life. He poisoned you, and kidnapped you, and made you so sick and it worried *me* sick. And then to find out you'd met and fallen in love with Roger who we knew nothing about, I worried more. But while I saw how much he loved you, and how happy he made you, I *still* worried."

She shook her head sadly. "I don't know if you'll ever be a parent. I don't know if you'll ever get these feelings that I'm having. Feelings of fear and danger, and of wanting to save you from everything and everyone. You were always the quiet one. The one who did as he was told and never caused problems, was never in trouble like your older brother." She looked pointedly at Carlos who shrugged. "And you weren't the baby that everyone always said was so adorable with his black hair and big blue eyes. But you were still *my* baby. You're *all* my babies, but I worry more for you. And no mother wants to go through what I did. Nearly losing all of her babies at one time. So, because Pedro and Angie need to be here, and Carlos and Viv have decisions to make, I want to offer you something special."

"What is it, Mama?" Tomas asked, feeling the love flow from her.

Taking a deep breath, she let it out slowly. "I want the two of you to travel the world. Permanently."

"What?" came four stunned replies.

"I want the two of you to pack those fancy luggage sets of yours and travel the world. Wherever you want to go, whenever you want to do it, however long you want to stay. It's up to you. That's why I set up the bank account in both your names, so you will have money any time you need it. And I want you to fly first class everywhere. I want you to stay in the best hotels, I want you to *do* everything, *see* everything, *try* everything. I want you to go and live your lives knowing that I have your backs and will support you. *Always.*"

"Mama." Tomas's head was flicking back and forth. "No, I—"

"Don't refuse me, Tomas. I am doing this *for you.* To get you out of porn, to give you time to spend together. After Luiz," she shook her head, "you need to live life, Tomas. Not be stuck in one place. You left home so you could see the world. Well, now I'm giving you the financial support to do so. Go and see the world, Tomas. It's *your* time to live."

"Mama," gushed out of him as he stared from his mother to Roger, to Carlos and Viv, to his father, who looked equally as shell-shocked.

"Listen to me, Tomas, because I am dead serious." Jenny held onto his hand. "Something bad has happened to you, and I am trying to make up for it. Now, I don't know what it is I'm feeling, but I know I need to do this, and you two need to travel and see the world. My hope is that you make it home for those important days, the rest of the time I want you to travel, so I'm not taking no for an answer. And the first place I want you to go is back to Australia to see your family." She glanced at Roger. "And maybe your family as well."

"I don't think so, Mrs S." He shook his head.

"I want you to try," Jenny continued. "*For me.* It's important you at least try. Mum and Dad are leaving this weekend, and I want you to go with them. Spend a few months there, travel, show each other where you were born and grew up, see the country. I want you to see your birth country. And then you can come back for the births of your nieces or nephews."

"Mama…I don't know what to say." Tomas was dumbfounded. He had wanted to leave Mykonos to see the world, and while he hadn't gotten far, he had met his soul mate in Roger, and that was worth everything. Now his mother was offering them the opportunity of a lifetime to travel around the world first class.

She read his mind. "You told me you wanted to see the world, well, now's your chance. See the world, Tomas. Do this for me. Because my gut is telling me it's important."

With another glance at Roger, who nodded enthusiastically, Tomas took a deep breath. "Okay, Mama, we'll do it for you."

Her head fell to his hand that was encased within hers. "I cannot tell you how happy that makes me. I *need* you to do this." She looked up with tears in her eyes. "I *need you* to do this. *You* need to do this, and I know one day it will all make sense, but I can't even tell you when."

"Okay, Mama." He burst into tears. "Thank you so much for this." He hugged her as he hadn't since he was sick. She was always taking care of him through thick and thin, and it had been horrendous the things he'd gone through, now she was giving him a chance to see the world.

"Right, now, you're leaving with Mum and Dad on Saturday, and you'll be back in June. That gives you three and a half months," Jenny said.

"But that means I'll miss your birthday and anniversary," Tomas wiped his face.

"And just this once it won't matter. Because the best present is knowing my son is alive and doing what he wants to do," she told him. "It's going to be hot in Australia, so you'll need summer clothing. We can go shopping, so you have enough to start with, or you can buy what you need along the way. Wherever you are you can buy whatever you need. Okay."

"Okay, Mama." Hugs and kisses went all round before she showed them the brochures she's collected from the travel agent.

Carlos joined his father at the window as he stood looking out over the park. "What the hell was that?" he asked in a hushed tone.

Spiros shook his head. "When your mother has a feeling, you go with it because she's usually right. You know that."

"But what feeling is she having now? Giving Tomas and Roger money to travel, all but demanding me and Viv move here? Something's wrong, Papa."

"I know." Spiros sighed. "I know." He watched his wife and saw the happiness on her face. She had told him of her fears for Tomas weeks ago when she'd shared her plan. She couldn't tell him then, just as she couldn't tell Tomas now. But for her, the feelings were very real. And when she felt them, you listened and took note.

But something was nagging *him*. It was the change in her. The change that he should have expected and he didn't like, because deep down inside he had a feeling himself. A feeling that he was losing his wife.

Pedro and Angie joined them for dinner at five and they sat around discussing the gift Jenny had given Roger and Tomas.

"Why can't *we* get a bank account?" Pedro argued.

"Because you have a well-paying job," Jenny replied. "What is it? A thousand a night? That's more than what most people make in a month." She took a sip of wine.

"Actually, Eddie gave me a raise after New Years. It's fifteen hundred a night now." He grinned. "Plus the money from the movies.

I got another one this weekend."

"And along with Angelina's fortune, they are the reasons why I haven't given you money. You earn a fortune from DJing and still have money from your movies. Just as Carlos has his movies and Viv has her modelling. Tomas and Roger are out of work, and I want them to see the world. They have the time. I've given them the money. Besides which, they don't have babies on the way to take care of, so they can afford to travel," Jenny said. "You two need to prepare for children and have to have a stable home. You can't be running off travelling with a baby. It's not doable unless you have nannies."

"Yeah, yeah," Pedro grumbled, finishing his meal. "They don't have babies to worry about."

"Hey," Angie cried. "I hope you don't have that attitude in four months." She stroked her belly. "You'll be doing babysitting duty you know."

Pedro shook his head. "Won't have time, babe. I work nights and sleep days. When will I get to look after a kid?"

She playfully slapped him on the arm. "I have to look after *you,* so *you* can look after *our* kid."

"I'm a man now, I don't need to be looked after," he protested.

Carlos and Tomas laughed. "Yeah, right," they said in unison.

"Hey!" Pedro's protests continued. "I didn't get myself poisoned by a lover," he pointed to Tomas, "and I didn't get another person kidnapped," he told Carlos. "Luiz and Aneeka, remember!"

Both boys frowned, but Tomas's was deeper. Luiz had been his first mate, his first attraction, his first lover. And he'd wanted him desperately, but couldn't have him, and it was a choice he'd made. *Maybe things would have turned out differently if I'd chosen Luiz?* he thought, thinking back to the guilt he'd had over being with an engaged man. *If I'd taken him back, imagine how different life would be now.* He glanced at Roger who was frowning back. *I wouldn't have this amazing man in my life. I wouldn't know true love, pure love. And I wouldn't be married to him.* The frown was slowly replaced by a tender smile as he gently touched his lover's face. *I love you* he mouthed and received one in return.

"I didn't get Aneeka kidnapped, she got herself involved," Carlos was saying. "She took those photos, and if she hadn't, that probably wouldn't have happened." He shook his head. "No way am *I* responsible."

"If it weren't for *those photos* you would have been arrested for your girlfriend's murder. But you *are* responsible for Barbara Weston who then latched onto Pedro," Tomas reminded Carlos.

Carlos groaned. "I'm not responsible for that whack job either."

"The hell you're not!" Pedro jumped back in. "You refused her in high school, dumped her last summer, and then she went cuckoo after the legal letter from Papa *and* attached herself to me, following me to New York, sending us those horrible gifts." He pointed a long finger at Carlos. "*You* made her a nut job."

Angie thought back to the gifts from Barbara as she played with her brand-new bracelet. It was a Valentine present from Pedro and matched the necklace he'd given her for Christmas. And even though she couldn't be sure, she figured Jenny had been behind the idea. It was even engraved, and she doubted he would think of that. Taking a deep breath, she put Barbara out of her head and slid a hand over her belly, feeling the baby kick. "Hey." She grabbed Pedro's hand, bringing an end to the conversation. "It moved."

With wide eyes Pedro spread his large hand over his wife's burgeoning belly, feeling the tiny kick from inside.

Jenny smiled. "It's quite something, isn't it?"

With a small shake of his head, disbelieving, almost, what he was feeling, he looked at Angie. "It's moving."

Her smile radiated her happiness. "Yeah."

Sliding his arms around her, he pulled her close and kissed her. "I love you, Angie.

"I love you, too." She kissed him back.

"We're pregnant, too, you know." Carlos rolled his eyes and waved a hand at Viv's stomach. "Baby over here too."

Viv looked radiantly happy. The small ruby heart earrings in her ears sparkled in the light. They were her Valentine's gift from Carlos.

Everyone at the table groaned.

"Jesus, Carlos is making it about Carlos again," Tomas said, rolling his eyes and sighing.

"He never gives up, does he," Pedro replied, looking at Tomas. "It's always about him."

"Always." Tomas agreed, nodding at his younger brother across the table.

"I didn't say it was," Carlos said to more groans. "But you two aren't the only ones in this family having a baby."

"Didn't say we were," Pedro told him. "Your attitude's gotten way out of hand since you won the best cock award last year."

"No, it hasn't. I'm still the same old Carlos I always was. But speaking of the porn awards." He licked his lips in preparation. "The both of you will no doubt be nominated this year, along with Roger."

"Can we *not* talk about that stuff?" Jenny stood. "How about you help me clear the table instead."

After the boys had washed and dried the dishes, Carlos pulled them aside. "Look, I know you two are out," he said to Tomas and Roger. "But Pedro's still got a way to go, and I'm writing now, but remember in Athens when we met each other's bosses? There was mention of a movie together."

Tomas frowned at what was coming. "I remember."

"What are you getting at?" Roger asked.

"Well, before I was kidnapped I'd been working on an idea that Harry had come up with. Something about a golden god coming down from the heavens above to bed all the women."

"Oh, God." Pedro rolled his eyes. "All about *you* again."

"No, no, listen," Carlos encouraged him. "I had scripts written up, but once we were all back together and here in New York, I started writing and came up with a movie. One that could potentially be split into three to showcase *each Greek* God."

"So, there are *three* Greek Gods in your movie?" Tomas asked. "Are you going to play all three?" he deadpanned.

Carlos shook his head in disbelief that Tomas hadn't caught on.

"I think he means *all three* of you," Roger told Tomas and tried to control his laughter.

"Yeah, I did get that." Tomas gave him a half grin.

"Absolutely," Carlos said. "All three of us make a move. A *full-length* movie so it can be cut up or kept together, whichever way our bosses want to do it, and everyone makes money."

"I don't want to do any more movies." Tomas shook his head wearily. "I'm over it."

"Not even if Roger was in it?" Carlos asked.

Tomas sighed and wrapped his arm around his lover's waist. "I don't know. I'd have to see a script and think about it. But right now, I *really* don't want to do any movies."

"Fine. That's fine. As long as you read it and think about it. Harry's already seen it and has spoken to Greta and Marcus. Obviously, as your ex-bosses, it will be up to them as it will be for their companies, but it could be a one-off." Carlos looked at his brothers. "This is going to be mega huge, I can feel it in my bones. You know, like Mama got today with you two. I can't describe it and don't know what it is, but *I know* it's going to be mega huge."

"Do you have a copy? We'll read it on the plane when we leave, and then think about it over the next few months," Roger said.

"I'll get you copy tonight."

In the living room, Jenny and Spiros were standing by the window while the boys were huddled in the kitchen.

"Jenny, what is going on?" Spiros asked.

"I'm worried about my sons, that's all," she said, a deep feeling of dread churning in her gut. She knew what was coming, had probably known it for some time, and hated that it was happening. But it wasn't happening tonight. Not on her watch. Removing herself from the situation, she hurried over to her sons. "It's time for you to go, Pedro, you don't want to be late."

"Not that I'll get anywhere in this snow," he said, and they turned to look out the windows. "Looks like we're being snowed in."

"I hope our flight isn't cancelled tomorrow," Viv said from next to Angie on the couch. "I have a shoot next week."

"Oooh, what for?" Angie asked.

"Maternity wear." Viv laughed.

Jenny took a deep breath. "You go to work and be safe. The rest of you come and sit in front of the fire. We'll talk about your trip back to Australia." She was determined to talk about anything but going home because she knew Spiros would fight her. And she didn't want that tonight.

"Have you thought about where you'll go?" She pulled Tomas down beside her on the couch. "Obviously back to Armidale. But you really should stay in Sydney and see the sights. And then there's Melbourne, the Gold Coast, Ayer's Rock. There's so much to see, and you'll be going back in summer and having a nice autumn, and then you'll be back here for this summer, so you won't be cold."

"Haven't even thought about it, Mama, it's all so new to digest. But we'll definitely go home and see the family," Tomas said.

"Good. You'll get to spend time with your cousins again. And Roger, you'll get to hear even more stories of Tomas and the boys when they were little."

"Can't wait." He grinned from his spot beside his husband. "Even more stories about what a manwhore Carlos was as a child."

"Hey," Carlos protested. "I wasn't a manwhore as a child. I only became one at eighteen."

"Oh," Jenny groaned. "We don't want to hear about your sexual exploits Carlos. Look at what you did to poor Barbara Weston."

"Mama, she was a whack job all the way back in high school. *No one* wanted her then," Carlos said.

"But *you* wanted her last summer," Tomas reminded him.

"I didn't know who she was," Carlos defended himself. "I didn't even remember her name after she'd told me. And I certainly didn't recognise her."

"Oh, of course not." Tomas grinned.

"It's not like that…" Carlos thought a moment. "Well, all right, it is. But I only had sex with her once last year, and that was enough. I didn't know we went to school together, and I certainly didn't remember rejecting her back then. Too many other girls to go after."

"Well, thanks to you, I got some pretty sick gifts and a dead father," Angie said quietly from her spot on the couch. "That whack job you ignored in high school, and fucked last summer, stalked us and killed my father." Everyone in the room went quiet, and the frivolity died.

Jenny went to sit by Angie's side. "I'm so sorry." Putting her arm around her, she rubbed Angie's arm. "It seems a lot of people were involved in the tangled web of the Stephanopoulos family last year, and some of you suffered more than most. I'm so sorry."

Angie wiped away her tears. "Considering what my father did, I'm glad he won't be around the baby because he'd be nothing but a bad influence. But that doesn't mean it's an easy subject to talk about."

"Of course not," Jenny agreed. "Let's change the subject."

"Sorry, Angie," Carlos murmured. "I keep forgetting what she did."

Angie shrugged. "So do I."

Spiros sat back and watched his family. His in-laws, Matthew and Sarah, chatted about the family back home with Roger and Tomas, filling them in on what had been happening. Angie and Viv talked about the latest fashion about to hit the European runways that they hoped would come to America. And Jenny flitted back and forth in and out of conversations, talking about maybe one day revisiting Australia. Maybe, when the babies were older and could travel, she'd take the whole family. It had been nearly eleven years since they'd been there, and so much had happened. And most of that was in the last eight months.

He sighed and watched her get cookies for everyone, avoiding eye contact with him when she offered him one. He nibbled on a heart cookie she had made for the family, and saw her fiddle with the silver heart locket he'd given her for Valentine's Day. It was similar to the necklaces the girls had received for Christmas, as he'd gone to the department store and bought her one.

He knew what was coming. At New Year's he'd agreed to stay until the boys' birthdays, and then they'd leave and go home with Jenny coming back for the summer. But his wife wasn't the only one who had gut feelings. So did he. And his gut was telling him his marriage was in danger.

*****

For two days they were snowed in, and the weather was so bad the airports were closed, which meant Carlos and Viv didn't go home. Juilliard was closed, and only Pedro ventured out to work. Everyone else stayed in front of the fire keeping warm, and talking about Tomas and Roger's trip back home.

Except for Spiros, who knew that broaching the subject was a no-no where Jenny was concerned, until he couldn't take it any longer. He saw her go upstairs for something and bit the bullet. Following, he closed the bedroom door behind him. "We need to talk about going home."

She stopped short, magazine in hand, and instantly hardened. "I don't want to talk about it." She tried to pass him, but he blocked her way. "Spiros."

"Jenny," he said forcefully, holding her by the arms. "We need to talk about it. You asked me to stay until the boys' birthdays, and that was three days ago. Your parents are leaving when the weather clears and taking Tomas and Roger with them. Carlos and Viv will be back in L.A., and it's time for us to go back to Mykonos." The anger simmered lightly inside of him. They'd already spent too much time away from their home, and it was time to let their children go.

Anger burned inside of her. She'd never felt as angry at her husband as she did now. When he'd asked her to leave her family, she went willingly, but sadly. She left behind brothers, sisters, parents, cousins. They uprooted the boys all to go across the other side of the planet back to *his* homeland because his father had died. But times had changed. And while they had a decent life, it was changing again, and Jenny no longer felt at home on Mykonos. With the boys gone, what did she have besides Spiros? As much as she loved her husband, she just didn't know if that life was enough anymore. If *he* was enough anymore. Tears welled in her eyes. "I love you, I do. So much." Her fingers traced his lips. "But Mykonos isn't my home anymore."

"Jenny." He frowned in despair. "Don't say that."

"My babies aren't there anymore." The tears flowed, and she choked.

"It's not enough without them."

"You must have known at some stage they would leave home." He took her into his arms.

"But I always thought they'd live nearby, get married and have babies of their own, not move half way around the world."

He sighed. "I know. I expected that too, but that's not what's happening, and we have to let them go. It's time for us to go home."

She pulled back and wiped her face. "I want to stay in New York, and I want you to stay with me."

"What!" He studied her face. "I have a business. We have a home."

"*We have a house*," she corrected him. "It's not a home *without our children*. And I don't care about the meat shop. That's your inheritance, not mine, not the boys'. You took it over, but that was your choice. Times have changed, it's time to make new choices, and I choose to be with my babies. Pedro and Angelina will need help, and I plan on being here to give it to them."

"Jenny…you know I can't give up the shop."

"I don't care if you give it up. Retire, sell it, let Christo run it. I want us to live *here* now. Why can't you understand I won't live without my babies?" Pulling out of his arms she flung open the door and went downstairs.

"Jenny," Spiros yelled, following her. "Mykonos is my home, *your* home."

"Not anymore," she yelled back, surprising everyone who was there. She dumped the magazine on the coffee table.

"What do you mean *not anymore*?" Spiros came into the foyer living area. "That's where we've lived for ten years."

Jenny moved back to face him. "That was *your* parents' house, and it wasn't until your mother died that it became ours. But times have changed; it's time for us to start a new chapter of our life. Why can't you see that?" They stood between the stairs and the living room, a standoff between two stubborn people.

"*Of course* we can start a new chapter. I never said we couldn't," Spiros said. "The boys have moved out now, it's us again, just like when we were first married before Carlos came along."

"Oh, so you expect me to be alone, have nothing to do, and worry about getting *your* dinner on the table by the time *you* get home because I don't have a job."

"Your job was to be a good housewife and raise our sons."

"Ha! Is that all I was?" Hands on hips, she faced off with her husband, completely forgetting her children and parents who stood wide-eyed. "Because *I* had no friends, no job, no family except for the boys for ten years. *Your* family wanted nothing to do with us and shunned us, and the local community didn't care for an outsider. *Your* family didn't even care about *you*," she told him. "Don't you remember how it feels to be in a new country with new things? Or have you forgotten that you made a *choice* to move to Australia off your own back? No one made you go there Spiros, you made a choice, and *I'm* making one now."

The boys stood side by side having never seen their parents in such a heated argument. And needless to say, fear was flowing through them.

"*Of course* I remember making a choice. I wanted to see a new land, start a new life. You were the first person I saw when I walked off the boat." The memories came flooding back for Spiros. Walking down the gangplank onto the dock to see a beautiful brunette with a smile that lit up the world. "You are also the only woman I've ever fallen in love with. The only woman I ever wanted to marry. And you said yes, Jenny, or have you forgotten?"

Oh, how could she forget! The sight of Spiros walking down the gangplank made her heart flutter and her stomach do flip flops. The tall, muscular, tanned Greek was different to the boys in her neighbourhood, and he moved in right next door. "I haven't forgotten saying yes to you. I loved you just like I do now. That's why I want you to make another change. So that we can now enjoy our later years while we still can and see the world before it's too late. Why do you have such a problem with living here?"

"Because our home is Mykonos," he said stubbornly.

"Our *house* is in Mykonos," she corrected.

"So is my shop and our friends," he reminded her.

"What friends? We sure as hell have no family there. I left my family in Australia for you to move to a country I didn't know. I sacrificed *my* life for you, Spiros," she all but yelled. "*I* left *my* home for your parents' house, for *your* father's shop. The only time it was a home was when the boys were there, and now they're not."

Angie hovered behind Pedro, clinging to him. She flashed back to her parents' arguments and how she would hide behind doors and watch and listen. The panic rose, and she tried to swallow it, but her throat closed and she choked on her tears and childhood fears instead.

Viv put an arm around her and pulled her back, motioning for her to stay quiet.

"But that doesn't mean we just abandon it," Spiros argued.

"I'm not asking you to abandon anything," Jenny cried, frustrated that he was fighting her. That *she* was fighting *him*. "I'm asking you to make a choice, together, to move on to a new chapter in our lives. I don't want to go back to Mykonos, Spiros."

"What? Ever?" He frowned deeper, disappointed and angry with his wife who had been so loyal, so loving, so giving, and now she was so angry.

"I don't know," she said, waving her arms in frustration. "For a few years. I don't know. I don't know if I'll ever go back. I haven't gone back to Australia, I'm not upping and moving the family there."

"Oh, well, thank God for that because that's even farther away," he spat.

She froze. "What!"

He sighed. "Jenny, I didn't—"

"*You,*" she spat, "made the choice to move to *that* country and start a new life. *You,*" she pointed her finger, "chose to marry an Aussie girl and start a life, a business, a family with her. *They* were *your* choices. Do *you* regret *them*?" She stood toe to toe with him. "*You* had no problem moving to the other side of the world. *You* had no problem asking me to move our three boys and our home to the other side of the world. In fact, I remember the guilt trip sob story you spun me about your father, and your mother being left alone even though *you have siblings* who could have taken care of her and the shop, and how *you needed* to be the head of the family and take over and be the big man."

Her eyes spat fire at him. "I remember *every* word you said to convince *me* to leave *my* family and move back to *your* homeland. *I* sacrificed my family, my home, my life for you, Spiros Stephanopoulos, because that's what *I chose* to do. Because I love you, you are my husband, and we are a family. And yet all you have done since New Year's is try and persuade me to go back to Mykonos even though you *know* I don't want to leave my babies alone."

"They're not babies anymore, Jenny, they're grown adult men," Spiros reminded her. "It's time for you to cut the apron strings and let go."

"Oh, like your parents did with you. Oh, wait, *your* father disowned *you*," Jenny spat, waving her finger to emphasise her words as she shook. "*Your* father no longer wanted you if you left Greece. And here you are telling *me* to cut the apron strings. *I* will never abandon *my* children." She let her words sink in as she gasped for air. *Where in God's name is this coming from?* she thought. The anger, the hatred, the resentment.

Spiros seethed. Never in all his years, all the time that they had been married or together, had he seen her like this. So angry, so alive with fire, so resentful of his decisions. He didn't like what he was seeing and didn't know if he wanted to continue seeing it.

"Mama, Papa." Carlos stepped forward. "Stop this now." He had never seen them so angry, so hostile in his entire life. And it was scaring the hell out of him.

"I am not abandoning *our* children," Spiros hissed, seeing the angry daggers shooting from Jenny's eyes. "I am letting them go to live their own lives."

"Yeah, like *your* father did," she sneered. "He had no problem letting *you* go."

"How dare you!" Spiros raised his hand ready to backhand her.

"Papa, no." Carlos sprang into action, stopping his father from raising his hand any further while Pedro and Tomas sprang to their mother's side as she shrank back in fear. "Papa, no." Carlos grabbed his father's face and made him look at him, seeing the wildness in his eyes. "How could you *ever* raise your hand to Mama? That is *not* what you taught us."

Spiros snapped out of it. Looking into his eldest son's eyes, he saw the horror and realised he'd raised his hand. Letting it drop, he hung his head in shame, hearing the girls crying, seeing them cling to each other. "I'm sorry."

"So am I," Jenny said. "I gave up everything I had for you, Spiros. I packed up the only things I had that were precious to me, my babies, and took them away from everything we had…*for you*…to take over your father's business. A man who abandoned you. A man who disowned you. Just so you could be the *man* of the family." She felt her sons' strength flow into her as they held her. "I left everything behind for you, and you can't even relinquish the damn shop for me now. You can't even take early retirement, or long service leave, or whatever," she screamed, "to make the move to New York with me now. How do you expect me to live without my babies? How do you expect me to live without my grandbabies? What if Angie needs me in the middle of the night? What am I supposed to do from *fucking* Mykonos!" She shocked everyone by swearing.

Because Jenny Stephanopoulos *never* used that language.

"In Australia, if I needed help with the boys, my parents were only minutes away, and I could call them, and they'd come running to help me, or I could go to their place. But what the hell can I do from Mykonos? I can't run to Angie's if she needs help because she'll be on the other side of the *fucking* world. What the fuck am I supposed to do from *fucking* Mykonos? Tell me, Spiros. How am I supposed to help my daughters-in-law with *our* grandchildren if I'm in Mykonos? Why can't you understand what I'm saying?" she screamed, her breath coming in short gasps. "Why do I have to give up everything *again*?"

Her tears poured down her face. "Why do I have to give it up again? Why can't *you* give it up for *me* for once? I lost my babies last year, and you wanted to disown them because you believed they were criminals when they weren't. Well, *I* believed in them, and *I* won't leave them. *Ever.* They are *my* babies, and I will *always* be here for them." Wiping her face, she saw everyone was in tears.

Taking a few deep breaths, she spoke once more. "If you can't do this for me, Spiros, if you can't sacrifice for me *for once*, then we…then we just aren't going to work anymore." She shook her head and heard the gasps. "I'm not giving up what I want anymore. So you can take it or leave it."

His heart thundered in his chest, and his blood sped through his veins as he stared at his wife along with their sons. "Jenny."

Still shaking her head, Jenny went on. "No, Spiros. If you can't sacrifice for me now, then there's no point. Go back to your home in Mykonos, because *my* home is here now, with Pedro and Angelina. *They* need me. You don't."

"Jenny…no…" Spiros was astounded. His Jenny, walking away from their marriage?

"Mama." Carlos looked from one parent to the other, as wide-eyed as everyone else in the room. "Mama, no."

"No, Carlos," she told him. "I sacrificed everything for your father so he could be with his mother after your grandfather died. I gave up everything. And now with his family gone, and you three and your partners here, this is where I want to be. And if your father can't understand that, and realise that the meat shop isn't even remotely important anymore, and for the most part, neither is Mykonos, then clearly, he doesn't get that home is where the heart is, and that is where my family is. And the family is here, and this is where *I* want to be. Then we have no more to say about it."

She gazed at her husband through tear-filled eyes. "I'm staying here, Spiros. You can go home, go back to that lonely little house, that lonely little meat shop. If that's where you want to be, then you're free to go."

"Jenny." He was confused, angry, didn't know which way to turn. And here was his wife staring at him with empty, soulless eyes. Eyes that had no love for him in them anymore. Not knowing what to do, he stepped back, heaved a sigh, and grabbed his coat from the closet. "Jenny." He turned to her only to be met with her back as she turned away from him. Frustrated by her rejections, scared by the turn of events, worried about the freaked-out expressions of his family, he walked out the door. Instead of waiting for the elevator, he headed down the stairs.

"Jennifer."

"Don't," she told her mother. "My husband, my problem."

"Mama." Carlos went to her side. "What the fucking hell!"

Jenny watched. Watched as Angie ran into Pedro's arms. Watched as Roger comforted a crying Tomas. Watched as Viv stood in the middle of the living room as stunned as everyone else. Watched at the window as Spiros left the building, turned up his coat collar, and took a left down the avenue. Watched while her husband left her. Watched as her tears fell. Watched as her marriage fell apart.

Spiros wandered aimlessly. He had no idea where he was going. No idea about direction. No idea about neighbourhoods. All he could think of was the cold, empty look in his wife's eyes.

The sky grew darker, the air grew colder. Pulling his collar tighter, he came to a stop on the snow-filled pavement in front of a sign that said *Ouzo Here.*

A sigh escaped him. *Well, that's gotta be a sign.* He entered the small bar somewhere in New York that instantly felt warm, yet was somehow still unwelcoming. Making his way to the bar, he motioned at the bartender.

"What can I get you?" The battle-worn, fifty something barkeep, asked.

"Ouzo, and keep it coming," Spiros said.

"Sure you can handle the stuff?" the bartender asked. "We've just had it in a few months, and no one can seem to handle it." He poured a shot and set it in front of him.

"I'm Greek born and raised. We drink ouzo for breakfast, lunch and dinner." Spiros sat down. "Keep them coming."

"Okay, if you're sure."

"You know what, just leave the bottle," Spiros said.

The bartender laughed. "Okay, your funeral." He left Spiros to drown his sorrows in the bottle of Greek liquid.

Spiros downed his drink, then another and another, doing a fourth before stopping to take a breath.

A woman sidled up to him and ordered a martini. "You look like you got sorrows to drown. Mind if I join you?"

Spiros looked around. "Can't stop you." And down went a fifth.

"Need a shoulder to cry on?" She sipped her drink, eyeing the Greek stud beside her. "I have good shoulders."

Down went the sixth shot of ouzo and he finally glanced up. "Jenny?"

The woman blinked. "Who?"

"Oh." Spiros cleared his eyes. "Sorry, you look like my wife."

"If you have a wife, what are you doing here?"

Down went a seventh. "Fucked if I know."

"That bad?"

"Worse than bad."

"Marriage ending?"

Down went an eighth. "I don't know."

"Fight that bad?"

He sighed. "We've never fought…until now."

"So why now?"

"Because she wants to stay here in New York and I want to go back home."

"Where's home?"

"Mykonos." A ninth followed the eighth.

"Nice. Why doesn't she want to go home?"

"Our youngest is here with his young wife, and they're having a baby."

"So, she wants to stay to help?"

"Yes." A tenth flowed down his throat smoothly.

"And what's wrong with that?"

"Nothing."

"Then why are you here?"

"Because she promised me she'd come home after New Year's, and then she made me stay until after their birthdays, and now she doesn't want to go home at all."

"And what's wrong with that?"

Spiros tipped his head back and drank the rest straight from the bottle.

"What's wrong with that?" The question was repeated.

"I don't want to live here. I want to go home." He ordered another bottle and promptly received it.

"And so instead of sorting it out with your wife, you're here getting drunk?"

"Yes."

"That doesn't seem like a very mature thing to do."

"I don't feel very mature right now." He drank half the bottle. The liquid burned his throat as it slid down into his gut. "I feel like getting drunk."

"And how many bottles of that stuff does it take to get you drunk?"

"At last count, five."

"Better keep them coming then."

*****

Jenny fretted, and paced back and forth in front of the windows in the penthouse hoping to catch Spiros coming home.

Everyone sat on the couches, silent in their own worries. Angie was snuggled up next to Sarah, who held on tight. For Sarah, Angie was a granddaughter straight out and she treated her as such.

Glancing at the clock as it struck ten, Jenny paced more, counting her steps as she went. Silently hoping, *praying* that Spiros came home. *Please God, let him come home so we can work this out. Why is he being so damn stubborn? Why is he so damn stubborn?*

Tomas looked from Jenny to Carlos, who was just as worried, to their grandparents. *Do we say something?* he mouthed to them and received a shake of their heads in return.

"Oh, for God's sake we have to," Carlos exploded into the quietness. "Mama." He marched over to her. "What in the hell is going on? Should we be out looking for him so you don't have to wear out the carpet?"

"Carlos," Matthew warned.

"No, Grandpa." Carlos glanced over his shoulder at him. "Mama." He took hold of his partially stunned mother. "Mama, you and Papa have never fought, never raised your voices at each other. What the hell is going on? Do you *want* a divorce?"

A weary breath came out of her. "No, of course not."

"Then what?"

She crumpled. "I'm sick and tired of giving up everything. Why can't he give up something for me for once? Why is it always me? No more." She stared into her son's eyes that matched her own. "No more am I going to sacrifice. I am *not* giving up what I have for a lonely little house on Mykonos. Not anymore."

"So, you're willing to let Papa go home by himself and then what? You'll never see him again? You'll get a divorce?" he asked.

She looked up sharply. "No...I...don't know. What I *do* know is that I want him to give something up *for me* for once."

"Oh, Mama." Carlos hugged her fiercely. "Oh, Mama, please fix this. Please make up with him. Please."

Her tears fell. "I don't know if I can."

*****

Spiros downed his fifth bottle of ouzo and drunkenly slammed it onto the bar. "And another," he slurred to the barkeep.

"I think that's your limit," the bartender said. "You've already made it further than anyone else, so I'm shutting you off."

"But I want another bottle." Spiros was in an argumentative mood.

"How about I take you home," the woman said. She'd been by his side all night, egging him on to drink, watching as he slammed back bottle after bottle.

"Home?" He wearily looked up into the face of his wife. "Jenny?"

The woman laughed. "That's the second time you've called me that."

"You look like her," Spiros slurred. "Brown hair, blue eyes."

"A lot of us have brown hair and blue eyes. Why don't I take you home?"

"Home? I don't have a home. My home is in Mykonos." He wobbled back and forth on the stool.

"How about you come with me, and I'll show you *my* home," the woman seductively purred, lightly trailing her fingers across his shoulders. "It sounds like you need to keep partying."

He looked to his left and found her breasts snug in their silky blouse, and felt a stirring in his pants. Was he having a hard-on for another woman? No, he couldn't possibly be.

"Let's get you home so you can keep drinking." The woman bought two bottles and led a drunken Spiros outside where she hailed a taxi and took him back to her place.

"Where are we?" He weaved back and forth as she unlocked her door.

"Home. Come in." Letting them in, she gave him another bottle. "Here, drown your sorrows."

He uncapped it and swigged back half a bottle before taking a breath.

"Now, tell me all your troubles and let me help you," she murmured, sliding her hands under his jacket.

He spilled his guts, telling her all the sordid details of the last eight months and how Jenny didn't want to go back home while he finished the bottle and downed the second.

"It sounds like your wife isn't very understanding." She breathed into his neck. A plan had formulated in her mind and she planned on bringing it to life.

"No, she's not. I don't feel good."

"Let's get you into bed, shall we." The woman led him to her bedroom where she flung back the covers and helped him out of his clothes before sitting him on the bed. "You rest, and I'll see you in the morning."

He lay down and spread out, asleep within moments.

"And now for the main act," she murmured. He only had his boxers on, and she awkwardly pulled them down so he was completely naked in her bed. "Oh, my God," she breathed. "You're magnificent." She stroked his penis and it rose to attention. "Oh, how I wish I could, God I want to so badly." Feeling it in her hands, she ran her hands over his body, kissing him, imprinting him. Unable to help herself, she quickly undressed and lay beside him, rubbing herself against him.

He rose higher and shifted. "Jenny?" he murmured, turning for her.

"Oh, I definitely am tonight," she whispered.

*****

Jenny had paced the entire time, pacing herself into exhaustion. Spinning her rings on her finger, looking at them thoughtfully. Studying them, trying to remember how important they were. Their own wedding had been simple. All of her family, none of his. But that didn't matter. All that mattered was the fact they were in love, that they loved each other, and both of them took their vows seriously. She had, all of her marriage. She had her parents to look up to. They were still married over fifty years later, and still in love, and she admired that. They were her role models. The two people in the whole world that she looked up to, and she wanted a marriage just like theirs. And as far as she knew, Spiros had taken them seriously. Neither one of them ever strayed. Never wanted to. But now…

Having not stopped the pacing, Jenny had finally collapsed onto a couch and fallen asleep sometime in the early hours. Everyone had stayed curled up on a couch, or in a chair somewhere waiting for Spiros to come home.

But he did not.

She woke, her eyes shot open, and she was up in an instant looking at the clock. Six-thirty.

Racing upstairs, she found the bedroom empty, racing back downstairs she called Brewster, but he hadn't seen Spiros either. Sighing, she put the kettle on.

Pedro, just home from work, padded softly into the penthouse. "Mama. Is he back?"

She looked up through gritty swollen eyes. "What are you doing here?" she whispered. "You should be asleep. Go home to bed."

"No, Mama. No," he said quietly and took her hands in his. "Is Papa here?"

She shook her head. "No."

He sighed. "Oh, Mama." Taking her into his arms, he hugged her, resting his chin on her head. "I don't want you two to break up."

"Well…I hope we won't," she murmured. "But I have a bad feeling about this."

Carlos and Tomas joined in the hug, weary-eyed and tired.

"Oh, Mama," Carlos murmured. "How do we fix this?"

She smiled half-heartedly at him and ran her hand through his hair. "You can't. Only your father and I can." The kettle boiled and they made coffees for everyone, taking them over and waking the others. Jenny stoked the fire and threw more wood on, and waited once more for Spiros.

*****

The woman awoke to a cold wintry day and looked at the man beside her.

Spiros Stephanopoulos.

In her bed.

A Cheshire cat grin slid across her face, and she stretched before sliding out of bed. Grabbing a silk robe, she padded into the kitchen and made breakfast, then carried the tray into the bedroom to see him waking. "Good morning," she murmured, sliding onto the bed beside him.

"What? Where?" He ran a hand over his face. "Where the hell am I?"

"In my apartment," she said holding out a cup of steaming hot black fluid. "Coffee?"

He didn't take it. "What the hell! Where am I?" Realising he was naked, and in another woman's bed, he panicked. "Who the hell are you?" Bolting out of bed he dressed as fast as he could. "*Who* the hell are you, and how the hell did I get here, and *where* is here?"

"I met you in a bar last night getting drunk on ouzo."

Looking down, he realised what he'd done. Guilt poured into him. "No, no, I wouldn't...I didn't...no. Oh, God no." He fled into the main room and found the door, flinging it open to run down five flights of stairs and into the street before throwing up in the gutter. It wasn't just the alcohol, it was the guilt. Both were hitting him and hitting him hard. "No, no, I didn't. I couldn't. Oh, no...Jenny," he groaned, choking on sobs, falling to his knees and crying, more than he ever had in his entire life.

"Are you all right?"

Spiros looked up into the face of a stranger. "What?"

"Are you all right?" The man looked at him oddly.

Wiping his face, Spiros climbed to his feet. "Yeah, yeah, I am, thanks."

"Okay." The man walked off.

Looking around, Spiros knew he couldn't go home, not now, not yet. Seeing the park across the road, he wandered over and found somewhere to sit and cry.

*****

Jenny glanced at the clock. Twelve-thirty. Right on the dot.

Sarah and Matthew, and Tomas and Roger had delayed their plans due to the weather and what was happening. The same with Carlos and Viv. Pedro was snoring softly on a couch, and Angie clung to everyone.

Jenny watched the clock tick over to one, and then two, and finally Spiros walked through the door.

Everyone stopped, waiting, and silence filled the room.

He looked at Jenny, head slightly bowed, eyes moving down, his face red with shame. His clothes were rumpled and reeking of alcohol. "I'm so sorry." He sadly shook his head. "I'm so sorry." He walked up the stairs leaving everyone wondering what had just happened.

After a few moments, Jenny cleared her head and flew up the stairs to find him in the shower. She waited on the bed to continue the conversation. But when he came out, he brought his toiletries with him, quickly dressed in his old clothes, and pulled out his old battered suitcase and started filling it with the clothes he had brought from Mykonos.

"What are you doing?" Jenny stood and faced him. "Why are you packing? And why are you using your old case?"

"I'm going home," was all he said.

A sob leaked out of her throat. "You're leaving me?"

He stopped. "I'm not…I don't…" With a desperate shake of his head, he finished packing and closed the lid. Finally looking at her, his face crumpled. "I'm so sorry. I can't do this. I can't be here. My place is at home, and so is yours."

"Not now," she replied, confused by what he was trying to say. "Not at the moment while they're still so young and having babies."

"I know, and that's why I'm no longer asking you to come home," he told her. "I can't take you away from them. But I can't stay..."

"Why not?" She was so damned confused.

"Because I'm not the man you married. I'm not the man you need anymore. I've done wrong by you, Jenny, and I am *so* sorry." He sobbed. "I'm so sorry." He all but collapsed into her arms.

"Spiros, what's wrong, what happened?" That damned feeling of dread made her stomach plummet. "What's wrong, Spiros?"

He straightened and breathed in. "I can't be your husband anymore." Just saying it killed him. But after all the hours he'd sat thinking in the park, he realised she was better off without him. If he could so easily cheat on his beloved Jenny, then he was not the man she should have. Grabbing his case and carry-on bag, he left her and went downstairs. "I'm leaving," he told everyone who stood around staring in shock.

"Papa, no," Carlos whispered.

Jenny slowly descended the stairs to stand beside him. "What the hell did you just mean, you can't be my husband anymore?" she asked through gritted teeth.

The guilt swept over him, and he couldn't look at her.

"Spiros, what the hell have you done?" Her voice rose, almost hysterically.

Worried, her sons gathered around her.

"Papa?"

Spiros finally looked up. "I'm so sorry, Jenny. I didn't mean to. I never meant to. I don't even know how it happened, but you're better off without me. Better off if you stay here with your babies than being lonely in Mykonos with me."

"What do you mean you didn't mean to? What didn't you mean to do?" The fear made her ill. The love made her blind. "Spiros," she managed in a squeaky voice as her throat constricted.

He sobbed and glanced away. He didn't want to tell her, didn't want to destroy her, but he owed her the truth. "I got drunk at a bar and woke up in a woman's apartment." The terror clenched his stomach.

"You…what…?" Jenny tried comprehending through her tears.

"I got drunk and woke up in a woman's apartment…in her bed… and I'm leaving because I'm no longer good enough for you, Jenny Marsh. I've failed you as a husband, and I am so, so sorry." His shame made him unable to look at anyone.

The truth dawned on everyone. His words sank in, and Jenny felt her chest, her body, implode. "No," she whispered. "No." She collapsed into her son's arms.

"Mama." They lifted her back up.

"No," her voice grew louder. "No!" she screamed, her body collapsing. "No. How could you? How dare you? Get out, get out," her voice rose to high decibels. "Get out and never come back. I never want to see you again. Get out, get out." She ripped her rings off and threw them at him. Her hysterics sent him out the door, into the foyer, out of the penthouse, out of her life.

As the elevator doors closed on him, he sobbed. Sobbed for the man he was, sobbed for the marriage he'd ruined because he couldn't give his wife what she wanted.

"Ah," Jenny screamed, collapsing onto the floor where the screaming continued.

"Oh, Mama." The boys kneeled beside her, trying to comfort her, trying to take her pain away.

"Oh, my God," Viv whispered. "He cheated on her."

Angelina was crying. "I don't want Mama and Papa to break up, they're all I have."

"Neither do we, sweetie," Sarah comforted her. Watching her daughter screaming on the floor, she knew there was nothing she could do for her. As she'd said the night before, *my husband, my marriage,* so she had to leave Jenny to deal with it. But that didn't mean she wasn't heartbroken for her daughter.

"Ah," Jenny cried in pain. "How could he, how could he?"

"Oh, God, Mama." Carlos had no idea what to do to make things better, so frantically looked at his grandparents. He had to step up and be the man of the family now. The head of the Stephanopoulos family.

Through swollen tear-filled eyes, Jenny saw the glisten on the floor and quickly scrambled over to collect her rings. Holding them, looking at them, trying to remember what they meant. Something once. Nothing now. Curling up her hand, she sobbed.

Brewster found Spiros a taxi, and he made his way to the airport. Come hell or high water he was going to get a plane home. Come hell or high water he had to get the hell away from Jenny. He had ruined everything. Everything he had, everything he held dear. He had ruined it with his selfishness and greed. With his anger and stubbornness. He'd ruined the rest of his life.

Finding planes were taking off once more, he boarded one for Greece. All he had was his battered old case and clothes he'd come with. He'd left the new luggage set, clothes and watches in the penthouse. They weren't him. Never were, never would be. He was Spiros Stephanopoulos. A Greek boy who grew into a Greek man and had the love of his life by his side. A love that he had destroyed in one fell swoop. A life he had destroyed in one foul night. A night that he would regret for the rest of his life.

I will never forgive myself for what I have done. I will never forgive myself for destroying a woman, a family, a life. Looking down at his wedding ring, he didn't know whether to keep it on or take it off. *I need to leave it on. Leave it on as a reminder of the woman I left and the life I destroyed, so I never forget it, or forgive myself for the rest of my life.*

*****

Jenny's sobs slowly stopped. Her nails dug into her hand. She was deaf to all sounds. Blind to all things. Getting to her feet, she walked upstairs to their bedroom and stood in the doorway, looking at the bed. The bed where they'd made love every night, during the night, and sometimes in the morning. But she couldn't stay there now. Couldn't sleep in that bed. Be in that room. She just couldn't.

Turning, she walked across the hall into the spare room that

Tomas and Roger had used when they were sick. She shut the door and sat on the side of the bed, staring out the window at the snowy park. She was empty. There was nothing. Nothing now, but it would be back. The build-up of pain, torture, hatred. It would all be back and then some, but for now, there was nothing. She was empty.

Still clutching her rings, she let herself fall sideways and managed to pull the cover over her. That was where she would sleep. That was where she would stay.

Downstairs it was panic stations.

"What the hell did we just witness?" Carlos wiped his face. "Yesterday Papa tries to hit Mama, and today he's left her? What the fucking hell?"

"I don't get it," Pedro breathed, while Angie clung to him. "What the hell has happened between them? I thought they were happy. They were happy the other night at 69 for our birthdays." He looked from Carlos to Tomas who was being held by Roger. "Right?"

Tomas looked up. "They *looked* happy," he stuttered through tears. "They looked happy at Christmas. Look at the presents they gave each other."

"Yeah, but Papa wasn't thrilled with Mama buying this building for us. He thought it was too extravagant. That the watches were too much. They've never fought over money before," Pedro said.

"But this is about more than money," Tomas told them. "Papa's sticking to Mykonos, and Mama wants to be here with us."

"So why doesn't Papa get that?" Carlos waved a hand around in anger. "Why doesn't he get that we all left Mykonos to see the world and do other things?"

"Because he's a proud Greek man who's incredibly stubborn," Matthew said, and the boys turned to look at their grandfather.

"That's not good enough," Carlos replied. Frowning, he tried to remember the last time they'd been absolutely, totally, completely happy. Australia. Before they had been shipped halfway around the world. He'd been shunned like his mother, but the girls loved him, and that's what kept him going. That, and knowing wherever he was, his mother was always there to look after him and support him. And now it was time to support *her*. Now, after his father admitted to cheating on his mother, he had to do more than support her through it. He had to step up and be the man of the family, the *head* of the Stephanopoulos family when his gutless father couldn't be.

Turning slowly, his eyes laid upon Viv who stared back in shock. "Viv…when you married me…you realised what kind of family I came from, right?"

She nodded, having no idea where he was going with it, but took note of the deadly serious expression he had on his face.

"That we are close…that Mama raised us to love and support one another, and whenever we were in need, the others would be there."

"Yes." She finally understood.

He breathed in. "Well…now I need to be here. For Mama, for Pedro and Angelina. I need to be here to support the family, and to take charge as the head of the Stephanopoulos family."

She stepped closer. "Whatever you decide, I will understand."

"But will you support it?" The urgency all but leapt from his eyes.

Her own urgency was in her nodding. "Yes."

"For however long it takes?" He searched her eyes.

"Yes." She stepped closer.

Another breath. "Then I need to be here. To stay here for however long it takes, and be the head of the Stephanopoulos family."

"What?" Pedro frowned. "You're not Papa."

"*But Papa's not here.* He cheated on Mama and walked out on her, and now I need to take charge of the family like Mama always taught me to do." Carlos choked back a sob that threatened to overtake him. "Papa's gone, Pedro." He shook his head. "He's gone."

Pedro's face crumpled, and the tears fell. He clung to Angie as she clung to him. In all of his twenty-one years, he'd never seen them fight. Never heard raised voices until Carlos had run out in the middle of the night, then on their return to Mykonos, but that hadn't lasted long. Now his family was destroyed when they had tried so desperately to keep it all together.

Carlos slowly walked over to him, holding an arm for Tomas to join them. They converged. "We have to be men now. We have to take charge, and I need to step up as head of the family. That's what they taught me to do." He rubbed Tomas's back. "Mama fought you hard to take that holiday. I think you should still go."

"No," Tomas protested. "She needs all of us."

"No," Carlos told him. "She wants you and Roger to travel the world and be happy after everything you went through. Pedro and I are going to be fathers, we need to be here. So you go and enjoy yourselves."

"How are we supposed to do that when our parents' marriage just fell apart?" Tomas cried. "I'm not going to be happy traipsing around Australia while she's here heartbroken."

"It's what Mama wants you to do," Carlos said. "She wants you to travel, Pedro to DJ, Angie to go to school, and me and Viv to move here. And that's what we're going to do. We're going to do what Mama wants and make *her* happy."

"I don't want them to fight," Angie sobbed from Pedro's arms.

"Neither do we, babe," Pedro consoled her.

"I want my Mama." Angie tore herself away from her husband and flew upstairs to the bedroom.

"Angie, no," Pedro called, starting after her.

"No." Carlos stopped him with a hand on the arm. "Let her. She might help Mama. They have a special bond that none of us understands."

Reluctantly, Pedro nodded and stepped back.

Not finding Jenny in the bedroom, Angie ran into the bathroom. And not finding her there, ran back into the upstairs hall. Seeing the door opposite, she barged through and found Jenny buried under the comforter. "Mama?" came out in a little girl voice. "Mama?" Slowly moving to the side of the bed, she went to her knees, all but burying her head in the covers. "Mama?" Her hand slowly snaked out to pull the comforter back to reveal a crying Jenny. "Mama?" Her bottom lip quivered. "Please don't die."

Jenny's eyes flew open. She stopped crying and frowned, her sorrows forgotten for a second. "Angie? I'm not dying. Why would you say that?" She stroked her daughter's tear stained face. "I'm not dying."

"My real Mama died after a fight with Daddy. She used to bury herself in bed after they'd fight." She clung to the comforter. "I don't want to lose you, too. Then I'll have no one but Pedro, and I'll have to have the baby and look after it all by myself," she sobbed.

Jenny sighed. "Oh, sweetie, no, come here." She pulled Angie onto the bed and flung the comforter over both of them. "I'm not dying. My heart is dead, but I'm not dying. I'm not leaving any of you." Wrapping her arms around her daughter, she held on tight. "I'm going to be here when the baby comes, and I'm going to help you raise it. It's what we do in this family."

"It's moving."

Jenny's hand went to Angie's stomach. "It's growing."

"And I'm getting bigger," Angie groaned.

A small sigh came out of Jenny. "You'll get bigger yet, sweetie, just you wait."

"Aw, Mama, don't tell me that."

"It's what's going to happen," Jenny told her. "Whether you like it or not." Another sigh left her. "And I need to get on with life whether *I* like it or not." Looking at her hand still clenched around her rings, she knew she had to make a decision. And she couldn't stay in bed. As much as she wanted to give up and hide under the covers, she couldn't. She had two grandbabies on the way. "Come on, let's go downstairs." Patting Angie's arm, she moved the covers, and Angie rolled into a sitting position. Jenny sat beside her, staring at her hand as it lay in her lap. Finally, she uncramped her fingers to reveal three rings. Engagement, wedding, eternity. Memories came flooding back of when Spiros proposed, down on bended knee holding up the box. She'd said yes, and he'd tried to put the ring on her right hand. But she'd laughed and reminded him that she was Australian and they wore it on their left hand. So, on her left hand he'd put it, while he wore his wedding ring on his right ring finger. Sighing deeply, she picked up each one and put them back on. A frown as deep as her sigh etched on her face.

"Mama, why are you putting them back on?" Angie thought it was strange since Papa had left and Mama had ripped them off and thrown them at him.

"Because for better or worse we *are* married," she told her. "And until he serves me divorce papers, he is still my husband." Straightening them, she let out another sigh. "Come on, let's go downstairs." With her arm around Angie, they walked down to the silent stares of blue, green and brown eyes looking up at them.

"Mama." Carlos stepped forward. "Are you okay?"

A sad smile touched her lips. "No, and I probably never will be. But I can't hide away forever. We have babies to prepare for."

"Mama," Carlos went on, noting the sadness etched on her face that had suddenly made her look twenty years older. "We've made decisions."

"Why?" she asked.

He blinked. "What? What do you mean, why?"

"Why do you need to make decisions? This is happening to me, not you, or Pedro, or Tomas. Your father and I will sort this out."

"Will you?" Pedro asked, standing behind his brother. "Mama," he shook his head, "this has *never* happened before."

"I know, and that is why we will all get on with our lives and do what we had planned to do." Jenny smiled softly at her youngest.

"That's what I was saying," Carlos tried again. "As the man of the family now, I need to be here with you. *For* you, and that's why I'll be staying from now on."

"What?" It was Jenny's turn to be surprised. "You've decided to stay?"

"*I* will," Carlos explained. "Viv will fly home as planned, pack up our stuff, and sort out her work schedule, then be back in a couple of weeks. But I'm staying here for you, Mama. As the head of the family now, I need to be here."

"Oh." Jenny's appreciation was felt through her whole body. "I can't believe you're doing this. Viv?"

Viv walked up to her husband's side. "He has a job to do, Jenny, and I'm standing by him. Besides, I have a feeling once the babies are born, everyone will come together, and everything will be sorted out. I have no problem moving here for a while…now that this has happened."

Jenny's heart went out to her daughter-in-law, and she hugged her. "Thank you so much for understanding."

"Of course." Viv patted her back. "Always. Besides, I expect him to do the same for our family. Stand up and be the man."

"It's a pity my husband didn't understand." Jenny pulled away and spied Tomas. "I still want you to go travelling with Roger." She moved over to him as he shook his head.

"I'm not leaving. I'm not going anywhere," he said. "End of discussion."

"It's not the end of discussion because we already discussed it and you already *promised me,* Tomas," she reminded him. "*None of you* can solve my problem with your father. I have no idea if *I* can solve the problem with your father, but I'm sure as hell not about to let it ruin your trip back home."

"But Mama," he cried, nearly stomping his foot in childish defiance. "I don't want to leave you."

"I understand that." Jenny took him by the arms. "But don't fight me on this, Tomas. I *need* you to do this, it's important to me that you travel and see the world. You *promised* me you'd go. So you're going."

"Mama." He was frustrated that his mother was making him go, when all he wanted to do was stay and be by her side to comfort and look after her the way she had him during his illness. He didn't understand why she was making him go. But, he *had* promised. Hanging his head, he mumbled, "I don't want to."

"You're going even if I have to carry you onto that plane, Tomas Stephanopoulos."

Reluctantly, he looked up, pouting his lips, whining as his brothers had at times. At the end of the day, he *was* only twenty-three. A legal adult, but not necessarily a fully matured man, especially when it came to his parents' breaking up. "All right. But I *really* want to stay here with you."

"You're going," she said and turned to her parents. "If you don't want to leave today then we'll call up and change it for tomorrow. It's probably too late and too cold now anyway." A quick phone call and plans were changed.

March 1978

"Oh, my God, I can't believe I'm forty-one," Viv groaned. "Forty was bad enough."

"Wait until you get to fifty," Jenny told her in all seriousness.

"Oh, God no." Viv pretended to pull out her hair. It was March, and Viv's birthday. The family that was left was celebrating with a meal at a fancy Italian restaurant. Being Saturday, Pedro had the night off, and Angie and Viv were a month bigger.

"Don't worry, Viv, you're still hot," Carlos consoled his wife. "And still completely fuckable."

"Carlos, that's gross," Jenny chastised, frowning at the turn of phrase, and getting a blush from him in return. "Did Tomas call today?"

"Yes, he did. He's enjoying his time with family and taking Roger around the place. He's glad you made him go," Carlos said, hiding behind his wine glass in embarrassment.

"Good. That's what I wanted." Jenny sipped her wine. It was a hundred dollars a bottle, but she didn't care. Hadn't cared about much since Spiros had left. Had just stayed inside looking after Angie and Viv, teaching them how to change nappies on teddy bears, and what food was best for babies.

Viv had packed up her house and rented it out, moving half of her and Carlos's things to New York, where they planned on staying for some time and putting the rest into storage. Plus, she still had

"

modelling jobs, and Carlos was producing more scripts than ever.

Jenny had bought him the latest typewriter to help. She'd been quite the typist in her day and helped him by typing them up. It kept her mind and the days busy, even though her nights were still cold and lonely. Pedro had finally finished off his eight movies and was done with his contract, which she was glad about, and she had taken up knitting again, knocking out bootees, bonnets and blankets. But now they were out celebrating.

"Oh, that was a delicious meal." Viv touched her napkin to her lips. "Thank you so much, all of you. And the bracelet is beautiful." She squeezed Carlos's hand. "Thank you."

"You're welcome, my darling wife. And since I have no idea what else to get you, you'll be getting a lot of jewellery from me." He kissed her, so abundantly happy with his life.

A sad smile came to Jenny's lips. God, she missed Spiros. Missed him kissing her, holding her, making love to her. But he hadn't called, and there had been no papers for divorce, so seeing her sons with their partners made her incredibly sad.

"Oh, Mama, sorry, we forgot." Carlos saw the look on his mother's face.

"No, no." She waved a hand. "Don't stop loving each other on my account. What's happening between your father and me is our problem. Don't let it ruin your marriage."

"But seeing us makes you sad," he said.

"Only sad for *my* marriage, not for yours. I'm overflowing with love and happiness for yours. But I've had enough, so I'm going home. If you want to continue then do so, don't let me stop you from celebrating." She waved the waiter to bring the bill and paid for the entire thing, including the meal she'd had sent out to her driver.

"No. I'm done for the day too." Viv struggled to her feet. "I'm more tired these days and would like to snuggle with my husband."

"We'll go then," Jenny said, and they retrieved their coats from the cloakroom and walked outside to their car. The driver exited the car and opened the door for Pedro and Angie who climbed in.

"Jenny?"

Jenny turned and saw Gardo walking up to her. "Oh, Giancarlo, hello. I haven't seen you in a couple of months. How are you?"

His heart had warmed at the sight of his Jenny with the blue eyes, noticing two sons and daughters-in-law. "Busy," he said, watching her intently. "Out celebrating?"

"Viv's birthday," Jenny said, noting how happy and healthy he was looking.

"The rest of the family with you?" He hadn't seen a man, and didn't know what Spiros looked like except as a spitting image of Tomas.

"Tomas and Roger are travelling in Australia and seeing my family."

"And…your husband?" Curiosity got the better of him and he stepped closer, his eyes flicking from her to the car and back.

"He's in Mykonos," she finally said.

"What!" He was stunned. Her husband had left her alone.

"He went back to Mykonos," she said, unable to look him in the eye.

"He's not here celebrating with you?"

She pursed her lips and breathed. "Not at the moment. He had to get back for business. Look," she glanced at Carlos who was waiting by the car door watching curiously, back to Giancarlo, "I have to go. It was nice seeing you again. Goodbye."

"Yeah, bye." He watched her climb into the car with Carlos right behind her, watched until the driver drove off. *Spiros is back in Mykonos? How long has he been there and how come I didn't know about it?*

April 1978

They finished a boisterous rendition of happy birthday and watched Angelina blow out nineteen candles on her red heart-shaped cake.

"Yay me." She clapped excitedly, disbelieving that she was not only nineteen, but married with a baby on the way.

It was April, the weather was warming up, the girls were seven months pregnant, and the family, along with Maggie, was celebrating at Angie's favourite restaurant, a '50s-themed diner full of checkered flooring, jukeboxes, records on the wall, and roller-skating waiters. Kind of like a funky version of *Arnold's* from *Happy Days*.

Jenny had supplied the cake, and the diner had provided the burgers, fries and shakes, something Angie had been craving for the last month.

Cutting a slice, Angie shoved it into her mouth and her eyes closed. A groan escaped her. "Oh, my God this is so good."

"Don't talk with your mouth full." Jenny laughed, glad her children were happy. "Did Mum and Dad call? What about Tomas and Roger?"

"Called today," Pedro replied. "Left messages on that new fandangled answer machine thing you bought us." It was a weeknight, and Pedro had the night off from 69 to celebrate his wife's birthday. Watching her stuff another piece into her mouth he asked, "Are we getting any of that?"

"Nope." She shook her head and ate a third piece, with Maggie eyeing her and the cake with envy.

"How are they?" Jenny asked. "The boys."

"Good." Pedro turned back to his mother on his right. "Happy."

"Good." Jenny nodded. "That's what I wanted."

"So, what *was* that gut feeling of yours that made you do that?" Carlos asked.

Jenny shook her head slightly. "I don't know. What I *do* know is it had to do with what Luiz had done, and that he was so sick because of that bastard that my motherly instincts went into overdrive. I have a really horrible feeling that what Luiz did will have massive repercussions for them...and we won't be able to do anything about it."

"What sort of repercussions?" Carlos frowned. "Is there something we should know?" If his brother was still sick, he wanted to know so he could do something.

Jenny sighed. "I don't know, that's just it. I *don't* know. What *I do* know is that I need to give them whatever they want, and send them wherever they want to go as long as it makes them happy. I *need* to make them happy. *Make sure* they're happy."

"So then, what do we do?" Pedro finally received a piece of cake as Angie cut it up and passed it around.

"Love him, support him, make him happy. Spend quality time with him, make sure he knows you love him. That's what I want for all for you." Jenny smiled at her baby.

"Oh, my God, I feel sick." Angie slumped in her seat between Pedro and Maggie.

"That's what you get for eating all the cake." Pedro wiggled his brows at her.

"Ugh," she groaned. "That was so good, but so sickening. But hey, I haven't had a cake *for years.* Not one that really mattered anyway."

"Your father didn't celebrate?" Jenny asked, before taking a bite of the delicious vanilla and chocolate marble cake she'd made.

Angie shrugged. "He gave me a cake, he gave me a present, he gave me money. But it wasn't the same without my mother there. And after last year, now I have all of you to celebrate with. A husband, a brother and sister-in-law, a new Mama." That elicited a Jenny smiled. "And a new Papa." Angie saddened at those turn of events.

"I'm sorry," Jenny said. "He probably doesn't know it's your birthday. I always took care of stuff like that."

"Has he called at all?" Carlos asked.

Jenny shook her head. "No. A part of me expects him to. A part of me doesn't."

"That's not good enough, Mama," Carlos replied. "He's not being much of a man."

"Don't say that," Jenny told him. "Please don't disparage your father. He was a good man for nearly twenty-eight years and something happened. We had a good run."

"If he wanted a divorce he would have sent papers," Pedro added. "Has he?"

"No." And that's why Jenny held out hope that her marriage could and would survive.

"So there's a chance then?" Angie asked hopefully.

"There's always a chance, Angie. There's always a chance," Jenny said.

May 1978

"Mama, happy birthday," Tomas shouted down the line from Australia. It was the third week of May and Jenny's birthday.

"Oh, God, Tomas, what time is it?" Jenny cried. She'd heard the phone in the middle of the night and stumbled downstairs to answer the incessant ringing.

"Seven at night," he said.

"It's the middle of the night here," Jenny replied with a yawn.

"But it's your birthday," Tomas said.

Jenny laughed. "It was my birthday yesterday, and I thank you for calling, but it's only," she glanced at the wall clock, "five in the morning." She had hit the big 5-0, but hadn't felt like celebrating it even though the kids had.

"Damn, I didn't time it right. We couldn't figure it out. Did you get your presents?" He'd sent over albums full of photos from the whole family, plus pictures of their holiday around Australia so far.

"Yes, I did, and I love them."

"I miss you."

"I miss you, too. That's why these photos are so special. I love them."

"Good. What did the others get you?"

"A picture of the four of them with happy faces painted on Angie and Viv's bare stomachs."

"Oh, God, they didn't?"

"They did. Plus, the usual suspects of perfume, flowers and chocolates."

"Of course. That's what we get you every year."

"I know, and I can't wait to see you."

"I can't wait to see you. Only a few more weeks."

"How's the holiday going?" She curled up on the sofa.

"It's amazing. The weather has been perfect, the family are awesome, and the scenery is beautiful. We're seeing places neither of us has seen before."

Jenny spied one of the albums beside her on the couch in the sitting room and flicked through it. Tomas and Roger on the Harbour Bridge in Sydney, on Ayer's Rock in the Northern Territory, on the beaches in Queensland. They were happy, healthy and in love. "And that is what I wanted. For the two of you to see the whole world and be happy."

"And we are, Mama, we are."

"Good."

"Have you heard from Papa?"

"Not yet."

"Oh, Mama." His voice fell.

"I probably shouldn't expect to. We *are* separated after all."

"But Mama, you're his wife, the mother of his children."

"Don't worry about it. There's still time for him to call. It's our anniversary tomorrow." She thought about celebrating her 26th wedding anniversary all alone and didn't like it one bit.

"Oh, no, I forgot about that. I hope he doesn't."

"So do I."

"Okay. I'd better let you get your beauty sleep. I love you, Mama. Happy birthday and happy anniversary."

"Thank you, my darling. I love you, too. Come home soon."

"We will, bye."

Hearing the dial tone, sadness came with it. Replacing the phone, she picked up the album they'd all been poring over the day before and started through it again. The happiness she felt at seeing them together was warming her. They loved each other so much she knew they were soul mates in every way, and wanted it to stay that way.

With a sigh, she glanced at the clock and saw it was now seven. She thought about going back to bed, but was interrupted by Carlos and Pedro bursting in.

"Oh, you're up." They bounced over to her and smothered her in kisses.

"All right, enough already," she cried, and quickly put the album on the coffee table. "What are you two doing up so early?"

"We thought we'd make you breakfast in bed."

"Except I'm not in bed," Jenny said, wrapping her robe around her. "And you don't need to make me breakfast."

"Can you make us breakfast, too?" Viv asked as she and Angie waddled in wrapped in their dressing gowns and slippers. They sat beside Jenny on the couch, bulging at eight months along.

Pedro grabbed blankets from the back of the couches and laid them over the three women in his life. "This is your bed, we will make you all breakfast."

"Yay," Angie cried happily. "Food."

Viv laughed. "That's all I think of too."

"I'm always hungry," Angie complained. "And I wonder why I'm a blimp."

"Oh, you are not." Jenny laughed. "The baby's growing, it needs more food."

A few minutes later they were treated to food made by the boys. Scrambled eggs, bacon and tomato on toast, a Stephanopoulos staple. Passing out trays of food, Carlos crowded next to Viv under her blanket, and Pedro pushed the ottoman against the couch to sit cross-legged on it facing Angie.

"Mmm, this is good," Angie said, shovelling a forkful of eggs into her mouth while resting her feet on her husband's leg.

"That's coz I made it," Carlos said before swallowing tomato and eggs.

"Well, your mother *has* been giving you lessons," Viv said, finishing off her toast.

"Yes, I have, and scrambled eggs are not that hard," Jenny replied.

"Has anyone called?" Pedro asked.

"Your brother rang at five this morning."

"How is he?" Pedro scooped eggs onto his toast.

"Happy, healthy, just like in the photos."

"Yeah, great pics. I'm jealous." Pedro swallowed the rest of his egg toast. "I'd love to go home and explore Australia."

"You can when the baby's older. You'll need to decide where you're going to settle down permanently once school's over," Jenny said. "You have two countries to pick from. "Australia or Greece."

"Speaking of Greece, has Papa called?" Carlos asked.

"Not yet." The disappointment stuck in her gut.

"Aw, Mama."

"Don't worry about it. As I told Tomas, we *are* separated."

"Not the point," Carlos argued from the other end of the couch.

"Exactly the point," Jenny argued back. "I just have to face the fact that my marriage is over."

"Mama, no." Pedro frowned in disbelief.

"Yes, Pedro." She looked her son in the eye. "Now don't some of you have school?" She turned her attention to Angie who groaned.

"Ugh, I don't wanna." She flung her head back and closed her eyes.

"Well, you hav'ta," Jenny said. "So off you go."

"I'll be glad when the school year's over. Just a few more weeks," Angie said as Pedro helped her stand.

"And then you'll be having a baby." Jenny ushered the others out. "I'll do the dishes, you all go."

"Bye, Mama, see you later."

"Yes, I'll see you later. I have some errands to run." After closing the door, she dealt with the dishes and was heading upstairs when the phone rang. She ran over to answer it. "Hello."

Silence.

"Hello?"

Silence.

"If there's no one there I'm hanging up."

Silence.

She hung up and walked back to the stairs only for the phone to ring. "Oh, for goodness sake." She picked it up. "Hello?"

Silence.

"Hello? Is this a crank call?"

"Jenny."

Every emotion thundered over her. She knew her husband's voice. "Spiros."

He breathed in. "I didn't…want to call…I wasn't sure I should. I didn't want to ruin yesterday…"

She didn't know what to say. A million things went through her head *to* say, but she didn't actually know *what* to say.

He gripped the phone tightly as he gazed around the lonely home in Mykonos. "I miss you," he whispered, tears flooding down his worn, etched face now covered by a full beard and longer hair. He hadn't bothered shaving or getting a haircut, cooking or cleaning. He didn't have the heart. It was *their* home. His and Jenny's and the kids'. But for the last three months it had been an empty shell. A shell he deserved to die in. To suffocate in.

Tears dripped into her dressing gown. "I miss you, too."

"I'm so sorry I screwed everything up. You have no idea how much I regret everything I did. I've ruined everything, and you don't deserve that." He glanced around his lonely, cold home. Lonely without her body. Cold without her love. "I wasn't sure if you'd want me to call. If you'd want to hear my voice. Want anything to do with me." Looking at his hand, he saw his wedding ring. It had stayed there and would until his dying day.

"I wanted to," she whispered. "I want my husband."

"I know you'll never forgive me, Jenny," he sobbed. "I know I can never make it up to you. You deserve a man who will never cheat on you. Never do what I did. I dishonoured you. I dishonoured our marriage, and that's not right. You deserve better, and I don't deserve you."

"Oh, Spiros." The pain in her heart over what had happened was nothing compared to the love she had for him. "Please," she begged in whispered tones. "Please come home."

He shook his head. "I am home, Jenny. I'm where I deserve to be. Alone in the place I fought you so hard for, and this is where I'll stay until my dying day."

"My, God, you're a stubborn man," she spat. "Are you even coming for your grandchildren's births? You forgot about Angie and Viv's birthdays!"

"I didn't know when they were."

"Why didn't you call your sons and find out?"

"I knew they wouldn't talk to me."

"You knew no such thing. You have become such an infuriating man, Spiros Stephanopoulos. Stubborn and infuriating, automatically thinking that you're right and no one else is, so everyone has to suffer for your stupid, stubborn pride." She slammed down the phone and instantly regretted it. "Oh, why did I do that?" she wailed. "Why did I let him get to me and make me angry? Oh, God, have I just ruined everything again?" She sobbed quietly for a few moments before wiping away her tears, shaking herself off, and going to get ready for the day.

Two hours later, she was coming out of the pharmacy when she ran into Giancarlo Gardo.

"Jenny." He was shocked to see pain on her face, and no happiness radiating from her as it usually did.

Jenny glanced up. "Giancarlo. I haven't seen you in ages. How have you been?"

"Not too bad until recently. A bit of a bug." He took in her spring dress flowing around her shapely legs. Her hair was pinned up and made her neck look longer.

"Yes. I remember the terrible flu Tomas and Roger had. It was horrible. I hope you don't have it."

He coughed. "A bit of hay fever I think. Change of season and all that. How's the family?"

Jenny smiled sadly. "Viv and Angie are weeks away from giving birth, and Tomas and Roger will be flying back from Australia."

He hated bringing up the subject. Really, he did. "And…is your husband back? You must be both excited." He was intrigued, but confused by the way her face fell. "Jenny? Is your husband not back?"

Taking a deep breath, she steeled herself. "No. Spiros left in February. He hasn't been back because he left me. He left me, and we are separated." A sob caught in her throat.

"What!" He was astonished, shocked and ecstatic. "What do you mean he left you? *How* could he, *why* would he? You're an amazing woman, Jenny."

She smiled sadly at his compliment. "Bad things happened, and he left me. I really must go. It was nice seeing you again. Goodbye." Unable to look him in the eye, she hurried away.

Well, I'll be fucking damned, he thought. *He fucking left her. How the fuck could he leave her? Why the fuck would he leave her? It doesn't make sense. The way they had been. The way she had been. Happily married for nearly twenty-six years and he ups and leaves her. What the fuck is going on?*

That night, as Giancarlo laid in bed, distracted, one arm under his head, the other on his stomach, he felt Sheila move beside him.

She woke, seeing him thinking about something. "What's got you so distracted tonight?"

"Huh? Nothin'." He went back to his thoughts.

"Bullshit!" She nestled into the pillow. "You were distracted when you got here, you were distracted during sex, now here you are lying awake thinking of something. Spill it."

He breathed in and let out a long sigh. "I ran into Jenny Stephanopoulos today."

She froze, and after a few moments managed to speak. "And?"

"And she told me her husband had left her back in February and gone home to Mykonos. They've separated."

"You're kidding?" That intrigued her. "I didn't know that."

"And why would *you* know? You two bosom buddies?" he sneered. "I ran into her in March, and all she said was he was there, nothing else."

Well, she thought, *did I do that?* Out loud she went on. "I suppose after everything that happened there was bound to be friction. Problems, a separation."

"I didn't expect it from *them,*" Gardo replied.

Wanting to change the subject because of the guilt she was feeling, she reminded him she had work tomorrow and to go to sleep. Back in February, she had scored a part-time job and loved it. She was working at the American Museum of Natural History three days a week, as well as a couple of days a week in an upmarket recycling opportunity store. The number of classic and vintage brand name clothes she'd been able to buy was ridiculous. Snuggling down, she thought about all she had and none of her guilt.

But her guilt ate her up over the next week, and Gardo noticed.

"What's wrong with you?" he asked on a sunny late May day. He'd been sleeping almost full-time at her house with no real need to go home to his.

"Nothing," she muttered, getting ready for work.

"Bullshit!" he replied. "Ever since I told you about the Stephanopouloses separating you've been acting weird."

"It was a shock is all." She slid her white blazer on over the matching pants. "After the way they acted and carried on, you'd think they were Joseph and freakin' Mary."

"No. There's more to it than that," he said. "Much more. You've got guilt written all over your face."

She looked up, knowing that her face was on fire.

He read her expression, and over thirty years of detecting experience kicked in. *"What did you do?"*

She swallowed. "Nothing." She grabbed her bag, locked the windows, and made sure her cats had water.

"What did you do, Sheila?" he bellowed, knowing something was seriously wrong.

"Nothing," she cried as he pinned her against the wall next to the door she had tried to escape through.

"What did you bloody do?" he breathed over her.

Biting her tongue, she tried to stop her tears. His size and voice alone scared her when he was in cop mode, and now she was shifting on the spot trying to get away.

"What did you do?" He leaned over her, trying to scare her into telling him. "Is it about Jenny?"

Glancing up at him she crumpled. "I did it."

"Did what?"

"I didn't mean to, and nothing happened," she wailed. "He was drunk, I had a crazy plan to get back at her, but nothing happened."

"What didn't happen?" He was breathing fire now.

"Spiros didn't happen."

His eyes narrowed, and his anger boiled up, simmering just short of the surface like a volcano. *"What did you do?"* His voice was low and menacing.

The tears poured forth. In that moment, she had never been more scared of losing the man before her. And for all the guilt since the deed, she hadn't actually done anything. "I was at a bar and he was getting drunk. When he was really drunk, I brought him back here and put him in my bed. I took his clothes off and…"

Gardo seethed. The woman he'd been seeing cheated on him. On *him*, on Giancarlo Gardo. "You cheated on me?"

"What!" Sheila looked up in shock. "No."

"Keep going."

"Well…at first I thought of doing it. I wanted to see how big he was, and he's as big as his son Tomas, and he looked so good naked that I got in beside him, but when he was kissing me he thought I was Jenny and was calling her name like you do, but all it reminded me of was you, and then I couldn't do anything because I wanted you and not him, so I pushed him away and he fell asleep, and put a pillow between us and went to sleep too, but when I made him breakfast in the morning he freaked out and ran before I could explain that nothing happened." She finally stopped babbling to take a breath. "I didn't do anything I swear. We didn't have sex. I couldn't."

"Because he wasn't me?" Gardo shoved her away. *"Do you realise what you've done?"* he bellowed. "You've ruined a marriage. You've ruined a family."

"It's not my fault he ran out before I could explain," Sheila cried.

"You shouldn't have done it in the first place. You should have called him a cab and sent him home." He stalked around the apartment, hands on hips, his size taking up half the space. "What the hell am I gonna do now?"

"Why do you have to do anything?" she asked softly.

"Because she deserves to know the truth," he told her. "So she can put her marriage back together."

"But I didn't do anything?" she wailed. "I stopped because I didn't want to be with him. I wanted to be with *you*."

"Cold comfort," Gardo yelled. "Now I have to come up with a lie to save your sorry ass." He slammed her back against the wall. "You took her money. She gave you *five million dollars* when she didn't have to, and you took it. Is this how you repay her?"

"No," she cried out. "I wanted to, but I couldn't. I wanted to get to know him, to see what was so special about him. Hell, you're one to talk. You've had a crush on her since you met her."

"But I've never taken advantage of her, or tried to break up her marriage." He shoved her back. "Now I need to tell her. And I should, by right, tell her *you* did it. But for some stupid reason, I feel I should protect you."

"Nothing happened," she said again through her tears. "I couldn't. He wasn't you, and I wanted *you*."

"So why the hell did you do it?"

"I'm sorry. I'm sorry. I was stupid."

"Why the hell should I lie to protect you, Sheila, why? Tell me why *I'm* thinking of lying to protect you?" He stood as wide as he could, with his hands on his hips, over her.

She sobbed quietly for a moment. "Because you love me."

He laughed, and the raucous sound echoed around the room. "*Do I? Do I love you?* Coz I sure as hell have never had *that* thought. Tell me why I should lie for you? Why should I lie to protect you from the wrath of Jenny Stephanopoulos? Who *I know* would hunt you down and kill you? *I've seen it in her eyes.* She would *kill* for her family."

"You can't let her kill me," Sheila pleaded.

"*Why the hell not?* What you've done is deplorable, disgusting, unforgivable."

"Please forgive me, Giancarlo. I had no idea what I was doing. I was stupid and thinking stupid things," she begged. "Please, please don't tell her it was me."

"And why the hell not?" He crossed his arms, and the bulk of his muscles bulged.

She cringed, head bowed, unable to look at him. She had only found out two weeks ago and wasn't even sure how far she was.

"Tell me why I shouldn't tell Jenny Stephanopoulos that you set her husband up and succeeded in ending her marriage. Tell me why I should lie to protect *you,* of *all people?*"

After a long silence, she answered. Taking a deep breath, she said, "Because I'm pregnant."

"What!"

She finally looked at him. "Because I'm pregnant."

His arms fell to his side, his brows slid down, etching the gap between them into a deep crevice. "What!"

"I went to the doctor a few weeks ago for my yearly check-up. I'm pregnant."

"Is it mine?" he asked seriously

"Of course it's yours!" she exclaimed, almost indignantly.

"Not that *I* can be sure." He gave her the once over.

"Giancarlo, you're the only man I've slept with. The only man I've had sex with in the last twenty-seven years. Of course it's yours," she said, exasperated.

"How can *I* be sure?" he asked in all fairness.

"Because." She breathed. "I haven't slept with any man besides you."

"Spiros Stephanopoulos."

"We slept in the same bed. I *didn't* have sex with him."

"How can *I* be sure?" His brain was not computing the information.

"Because I'm telling you the truth. Besides, if I *was* pregnant to him I'd be showing by now, and I'm not, because I didn't have sex with him. I've only had sex with two men in my life, and one of them is you."

A deep sigh emanated from him. He was angry, he was pissed, he was absolutely disbelieving that at fifty-three he was going to be a father. He didn't know what to do. He didn't know what to say. What the hell *could* he say? Sheila had gotten herself into a mess, and now he had to fix it.

A baby. For fuck's sake, a baby! She was having a baby. No, it couldn't be happening. It must be a mistake. It must be wrong. "You're too old. How are you pregnant?"

She took a breath and shrugged. "Apparently, it's a miracle. I'm still trying to come to terms with it. I have more tests done in a few weeks."

His breath came out hard and fast. "Weren't you…I used…"

"Protection?" She cocked a brow. "It doesn't always work. I think there were times we didn't."

Stunned into silence, it was broken by a loud knocking on the door. Flinging it open, he saw Officers Burns and Devron standing in front of him. "What do you two want?"

Two stunned faces looked back at him, to Sheila, to him.

"There were, ah, calls of a domestic disturbance," Burns slowly said, unsure of how to proceed and wondering about the relationship happening before him.

"We were arguing. Two people having an argument. It happens all the time." Gardo grabbed his jacket and stared for a moment at Sheila who stood quietly, ashamed and guilt-ridden, before walking out the door and closing it behind him. "Tell the person who complained to mind their own damn business," he said, walking down the stairs and pulling on his blazer. "People argue all the time, get over it."

"Sir. You really want us to tell them that?" Burns asked as they followed.

Gardo stopped at the main door, hand on the knob, and looked at him. "Yes." Throwing back the door, he strode to his car.

"Jesus. I didn't know Gardo was seeing a woman." Devron stood with his hands on his hips, watching the detective screeching down the road.

"Not just *any* woman," Burns told him, getting a curious look in return. *"Sheila Manning."*

"Manning?" Devron thought about the name and where he'd heard it.

"As in…*Luiz Manning* and the *whole* Stephanopoulos family," Burns reminded him.

Devron's eyes lit up. *"Get out! That's* her? She definitely doesn't look how *I* imagined."

"Word on the street is, that Jenny Stephanopoulos gave her money from the Papadopoulos estate that she inherited. Sheila was suing for bucket loads, Jenny gave her some."

"Whoa! Really? So how'd she and Gardo get involved?" Devron asked as they went back up to the fifth floor.

"No one knows. Unless it was after the whole investigation. She was Luiz's mother, and his father was Andros Poulos. Remember him?"

"Yeah, I certainly do." Devron knocked on the complainant's door, and it was answered by a timid man in spectacles.

"Yes?" He pushed the spectacles up the bridge of his nose. His long brown cardigan hung on his slender frame, and his shoulders were hunched as if burdened by a million things.

"You're the one who called about the domestic?" Devron asked.

"Yes."

"It was simply an argument between a couple. The man who's there is a detective, and he was arguing with his lady friend. That's all. As *he* said, people argue all the time. So that's all you heard."

"Yes, well, it didn't sound like just an argument. I kept hearing thuds," the man murmured. "Like things were being moved or shoved."

Sheila pulled her door closed, and the officers turned around. "What you heard was a private argument between my boyfriend and me. It's none of *your* business, and I'll remind you to mind your own and stay out of others." She sneered at the man in the opposite apartment. "I've been here for five months, and you've been nothing but a busybody, always complaining about everyone else. Mind your own damn business." She sent a scathing look his way before quickly going down the stairs. She needed to get away from them, from him, and get some air. She had a lot to make up for, especially with Giancarlo, and hadn't meant to let the information out like that. She had been waiting for the test results before telling him, but she hadn't a choice. She didn't want the wrath of Jenny Stephanopoulos and her family on her. Her life had been good the last six months, with a great apartment, nice clothes and furnishings, and a man she loved dearly.

Loved!

Yes, she loved Giancarlo. Had realised it in February, that night Spiros was snoring his head off beside her. She couldn't have sex with him because he wasn't Giancarlo. *He* wasn't her lover, Giancarlo was. And he was all that mattered after three years of them seeing each other. He was all that mattered now. Him and the baby.

*****

Giancarlo paced his office. Ten steps across, ten steps back, repeated and repeated and repeated, back and forth for hours. He did no work, made no calls, just paced and played with a rubberband, stretching it, snapping it, winding it around his forefinger over and over. He had to come up with a way to break it to Jenny. She deserved to know, but how was he going to tell her? What was he going to say without dumping Sheila in it? She was pregnant. What the fuck! How the fuck did that happen? He'd figured his seed was too old and her eggs were past their use by date. But then who the fuck would have thought that would happen?

Holy fucking shit balls? I'm going to be a dad. But I'm too old. Fuck, I'm fifty-three, nearly fifty-four, and I'll be turning fifty-five the year the kid's born. I'll be sixty-five when the kid's ten, seventy-five when he's twenty and going off to college. Eighty-five when it's thirty and probably dead by the time it's forty. Fuck. How the hell am I going to be a father?

He thought about Sheila's experience with Luiz, and didn't know what sort of mother she'd make. *What if we're both fuck-ups? What if the kid turns out to be another whack job? What do we do then?*

Could he raise a kid? Could he be a father? A good father, and not some guy who was only there when he wanted to be... But a good father who was there all the time to wipe up tears and blow noses, clean scraped knees and kiss goodnight. Could he be *that* kind of father?

Fucked if I know, I've never been a father before.

There's a first time for everything, floated through his head.

Yeah, but it's a bit too damn late for this.

It's never too late...

He stopped.

Stopped pacing, stopped snapping the rubberband.

Fucking hell, I'm going to be a father.

*****

"Oh, my God, Tomas!" Jenny cried as her son and his husband came through the door.

"Mama!" He scooped her up into his arms and swung her around. "Oh, my God, it's so good to see you." He'd missed her terribly while back in Australia, and wished she had been there.

"Oh, my baby, you're back." Smothering him in kisses, she saw Roger over his shoulder. "Roger, how are you?"

"Good thanks, Mrs S." He helped her parents into the penthouse.

"Mum, Dad, back again." She didn't stop squeezing her son while talking to her parents.

"We had to come for the great-grandbabies." Sarah set her bag down. "We brought lots of presents."

"Mama, all right." Tomas laughed as she went back to kissing him, and set her down. "Enough."

"How do you feel?" She studied his face, turning it left and right. "Good, bad?"

"Fine." He smiled. "I'm not where I was before all of this, but my life has changed, and I feel good for what it is. We eat good food, go for runs, and workout. It's *all* good."

"But you don't feel like you did before you were poisoned?" The worry crept into Jenny's heart.

He shook his head. "No. I can't put my finger on it, but I just feel different."

"Obviously, the poison did something to you," Jenny fretted. "I don't want you to be sick." She brushed his hair out of his eyes. It was a little longer and in a different style, but still as black as night.

"I don't know if it did, but still, I feel good for what it is," he repeated.

Jenny's gaze moved to Roger. "And did you connect with family?" she asked hopefully.

He shook his head as sadness fell over him. "I tried, Mrs S. Called my parents, my siblings, none of them wanted to know."

"Oh." Jenny felt his sadness. "I'm so sorry. I was hoping they might have changed."

"So was I, considering you had all accepted me. But no, nothing's changed," Roger told her sadly.

Tomas decided to change the subject. "Where are the others?"

"Angie's taking a nap with Pedro, and Carlos and Viv are doing last minute things," Jenny told them.

"Everyone ready for babies to come?" Tomas asked, his hands lingering at his mother's waist.

Jenny laughed. "I don't think so."

Tomas's smile faded. "And Papa?"

Jenny took a breath. "He called after you did for my birthday."

"Is that all?" He stared deeply into her eyes to find the answers he was seeking.

"That's the last time I heard from him." She released him from her clutches. "How long are you staying?"

Tomas exchanged glances with Roger. "A month or two. We were hoping to get to Europe for a part of summer and then spend autumn traipsing across the countryside."

"Oh, that sounds wonderful." She sighed. "I wish I could go with you. I'd love to see Paris and London in the summertime."

Tomas brightened. "I wish you could too, Mama. I'd love to see Europe with you and the family, but you'll have grandbabies to look after."

Carlos came bursting through the door. "Hey! Brewster said you were back."

"Speaking of babies…" Tomas grinned. "Carlos!" He hugged his brother tightly. "Good to see you."

Carlos hung on, remembering his mother's words at Angie's birthday. *Love him, support him, make him happy. Spend quality time with him, make sure he knows you love him.* "Ah, good to see you too. I love you, bro."

A micro frown slid over Tomas's face. "I love you, too. What's wrong?"

"Nothing's wrong. Why would there be anything wrong?" Carlos pulled back. "I'm not allowed to tell my brother I love him, and have missed him, because he's been traipsing around our home country for months, and we haven't seen him, and I'm jealous? We've spent ninety-nine percent of our life together. I do miss you and Pedro when we're not together, you know?"

Tomas quizzically looked from Carlos to Roger and back, wondering where all this was coming from, and remembered when they'd all caught up with each other at the airport in Chicago. Until then, they hadn't really spent time apart, and he'd missed them terribly. Even though they were all off having their own adventures, it had been awful being apart. "Ah, yeah, I missed you, too. And yeah, it *sucks* travelling around Australia." The grin was back in place, and he realised how much he *had* missed everyone, especially his mama.

Viv trundled through the door. "Sorry I'm late, had to stop for a pee first."

Tomas turned to her. "Whoa, Viv, you're huge!"

"Geez, thanks." She rolled her eyes. "And you're all tanned and toned. Look at you two." She hugged her brothers-in-law. "Here I am a beached whale, and you two look better than ever."

"Oh, for heaven's sake you're not a beached whale." Jenny laughed. "Far from it."

"Maybe not, but I need to sit." Waddling over to the sitting room, she plopped down. "*Oh, God* that's good. My feet are killing me. Carlos, come massage." She waved a finger at him and pointed to her feet.

"Yes, Viv." Carlos dutifully went over and started massaging.

"Wow, since when did he think about others instead of himself?" Tomas quietly asked his mother.

"Since stepping up to be the man of the family," Jenny told him. "You boys want something to drink? It's warm out there. Mum, Dad?"

Pouring drinks and sitting around chatting, Angie made her way to the penthouse and joined them.

"Hey," she cried. "When did you two get here?"

"An hour ago." Tomas leapt up and hugged her, then rested a hand on her stomach. "Wow, any day now."

"Yeah, but I'm hoping Viv will go first so I can see what I'm in for," Angie replied.

"Oh, sweetie, I don't think you have any idea what this is going to be like," Viv said. "And neither do I."

"I know, that's why you can go first so I can see, and then decide whether I want to go through with it or send it back for a refund," Angie cheekily said.

"Oh, Angie, it's not as if you can say no at this stage," Jenny said a broad smile.

"Oh, I know," Angie replied. "It's just, regardless of all the books and videos, it's scary having a baby." She sat beside Viv on the couch.

"Try having one in the fifties," Jenny told her. "We didn't have the technology you have today."

"Try having one in the twenties," Sarah said. "*That* was horrendous. Women lost babies during childbirth, or lost their own lives. God knows why I had as many as I did."

"Because protection wasn't around then like it is now," Jenny told her.

"Fat lot of good *that* did us," Viv said to Angie.

"You got that right," Angie agreed.

"Then you shouldn't have had sex," Jenny said as Pedro walked through the door wearing shorts and a t-shirt.

"Who shouldn't have sex?" He yawned and ran his hand through his already ruffled hair.

"You and Angelina, and Carlos and Viv," Jenny went on. "We're talking about having babies and using protection."

"Well, that's something *these two* will never have to worry about, hey bro." Pedro pulled Tomas into a big bear hug. "Ah, I've missed you," he growled, lifting his brother.

"I missed you, too, little bro." Tomas hugged back fiercely.

"Get in here, Roger," Pedro said, and the three of them hugged it out.

Jenny smiled. It brought such joy to see her boys happy and loving each other.

Pedro finally let go. "How's the rest of the fam? Oh, hey, Grandma, Grandpa." He walked over and kissed them both. "Everyone else good back home?"

"Very good," Sarah replied. "All send their love and support, plus a whole bunch of baby presents for you both."

"Cool." Pedro eyed the bags by the door. "Any for us?"

"No, just the babies." Sarah smiled at her grandson.

"And when are you both due?" Tomas sat beside his mother on the couch.

"This week," Viv said. "Any day now, actually."

"Next week," Angie added. "But the doctor said the baby could just come when it wants."

"Do you have everything then?" Roger asked. "Learned how to put nappies on and how to bottle feed, and get it to sleep?"

Angie grinned. "We know how to change a diaper on a teddy bear."

"What?" Roger frowned and looked at Jenny who laughed.

"I used a teddy bear for them to practice on," Jenny said.

"Oh, right," Roger said. "Practice makes perfect."

"Not quite." Angie giggled, remembering back to the lessons. She caught Viv's eye and laughed harder.

"What's so funny?" Tomas's puzzled expression showed he had no idea.

"Let's just say that if the poor teddy is anything to go by, the babies are going to have a hard time getting their nappies changed," Jenny told him.

"Poor Teddy," Angie said. "I pinned the diaper right to him."

"And I kept pinning mine the wrong way, so it kept falling off," Viv added.

"Ah, geez," Tomas groaned. "I feel sorry for those babies."

Jenny laid a hand on Tomas's arm. "Tell us about your holiday?"

Tomas and Roger took it in turns telling them all about their adventures. "We celebrated Roger's birthday on the Great Barrier Reef, soaking up the rays on the beach, staying on the different islands. It was *glorious.*" He gazed adoringly at his husband. "He turned the big 3-0."

"Oh, happy birthday," Jenny said. "You should have told us when your birthday was; we could have gotten you a present."

"Believe me, Mrs S, the whole world trip is enough of a present," Roger assured her. "On top of the amazing luggage set, it was more than I could ever ask for."

"I'm glad you're both happy." Jenny smiled lovingly at her son. "It's worth it to see how happy you are."

June 1978

After a couple of days of catching up, Carlos bought up *The Greek Gods* movie. "Look, Harry's coming to New York if we agree to do this movie. Greta's got the set done, Marcus will probably want his share. Are you guys in on the movie?"

"Does it really mean that much to you?" Tomas asked. "That stuff's behind us now."

"Yeah, but just imagine the *three of us* in a movie. You've read it. You two would be together, and it's only Pedro and me doing the deed with multiples."

"Not that I care to do it anymore, either," Pedro said.

"The two of you are out of your contracts. I'm done, but Harry has me under a script contract which I don't mind. He owns the scripts, he'll make the money. But so will we as the stars since Greta and Marcus won't get what they're expecting. They'll only get a bit because they were your bosses. Most of the money goes to Harry and us."

"I make money from DJing," Pedro said. "I got another raise last week. Two grand a night. That's ten grand a week. I don't need money."

"Oh, well, lucky you, but this will be massive, I promise you," Carlos said. "We *need* to do it. Our movies are the biggest selling porn movies of all time. Imagine *all three of us* in one movie. *Together!* Greek Gods descending on Earth to bed all the women, ah, and men, we want. But, of course, Roger will capture Tomas's attention, while a bevvy of women will attract us," he said to Pedro. "We *need* to do it. Imagine the legacy."

"And will your legacy also be as a writer, or are you getting out of the business?" Roger asked.

"Harry has me for a hundred scripts, I've written eighty of them, and even he sees this will be the best he's ever made. After that," he shrugged, "who knows. The world is changing. *Times* are changing. We *need* to do this."

"You sound like Mama." Pedro stretched out on his deck chair. They were on the rooftop terrace they'd been utilising in the warm weather. "What's this *need?*"

"I don't know." Carlos shrugged again. "It's just deep in the pit of my stomach. My gut is telling me this will be huge and we'll regret it if we don't do it. So, what do you say? Greta has the stage ready to go 'cause she thinks it's a goer."

The boys traded glances, reluctant to partake in another movie. But somehow, they all knew they'd do it.

*****

Giancarlo finally grew the balls to call Jenny. He'd paced his office for three days straight back and forth, even sleeping on his couch because he didn't want to go home to Sheila, and didn't bother going home to his house. He knew he had to call, and knew it had to be now.

The phone rang, and Jenny ran to answer it breathlessly. "Hello."

"Ah, Jenny? Giancarlo."

"Oh…hello Giancarlo, good to hear from you. Is everything all right?"

"Ah…no…it isn't…can you come down to the precinct? I need to talk to you."

"Oh…why? The boys are all home, and the girls are close to giving birth. Is it important?"

"Extremely. I need to tell you something that will solve a massive issue. Please."

"Ah, oh, okay. I'll be there soon." With a frown on her face, she set the phone down. "That was strange."

"What is it, Mama?" Angie asked from the couch. Swollen feet up on the ottoman, she was rubbing her enormous belly, and glad to finally be out of school.

"Detective Gardo wants to see me. I have no idea why, but I'll have to go to the precinct to talk to him. Can you tell the boys when they come down?"

"Sure."

"Okay, I'll be back soon."

Fifteen minutes later, she was climbing the stairs to Gardo's office. "Giancarlo?" She stopped in the doorway. "You wanted to see me?"

He stopped stretching the rubberband in his fingers and stood still. The sight of her in her blue summer dress moved him, but didn't arouse him. "Ah, yes, please come in. Close the door."

Doing as she was told, she stood in front of him. "It must be important." He looked as though he hadn't showered in days, and his clothes were rumpled and stained. "How have you been? You look like you need a shower."

"Tough case," he said, staring into her big blue eyes. Blinking, and looking at her, he tried to get the balls to tell her.

"What is it? Does it have anything to do with my boys?" She felt tendrils of fear rising from the pit of her stomach.

"What? Ah, no, but it does have to do with your family."

"How?"

Letting out a huge sigh, he started the story. "During the process of an investigation, in a bar, I noticed a picture on the wall of a man with five bottles of ouzo in front of him. He looked familiar, and I asked who he was. The bartender said he was a Greek guy by the name of Spiros—"

"My Spiros?" she interrupted

He blinked slowly and continued. "He had downed five bottles and set a record for the bar. I realised that he *must* have been your Spiros because he looked like an older version of your son, Tomas."

She swallowed a painful lump. "Is this going somewhere?"

"I asked some more questions, and found out that a woman had bought two more bottles and walked him outside and hailed a cab. Now, you had told me that he left in February…and the timing was right." He watched her downcast expression. "So, out of curiosity, I rang the cab companies and had them trace that ride all the way back and was given an address. I went and spoke to that woman who lived there."

"I don't want to hear it," Jenny cried. "I don't want to hear what happened." She turned to leave.

Giancarlo grabbed her by the arms and turned her to face him. "You need to hear this, Jenny. It's vitally important for the sanctity of your marriage."

"How can hearing those sordid details save my marriage?" Tears flowed, lips quivered. "It's over, he slept with her."

"No, he didn't."

Inhaling a sobbing breath, Jenny stopped. "What?"

"He didn't sleep with her," Gardo said and sighed. "I asked the woman a lot of questions, and she told me that her husband had died six months earlier. That her friends kept pushing her to get out and meet men. Well…she went to the bar and saw your husband knocking back the alcohol and started up a conversation. He told her how bad things were and they drank together. At the end of the night, she took him back to her place and helped him into bed. He was blind drunk, and she took his clothes off, but he fell asleep, and she ended up sleeping on the couch. When he woke, she had made breakfast and was trying to tell him when he flipped out and ran out of her place. She swore on a stack of bibles nothing happened because she realised that she wasn't over her husband, and just couldn't be with another man. It was just a terrible case of misunderstanding."

Sputtering sobs came out of Jenny. "They didn't have sex?"

"No." He shook his head. "No, they didn't."

She collapsed into his arms, crying against his broad chest. "They didn't have sex?"

He held her, stroking her hair, kissing the top of her head. "No. No, they didn't." He held her while she sobbed. Sobbed for the months of pain and heartache, sobbed for the months of loneliness after the end of her marriage.

"Oh, my, God," she stuttered through her tears. "He didn't cheat on me. He didn't cheat on me." Finally raising her head, she looked him in the eyes. "He didn't cheat on me?"

"No." He gently wiped away her tears and knew this was probably the last time he'd see her. "Jenny, he didn't sleep with her. It was all a big fat misunderstanding."

Her fingers joined his in wiping away her tears. "Yes, yes, I can fix this. I can have my husband back. Thank you, thank you so much." She kissed his cheek, and crying tears of joy after four months of tears and pain, she left.

Giancarlo stared at the closed door. She was gone, and he was a wreck. A weak, insipid wreck. But he couldn't put Sheila in it. Not with her having his baby. Whatever she had done, for whatever reason she had done it for, he had to protect her and their child. His eyes closed. He knew this was the last time he'd see Jenny. Jenny with the blue eyes Stephanopoulos. Jenny who laughed and smiled and lit up his life. But he felt no regret. Only a morsel of sadness. Because whatever he had been looking for, and thought he'd found in Jenny, had actually been under his nose all along, except he hadn't seen it. Because he hadn't supported or encouraged it. The change. And now that he'd been used to it for six months, he realised what he'd wanted was always there, it just needed caring for. What he'd always wanted, and needed, was Sheila.

Jenny flew into the elevator then into the penthouse, slamming open the door and not bothering to shut it. She flew to the phone and dialled long distance, waiting for him to answer.

"Mama?" Carlos shut the door. "What's going on?" Everyone hovered around, and the girls came out of the kitchen eating bags of cookies.

Spiros was up going over the account books when the phone rang. "Stephanopoulos residence."

"Spiros, Jenny," she said excitedly. "You didn't cheat on me. It's all been a big fat misunderstanding. You didn't have sex with that woman, you didn't cheat on me. So, pack your bags and come home. The girls are due to give birth, and you need to be here. Come home, Spiros."

Murmurs and joyous looks went around the room.

"Wait, Jenny. What are you talking about? I know what happened."

"No, you don't for God's sake. You only think you do in your own bloody stubborn way again. Giancarlo saw a picture of you on a bar wall and found out about the woman. He tracked her down, and she admitted nothing happened. She was going to explain it to you over breakfast, but you ran off before she could. So, all this time you thought you'd done something, you hadn't. All this time we could have been together but weren't, because you didn't bother finding out what really happened. And the last time you did that you gave up on your sons all because of Stefano bloody Papadopoulos. Well, *no more,* Spiros. *No more* arguments. *Nothing happened,* so you can come home."

Spiros was disbelieving. "You mean…you mean nothing happened, and I've…I've been exiling myself for nothing?"

"Yes, you idiot." Jenny laughed almost hysterically. "You've done this to us all because you couldn't work it out. You need to come *here,* Spiros. This is our home now. You need to be here with me, with our boys, with the babies. They're due."

"I know." He sobbed uncontrollably, still not registering that he hadn't slept with anyone, and that he had ruined it all himself. Ruined his life, ruined his marriage, possibly ruined Jenny's love for him.

"Then pack up and come home," Jenny told him. "We're all here. Tomas and Roger are back. Mum and Dad are here."

"Tomas is back," Spiros said. Looking around he saw nothing. Nothing but a lonely, empty house. Empty of love, empty of happiness, empty of his family. They weren't there anymore. They had struck off to a new land for new adventures just as he had, and what his father had done to him gutted him. Made him feel unloved, unwanted. And now his sons had done the same things, and he'd stubbornly refused to go along with his wife and move to be with them. And that stubbornness had cost him his family, his wife, the love of his life. No more. No more life without Jenny. No more life without his family. Mykonos was dead to him. Mykonos was no more.

It was time *for him* to sacrifice for his wife, for his family, instead of her sacrificing for him.

"Spiros?"

Letting out a deep relieving sigh, he said, "I'll be there as soon as possible."

Jenny glanced at Viv as she stood clutching her stomach, a small puddle of fluid between her legs on the marble floor in front of the door. "You'd better hurry, Viv's water just broke." Her words freaked Carlos out, and everyone went into panic mode.

They rushed Viv to Mount Sinai hospital and into maternity, but after an examination found she was barely dilated.

"Ow, it hurts," she cried out, clenching her jaw. "Make it go way." She was in a white gown and had her hair tied up on top of her head. Leaning back, she looked deathly white against the white sheets.

"We can give you some gas, Mrs Stephanopoulos. But it looks like we could be here for a while." The doctor, a tall, good-looking, blue-eyed curly-haired brunet, pulled off his rubber gloves. His name tag read Hardcoe.

"Oh, God, yes please," Viv gasped. "Gimme now." She snatched the mask they offered and inhaled as deeply as she could before letting out her breath slowly.

"How long will we be here for?" Carlos was rubbing her shoulder.

"Well…some women are in labour for up to forty-eight hours," Hardcoe said.

"Oh, Jesus." Viv breathed in again. "I don't want to be in pain for that long."

"The pain's going to get worse," Hardcoe replied. "I'll be back later to check on you."

"Oh, God, tell me it's not going to take that long," Viv groaned. "I couldn't bear it."

Jenny patted her hand. "It very well could be, so since there's no point the rest of us being here, we'll go and give your apartment a freshen up for when you come home."

"No! Please don't go, Mama." Carlos's eyes were saucer wide and scared as hell.

Jenny almost laughed at him. "You don't need me right now. You just need to take it easy and call me when she's fully dilated, and then we'll come running."

"Ugh, don't leave me." Viv reached out, feeling so weak and pathetic. This was more pain than she'd ever felt in her life, and if she couldn't deal with *this*, how was she going to deal with the birth?

Jenny kissed her on her sweat-dampened forehead. "We'll be back later, Viv. You have a long, long way to go." They left them to it and walked out the door.

"*Oh, God no*," Viv wailed, panicking at the thought of going through this alone. "I don't want to do this, I don't want to do this. *Why did you do this to me, Carlos?*" Her voice had risen with every word.

"Hey, it wasn't just me participating all those times. It was you too." He dashed out the door to his mother.

"*Don't you leave me, you bastard,*" Viv screamed after him.

Carlos stopped short at the ferocity of her insult and saw everyone turn around in surprise. "I'll be back in a minute," he yelled in return and walked a few steps along the corridor to his mother. "Mama, what about Papa?"

"What about him?" Jenny asked.

"What happened? How did you find out, and what actually happened?"

Jenny smiled. "Don't *you* worry about that now. Your father and I will talk when he gets here, and we'll sort it out then."

"So…he didn't cheat on you?" Carlos continued uncertainly.

"No, he didn't." She smiled like she hadn't done in months and kissed her son. "Have fun with Viv, and don't forget to call."

They made it home and spent the next few hours cleaning their apartment. Vacuuming, dusting, changing the sheets, and having a summer clean, only then did Jenny go up to the penthouse to await her husband and clean up the bedroom. She hadn't slept in the bed for the last four months, having moved most of her things into the second bedroom and bathroom. But now it was time for a clean and air out. While moving her things back in, she straightened his clothes and accessories, and lined up the shoes, because he hadn't taken anything except his old clothes and case. Changing the bed, she tidied the room, and placed clean towels in the bathroom. She freshened up the spare room the same way, then put a load of washing on. An hour later, she was done and still waiting for her husband. The phone rang. "Spiros?"

"No, Mama, it's me. Papa there yet?" Carlos asked.

"Not yet. But then it could be a while. How's Viv?"

"In pain and two centimetres dilated."

"Oh, well, that's not much. It *is* going to be a long one."

"Yep." He sighed. "The doctor's looking in on her and she's sucking back that gas, so she's not too bad."

"You tell her to hang in there and we'll be in when she's close."

"Okay. Love you, Mama."

"Love you both, bye." She looked up as Tomas and Roger came in. "What have you two been up to?"

"Took a jog around the park," Tomas said, slightly damp from a shower after working up a sweat. "Got some exercise after being on the plane all those hours. "Papa called?"

"No. He's probably on a plane himself. But I just hung up from Carlos. It's still slow going."

"So, the baby's not coming yet?" Tomas asked, having no idea about babies and the timetables they kept.

"No. But it's just as well you arrived back today. You would have missed out on all the fun." Jenny grinned at her son.

The day turned to evening, and they had a filling dinner before sitting on the rooftop terrace to enjoy the last rays of light before night-time.

"I love the city in the summer," Jenny said, breathing in the scented air. "I went for a walk in the park the other day. It's so beautiful. We'll need to take the babies to feed the ducks."

"I just wish this baby would get out of me already," Angie groaned. "I'm huge!"

Jenny laughed a light, happy laugh. Everything was happening and coming together. "You're not huge. I was bigger than you when I had Carlos. *I* was huge."

"How big, Mama?" Pedro asked, reclining on an outdoor lounge.

"As big as a house," she teased, seeing how happy he was as he sat beside his wife.

"No wonder, with that big head to push out." Pedro grinned.

"Yep, he definitely had a big head," Jenny said.

They sat and talked and drank until the phone rang and Jenny flew down to answer it. "Yes?"

"She's three centimetres dilated and off her face on gas," Carlos said. "And I'm worn out, so they've set up a cot for me in her room. It's already midnight and I'm gonna *try* and get some sleep."

"Okay. Call anytime if you need anything."

"Is Papa there?"

"Not yet."

"Okay…bye."

She replaced the phone and turned for the stairs, but stopped short when she saw a man in her doorway.

"Jenny."

She sucked in air. "Spiros?"

"Jenny."

"Spiros!" She flew into his arms and he picked her up, kissing her as he hadn't in so long. Feeling the rough texture of his beard, she pulled away and stared at his face. Her fingers ran through the beard. "No, don't like it, get rid of it."

He laughed. "My Jenny." He let her slide to her feet, but kept his arms around her. "My Jenny."

"My Spiros." She smiled brighter than she ever had.

Lightly brushing her hair off her forehead, he drank in her features. Her eyes, her nose, her lips. They were turned up in a smile so bright it blinded him. He hadn't seen that smile in months, even though it felt like a lifetime. "My Jenny, oh, how I've missed you."

"Not that you had to. If you hadn't exiled yourself by leaving, we could have sorted this out when it happened," she told him.

"I know." He groaned. "I was so stupid as always. Only thinking about myself, thinking *I* knew better. And now I've missed out on four months with my family, *your* birthday, and *our* anniversary when I've never done that before."

"It's over now, all is forgiven. Nothing happened, and it's over. You're here, and the babies are coming, and we'll all be a happy family once more. Let's move on from here."

He nodded. "How is Viv?"

"Three centimetres dilated. It will be a while."

"Just like you with Carlos." He remembered before looking around. "Where is everyone?"

"Up on the terrace. We have a rooftop terrace you know. The view is spectacular. Come on, we'll put your things away and go upstairs." Locking the door, she spied his old suitcase and carry-on. "You bought that old thing back?"

He laughed. "It's actually filled with stuff I didn't want to leave behind. Pictures, photo albums, bits and pieces I didn't think you would want to do without. I have a change of clothes in the bag. Figured I'd just use everything you bought me that I left here."

"Finally," she told him. "They've been going to waste, and thank you for bringing the rest of the photos. I had the baby albums, but wanted the rest of them. As for my clothes, they don't matter. I had the few bits of jewellery I owned and my favourite clothes with me. Most of the old stuff will go to Goodwill."

"The rest of my stuff can be donated if we ever go home," Spiros said. "I don't have much anyway."

She smiled. "We will. *One* day. Did you put dust covers on everything?"

"Hadn't taken most of them off."

"Spiros! What have you been doing for the last four months?" Jenny stared, astounded at his words.

"Wallowing in my exile, my self-pity, my stupid stubbornness," he joked.

She kissed him. "Well, no more. Let's go up." After depositing his things in their bedroom, she took him up to the brightly lit terrace. "Tomas, this is what you'll look like when you're old and hairy." She led Spiros through the door, and everyone looked up.

"Papa!" Pedro and Tomas bolted over to their father for hugs.

"Papa, you're back."

"Yes, for good this time," he told them, holding his sons tightly.

"You're not leaving again?" Tomas asked, stroking his father's beard, having never seen him with one before. "Weird."

"No, I'm not. I was stupid and stubborn, but not anymore. This time your mother gets what *she* wants. Besides, Mykonos is far too lonely without my family. And how are you feeling? Good?" He looked from one son to another.

Tomas smiled a match to his father. "Feeling good, Papa."

"Hey, don't forget about me," Angie cried. "Someone help me up."

Roger laughed, and gave her a hand out of her seat, helping her over to the reunion.

"Papa." She joined in the hug, and he held her fiercely. "I missed you."

"I missed you, Angie. I'm so sorry I forgot your birthday. I didn't know when it was and was too proud to call to find out."

"It's okay, I understand. As long as you're back and not going anywhere," she replied, hugging him as tightly as she could.

"I'm not going anywhere," he told her.

"Good." She looked up at him. "You need a shave."

"And a haircut," Jenny added. "We'll have to get you one in the morning before going to the hospital."

"Was that Carlos on the phone?" Sarah asked as they gathered round.

"Yes. Viv's not even half done, so she won't pop until tomorrow. May as well get some rest, and we'll go in the morning. He'll call if anything happens. Go and get some sleep."

Making sure everyone left safely, she locked the door and took her husband upstairs, making him shower and shave while she prepared the bed. Finally, they were together and wrapped tightly in each other's arms, naked, making love as they hadn't done in months.

She orgasmed as she hadn't done in months, and when it was over, lay back while his moustache did the deed with her nipples. "Ah," she breathed as he sucked. She peaked, and another orgasm rolled over her before she fell asleep in her husband's arms, exactly where she needed to be.

*****

The next day, after a quick breakfast and a haircut for Spiros, they all gathered at the hospital at ten.

"Arggghhh," Viv growled. "Get it out of me."

"You don't have long to go," Doctor Hardcoe told her. "You're almost there. Have some more gas."

Viv sucked back and relaxed.

Carlos looked from her to the doctor before noticing his parents in the doorway. "Papa!" He ran outside and into his father's arms. "Papa."

"Carlos." Spiros hugged his son. "It is so good to see you. How's Viv?"

"Nearly there." Carlos pulled back and took hold of his father's face so he could stare into his eyes to see the truth. "Are you back for good or running away again?"

"Carlos," Jenny warned.

"No, Jenny, he has a right to ask. I'm staying," he told his eldest. "For good."

"So, I can step down as the head of the family and just enjoy being Carlos again?"

An amused look crossed Spiros's face. "Well, of course you can."

"Good, coz I need a break," Carlos said, exasperated. He let go of his father's face. "Viv has yelled at me all night, and I need some fresh air and a drink."

"You go and take five minutes, and we'll stay with Viv," Jenny said. "Take your brothers with you."

"Okay, Mama. See you soon." They left for a bite to eat and fresh air.

Jenny turned to Spiros. "The day you left he really stepped up to the plate. He made the decision to be the man of the family and stay and look after me, Pedro and Angie. He insisted Tomas and Roger go on their holiday, and told Viv they were staying. She agreed, and went back to L.A. for their stuff, and they've been here ever since. Our son really came through for me. We've taught him well, and he showed me that he remembered and took in everything that we'd taught him. I'm proud of him. You should be too. I think the last few months showed all of us he can really step up and be the man he needs to be to head his own family."

"I'm glad," Spiros said. "I'm glad that he listened and showed that he could be the man we trained him to be. *Unlike* me. I ran like a coward and left my family behind like an idiot." He shook his head in dismay, closing his eyes against the horrible memories.

"And we'll talk about that when we have a moment to ourselves. But right now, we have Viv to keep company," Jenny said. They entered the room with Angelina and Jenny instantly felt sympathy. "Poor Viv. I know what it's like. But once the baby's out, you'll forget all about it."

"Oh, God, I hope so," she moaned. "Hey, Spiros is back." Her eyes were hooded, and she sounded drunk.

He laughed lightly. "Viv. How are you coping?"

"Oh, not good. Every contraction's intense and I can't wait for it to be out of me."

"Not long now and then it will be out, and you'll have God knows how many stitches to contend with. Peeing will be painful, and you won't be able to have sex for oh," Jenny playfully glanced at Spiros, "at least six months."

"What! Well, after what he did to me he ain't gettin' any until he's my age!" Viv's head lolled back and forth as she waved her hand to make a point.

Jenny laughed as she hadn't in months. "Oh, my God, that's funny. You do know if you wait until he's forty-one, you'll be fifty-seven?"

"Ah fuck it!" Viv groaned through clenched teeth. "This is too much to go through again. Argh." Her body rolled forward as she screamed.

Jenny grabbed her, Spiros held her hand, and Angie backed away in fright.

"Get this thing out of me," she growled. "Get it out now."

"It will be soon." Jenny rubbed her back. "It will be soon. Suck some more gas."

Viv inhaled and kept inhaling as the doctor came in with an army of nurses.

"Let's have a look…" He lifted the sheet. "And you're crowning.

Okay, it's time to give birth."

Her legs went up in stirrups, and the nurses lifted the back of the bed and shoved pillows behind her.

"Viv." Carlos came barrelling into the room. "Is the baby coming?"

"No, you bloody dickhead," she screamed. *"It's taking a bloody holiday…of course it's fucking coming!"*

Carlos stopped at the bed in shock, eyebrows raised, mouth open.

"The baby's coming out," Hardcoe said, ignoring the outburst. They'd heard it all before anyway. "It's on its way…now."

"Now you can take over." Jenny relinquished her spot to her stunned son. "We'll just wait outside." They left them and waited with the rest of the family in the waiting room down the hall, hearing Viv growl all the way through and trying not to laugh with what she was screaming at Carlos.

"Ugh." Angie buried her head in Pedro's chest. "I don't want to do this. Listen to her. I don't want to go through that."

"Aw, babe, you're gonna have to," Pedro comforted her.

"Ugh, but I don't *want* to. I don't want to be in *that* pain," she wailed.

"You don't have a choice sweetie. It's a part of giving birth," Jenny told her, hearing Viv's screams get louder. Unable to help herself, she cringed at the memories.

"Come on, Viv, one more," Carlos encouraged her. "Push."

"I am pushing," she growled between clenched teeth. *"You* try pushing a damn bowling ball out of a tiny hole, you arrogant prick. I'd like to see you push it out of your ten-inch cock, you fucking porn star! Argh!"

Carlos blushed at Viv's language, but there was no time to be embarrassed considering the position Viv was currently physically in.

"Keep pushing," Hardcoe said, pulling the baby out. "And she's out."

"She's out?" Carlos looked at the blood-covered baby in his hands. "She?"

"You have a daughter," the doctor told him as the nurse wiped her down and then placed the baby on Viv's chest. "You have a daughter."

"A daughter?" Viv asked dazedly, looking at the baby wrapped in a towel in her arms. "I have a daughter?"

"*We* have a daughter," Carlos said, still clinging to her for support. "We have a baby, and she's beautiful." He gazed over Viv's shoulder to stare into the huge blue eyes of his daughter. His little girl. His beautiful little girl with the little tuft of golden-brown hair coming out of the top of her head. He imagined a light blue ribbon holding it together. A sob came from him. "I'm a father. I have a daughter."

Viv was crying, but looked into his eyes anyway. "*We* have a daughter."

Gazing into his wife's eyes, he nodded. "She's beautiful."

While the doctors finished with Viv, some of the nurses took the baby and weighed and measured her, and washed her over before handing her back to the proud parents.

"We'll take you to your room shortly. Everything's done. Congratulations."

"Thank you," Carlos said, glancing from the doctor to the baby. "We have a daughter." He couldn't stop saying it. Couldn't stop thinking it. *He* had a daughter. A baby with Vivian Villiers, super model, super wife, super mum. She had given him a beautiful baby girl.

"Oh, my God, she's beautiful," Viv said, gazing into the big blue eyes of her brand-new baby girl. "You're so beautiful, so, so beautiful." She touched her finger to the tiny nose, and a tiny hand reached up and hooked on. "Oh, my God, look at you, you're holding Mommy's hand. Carlos…" She looked at him, light shining from her eyes. "She's holding my finger."

A half-sob half-laugh escaped him. "She is, she is. Look at her. She's so beautiful."

"We're going to move you now," a nurse said as orderlies came in.

"Okay," Viv said. "Can I keep holding her?"

"Of course you can. She *is* yours."

As they were wheeled out into the hallway, Carlos saw his family making their way slowly toward them. "It's a girl," he called. "I have a daughter." He double fist pumped and turned to follow Viv.

"Oh, my God, a girl," Jenny cried, covering her mouth with both hands. "A girl." The tears flowed. "We have a girl."

Spiros took her into his arms. "We have a granddaughter."

Slowly, through sobs, she looked up at him. "Yes…a granddaughter."

He nodded, a smile covering his face. "A grandbaby." As she buried her head in his shoulder, he watched his sons hug and celebrate. His in-laws were now great-grandparents, his sons now uncles. It was a moment to celebrate, a moment to rejoice. A moment to come together and be a family and he'd nearly missed it. But no more. No more running out on anything. No more missing out on his family. He was here to stay.

Jenny pulled away. "We need to go see her, come on." Moving down the hall, they found Viv's room and all piled in. "May we?"

Carlos stepped back from Viv's side. "Of course. Come and see your granddaughter." With his arm out, he welcomed them in to his little family and slid his arm around his mother's shoulders. "You have a granddaughter, Mama."

Jenny stood by the bed and leaned in, staring in wonder down at the tiny little cherubic face that stared back. "Oh…" Her lip quivered. "She's beautiful. She looks just like you," she told Carlos. "Little tuft of brown hair, big blue eyes. She's beautiful." Tears flowed down her face. "Just beautiful."

"Ah!" the baby cried, giving a frown and a pout in return.

"I know, Mama, I know." Carlos kissed her temple.

"What's her name?" Jenny asked, gently touching the tiny hand resting on the blanket.

"Don't know yet. We haven't picked one out. Wanted to see what we got first," Carlos said. "But…regardless of what we *do* call her, another generation of Stephanopouloses has begun."

*****

While Carlos and Viv were taking a nap, Jenny brought Spiros up to date on what had happened.

"So…how did he find out?" Spiros asked as they sat in the park across from their home. "He saw my picture? I don't remember a picture."

"He was in the process of investigating a crime and was in the bar to ask questions. He saw your photo and asked who you were, and was simply told Spiros, a Greek guy. You had five bottles of ouzo in front of you, so you would have been blind drunk. They snapped a shot before you left."

"And do we know who this woman is?"

"Someone who'd lost her husband and her friends told her she needed to get back out there. You told her how bad things were, she felt lonely, and you both got drunk and ended up at her place. But she felt guilty over her husband."

He shook his head. "I don't remember much. I woke up, she had a breakfast tray. I realised I was naked in her bed and automatically assumed."

"Well, you know what they say about assume," Jenny said. "Those who assume end up making *an ass* out of themselves. And *you* certainly did that."

He grimaced. "I know. I was stupid and ruined our lives. Do we know her name?"

"No. Giancarlo didn't tell me."

"Could you ask him?"

She thought about it. "I don't think he'd tell me even if I asked. Something told me he was keeping her name out of it on purpose."

"Why?"

She shrugged. "Don't know. Maybe so I didn't do something."

"Would you?"

"Well, if nothing happened, and it didn't, probably not. But I still might have gone around for a little chat, like I did with Sheila."

"And what sort of chat would that have been?"

After a beat, Jenny replied. "A very forceful one."

*****

They visited Viv and Carlos in the hospital the next day, and Jenny was able to hold her grandbaby. "Oh, my God, look at you," she breathed. "You're *so* beautiful." The baby was fresh and clean and wrapped in a pink blanket that she'd made. She gently rubbed a finger over the baby's cheek, getting gurgles in return. "Oh, you're so perfect. So beautiful." A slight bounce to her movements kept the baby quiet as it gazed up at her with big blue eyes, the exact same shade as hers. "You have our eyes little one. Yes, your papa's eyes, and your grandma's eyes. Yes. They're *so* blue. And you are *so* beautiful, yes you are."

"How the hell can you do that when all she did was scream for me?" Viv asked, tired, but resting comfortably against several pillows in her private room.

"Probably because you're still stressed from the birth. Give it a couple of days to get relaxed and calm, and that will come through to the baby. They pick up on your vibes, feel it in your actions, hear it in your words." Jenny stared proudly down at her first grandchild.

Carlos sat beside Viv on the bed. "You're so good at this, Mama."

"Bet you're glad you moved here now," Jenny said.

"Oh, hell yes!" Viv sighed. "I know I'm going to need help for a while."

"You'll get used to it," Jenny told her. "You need to get a routine in place and stick to it. That's what helped me with you three, and that's what will help you now." She looked at her husband who was standing by her side, an arm around her. "Look at our beautiful granddaughter."

He beamed down on both of them. "I can't believe I'm a grandfather. I don't feel old enough to be a grandfather."

Laughing lightly, Jenny said, "I know what you mean. My babies are barely adults, and they're having babies. As far as I'm concerned, I'm still a mother."

"And now you're a grandmother," Carlos said. "But you'll always be *our* Mama."

"Absolutely," Pedro and Tomas agreed in unison.

Jenny smiled at her boys and slowly walked to them at the end of the bed. "Say hello to your uncles, baby girl. This is Uncle Pedro, and this is Uncle Tomas."

"Hello, little one." Tomas gently touched a finger to the baby's cheek. "Oh, you're so tiny. Look at you."

"Wanna hold?" Jenny asked.

Tomas stepped back in alarm. "What! No."

"Come on, you won't break her, just keep your arms tight. Here."

She placed the baby into his arms.

"Mama, no! I can't do this." But he grabbed on anyway and glared down at his niece.

"Don't be silly, of course you can. You have to," she said. "Just be gentle and relax. She'll sense your reluctance."

Holding on tightly, he breathed as the baby cried.

"It's okay, sweetie," Jenny crooned. "Uncle Tomas won't hurt you. It's okay." The soothing tones of her voice calmed the baby, and Jenny showed Tomas how to move.

He bounced lightly on the spot, staring down at the baby in his arms, a small smile crossing his lips. "Hey, baby," he said softly. "Hey."

The baby gurgled and blew bubbles.

"There you go," Jenny all but whispered, gazing at her son with an overwhelming abundance of happiness. "You got it."

He glanced at her and radiated his own happiness. "My niece."

"Your niece. Oh, do we have a name yet?" Jenny looked over her shoulder to ask.

"Not yet," Carlos said. "We're not sure whether to give her a Greek name or an American one. She'll get Stephanopoulos obviously, but we want to pick the right name to go with it."

Jenny turned back to her granddaughter. "You have time. You'll know which one suits her soon. Don't rush it."

Roger slid his arm around Tomas, who looked up at him.

"And you're Uncle Roger. Say hello to your niece. Baby, this is your Uncle Roger," Tomas told the tiny bundle in his arms.

"Ooh, ooh," the baby gurgled, staring at the two of them.

Roger gurgled happily right back. "Ooh, ooh."

"Ah," the baby replied, and everyone laughed.

"Well, you have baby talk down," Jenny said to him.

Angie groaned softly and rubbed her stomach.

"You okay, babe?" Pedro hugged her close as they stood around Tomas.

A weary sigh came from her. "Baby's moving a lot and causing some pain."

"Maybe we should get you looked at by the doctor. The baby could be coming," Jenny said. "Has your water broken?"

"Mmm, I don't know." She shrugged. "What's it feel like?"

"Like your bladder has burst and you're having a weird pee from the wrong place," Viv said.

"Oh, I had that this morning," Angie said. "I thought that was normal."

"Oh, no, it's not," Jenny said. "Come on, you're in labour, and you're going to see the doctor." Grabbing her arm, she led her out of the room with Pedro following.

"Wait! What about the baby?" Tomas cried out.

"It's okay, stay calm," Roger soothed his panic-stricken husband. "Take a breath, you won't drop her."

Tomas relaxed and looked back at his niece who was drifting off to sleep.

Spiros moved over to them and kissed Tomas on the forehead. "You're doing fine. Don't worry." He proudly looked at his son and wrapped his arms around both him and his granddaughter.

*****

"You're definitely dilated." Hardcoe finished examining Angie. "We need to admit you because I doubt this one will take long. When did your water break?"

"About eight this morning," Angie told him, feeling sick to her stomach with fear about giving birth.

He glanced at the clock and made some notes on his clipboard. "It's ten now, so only two hours ago. But you're already eight centimetres dilated, so not long."

"I had Pedro four hours after my water broke," Jenny told everyone in the room. "He slipped out like an eel."

"Ew, Mama," he protested with a screwed up face. "Can you *stop telling everyone* that?"

"What! Well, look at you, all long and lean. No wonder you slipped out." She hid her smile behind a serious expression, laughing on the inside at his expression.

"This birth might be exactly the same," Hardcoe said. "We'll admit you, get you ready, and keep a close eye on you."

"Are you able to put her in a room near Viv?" Jenny asked.

"We'll try," a nurse said and gave Angie a gown to put on.

"What am I supposed to do with this?" Angie held it up with two fingers and curled her lip in disdain.

"Put it on," Jenny said. "If Viv can wear one, you can. Come on, I'll help you change."

A half hour later, they were in the birthing unit waiting for the baby when almost everyone walked in.

"And baby number two is on its way," Spiros said. Pedro had told everyone Angie was in labour.

"And getting closer," Jenny said as she finished braiding Angie's hair to keep it out of the way.

"How long?" Tomas asked, sitting on the end of the bed.

"An hour or two, if that, the doctor thinks," Angie said, rubbing her belly. "Thankfully, there's not much pain, just a lot of ache."

"Like a bad menstrual cycle," Jenny explained to ignorant facial expressions.

"Ew, Mama no. Leaving now." Tomas covered his ears and walked out the door with Roger following, and laughing at the histrionics.

"Yeah, I'd love to leave with him, but I don't want to leave Angie, so no more women talk, Mama," Pedro said.

"If you want to go, go," Jenny said. "We can stay awhile."

"You sure?"

"I'm sure, go."

"Thanks, Mama. Back soon, babe." He kissed Angie and ran after Tomas, grabbing him by the shoulders and leaping up.

"Hope he doesn't do that when the baby comes," Angie said, groaning at a cramp.

"He won't. He'll man up like Carlos," Jenny told her. "We raised our sons to be men, Angie. He'll prove that once he's a father. And except for work, he won't need to run off."

The boys met up in the waiting room.

"How's Viv?" Pedro asked Carlos.

"Resting," Carlos replied.

"Not staying with her?" Pedro crossed his arms and stood over his brother.

"Not at the moment. I wanted to talk to you lot about the movie."

Tomas groaned. "Now?"

"With Viv having given birth, and Angie about to pop, they'll be in the hospital for a while, so what better time to get it done. Three days tops. One day each to film. Coz once the girls come home, they *will not* want us to leave."

Pedro sighed and scratched his head. "Okay. If you can set it up, then I'll get it done. But give me a day or two once the baby's here so I can rest too."

"Okay, cool. Tomas? Roger?"

Tomas didn't care to do another movie, but at least he could be with Roger in it, no one else. And while the concept had been corny, his brother's script was good. He looked to Roger for confirmation.

"Do we need to sign a contract?" Roger asked.

"Nope. I sign on behalf of all of us, and we get the money," Carlos said.

"How'd you manage that?" Pedro asked.

"Harry owns my script, so he gets rights to the movie. I get rights to be stated as writer, co-producer, co-director. I sign on behalf of my family. I had a lawyer look over it, he said it was a good deal for us. Greta gets a cut for the use of the studio, nothing more."

"Will they all be there? We don't work for Marcus anymore," Tomas said.

"He'll probably be there, and Greta will probably want to watch Pedro since it's her studio."

"I just…I just want to feel comfortable," Tomas said. "I don't know these people."

"But you know me, and I'll be there the whole time," Roger said, rubbing his back in comfort.

Tomas smiled up at him. "Thank God for that."

"So, we'll get it done over the next few days?" Carlos crossed all of his fingers.

"Yeah, okay," Pedro agreed.

Tomas sighed, and Roger answered for both of them. "Agreed."

"Great. I'll call Harry."

A half hour later it was all set, and Harry was on a plane for New York.

An hour after that, Angie was giving birth. "Ooohhh," she breathed through clenched teeth and puffed out cheeks. "Ooohhh."

"Good, good, the baby's crowning," Hardcoe said.

Angie dug her nails into Pedro's and Jenny's hands. Both were in the birthing suite, one on either side. She had wanted Jenny in there as she had no mother of her own and wanted the extra support.

"Ouch, Angie!" Pedro forced her nails out of his skin. "Easy."

"Sorry, but you try pushing a kid out. You'd need something to hang onto. I am *never* doing this again for as long as I live."

Jenny watched her daughter's face, clenched in fear, and a need to deliver the human being inside of her. The pang hit her heart. The pang of remembrance. The pang of pain. Sharp and unending. So sharp it took her breath away until she remembered to breathe normally, but the pain didn't go. It just grew bigger and more painful. The more she looked at Angie's face. Her face. Her daughter's face. Tears came. They sprang to her eyes like tiny daggers, and she unsuccessfully tried to blink them away.

"It's coming," the doctor yelled. "Get ready to push."

Jenny pushed. Pushed with all her might as she gave birth to her baby. Her little baby girl with the black hair and blue eyes.

"Oooh," Angie screamed and the baby slipped out into the waiting arms of the doctor.

"It's a girl. You have a baby daughter." He held up a squirming, screaming baby with black hair and blue eyes.

Jenny's face crumpled, and she burst into tears as the little baby in the doctor's arms lay silent. No screams, no squirming, no nothing. "No," she cried. "No." Her cry turned to a scream as she bolted out the door and into the hallway.

"Jenny?" Spiros was holding a huge white rabbit he'd just bought. "Jenny?"

"No," she screamed and ran to him, past him, snatching the rabbit from his hands as she kept on going.

"Mama?" Angie cried out in the suite. "Mama? Where's Mama? I need Mama." She gripped Pedro's hand as he stared at the door in shock. "Mama," she screamed. "Mama."

"Papa, what the hell?" Carlos and Tomas moved after her.

"No! Give her some time," Spiros told them. "Just give her some time."

"But—" came two questioning and scared expressions.

"No," he said sternly. "She needs some space to take a moment. Leave her."

While the doctor cleaned and finished with Angie, the nurses saw to the baby before laying her in Angie's arms. A few minutes later she was wheeled out and to a room near Viv's.

"I'll be back soon, babe," Pedro said. "I need to find out what the hell just happened."

Angie was crying as hard as the baby. "I need Mama. I can't do this, Pedro, I can't do this without her. Why's the baby crying? Stop her crying?" A nurse took the baby, and Angie cried harder. "I want my Mama."

But Jenny was crying just as hard as her daughter-in-law, clutching that rabbit to her chest as hard as she could. Standing at the window of the waiting room, thanking God there was no one else around. "Oh, my baby," she sobbed. "My baby." The tears flowed, and her throat constricted, making it hard to breathe between the choking sobs. "My baby, my baby."

"We have to go find Mama," Carlos was saying when Pedro came up to them."

"*What is going on?*" he asked. "She bolted out of there and left Angie in tears. *What is wrong?*"

Spiros wasn't sure what to tell them, but he was sure his downcast expression said a lot. "Was it a girl?"

"What!" Pedro was confused.

"Did Angie have a girl?" Spiros asked tiredly.

"Yes," Pedro said. "We had a girl."

Spiros nodded, and a weary sigh came from him. He glanced at his in-laws and saw the same expression reflected on their face. They nodded. "Go and find your mother," he told the boys. "It's best coming from her."

"What is?" Carlos asked with a shake of his head.

"The truth," Spiros said. "Go and find your mother."

Trading glances, and with trepidation, they headed off in search of their mother and found her in the waiting room at the end of the hallway.

"Mama?" Carlos stepped up behind her and put his hands on her heaving shoulders. "Mama, what is it? What's wrong?"

She sobbed, her chin resting on the rabbit's head that was scrunched in her hand.

"Mama," Pedro said softly. "Angie's crying out for you." But that just made her cry harder.

Carlos gave him a dirty look for making her cry more, but Pedro shrugged in return. He didn't know what to do.

"Mama," Carlos tried again. "Papa told us to come find you. That it was best coming from you."

That made her head turn. She gazed at him through swollen eyes and breathed in stuttering gasps. "It was best coming from me?"

"Yes." Carlos nodded. "Does it have to do with Angie and the baby? Did something happen?"

"No, it didn't," Pedro told him. "It was fairly easy."

Carlos glanced at him. "Then what is it?"

Jenny hiccupped, and finally turned around to face her sons, still squeezing the life out of the rabbit that would need CPR to be resuscitated if she squeezed it any harder. "Angie...having a baby..." gasp, "brought back..." gasp, "memories..."

"Of what?" Carlos asked, gently brushing her hair from her forehead.

Gasp. "Giving birth."

"Well...you had three of us," Tomas said softly, seeing his mother's eyes lay upon his. His heart was aching so badly for her. "Mama?"

Her face crumpled. "After...I had Pedro...I was pregnant..." She sobbed.

The boys looked at each other in confusion.

"Mama?" Carlos murmured, his arm sliding around her shoulders.

"I was pregnant after Pedro," stuttering sobs, "the baby would have been born two years after you," sob, "two years…like all of you." She buried her head into the rabbit.

Carlos looked at his brothers. "Well," he started keeping his voice soft and low, unsure of where to go because he wasn't connecting the dots. "There *are* only three of us…"

Jenny looked up, gulping back air, her face flushed and hot. "It was a baby girl," gasp, "she would have been two years younger than you," she said to Pedro. "Angie's age. And I always imagined what she would have looked like," gasp, "long black hair and blue eyes. She would have looked like Angie. She would have looked like Angie," she sobbed.

"Oh, Mama," Carlos breathed. "We had a sister, but…" The light finally dawned and he slipped into shock. "Mama," he whispered. "Alena?"

She looked into his big blue wide eyes, and her head moved up and down.

"Alena was our sister," he went on. "The name you put on the Christmas bauble and stocking. Papa said it was for a relative no longer with us."

"It's true," Pedro said, digesting the information. "She's no longer with us."

Jenny sucked in air and wiped her face. "That's the name I gave her. I was six months pregnant. She didn't live. No one knows why. She didn't make it…she had big blue eyes and a tuft of black hair."

"Like the baby," Pedro murmured, finally understanding her reaction. "Oh, Mama. That would have brought back all those memories for you."

"It did," she gasped. "Bad memories. Painful memories."

"Why didn't anyone say anything?" Carlos asked. "No one mentioned it all these years. It was kept quiet. No wonder you have such a strong bond with Angie and treat her like a daughter. But why in God's name did no one tell us?"

"Because you were too young," Spiros said from behind them. They turned to look at him. "Because it was the fifties and no one ever talked about losing babies."

"You mean *you* never talked about it," Jenny said, angry at her husband. "All *I* wanted to do *was* talk about her. I cried, I sobbed, I fell apart, and all I wanted to do was have you there with me, *crying* with me. But you weren't."

"Jenny," Spiros said softly, aching for his wife. "We both chose to not tell the boys because they were too young. And that going and spending time with your relatives would be beneficial for all of you, so that when you came home, you could get back to looking after them. They were young. They needed you."

"I know," she said. "But I needed *you,* and every time I wanted you, you weren't there." The tears came again.

His heart broke all over again. "Jenny, that's not true. I *was* there. I held you."

"Oh, you were there physically, but not emotionally. There was not one tear from you, Spiros."

"That's not true," he stated.

"Well, *I* certainly didn't see any. *I* never saw you cry. You never talked to me about how *you* were feeling, if you were sad or not."

He sighed. "Greek men don't talk about those things. I went through it with my parents. They shut it all out and said nothing."

"Then you should have known better," she cried. "You should have known to not do what they did. Stop using your Greek heritage as an excuse for not doing things, Spiros." She felt her blood start boiling. "I'm *sick* of that bullshit. I'm *so over it.* I *don't* want to hear one more word about your Greek heritage. I've had enough. I needed my husband, and he wasn't there for me emotionally."

"I'm sorry," was all he said.

"So am I," she replied and walked past him.

After a few moments of traded glances and shrugs, the boys followed.

He let them, knowing that this had always brewed under the surface. Knowing that Angie had taken Alena's place in the family, but he hadn't known what to expect with the birth. She'd been all right with Viv's, so he didn't think Angie's would be bad. Breathing in, he removed his wallet from his back pocket and pulled out a well-worn picture of Jenny at six months pregnant with the boys gathered around her. Another photo had her holding the baby. He had taken a camera to the hospital and taken photos as they allowed her to hold her dead child. Jenny's face was red from crying, holding a baby she would never get to hold again. A few days later they had their baby girl cremated, and her ashes were kept in a beautiful urn on Jenny's bedside cupboard. Even now, when she'd moved to New York with the boys, she'd taken it with her. Alena was with them…always.

Putting his wallet back in his pocket, he went in search of his wife, finding her standing in front of the nursery window looking at her grandbabies, her fingers on the glass as she watched. He stood behind her. "I never forgot our daughter." He held the two photos in front of her.

She glanced at them and looked up in surprise. "You still have these?" She took them from him. "You still…"

"Of course. They've been in my wallet since I took them, along with pictures of the boys."

She stared at the photo of her holding Alena and tears started again.

"I never cried in front of you Jenny because I wanted to be your rock. If I fell apart as well, the boys wouldn't have someone to look after them. I wanted to be the shoulder you cried on, the rock you relied on. But in private, I cried like a baby. I just didn't want you or the boys to see it."

"Why not?" she asked. "I needed to know you were upset too. That *she* mattered to you."

"She did." He frowned in pain. "She did, so much. But I had the business to run and food to put on the table to provide for you and the boys. They needed to know Papa was there for them, so I cried at night when they were in bed. When you went away, I'd tuck them in and stand there watching them sleep. My boys needed me to be strong. So I cried when no one was watching."

Her face screwed up, and her arms went around him. "Oh, Spiros."

Down the hallway, Carlos leaned against the wall. All three had just come around the corner and stopped to observe their parents.

"So…everything is okay again?" Pedro stood behind Carlos, one hand on the wall, one on his hip.

"Looks like it," Carlos said, watching them closely. "God, I can't believe we had a sister."

"Yeah," Tomas murmured. "Poor Mama. Imagine losing a baby, and then you end up with a daughter-in-law that would be just like her."

"That must be hard," Pedro agreed. "But she seems to love Angie like a daughter. So, obviously, there's no problem."

"They do have a special bond," Carlos added. "Angie calls her Mama and needs her like a mother."

"I thought it was awesome of Mama to take her on like she did. I thought it was Mama just wanting a daughter after having the three of us," Pedro said.

"She did." Tomas looked at him. "Angie was *and is* the substitute daughter she didn't get."

"Do you think things will get back to normal?" Pedro asked his brothers, searching his parents' body language for any sign of further problems.

Carlos watched his parents hugging. "I think from now on things will be different. But better, more open, more honest."

Jenny pulled out of her husband's arms and looked down at her two granddaughters lying side by side in their cribs. Viv and Carlos's daughter was quiet and sleeping, while Pedro and Angie's daughter was screaming her head off. She laughed. "Look at them. So different."

"They are," Spiros agreed. "Just like Carlos and Pedro. I can see why you wanted to be here. Why you couldn't be in Mykonos away from them. The family's definitely here now."

She stood staring at them, nodding in agreement, holding the photos close to her, watching her baby girls lie side by side, so different in looks, and clearly so different in personality. "I wonder what names they'll come up with."

"Haven't even thought about it," Pedro said as the boys came up behind them. He leaned between his parents, an arm around each one. Tomas stood to Jenny's right, and Carlos stood to Spiros's left.

"You've both had nine months to come up with names," Jenny said.

"We know, but we also had other things to do," Pedro replied. "Like work and school."

"Well, now that you can see them, and watch them, a name should come." She held the photos out to show the boys. "Your sister," she said sadly.

They crowded around and gazed at the photos. Their tiny baby sister asleep forever in their mother's arms.

"Oh, Mama," came in sad murmurs. "She looks like the baby."

"And now I need to go and explain myself. Is Angie asleep?" she asked Pedro.

"Probably, but she was crying for you, so maybe not," he said.

Jenny nodded. "I'll go and see her." Leaving them to watch over the babies she made her way to Angie's room, finding her crying, sniffing, and lying on her side clutching her pillow. "I need to apologise."

"Mama?" Angie perked up. "Mama?"

Jenny moved to the bed and took her eagerly outstretched hand. "I'm sorry for running out on you when you needed me." Wiping her tears, she went on. "It brought back some memories for me."

"Good memories?" Angie asked hopefully, glad her mama was back.

"No, sweetie." Jenny shook her head and pulled the chair over. "And I need to explain why." Taking a deep breath, she said, "I became pregnant after Pedro. And I had to give birth early. To a little girl. She wasn't…alive…"

"Oh, Mama…she had passed?" Angie said softly.

Jenny nodded, trying not to cry. "I had a baby girl, and I lost her." She showed Angie the picture of her pregnant, the boys around her. She was wearing a yellow and white sundress. The picture was old and crinkled.

"I'm so sorry, Mama. I can't imagine losing a baby. What happened?" Angie asked, tears in her eyes.

"No one knows," Jenny replied. "The doctors couldn't tell me why I'd lost her. But it hurt like hell to, and I've never fully gotten over it. She would have been your age, and I always thought she would have looked like Pedro. Jet-black hair, big blue eyes, about your height." She squeezed her hand and showed her the other photo. "My baby. Alena."

Angie took the photo and felt like weeping uncontrollably. "Oh, she's beautiful."

"Yes…she was."

"What happened? Is she buried in Australia?"

"No. We cremated her, and I have her in a small urn."

"The beautiful blue and pink container on your bedside table?"

Jenny smiled softly. "Yes."

"Oh, I love that, I didn't know it was an urn." Angie handed back the photos. "I don't know what to call her."

"Alena," Jenny said softly.

"What?" Angie's eyes flew to Jenny's. "No, I meant our baby."

"Alena." Jenny looked from the photo to Angie.

Angie blinked. "You want us to call her Alena?"

"If you want. I'm a big believer in reincarnation, and your baby looks just like her." Glancing down at the photo, a sad smile touched her lips. "I think she's back for another go. But it's up to you and Pedro. Don't feel pressured to call her that. It's entirely up to you. I just…after seeing her and seeing this photo again…it somehow seems right."

"And what about Carlos and Viv's baby?"

"Haven't come up with a name for her yet. But the two of them are going to be so different. With you and Pedro having black hair, and Carlos and Viv golden-brown, these girls are going to look completely different, and their names will be too. The only thing they'll have in common is their surname."

Angie smiled, tired after a long day, and rested her head on the pillow. "I'll talk to Pedro about names. See what he says."

"As I said." Jenny pulled the covers over her tired daughter. "It's entirely up to you."

*****

"Harry."

"Carlos."

"Let's get going, shall we! The set looks amazing."

"You can thank me for that?" Greta came over to them as they stood in her studio overlooking *The Greek Gods* set.

"Yes," Carlos replied. "Thanks, Greta, it looks amazing."

"I know. Who's recording first?" she asked.

"I will. The girls have had their babies and are spending a few days in hospital. It's the perfect time to get it done." He glanced over the fluffy clouds and ancient Greek street scenes. "I'll go and get ready, and we'll start filming." Changing into his chiton and golden crown, he walked on set, had a look around, and talked to the engineer about coming down through the clouds to the streets below. After a run-through with his female co-stars, everyone moved into place, and Harry called action.

Surrounded by clouds, Carlos lay back on his chaise longue eating grapes and blowing his own trumpet. He peered down through the clouds to the city below and spied a bevvy of beautiful woman. Floating down, he came to land in front of them. "I am Carlos, God of Greece, God of love." The girls tittered among themselves as he continued. "Who here wishes to serve me?"

"Oh, me, me," came several cries as the girls rushed forward.

Carlos clicked his fingers and an appropriately placed bed piled with cushions suddenly appeared. He led them to it, and they lay upon it eating grapes, drinking wine, and doing the deed. He bedded all of them, and after an hour Harry called cut after Carlos had ascended into the heavens on his cloud.

"How was that?" Carlos asked as he was lowered to the ground.

"Perfect," Harry told him. "Just need to get extra shots of the girls, and that's it. But your part is done."

"Cool." Carlos stepped out of the strap that had lifted him up. "I'll get Tomas in tomorrow and Pedro the day after."

*****

The next day, he came with Tomas and Roger, and they did a run-through. It wasn't going to be much. Tomas would descend and choose a man of his liking; that man would be Roger.

After changing, they took their places while Carlos stood next to Harry, who yelled action. Staring down from his spot in the clouds, Tomas descended to the streets of Greece where a group of men and women gathered. He walked among them to curious glances, the girls giggling and hiding their faces, the boys flexing their muscles and giving him the eye. Coming upon an attractive man lifting iron bars in a metal workshop he said, "I am Tomas, God of Greece, God of muscles. Do you wish to serve me?"

Roger eyed him up and down, nodded, and moved over to Tomas. They both ascended to the clouds where they made love in the heavens, revelling in the peace and quiet away from the rest of the humans. Once they were done, Tomas sent Roger floating down to the ground and flew away home.

"And cut," Harry bellowed. "Well…" He leant back in his chair and puffed his cigar. "I've seen your brother's movies, but I've never actually *seen* two guys having sex."

Carlos stood staring in disdain. "I can't believe I just watched my brother and brother-in-law have sex. Fuck, they're bigger than me."

"Oh, they certainly are," Harry agreed. "Makes me wish I'd found *them* first."

*****

With the girls still resting in hospital, Pedro came in for his turn in the film. He lay in the clouds strumming his harp and descended into the city. "I am Pedro, God of Greece, God of music. Who here wishes to serve me?"

He took a group of beautiful girls to a party where he played his tunes and danced the night away on the dance floor, taking any girl he wanted, any time he wanted. And when it was all over he ascended into the clouds.

After three days, the movie was done.

"And that's a wrap," Carlos called, having been there all day. "Pedro, get changed; we're done."

"And I'm back at the hospital," Pedro told him before he headed off to change.

"Wait for me, and we'll go together," Carlos yelled out. "Harry, you editing? I want to see it before we go with it."

"Of course," Harry said from his chair. "This movie needs to be perfect before it's released because it's going to be the biggest release of summer. *The year.*"

"It's coming out that quick? We're already June," Carlos said.

"If I work the next couple of weeks on it, it will be out in August, in plenty of time for the porn awards."

"Good." Carlos nodded, seeing Pedro dressed and walking toward them. "I want it to be the biggest bonkbuster that ever hits the porn awards *and* the industry."

"Oh, it will be, my boy," Harry said. "I'll make sure of it."

"Great, we're gonna go, job well done all," he called out, and Pedro waved goodbye, leaving Harry, Marcus and Greta to talk.

"I *cannot believe* I saw all three of them," Greta said as she and Marcus crowded around Harry's chair. "I thought Pedro was good, but fuck me, Carlos and Tomas."

"Tomas and Roger have been our biggest couple," Marcus said. "Movie-wise *and* size-wise. This movie's going to be *huge.*"

"It certainly is," Greta agreed. "Considering the size of all of them. Even Roger is massive."

"They all are," Harry said, giving himself a silent pat on the back for leading Greta and Marcus on. "Not only are they big, but the movie's going to be huge. It will blow everyone's mind and smash every porn award there is." Greta and Marcus looked at him in surprise and excitement. "Oh, yes," he told them. "This is a *multi*million-dollar movie."

*****

A few days later, they brought the babies home from the hospital and laid them in their cribs.

Viv and Carlos's daughter slept the whole time, wrapped in her pink and blue blanket, whereas Angie and Pedro's cried non-stop.

"Why is she crying?" Angie covered her ears. "I can't stand it."

"Well, this is what you get for having sex at eighteen. A baby," Jenny said, patting the baby on the back. "She senses your frustration. Just calm down, and it will get better." The baby's crying drifted into gurgles. "There, there, sweetie, it's okay. This is your home now.

Everything looks different, everything looks weird, and you have to get used to it. But we're all here for you. Yes, we are."

For Jenny, two granddaughters offered a second chance at raising the daughter she'd lost, and as much as she wanted to call the younger baby Alena, she couldn't because they hadn't chosen a name yet. But she had a bonded spirit with that baby and knew it was her Alena come back to them. Walking around the nursery, she pointed out all the things to the baby as she lay on her shoulder. "And this is your cot, filled with lots of teddies, and this is the chair Mama will sit in to feed you. Yes. This is your room, sweetie. This is where you'll sleep and grow up."

Pedro stood beside Angie in the doorway, astounded that his mother had stopped the baby's cries.

Angie looked up at him. "I don't know if I can do this," she whispered.

He gazed down at her. "Mama has taught you everything you need to know. She'll be here when we need her. But we have to get used to being parents." He watched his baby sleep in his mother's arms.

Jenny saw them and smiled. "Thought of a name yet? Because calling her *baby* sounds weird." She shifted and laid the baby in the cot. The baby gurgled and cried out, but Jenny patted her tummy. "Shhh, Bubba, time to sleep. Shhh." The baby settled and drifted off.

"Not yet. Angie told me what you said about calling her Alena," Pedro said, watching his mother's face for a sign.

Jenny straightened. "That's entirely up to you. Don't feel pressured, don't feel you have to, but we can't keep calling her *baby,* now can we."

He grinned. "Suppose not."

Angie sighed. "I wish she'd do that for me." She gazed at the tiny human being sleeping in the crib. "I couldn't get anything right in the hospital."

"You just need to calm down." Jenny led them to their living room where Spiros sat. "You need to take a deep breath and breathe. Everything's going to be okay." She sat down on a couch. "Just keep breathing and stay calm. The baby will be calm too."

"Was Pedro? Or Tomas or Carlos?" Angie asked as she sat next to her.

Spiros laughed. "Oh, hell, no! Well, Tomas was, but definitely not

Carlos. He was a rambunctious little kid that didn't stop moving. Always on the go, wanting to explore everything, wanting to put everything in his mouth. You name it, he did it."

"Yes, Carlos was definitely a handful, where Tomas was so quiet you'd forget he was there," Jenny added.

"Carlos always had to be the centre of attention," Pedro said from his seat next to his father. "And that hasn't changed."

"Whereas Tomas has always been quiet, observant, a keep to himself kind of soul. Slept a lot as a baby, which is what I think Viv's baby might do." Jenny crossed her legs and straightened her skirt.

"Which would be surprising since she's the spawn of Carlos." Pedro cheekily grinned.

"Pedro, don't use that word," Jenny chastised. "We don't know *how* she'll turn out. In a year, the babies could both be the complete opposite of what they are now." She patted Angie's hand. "Pedro was a bit of both. He slept a lot and then he was awake a lot. When he was with Carlos he wouldn't stop, when he was with Tomas, he was quiet and observant. But the one thing he always did was dance everytime we put a record on."

Pedro's grin extended across his face, and his blue eyes sparkled. "I love my music."

"You always did," Jenny said. "Now you can introduce the baby to it, and I think while she's sleeping you should both relax and breathe. If she wakes, just check her nappy, or feed her. All you have to do is pick her up and hold her like I did. Stay calm, keep your heartbeat down, and it will keep her calm too. If you aren't breastfeeding, you'll need to make up a bottle, and I've stocked your cupboards with all you need. So we're going to go and let you all rest."

"No, don't go!" Angie clutched her hand. "I won't know what to do."

"Of course you do," Jenny told her. "Just breathe, stay calm, and let your love for her flow through you. That's the most important thing. That she feels your love for her. Smile at her, speak gently, show her you love her. Now, get some rest. It's what you'll have to do from now on, rest when she does." Jenny and Spiros left them to it.

Pedro sat beside Angie on the couch. "It's going to be okay, babe.

Just breathe."

"How can I breathe when I have a human being to look after?" she said. "This is all too much. I can't do this." Her heart pounded in her chest, and her adrenaline flew around her body. She was wired and had no idea what to do.

The baby started crying.

"Looks like you'll have to. Come on, we'll do it together." Pedro pulled a reluctant Angie to the bedroom, but she refused to enter, so he went to the crib. "Hello baby, it's Papa. What's wrong with my precious little girl," he crooned and carefully picked her up and held her as his mother had. "What is it, my baby? Are you hungry? Need a new nappy?" Gently rubbing her back, he found her cries diminished, but didn't stop. "Let me check your nappy." He looked and saw it needed changing. "Okay, Mama and I are going to change you, that's why you're crying, yes, it is. Angie, how do you do a nappy?"

"I don't know." She stood frozen.

"Come on, Angie," he said softly. "Come and fold a nappy for me and we'll do it together. Come on, don't be scared."

"I don't know, I don't remember," she said crossly and made the baby cry.

"It's okay," Pedro soothed both of them. "Angie, calm down and think. Don't let your emotions frustrate you. This is your daughter, *our* daughter, *we* made her, our *love* made her, and you wanted to keep her, so let's do this together. I'll keep her calm, and you do the nappy."

On the verge of frustrated tears, Angie wiped her face and picked up a nappy from the shelf of the change table. Laying it out, she started folding. "No, that's not right." She tried again, but couldn't get it, throwing it down in frustration.

"Calm down, Angie," Pedro said, putting an arm around her. "It's okay, take a deep breath, breathe, now try again."

She breathed while Pedro took care of the baby and tried to remember what Jenny had taught her, coming up with the perfect nappy ten seconds later.

"Okay, now let's change her." Pedro laid the baby on the change table, and together they removed the soiled nappy.

"Ew!" Angie screwed her nose up and flicked open the nappy bin. "Gross."

Pedro laughed. "You know they'll need washing."

"I'm not washing them," she adamantly protested.

They cleaned the baby and pinned on the clean nappy, re-dressing her while she gurgled.

"Now, it's your turn," Pedro told Angie as he gently stroked the baby's head. "She looks like an Alena. The name does suit her."

"But do we want to use a name when Mama already has?" Angie asked, looking down at her tiny offspring.

Big blue eyes stared up at her, and the little tuft of black hair was being pushed back by Pedro's hand. The baby was going between frowning and euphoria at her daddy's hand moving over her face and head. But her hands in her mouth helped calm her. "Ooh, ooh," she gurgled, making her mother smile.

"Do you like the name, Alena?" Pedro asked the baby.

"Ooh, ooh," came the reply.

"Looks like she's on board." Pedro looked at Angie to see her smiling down at her. "What about you, babe? Think it's a good name?"

Angie looked from her baby's big blue eyes to her husband's. "I think it rhymes too much with mine, but…it is nice." Gazing down at her baby, watching her shove her fat little fists into her mouth, she felt that burst of love Jenny had said she would get. The burst of love that flooded her whole body telling her she'd do anything for her daughter. Love her with every fibre of her being and protect her until the end of time. Sliding her hands under her, she lifted her into her arms. "Hey, my little girl, is that the name you want?" Holding her against her shoulder as Jenny had taught her, she patted the baby's back. "Is that the name you want, huh?" She received gurgles in return and felt the love flow for her daughter.

July 1978

Jenny spent the next month looking for a Greek Orthodox Church that would christen the girls, but not in the full Greek way. With one of them being half American, a quarter Aussie, and a quarter Greek, and the other three-quarter Greek and one-quarter Aussie, most churches didn't want to deal with a baby not full Greek. Finally, she found one that was willing to take both at the same time and not be so prudish about traditions. And the cheque for one thousand dollars helped.

The whole family stood in the small church and gathered round as the babies were christened in the oil bath.

"I christen thee, Diana Villiers Stephanopoulos." The priest dunked Viv and Carlos's baby into the oil, did the usual priest things, and handed the baby over to be cleaned and dressed.

Since the family was small, there were no godparents to help, just one more tradition not abided by. Although the boys had both suggested to Jenny that they pick Tomas and Roger as godparents, Jenny had talked them out of it. When asked why, she reluctantly admitted to her fears of something bad coming Tomas's way and that they shouldn't take the risk of something happening to him first. They didn't understand her fears, but abided by her wishes, regardless of how bad they all felt for doing so.

Watching Viv and Carlos dress a screaming Diana in her white dress, made for a change to Angie's baby, who lay quietly in her mother's arms. Once Diana was dressed, the ceremony moved on.

Angie and Pedro undressed their daughter, and the priest dunked her into the oil. "I christen thee, Alena Jennifer Stephanopoulos."

"What?" Jenny gasped, a hand flying to her heart as everyone turned to stare at her with smiles on their faces. "Oh." Her face crumpled. "You didn't."

Pedro smiled softly. "We asked her if she liked the name and she said she did. But we don't want to upset you, Mama. If you don't want us to use it…"

Jenny's tears were hot with love and joy. "I'm not upset, my baby. I love it, and I love the two of you and our beautiful baby."

Alena was passed back to Angie who wiped her down and dressed her. They finished up with a few bible passages, prayers and blessings for everyone.

"Thank you so much, Father." Jenny shook his hand. "This means so much to us." They left and went back to the penthouse. It was a hot July day, and they didn't want to be out in it with the babies, so they sat in the air-conditioned comfort of home.

"Oh, my babies finally have names." Jenny watched them sleep side by side in the crib she had set up in the living room of the penthouse. She'd brought a few extra things and set them up along the wall of the office for when she would be looking after them.

Pedro went over and stood beside her. "We didn't want to upset you by picking the name…but it seemed to fit."

Jenny turned her attention to her son. "That's what I told Angie. I'm glad you did." She waited as Angie joined them. "I think she wanted another go at living and knew that it wasn't her time with me. That's why she left." She reached up to caress her son's cheek. "She wasn't meant to be here with me, not that way, because she knew it was the two of you she was meant to be with. And that's why she's here with you two now. She's getting another go at life."

"Oh, Mama." Pedro kissed her temple. "I love you."

"I love you, too," Jenny replied. "And you," she told Angie. "And you, baby Alena." She reached down and touched both babies on the cheek with the back of her forefinger. "I love you both so much. Yes, I do. And you, too, Diana."

Leaving the babies to sleep, they poured iced tea and soft drinks and sat around chatting.

"When are you leaving, Tomas?" Jenny asked, sipping her iced tea.

"Next month," he said from his spot next to Roger. "The movie will be out, and we'll be gone."

"It's going to be an awesome movie, bro," Carlos told him and lifted his drink in cheers.

"Maybe so, but I *really* don't care anymore," Tomas replied.

"I can't believe you boys did that after promising to get out of it," Jenny complained. "You said once the babies were here there would be no more. And yet you left Viv and Angie in the hospital to do it."

"It only took three days, Mama." Carlos shrugged. "It's no big deal."

"*Of course* it's a big deal when *you promised*," Jenny told him. "I wanted you all out of it, and you go and make another one."

"It's all over with *now*, Mama," Carlos told her. "I still have a few scripts to go, and I'm thinking of doing other things. Like scripts for normal movies."

"That's good to hear. What about film school? You could learn how to make them," Jenny said.

"I'm getting all the practice I need working on set," Carlos replied. "But who knows, maybe I'll take some courses in other things."

"Mmm, good." Jenny brought her attention back to Tomas. "Where will you go next, do you know?"

"We're heading for London." Tomas grinned. "We'll travel all over Britain, Scotland, Wales, Ireland, and then move on to France and the rest of Europe."

"Oh, that sounds so nice. I wish I could go with you. Maybe next year we'll all take a trip there. The babies will be one and old enough to travel. Oh, yes…" Jenny became excited. "Let's all plan a summer European vacation, and then we can take the babies home to Australia to see the family. If we plan ahead now, we can organise our schedules around it."

"Sounds great," Viv said, and Carlos agreed.

"Ooh, I'd love to see Australia," Angie said excitedly.

"Or, we could go for Christmas and New Year's next year instead. It will be summer there and warm. We can chase summer around the globe," Jenny said. "Oh, that's given me so many ideas now." She jumped up and grabbed a pad and pen and sat down to write out her list.

"You know we have to get through *this* summer and Christmas yet," Spiros said.

"I know, but it doesn't hurt to plan ahead. And you boys will see what Europe's like, so you'll have to tell me when you come back for Christmas where the best places to go are, and then I can book ahead," she told Tomas and Roger.

"Are we talking the whole summer, Mama? I don't know if Eddie will give me three months off and again at Christmas," Pedro said.

"If he fires you so what, you can get another job when you come back, or not at all. We have money," Jenny told him.

"But I have a job," he argued.

Jenny shrugged. "Then he either lets you go, and takes you back, or another club will sign you up."

*****

"Well? What do you think of the rough cut?" Harry leaned back in his chair after showing the movie to Carlos. He'd stayed in New York to work on the movie.

Carlos had studied every scene as he sat watching. "It's good…"

"But?"

"But…I think it needs something to make it better."

"Like what?"

"Well…there are plenty of tits and crotch, and mouth around cock shots, but it just needs something else."

There had been plenty of close-ups of the boys, their whole body had been given close-ups as the camera had panned up and down slowly, covering their sizable manhood, especially when getting blown, and there had been face shots of them closing their eyes in ecstasy, or staring down at the women doing the blowing. But it needed something more…

"More shots of the girls? I have those," Harry said.

"Isn't the movie about us?" Carlos snickered. "What about music? It needs a bit more oomph. It needs…more slow motion scenes, more of the extras in slow motion…more of us in slow motion…like me flinging my hair back. It needs the right music on the right slow motion scenes."

"Okay. I'll get onto that and do another cut."

"We need to make it the best movie ever, Harry," Carlos said.

"Oh, we will, my boy." Harry puffed on his cigar and blew it out. "We will."

August 1978

On August the first, *The Greek Gods* was released to rave reviews. The boys showed up at the opening of the movie in Times Square, New York. A large segment of the street was blocked off for the opening, as many adult movie theatres were all screening it at once. They signed autographs and had their photos taken. Plus, they signed the posters of the movie that the manager asked for.

In L.A., Harry was out for the opening of the movie at *The Pussycat Theatre*, holding a huge after-party for anyone who wanted to come. In Miami, Marcus Seralift did the same, providing posters, and promoting Roger and Tomas's previous movies since they weren't there in person.

Greta turned up as Pedro's ex-boss, shaking hands with everyone as if she was responsible. "Yes, yes, it was my idea," she told a reporter on the red carpet. "As Pedro's boss, I suggested to Harry DeVille and Marcus Seralift that we do a threesome together. It finally came through, and here we are."

The boys stood in front of the movie poster in the lobby of one theatre, and had a million photos taken, chatting to reporters at the same time.

"Carlo, Carlo, is it true that you're a father now? You had a baby with supermodel, Vivian Villiers?"

The grin was ear to ear. "I have, I have," he said, standing with an arm around each brother. "We were married last November and have just become proud parents. Same as Pedro and his Angelina." He squeezed his brother's shoulder.

"And is it true you wrote this movie, Carlo?" another reporter asked.

"Absolutely. I started writing when I re-wrote the *Cabana* scripts. Then *The Meat Shop* movies, and now *The Greek Gods*. I've also written a hundred other movies for Harry DeVille and his company. Many are now in theatres for your viewing pleasure."

"Tomas, Tomas, what's it like being a gay man in porn?"

Tomas flinched then saw Roger nearby, giving him the thumbs up. "It's actually very easy, especially when you work with your real-life partner."

"Is that how you met Roger Dencott?"

Tomas wanted the ground to open up and swallow the reporters. He wanted all of this to be over. "No. I met him at a club and found out he worked in the industry. Eventually, I moved into the business too."

"Pedro, you're only twenty-one and a DJ at *Studio 69*. Which career will you continue?"

"DJing, absolutely, I love my music, and I'd rather do that than this. I only got into it because I saw my brother's first movie and was offered a bunch of money by Greta Von Burro. But my contract's over, and I have my wife and baby girl to think about. So this is my last movie."

"Is it the last one for all of you?"

Their eyes zoomed in on the person who'd asked. "Yes," came three simultaneous and determined replies.

"Okay, everyone, let's get into the theatre to see the movie." Greta waved the reporters away and ushered the boys and Roger inside. An hour later they emerged to thunderous applause, inside and out.

"Boys, you were a hit as I knew you would be," Greta said to them. "It turned out better than I expected."

"We know!" Carlos said. "I made sure of it. I wrote the best script, hired the best director, and worked with him to make it happen. It was the best idea I've ever had." He watched Greta's smile disappear.

"Your idea?" she said. "I'm the one that suggested working together."

"Yes, but *I'm* the one who wrote the movie, co-produced, co-directed, and made sure my brothers were as comfortable as possible doing it. So, exactly *what* did *you* do besides provide the stage and set?" Carlos asked.

"I provided the talent. All of those girls you and Pedro fucked, *my* talent!" Greta seethed.

"And *that's* all you get paid for," Carlos told her as he signed more autographs on the way to their limo. "The set, the stage, the talent. The rest of it was me, my brothers, and Harry. And now Greta, *we are* done."

The boys climbed into the limo, wound down the windows, and waved to fans as they left.

*****

"How'd it go in L.A.?" Carlos asked Harry on the phone the day after the premiere. Tomas and Roger were leaving later that day, and he wanted to know before they left.

"From early takings, and what I've been told across the country, we already have one million in ticket sales."

"And when will the video come out?"

"October first. Right in time for the porn awards."

"Cool, I'll let everyone know. Keep me informed, Harry."

"I will."

Carlos hung up and went to the penthouse to see Tomas and Roger holding the babies. "Hey. We made one million in sales on day one alone. I told you this movie was going to be huge."

Tomas looked up from baby Alena's cherubic face and big blue eyes. "Yeah? Well, I'm glad it's over."

"And the video's coming out October first in time for the porn awards," Carlos went on. "Are you boys coming back for that?"

"God, no!" Tomas wrapped his finger with Alena's fat little ones. "No way do I want to be there."

"But what if you win?" Carlos asked.

"Then accept on my behalf," Tomas replied. "I'm not interested in getting up in front of a huge crowd of people to accept a cock-shaped award. That's your forte. You accept for me and then you'll get twice as much time on stage. Twice as much exposure." He leant down and kissed Alena's forehead. "Besides, I'd rather be out of the country seeing the world than having a cock in my hand."

"Hey," Roger protested.

"I didn't mean yours." Tomas laughed. "I meant the award."

"I know." Roger grinned, bouncing up and down gently as Diana gurgled. They were standing in the sitting area of the penthouse; their luggage sets ready to go.

"When's the flight?" Carlos asked, standing in front of Roger and stroking his daughter's head. She gurgled and blew bubbles in return. "Hey, my little bubba," he said softly.

"Mama said we could leave anytime. She got us a private plane over there, but we'll have to use the normal airlines after that, and we're also catching trains and buses for fun. We've booked the Orient Express to Rome." Tomas's eyes glittered with excitement.

"Sounds cool, little bro," Carlos said, smiling at his brother's enthusiasm.

After their last meal with Pedro and Angie, they said their goodbyes and were wished luck with their journey.

"Don't forget lots of photos," Jenny told them. "Remember you have the money to stay where you want, and take lots of photos."

"Okay, Mama." Tomas hugged both parents. "Lots of photos and lots of presents for everyone. We'll see you for Christmas."

"Oh, can you come back a bit early?" Jenny asked as they settled into the limo. "Maybe for Thanksgiving?"

"We'll try, Mama. I love you."

"Love you, Tomas, Roger."

"Bye Mr and Mrs S."

"Bye." Carlos and Pedro waved goodbye as the girls stood holding the babies.

Jenny sighed, reluctant to let her son go, but happy he was seeing the world with the man he loved.

"Come, my love, let's go upstairs." Spiros led her inside, and she said a small prayer for her son's health and safety.

October 1978

"Hello, and welcome to *The Annual Porn Star Awards*," Carlos said from the stage of *The Pussycat Theatre* in L.A. He and his brothers had been asked to host, and the girls had encouraged them to do it since they'd probably never get another chance. Waiting for the screaming to die down, he grinned at Pedro who was beside him. "My name is Carlo Stefan, this is my brother Pedro Stefan." More screams. "Now, you might be thinking, but wait, isn't there another brother? And you'd be right. Our brother Tomas is travelling through Europe with his partner in crime, Roger Dencott." Even louder screams.

"Let's kick this show off with the best male newcomer in the industry," Pedro said and opened the envelope. "The nominees are…Vilos Meyer, Mikael Krevnokov, hey I wonder if he's related to Martine Krevnokov, Topher Star, Tomas Stefan, and me, Pedro Stefan. Am I allowed to give this away?" he joked. "And the winner is, hey, me, Pedro Stefan!"

He was awarded a silver penis and took to the microphone once more. "Thank you very much for making me the best newcomer. I hope it's because you like what I do as a DJ in my movies." Cheering came back at him. "Yeah, yeah, it's for my cock! Let's get on with the rest of the awards, shall we."

Carlos announced best director, which was won by Harry and himself for *The Greek Gods* movie. Best producer went to Harry, him, and his brothers for the same movie as they shared producing credits.

"Okay, it's time for the best cock award; an award I told Carlos I would win this year and beat him, so the nominees are." Pedro glanced through the names. "Ah, some familiar names here. Carlo Stefan." A thunderous applause went through the crowd, and Carlos grinned and waved to them. "Pedro Stefan." An even louder applause. "Tomas Stefan…looks like we're dominating, Roger Dencott." Wolf whistles sounded out across the crowd. "And Caden Carmichael. And the winner is…" He ripped the envelope open. "Oh, my, God, our brother, Tomas!"

Carlos laughed. "And you were so sure you'd be winning it." Taking the award, he gave his thanks. "We accept this award on behalf of our brother who is touring the world. We'll let him know how much you think of him. Next up is best actor." That award went to Carlos, and best movie went to Harry and the boys for *The Greek Gods.*

"Moving on, we have some new awards this year, and the first one is for best gay movie, so here we go." Carlos stood ready to read out the nominees. "*Mount Cockmore, Big Cock Avalanche, Big Cock in Little China, Cock A Doodle Do,* Jesus, they called a movie that? And *Mount Me Baby One More Time.* And the winner is…*Big Cock Avalanche* with our brother Tomas Stefan who happens to star in it with his partner, Roger Dencott."

Tomas and Roger also went on to win best gay love scene, another new category, plus best gay sex scene. Pedro won for best straight sex scene for his threesome in his first movie. They announced four more awards before they were done.

"Ladies and gentlemen, that is the 1978 Porn Star Awards. We are Carlo and Pedro Stefan, this is *The Pussycat Theatre* in Hollywood, and thank you all for being here. Goodnight." Carlos and Pedro waved to the audience as streamers and balloons came down.

Finally getting backstage, they were congratulated by Harry and Harriet, Greta, and Marcus who had flown in to accept the best gay movie award.

"And we're done," Carlos said, ready to rip off his tie. He and Pedro had dressed up in tuxedos for the occasion.

"Not yet, my boy. Since you had hosting duties it's time to take some photos," Harry said and led them back to the media room for the reporters to take snaps.

Holding the awards between them, Harry, Marcus, Pedro and Carlos all stood hanging onto silver penis statuettes, smiling for the cameras while Greta hovered nearby, hoping to get in on the action.

"This will be in all the rags next week," Harry muttered through gritted teeth. He hated having his photo taken, but couldn't wait to be in the magazines.

"We have to make sure to stock up on each edition. The family will be so proud," Carlos joked, smiling brightly for the cameras.

"Angie thinks it's hilarious," Pedro added. "She still gets off on all the magazines you were in *and* on last year."

"They could be worth a fortune in a few years," Carlos said. "I kept all of my copies too." They finished and made their way outside to the waiting limos.

"Coming to celebrate with us?" Harry asked. "We were able to get the same club as last year."

"No, thanks, Harry, we've gotta get a flight home to New York."

"This time of night?" Harry asked.

"Mama has a private jet on standby, so we'll get there faster. Call you in a couple of days about new scripts."

"Okay. Safe flight." Harry slapped him on the back in farewell.

The boys climbed into the limo carrying two boxes of awards. Between them, they had won fifteen, including Tomas and Roger's.

"God, look at these." Pedro stared into one of the boxes that sat between them. "That's quite a haul."

"It is." Carlos finally ripped off his bowtie and unbuttoned his shirt. "Adds to the ones I won last year. And they'll be the only ones you and Tomas win because you're done. So, no more awards for you."

"Yeah, I don't care," Pedro said with a soft grin on his face. "I'd rather DJ anyway."

They flew into New York in the wee hours of the morning and sneaked in to kiss their babies and wives good morning.

*****

"Mmm," Sheila moaned, waking as the baby kicked. "Mmm, stop that."

Giancarlo rolled over. "Baby kicking?" He placed a huge hand on her stomach and instantly the kicking died down. "You stop kicking your mama, little one."

Sheila felt the movement stop. "How do you get him to do that?"

"It's the tough nut approach. Take no prisoners." He rubbed his hand over her stomach, and while it was calming for the baby, it was arousing for her. He'd moved into her place full-time. For now. They had been busy making plans for the baby and knew her tiny apartment wasn't cutting it. After months of convincing, she'd agreed to move into his house in Forest Hills, as long as it had a complete makeover. His house was decades old and needed renovations if a baby was going to be living there. After to-ing and fro-ing he had accepted her offer of renovations that she would pay for. His money had bought the house, hers would make it presentable for her and the baby.

If she was going to make a home with Giancarlo, it needed to be safe and childproofed. She had all the floors changed, wiring, water and gas updated, the walls were replastered over fresh insulation, the roof retiled. She made sure she had her luxuries, a dressing room and large bathroom, plus two bedrooms and a bath for the baby or potential guests. The carport was updated, a new lawn and garden laid, plus the porch was rebuilt and painted. It was costing a pretty penny as the house was a gut job, but it was what she wanted and what the house needed. And she couldn't wait to decorate. They'd be taking her bedroom suite, lounge suite and appliances, but she wanted much more. Because for the first time in her life, she'd be having a real home to live in, with a man, and a baby on the way. She groaned.

"Still moving?"

"No. Turned on."

"Well, let me fix that." He pulled her into his arms and attached himself to her in every way, only pulling back when she was sated. "Enough?"

She sighed in delirious happiness. "For now."

"Speaking of, for now, I guess I'd better make it permanent." Rolling over and flicking on the bedside light, Giancarlo pulled a small box from the drawer. "I know it's not much, and you have money and all that, but this is all I could afford." He rolled back and presented her with a small diamond ring. "I'm no good at this, having only been married once before, and a million years ago at that. When my wife left me, I vowed never to go through that again. And I didn't. But after the last few years, and especially the last ten months, things have changed. And now with a baby on the way, I should make an honest woman out of you. So ah…will you marry me?"

Sheila had been staring at the ring. In all of her life, no one had ever proposed. Certainly not Andros, and after letting herself go had figured no one ever would, so she didn't know what to say. "Um…" she breathed, looking at the small diamond ring. "I'm…"

"I understand if you don't want to, probably too presumptuous of me."

"No," she cried. "I want to; it's just that no one's ever asked me before. I've never been engaged or married." She grasped both of his hands in desperation.

"So…do you want to be now?" He leant back on a pile of pillows.

She looked up into his blue eyes and beamed. "Do you want me to be your wife?"

"Well…ah…" He blushed. "I wouldn't be asking if I didn't."

"For better for worse, in sickness and in health?" she asked, her heart speeding up.

He smiled. "Yes."

"Then the answer is yes. Yes, I'll marry you, Giancarlo Gardo," she cried, watching him slide the small gold ring onto her finger.

"I…ah…thought we could make it official at City Hall before the baby comes," he said, pulling her into his arms.

She rested her head on his broad chest, staring at the ring, completely, totally happy. "We can. As soon as possible?"

"As soon as possible."

*****

"Yep, bro, won a tonne of awards. You more than the rest of us. You won best cock, outdoing Pedro who's bragged all year," Carlos told Tomas.

"Bet he hated that." Tomas laughed down the line from Germany.

"He did. But he won best newcomer, and we all won as co-producers. You and Roger won best gay love *and* sex scene, Pedro best straight sex scene. So, we're all pretty even."

"Keep mine and Roger's in the box, just put it in our apartment."

"Are you coming home for Thanksgiving?" Carlos asked.

"Unfortunately not. We'll be in Switzerland that day then head off to Italy for three weeks."

"Oh, a hop, skip and a jump from home."

Tomas's laugh tinkled across the seas. "I haven't heard that since Australia. But it's our last stop on this holiday. We've been all over Europe. It's amazing. It really is."

"It sounds amazing, and I'm bloody jealous." Carlos twirled the phone cord around his fingers.

"Don't be. Mama's bringing us all back next year to see the sights, so just you wait."

"I can't. It's a whole year away," Carlos complained. "As long as you're having fun though, that's all that matters."

Tomas smiled softly. "I am. We are. And we'll see you all for Christmas."

"Okay, see you then."

"Love to Mama and Papa and everyone else."

"I'll let them know, bye." Carlos went up to the penthouse and found his mother picking up Alena.

"Is Tomas coming for Thanksgiving?" Jenny lifted Alena into her arms. "It's going to be Alena's first Thanksgiving," she said in a childlike voice to the baby and received a smile in return. "Yesh, it is."

"Probably not. They'll be in, get this, Switzerland, and then on to Italy for three weeks."

"Ooh, la la." Viv picked up Diana and helped her into Jenny's arms.

Jenny took both babies. "Ooh, Italy," the childish voice continued. "You'll get to shee Italy next year, yesh, you will. But first, we're having our first Thanksgiving and our first Chrishmash. Yesh, we will. It will be Alena's first Chrishmash, yesh, it will." She pretended to munch on the baby's head. "Yesh, it will. And it will be Diana's first Chrishmash. Yesh, it will, nom, nom, nom."

Both babies smiled happily, reaching up to Grandma, able to sit on their own, able to reach up, able to communicate in their own special way.

"Yesh, it will be." Jenny hugged them tightly. "It will be your first Chrishmash, yesh, it will. Grandma loves you both sho mush. Yesh, she does."

*****

Sheila Manning became Sheila Gardo on October 20th, 1978. It had only been a week since Giancarlo had proposed, but both figured it would be better if it was done out of the way before she grew too big. Although at five months, she was already showing a huge rounded belly. She wore a simple white pantsuit, several sizes bigger than the one she originally had, and he wore a simple black three-piece suit with a white shirt. It was the suit he'd bought just to see Jenny that day many months ago.

He showered and put aftershave on, and she'd put her hair up, and added baby's breath, so she didn't need a bouquet. It was a simple, quick ceremony in City Hall. The paperwork dated and stamped made them official.

They were now husband and wife.

November 1978

In early November, the three boys celebrated their first wedding anniversaries, giving their wives gifts of jewellery, and their husbands gifts of eternity rings, with each one's initials and date on the inside, and the word *Forever* emblazoned on the outside.

Tomas thanked his mother for making them get married over dinner as he linked his fingers through Roger's. So happily devoted to each other, they were glad to be together for eternity. And Jenny knew deep down in her gut that they would be.

*****

At Thanksgiving, almost all of the Stephanopoulos family crowded around the penthouse dining table, said grace and gave their thanks.

Jenny and Spiros sat at each end, Carlos and Viv on one side with Diana between them in her highchair, and Pedro and Angie on the other side with Alena between them. The girls were now five months old and as noisy and boisterous as ever, throwing food across the table, causing much laughter and hilarity. And the girls fed off it, knowing they could make everyone laugh. For that would be their party trick as they grew older. If they could make people laugh, they could get away with anything.

Tomas and Roger celebrated Thanksgiving in Switzerland. Zurich to be exact. They spent the snowy day inside their hotel room, giving their own thanks that they had each other, and made sure to call Tomas's family, not just in New York, but back in Australia too. They also called Roger's friends in Miami. They would be leaving the next day for Italy, riding the Orient Express all the way there, and they couldn't wait.

Sheila and Giancarlo celebrated Thanksgiving in her apartment. It would be her first and only one as they were due to move into Giancarlo's house for Christmas. She just needed to add the finishing touches to it, and it would be perfect. They spent the day happily married and in love, as he'd gotten three days off, and they watched old movies and laughed at the corny comedies on TV.

December 1978

On Christmas Eve, Tomas and Roger made it home in time to see their nieces crawl across the floor toward the great big tree Jenny had set up, ready to pull it down on their heads. Laughing, Tomas and Roger scooped up the little ones, to their great delight, and flew them across the room to Jenny and Spiros whom they hugged fiercely and had missed terribly.

With hugs and kisses all round, the whole Stephanopoulos family celebrated once more, unwrapping bountiful presents that everyone had bought for each other, and Tomas and Roger had brought home from Europe, especially for the babies who were now six months old and happily ripping at the pretty paper and not caring about the present within.

Sheila and Giancarlo celebrated their first Christmas Eve together as husband and wife, putting the finishing touches on the huge tree that sat proudly in the corner of the new living room in Giancarlo's house. They'd moved in two weeks earlier after Sheila's final touches, and they were decorating the tree, like the whole house, with coloured lights, tinsel, and baubles. Presents sat around the tree, not many, but a few, for the number would soon grow as their child did, and she couldn't wait. For all the years she'd had with Luiz, not being able to buy him a lot of presents, or give him everything he wanted, she vowed this time would be different. This baby was wanted. This baby would be loved.

It would be so loved, that after a long discussion, Giancarlo had decided to retire from the force at the end of the year. That way, he'd have time to dedicate to his son, or daughter, and his new wife.

*****

On New Year's Eve, 1978, the Stephanopoulos family wandered into Times Square for the ball drop. They had missed it the year before because Tomas was sick and Pedro was working. He'd bartered the night off, and now they all stood in the freezing New York winter, waiting for it to fall. The girls were wrapped up tight, as were their mothers and fathers, and Jenny and Spiros celebrated another year together. Although their anniversary and her birthday had been all but forgotten, he'd more than made up for it since being back. And the girls being born had helped her immensely; especially knowing her little Alena was back in the family and could now have her stocking filled at Christmas.

Somewhere in the crowd stood Sheila and Giancarlo, celebrating their first New Year's as husband and wife. Neither had actually taken the time to be at a ball drop before. Sheila had never bothered as she had no one to go with, and even though she had attended the previous New Year's Eve at *Studio 69*, that had been the only time she'd gone out to celebrate. And Giancarlo had always been working, so had only seen it from a distance as he raced past after a criminal, or in pursuit of a murder of which many happened on New Year's Eve. But now he was retired, he had the time to take Sheila to celebrations, movies, the theatre and much more.

"10, 9, 8, 7, 6, 5, 4, 3, 2, 1, Happy New Year."

Spiros took Jenny into his arms and showed her how much he loved her. His sons did the same with their partners. They were thankful that all were well and not sick or working as they had been last year.

Giancarlo and Sheila locked lips, happy, but frozen in the wintry street. Smiling happily at each other they moved on, just metres from the Stephanopoulos family, not that either family noticed. They were too wrapped up in their own lives and eager to all get home to warm beds and hot chocolate.

February 1979

On Valentine's Day, 1979, the three Stefan brothers celebrated their 22nd, 24th and 26th birthdays in style at *Studio 69*. Just as with the year before, Pedro worked his decks with supreme finesse, playing all the latest tunes to get everyone's boogie shoes on. The babies were now eight months old, and being looked after by Jenny's parents who had come over for the boys' birthdays. Jenny and Spiros danced up a storm, Viv was dirty dancing with Carlos, and Tomas and Roger hung out with friends. All were enjoying themselves, having feasted on the cake Eddie had made. Last years had been such a huge success he'd had a similar one made, but this one had Pedro behind his decks, Tomas and Roger in a clinch, while Carlos had a woman on his cock.

The cake went down a treat, and all had a good time, especially the boys who were another year older, who all celebrated their birthdays together because Papa made Mama very happy every birthday and anniversary, which is why she'd had three children nine months later on Valentine's Day.

But it was not as if they were the only ones who had that special day for a birthday, for coming into the world right at that moment, at Mount Sinai hospital, in the same birthing unit as Viv and Angelina, with the same doctor and nurses, was James Giancarlo Gardo, son of Sheila and Giancarlo Gardo. Weighing in at 8 pounds 4 ounces, the baby screamed the birthing unit down, showing his laughing father what kind of son he would be, and his teary mother that he was going to be *exactly* like his brother, *especially* when he looked up and flashed his aqua blue eyes at her.

About the Author

L.J. has been writing since 2006, when her first of many novels, ***The Road To Vegas,*** was born. In 2016 she created the ***Porn Star Brothers*** series about three sizzlingly hot Australian born Greek Island raised brothers who became the hottest porn stars in '70s America.

L.J. lives in Australia, loves '80s music, disaster movies, and collecting Jackie Collins books as Jackie is her inspiration and mentor.

L.J. Diva is the adult pen name for author Tiara King. You can find more about Tiara on her website; follow her on social media, or visit her publishing house, Royal Star Publishing.

Socials

tiaraking.com.au/ljdiva

royalstarpublishing.com.au

Sign up for *Tiara's* Newsletter…

Make sure you're always in the know and never miss free exclusives, the latest news, book updates, and so much more with newsletters from…

tiaraking.com.au

Have you read these?

THE PORN STAR BROTHERS SERIES

Porn Star Brothers
Forever
Love Never Dies
Stefan: The New Generation
DeLuca
Spiros & Jenny
And Always

THE ILLICIT THINGS SERIES

Her
Him
Madam X

A NOVEL INVESTIGATIONS SERIES

Designs in Crime
A Killer Plot
Murder on the Set
A Novel Investigation (omnibus)

Or these?

NOVELS

Burning Desires
Anything for You
Falling for London
The Road To Vegas
Hollywood Dreams
The Billionaire's Dirty Little Secret

SHORT STORIES

The Body
The Perfect Plot
The Star of Your Own Crime Scene

www.ingramcontent.com/pod-product-compliance
Lightning Source LLC
Chambersburg PA
CBHW030012200726
48284CB00016B/65